KU-165-897

TRUST

MIKE BULLEN

LARGE
PRINT

First published in Great Britain 2015
by
Sphere
An imprint of Little, Brown Book Group

First Isis Edition
published 2016
by arrangement with
Little, Brown Book Group
An Hachette UK Company

The moral right of the author has been asserted

Copyright © 2015 by Mike Bullen
All rights reserved

Lyrics reproduced from 'Always' by Irving Berlin,
Sony/ATV Music Publishing.

All characters and events in this publication, other than
those clearly in the public domain, are fictitious and
any resemblance to real persons, living or dead,
is purely coincidental.

A catalogue record for this book is available
from the British Library.

ISBN 978–1–78541–291–2 (hb)
ISBN 978–1–78541–297–4 (pb)

Published by
F. A. Thorpe (Publishing)
Anstey, Leicestershire

Set by Words & Graphics Ltd.
Anstey, Leicestershire
Printed and bound in Great Britain by
T. J. International Ltd., Padstow, Cornwall

This book is printed on acid-free paper

For Rachel, Maggie and Lisa

TRUST

Trust wasn't something you could have in degrees; it was all or nothing . . . Greg and Amanda are happy. They've been together thirteen years, have two young daughters, and are very much in love. But Dan and Sarah aren't so fortunate. Their marriage is just going through the motions, and they're staying together for the sake of their son. When one bad decision sends a happy couple into turmoil and turns an unhappy couple into love's young dream, there's only one thing that can keep everything from falling apart: trust.

DISCARDED

SPECIAL MESSAGE TO READERS

THE ULVERSCROFT FOUNDATION
(registered UK charity number 264873)
was established in 1972 to provide funds for
research, diagnosis and treatment of eye diseases.
Examples of major projects funded by
the Ulverscroft Foundation are:-

- The Children's Eye Unit at Moorfields Eye Hospital, London
- The Ulverscroft Children's Eye Unit at Great Ormond Street Hospital for Sick Children
- Funding research into eye diseases and treatment at the Department of Ophthalmology, University of Leicester
- The Ulverscroft Vision Research Group, Institute of Child Health
- Twin operating theatres at the Western Ophthalmic Hospital, London
- The Chair of Ophthalmology at the Royal Australian College of Ophthalmologists

You can help further the work of the Foundation
by making a donation or leaving a legacy.
Every contribution is gratefully received. If you
would like to help support the Foundation or
require further information, please contact:

THE ULVERSCROFT FOUNDATION
The Green, Bradgate Road, Anstey
Leicester LE7 7FU, England
Tel: (0116) 236 4325

website: www.foundation.ulverscroft.com

CHAPTER
ONE

Greg Beavis lay awake in the dawn light that infiltrated the bedroom. He had an early train to catch and so had set the alarm for 6 a.m. If he hadn't, he'd have woken at six thirty. But because he had, he was fully alert at five thirty. How did the body know to do this? Greg had half an hour before he needed to get up, thirty minutes in which he could contemplate this irony (if indeed it were an irony and not, like rain on your wedding day, merely inconvenient). Alternatively, he could gently nudge Amanda awake in the hope of interesting her in an early-morning shag. Of these options, the latter was by far the more appealing but by an equal distance the less advisable. Amanda was a woman who valued her sleep and, though she enjoyed sex as much as the next person (and in this instance the next person was Greg, who enjoyed it a lot), something told him she would not appreciate being cheated of her last half hour of slumber. That something was experience.

Still, if the sex were good, it would be worth the grief. And sex with Amanda was always good, often great, even after thirteen years and two children. Greg cast a sideways glance towards her sleeping form. During the night she'd shrugged off the duvet, exposing the rise of her hips. The curve was a little more pronounced than when they'd first met. Amanda had been twenty-three then. Greg had been two years older than her, and indeed still was. It was only reasonable that in the ensuing years her figure should have filled out a bit. What struck Greg as remarkable was just how sexy she was, notwithstanding the gobbet of saliva bubbling on her lower lip.

Greg edged a hand across the no-man's-land of the queen-sized mattress, bringing it to rest lightly against Amanda's thigh. Troops in position, ready to commence engagement.

"And what do you think you're doing?"

Greg stiffened at the sound of Amanda's voice, or at least those parts that weren't already stiff did. He found her staring at him, one eyebrow cocked. This was one of Amanda's faculties: the ability to go from comatose to vigilant at the flick of a switch. No slow turn of the dial for her. She should have been in the SAS.

"Nothing," he improvised inadequately, withdrawing the expeditionary force that was his hand. He smiled sheepishly. It was this boyish charm that had first attracted Amanda to Greg and even now, as he stumbled among the foothills of middle age, she still found it appealing. In truth, it was not Greg that had woken her but thoughts of the day ahead. It was a Monday. That meant Molly had sport. But did she have a clean top? And where was Lauren's lunch box? Amanda couldn't remember seeing it the night before. Chances were their younger daughter had lost it again.

2

Amanda shot a glance at the bedside clock. No way was she getting up at 5.38a.m. to look for a bloody lunch box. Twenty-two minutes till the alarm was due to sound: plenty of time for a quickie, and a cuddle afterwards. To Greg's surprise and joy, Amanda manoeuvred across the cotton sheet and pressed herself against him, resuscitating his diminishing erection.

Greg needed no further invitation. He tenderly traced the outline of Amanda's jaw, a gesture she interpreted as romantic, but which was in fact a diversionary tactic allowing him to flick the spittle from her chin. Mission accomplished, he redeployed his hand to its earlier bridgehead on her thigh, advancing the fingers slowly northwards, increasing their pressure as they neared the delta. Amanda shuddered appreciatively. But then Greg heard a dread sound: a low rumble far off up the street that subsided then rose, louder, as it drew close. How could he have forgotten? Idiot! But perhaps Amanda wouldn't notice.

Fat chance. Her thighs tensed, and not in a good way.

"Did you put the rubbish out?"

Greg was torn between evasion and a flat-out lie. The momentary hesitation was enough to sink him.

"There's still time," she said.

For a glorious moment, Greg thought she meant for their shag, but this hope was dashed when she shrugged him off.

"And don't forget the recycling."

Greg had half a mind to argue. They could miss a collection. All right, their bin would be overflowing by the next, but there were always households with spare capacity: dinkys, or retirees, or that sad sack at number eighteen who Amanda suspected was a paedo. A week hence Greg could sneak out under cover of darkness and surreptitiously stuff their surplus garbage into their neighbours' wheelie bins, like a serial killer disposing of body parts.

"Go. Go!" Amanda jabbed a heel at Greg's buttocks with a little more force than was playful. The bin lorry lumbered nearer, the asthmatic wheeze of its air brakes provoking a frenzy of barking from the family's labra-doodle, Jess, who was shut in the kitchen. This in turn spurred ten-year-old Molly and her eight-year-old sister, Lauren, to leap awake in the room they shared, barrel along the landing and, without breaking stride, launch themselves on to their parents' bed.

There was no way Greg was getting his end away now. Accepting defeat, he gave his daughters quick hugs before hauling himself out of bed and towards the door, bending a little so as to hide the tumescence still apparent in his shorts.

Greg and Amanda lived in Stamford Brook, a characterless enclave of west London favoured by families who aspired to, but couldn't afford, neighbouring Chiswick. Eleven miles to the north and east, in the moderately leafier suburb of Muswell Hill, Greg's friend and colleague, Dan Sinclair, was still asleep. He had not had a restful night. Despite going to bed a little after eleven, it had been past one before Dan nodded off. He'd made the mistake of trying to calculate how

4

far short he was of his monthly sales target. Dan was good with figures but, not having a maths degree or Asperger's, struggled with percentages, particularly in his head. This had contributed to his insomnia, though not 50 per cent as much as the numbers he'd come up with. Three weeks into June, he'd only achieved 65 per cent of his forecast sales. That meant that, in the remaining quarter of the month, he still had a third of his target to fulfil. In percentage terms he needed to improve on his current performance by some . . . some . . . It was at this point that Dan had reached the outer limit of his mathematical ability; the answer lay across the border, beyond his grasp. But of one thing Dan was fairly certain: he was screwed.

He suspected Greg had already filled his quota, and this just made matters worse. Because, while the two were mates, they were also rivals. Or perhaps it was because they were mates that they were such rivals. Nine times out of ten Greg came out on top. In fact, in the three years they'd worked together, Dan had only outsold Greg on seven occasions, and never in consecutive months. In the early days Greg had crowed about each of his victories, but this had worn thin with repetition, and over time he'd let the results pass without comment, which Dan found even more humiliating. He longed for a triumph of his own so they could resurrect their competition. Ah, well; maybe next month.

At six fifteen Dan's clock radio erupted into life, John Humphrys' hectoring tone jolting him from a dream in which the slides of the Powerpoint presentation he'd been making to the Board had been in the wrong order. Could it really be morning so soon? In a little over an hour he and Greg were due to leave for Infotech 2014, a two-day conference for the UK's IT industry, usually held in attractive cities like Durham or Exeter, but which this year was taking place in Birmingham. Dan was not looking forward to it, and not just because it was in Birmingham. If there was anything to make him feel inadequate, it was forty-eight hours in the company of colleagues and competitors, all cocksure and confident, or convincingly giving that impression.

He fumbled for the radio's snooze button, silencing the *Today* programme presenter. How the hapless junior minister Humphrys was haranguing must have wished she had the same facility. From the en-suite bathroom came the satisfyingly forceful sound of their recently installed power shower. Sarah was up before him. Dan considered confiding in his wife his concerns regarding work, but knew that, in this instance, a problem shared was not a problem halved. Sarah would only worry that he was about to lose his job. And he wasn't. Not yet, anyway. You needed three consecutive months of missed targets before you were deemed to be in a slump and vulnerable, and this would only be Dan's second. Still, a trend was emerging. And that's what Sarah would focus on. Better that she live in a state of blissful ignorance, her mind filled instead with thoughts of . . . It occurred to Dan that he had no idea what was in his wife's head.

What was in Sarah's head was the song "Happy" by Pharrell Williams. It had been on the radio the previous afternoon when she'd collected Russell from swimming practice and it was proving impossible to shift. Still, it could be worse — something by Ed Sheeran or another of those man-child warblers, inexplicably popular nowadays. Stepping out of the shower, Sarah wiped a hand across the steamed-up mirror and considered her reflection. She'd had an hourglass figure in her youth, but now, at the age of forty-two, it was more pear drop, as though the sand had settled at the bottom, causing the glass to warp and buckle. Not for the first time, Sarah made a mental note to resume going to the gym. If only she could attend as religiously as they direct-debited her membership fees.

Sarah checked her breasts for lumps, a cursory inspection, but still more attention than Dan had paid them lately. It wasn't his fault. She knew he was worried about work. He tried not to show it, but, after sixteen years of marriage, he was an open book. In recent months not a particularly interesting one — nothing that would win the Booker Prize or even make the shortlist. Satisfying herself that the surface of her breasts remained flush, if not exactly firm, Sarah wrapped herself in a bath sheet.

Dan sat perched on the side of the bed as she emerged from the en suite. His pose reminded her a little of Rodin's *The Thinker*, had the sculpture been carrying a couple of excess kilos and the weight of the world's problems upon his shoulders. Poor Dan, she thought. I wish he could be happier.

"I've ironed you a shirt," she said, though she doubted this alone would lift his mood.

Dan turned to look at his wife. At five eight she was only an inch shorter than him, but she cut a more impressive figure, he thought. Statuesque. Handsome. His eyes were drawn to where her full breasts met, and where she'd tucked in her bath sheet. A second towel was wrapped around her head, worn like a turban to dry her shoulder-length caramel-brown hair. Dan wanted to desire her, but it's not something that can be forced. Perhaps if her first words to him on waking had not concerned ironing. Was this what their relationship had become? Mundane exchanges about laundry?

"Thanks," he replied.

In fairness, perhaps this was what a stable and lasting marriage looked like. After so long together it was too much to expect the flames of passion to burn high; enough, surely, that the pilot light was still aglow, providing warmth, if not heat. Dan and Sarah believed that they loved each other, in their own, undemonstrative way. They were content in, if not excited by, each other's company. And they never had fights, though perhaps this was due more to a lack of emotion than a shared empathy.

Dan leant on his knees and levered himself upright. He felt older than his forty-one years, closer to the end of the decade than its beginning. He sighed. He wasn't looking forward to the day ahead. Although at least he could face it in a freshly laundered shirt.

Greg picked up a framed photograph from his bedside table and made a pretence of considering it. Taken the year before, during an otherwise lamentable package holiday in Cyprus, it showed Molly and Lauren hugging Amanda, the three of them squeezed together more tightly than commuters aboard a Northern Line Tube. Greg had snapped the picture over dinner on the first night, before they'd realised that *Limassol* was the Greek word for "shit hole". His daughters' smiles were brighter even than the camera's flash. It was his favourite portrait of the three most important women in his life.

Greg shifted his gaze from this facsimile of the girls' faces to the real things, raised towards him anxiously. The children hung on his verdict, their young brows furrowed in apprehension. What a great age they are, thought Greg; so trusting, so gullible.

"I don't think I've room in my bag," he said, moving to replace the photo on the table and unleashing a storm of protest.

"You have to take it!" This from Lauren, although the younger, the sharper of the two, with the keener nose for injustice.

"You always do!" chimed in Molly.

"*Please!*" they chorused.

Teasing them like this wasn't cruelty, Greg mused, not quite. It was a game. They knew that ultimately he'd cave and, until that moment, could revel in the exquisite agony of pretending that some other outcome were possible. It was the same vicarious pleasure that he and Amanda experienced watching a horror movie, safe in the knowledge that the axe-murderer was trapped within the confines of the TV screen. But, enough. Molly looked like she might be about to wet herself. Time to put them out of their misery.

"I suppose I could make room," Greg allowed, stowing the photo in his overnight bag.

The girls' delighted squeals brought Jess bounding and barking into the room. Amanda leant against the door, watching this scene with wry amusement. She made no attempt to join the fun. This was Greg's moment with his girls. They wouldn't see him for the next couple of days; let them enjoy it. Amanda loved being their mother but imagined it must be bliss to be their dad. Talk about unconditional love. With her daughters' laughter trailing her out of the room, Amanda started down the stairs. She recalled that she still hadn't found the missing lunch box. Lauren must have left it at school. Again. Irritating bloody child!

Sarah cut Russell's chicken sandwiches in two, then caught herself before halving the wholegrain bread again. Time was he wouldn't eat them unless they were in quarters. Now the fifteen-year-old was mortified if his sandwich bag contained "kiddy" portions. Sarah smiled to herself. This must be one of those markers that indicate a new stage in life, like acne, braces or (though not in Russell's case — hopefully) breasts. She added a yoghurt sachet and digestive biscuit to his lunch box then, as an afterthought, tossed in an apple, hoping that her son might consume it before realising it was fruit.

Dan often gave Russell a lift to school on his way in to work, but today was taking a taxi to Euston Station.

10

Russell was grateful for the opportunity to catch the bus. He found being alone with his dad somewhat tortuous. Neither of them could think of much to say and used the car radio to mask the awkward silence that was intermittently broken by their awkward conversation.

Standing at the front door, Sarah bade her menfolk goodbye. Russell allowed her to brush his cheek with her lips, the faintest touch before he fled, though Sarah was grateful for even this brief contact. She missed the kisses and cuddles they used to share. They seemed such a distant memory now, though it was only in the last year or so, since he'd slammed the door on childhood, that Russell had withdrawn from her. Dan was more forthcoming. He hugged his wife and pressed his lips against hers, but it was inadequate compensation for the loss of Russell's display of affection.

Sarah closed the front door. She heard the latch take, the sound accentuated by the silence in the rest of the house, and retraced her steps to the kitchen. She had to clear away the breakfast things; there were clothes to be washed and an evening meal to plan — just for her and Russell, she remembered. The rest of the day loomed emptily in front of her. It was a daunting prospect.

It wasn't meant to be like this. When Sarah first met Dan, they had both been working for an office supplies company. Sarah had been PA to the Managing Director, Dan the new boy in the sales department. They'd started dating and, two years later, had married. When Russell came along Sarah took maternity leave, fully intending to return to work. But after six months she hadn't felt ready to hand her baby over to a childminder. Dan had supported her decision to stay at home. They could just about get by on his salary, and their financial situation would become easier as his income rose.

Except their outgoings rose faster. They took on a larger mortgage, expecting their family to grow. It hadn't happened. Sarah fell pregnant three more times, but on each occasion miscarried. Finally, they decided to stop trying. As Dan explained to friends, it wasn't the disappointment they couldn't bear so much as the hope. And their continued attempts to expand their family almost seemed like an indictment of Russell, as though he, by himself, weren't enough. Dan and Sarah resolved to appreciate what they had, not bemoan what they didn't.

Sarah had thought she might return to work when Russell started primary school, but neither she nor Dan wanted their son to become a latchkey kid. You didn't need a psychology degree to know that children fared better if they returned home not to an empty house but to a sympathetic ear, a glass of milk and a chocolate Hobnob.

When Russell graduated to secondary school, Sarah had felt her role diminish. He didn't need his mother as much, nor want her. At last she desired to go back to work, but had discovered that the attraction wasn't mutual. Her office skills were stuck in the mid-1990s, fossilised like an insect in amber. She could retrain, and for a while had tried. But whether it was down to hormones, age or disuse, Sarah felt that her brain had atrophied. She simply couldn't learn like she had in her youth. She found simple commands (control, alt, delete) difficult to assimilate and impossible to retain. She had had to face up to the fact that she was obsolete.

The phone rang. It was Veronica Bragg, a sometime tennis partner of Sarah's.

"Darling!" brayed Veronica. "I haven't seen you in forever! We must catch up. Are you free for lunch tomorrow?"

Tomorrow, the day after, the day after that. Sarah didn't much like Veronica, but in small doses she was preferable to solitude. They made a date for the following day.

"Night night, sleep tight, see you in the morning light. Night night."

Greg blew a kiss down the phone and mimed rubbing noses, to the right, to the left, to the right again. There was a strict choreography to his nightly bedtime ritual with Lauren, and Greg knew better than to mess with it.

"OK, into bed, sausage. Put your mum on now."

A moment later, Amanda's voice sounded in Greg's ear.

"Hey, you," she said. "How's the conference?"

How indeed? Every year it was the same. Greg looked forward to these two days away from the responsibilities of home, on expenses, in a four-star hotel. What wasn't to like? But the reality was always a let-down. Each year he saw the same old faces, except they were a little older, wearier and more alcohol-ravaged. Any influx of new blood simply served to remind him of the march of time: bright-eyed and ambitious youngsters elbowing a path through the crowd, shoving Greg and his contemporaries a little closer towards the exit. At thirty-eight, Greg was something of an elder among the tribe of salespeople (making Dan an eldest, he mused). The two were nonetheless respected elders, working for the British division of a multinational computer manufacturer. Between them they covered Greater London: Greg had the west, Dan the less glamorous and less lucrative east, but still the second most sought-after patch. Like Dan, Greg spent half his time on the road, with only Heart FM and the computer-generated voice of his Sat Nav (Natalie, Greg had christened her) for company.

That's where Greg would prefer to be now: out in the field, somewhere on the North Circular, the smell of a potential sale in his nostrils. But instead he was in Birmingham, stranded like a beached whale that's lost the will to live. At least the conference was good for networking. Many of his clients were here, affording him the opportunity to remind them that the next time they upgraded their systems (every two to three years in the fast-changing world of IT), he was their go-to guy. And already he'd made a number of new contacts, though only 5 per cent would ever amount to anything. Of course, Greg reminded himself, you didn't know which 5 per cent, so it was only in retrospect that you could separate the wheat from the chaff, whatever chaff was — belly-button fluff, something like that. If only the people weren't so dull. Strait-laced, buttoned-down. Like Dan, bless him.

Worse than the delegates were the sessions. The titles changed but the speakers remained as boring as ever, evangelising about arcane technological advances that only other geeks could get a hard-on for.

"I wish I could come home," Greg told Amanda now, in a tone that his mother, had she still been alive, would have recognised from when he was twelve and had been sent on an Outward Bound hike in north Wales.

Amanda laughed, which Greg didn't feel was an altogether sympathetic response. He was right.

"You say that every year," she reminded him. "And then you have a great time. Someone has a party in their room, you all get horribly pissed and you can't wait to do it again twelve months later."

"Perish the thought," said Greg morosely. "I'll be a year older then."

Two floors up and three rooms along, Dan was on the phone to Sarah.

"There was a fascinating session this afternoon — about the future of fibre-optic cable. I bet you can't guess the speeds they're talking of in two years' time."

It appeared Sarah had no intention of trying, as she changed the subject before Dan could continue.

"I think you need to speak to Russell when you get home," she said. "I was on the laptop earlier, checked the browsing history."

"I thought he always deleted that."

"He must have forgotten. He's been looking at some fairly dubious websites."

Oh God, thought Dan. Please don't let it be too perverse. Not animals. Or children.

"Like what?" he asked, not wanting to know.

"Bondage."

It was fortunate that there was a phone line and a hundred miles between them, or Sarah would have seen the guilty look that swept across Dan's face. The night before, he'd been watching a wildlife documentary while Sarah was having a bath. At least, that's what each had believed the other to be doing. Dan was in fact surfing the net and had happened upon a site he'd never seen before — the homepage of a dominatrix in Santa Fe. He'd been idly wondering what it was about New Mexico that made it such a Mecca for fetishists, when the door to the lounge had been flung open (or so it had seemed to Dan) and Sarah had loomed on the threshold.

"God, that's disgusting!" she'd blurted. Dan was not surprised by this reaction. Even when they'd been in the habit of regular sex — back in the day — Sarah had been conservative in her tastes, regarding anything more exotic than the missionary position as unsavoury or absurd. Dan was, however, surprised to have been caught; he'd thought his reaction, in slamming shut the laptop lid, had been faster even than his broadband connection. It was when he'd looked at Sarah, ready to confess his sin, that he'd realised her eyes were fixed not on the computer screen but on their forty-two-inch plasma TV. A cheetah was in the process of ripping a gazelle to bloody, high-definition shreds. Dan had casually laid the laptop aside, intending to delete the browsing history before he went to bed, but this task had slipped his mind. Thank God she suspected Russell.

"Well, bondage isn't so bad, is it?" he asked now, before remembering to add, "Assuming the women were willing participants."

"No, it was harmless enough, but even so. I think one of us ought to have a word with him. I could, if you like."

"No!" Dan was conscious of sounding a little too insistent; he adjusted his tone to nonchalant as he continued. "He'd be mortified if you talked to him about sex. Leave it to me. We'll have a man-to-man when I get back."

"That would probably be best," Sarah agreed.

Dan had no intention of doing any such thing.

Spend any time in Birmingham and, before long, someone will inform you that the city has more canals than Venice. Still, you'd rather be in Venice, Greg reflected, as he and Dan strolled after dinner through the evocatively named Gas Street Basin. This city-central marina of narrowboats and barges features on every picture postcard of Birmingham, evidence perhaps of the city's dearth of scenic sights. But Birmingham is not without other attractions. There's its rich culinary heritage, most notably that traditional Brummie dish, the balti. Try finding a good curry in Venice.

Awash with Kingfisher lager, Greg and Dan returned to their hotel. Greg hoped that Amanda's prediction might prove correct, that they would arrive to find the joint jumping, plans for a party being hatched. No such luck. A spattering of suits contaminated the bar, salesmen laughing loudly at their own piss-poor jokes. In one corner, a gym-toned woman in her late forties held court, wearing a tight jacket and tighter skirt, the colour of which matched her strident scarlet lipstick. This was Paula Stratton, a colleague of Greg and Dan's, but senior to them — a Regional Sales Manager. Were London her turf, she'd be their boss, but her patch comprised Manchester and the north-west — fortunately, from their point of view. Not for nothing was she known as Strap-On. This nickname would have been cruel and sexist had she not coined it herself. She went to great pains (other people's mostly) to live up to the reputation she'd so carefully crafted. Standing at the entrance to the bar, Greg and Dan exchanged a look. Each quite fancied another beer, but not that much. An early night suddenly seemed appealing. They discreetly withdrew. As Greg had feared, this year's conference was proving to be a bust.

This assessment was reinforced by the first session the two men attended the next morning. The hotel's cavernous conference hall was at best a third full; Greg suspected the other delegates must have been tipped off. The speaker was an American management guru who'd flown in from Seattle to deliver the keynote address. Jet lag could conceivably be to blame for his stuttering performance, but not for his complete lack of charisma. Greg, a full English breakfast settling on his stomach, struggled to stay awake as the lecturer monotonously read aloud the slides projected on to the screen behind him.

"This diagram represents the Johari window, comprising quadrants which heuristically facilitate interpersonal relationships."

Greg turned to Dan, who sat beside him taking notes.

"What's the title of this session?"

"Getting Your Message Across."

"Well, there's a definition of irony."

Dan shushed him. Greg wondered if it was too early for a Jack Daniel's. Quarter to ten. A tad degenerate. A change in the speaker's cadence drew his attention back to the stage.

"OK, we're going to have a bit of fun now; we're going to play a game!" Greg hadn't thought it possible for his spirits to sink any lower but now discovered that it was. "I want you to choose a partner, but not somebody you know."

"If this involves hugging, I'm out of here," Greg muttered to Dan. He felt a tap on his shoulder and turned to find, leaning across from two rows behind, an attractive young woman. "On the other hand . . ." He mugged at Dan.

"Hi! I'm . . ."

"Liz," said Greg.

"Oh! Have we met?"

"No. I can read." Greg gestured at the name tag she was wearing on her breast. A very shapely breast, he noted. Liz laughed prettily. She was in her late twenties, he estimated. Beside her sat her friend — Lynda, her badge announced — who was making the acquaintance of Dan. Both women were good-looking, though, in Greg's opinion, Liz, being a brunette like Amanda, narrowly shaved it. From the stage, the speaker's voice interrupted.

"Now, I want you to tell your partner something about yourself, something interesting, that very few people are aware of."

Greg hated party games. But he was prepared to give this one a go.

"You first," Liz said.

Greg considered his options. Something interesting but not widely known. Once, when he was sixteen, his mum had caught him wanking over a picture of Pamela Anderson. No, perhaps not.

"I can do this," he said, pulling his left thumb back against his wrist in a manner that appeared physically impossible.

"Oh my God!" Liz exclaimed. "That's repulsive."

Greg beamed. It was repulsive. And had he not been double-jointed, would have hurt like buggery.

"Your turn," he said brightly.

Liz bit her bottom lip, deep in thought. Full lips, Greg noticed.

"I'm a Sagittarian!" she finally declared.

Greg was acutely underwhelmed. He'd been hoping for a more salacious revelation, something juicy, like her lips.

"That's not very interesting, is it?" Liz asked.

Greg shrugged non-committally — agreeing, without the rudeness of actually saying it. Liz resumed the lip biting. She really was very attractive. Greg found it difficult to tear his eyes from the fold of skin trapped between her teeth, and made no attempt. Within his lower regions something stirred. It was not his full English breakfast.

"It's hard, isn't it?" Liz asked, and for a moment Greg thought she'd noticed. But she meant the task they'd been set.

"I'm allergic to peanuts?" It was posed as a question, presumably not as to whether she really did have a peanut allergy (Greg was prepared to take her word for that), but whether he deemed this admission of sufficient interest. It beat knowing her star sign, but not by much.

"I know!" Liz's eyes lit up, and she leant forward, gesturing to Greg to follow suit. Together they bridged the row between them. She brought her bitten lip close to Greg's ear. "When I'm sexually aroused, I purr like a cat."

There is a poison used by certain tribes in the Amazon rainforest that can render victims instantly paralysed. Liz's disclosure had a similar effect on Greg. He stood, rooted to the spot, his brain frozen like a crashed computer, unable to send commands to his limbs. Liz leant away but held his gaze. She smiled in a manner that Greg, had he had the power of speech, might have described as feline.

"If you'll resume your seats," announced the speaker, revelling in his role as game-show host. Greg somehow managed to drop his arse on to his chair. He could feel the heat of Liz's aura two rows behind him, but dared not look back. The lecture continued for another forty minutes; Greg did not take in one word.

CHAPTER
TWO

Can women have it all? It's a conundrum that is never resolved, and from the perspective of women's magazines, thank God for that, else they'd regularly be short of copy. But Amanda knew the answer: No. You can't be both a full-time mum and a full-time worker; the maths just doesn't add up. She was in awe of mothers who managed to hold down a nine-to-five job. How did they find the time? By having none for themselves, perhaps.

Amanda worked part time, twenty hours a week, but still never seemed to be on top of everything else she needed to do. Take today, for example. She wasn't due at the surgery until the afternoon. After readying the kids for school and dropping them off, she'd nipped down to Barnes to return a dress that had looked better in store than when she'd tried it on at home. Actually, "nipped" is the wrong word. You don't nip anywhere in London nowadays, not outside the exclusion zone of the congestion charge, anyway. The morning and evening rush hours had bled into the middle of the day, until they'd joined up somewhere around lunchtime and filled the whole of the working week. Ah, the joy of living in the capital.

It had been Amanda's plan to take Jess for a walk on the way home. Stuck in traffic, she was ready to nix that idea. But the labradoodle hadn't been out yesterday, either. Amanda made the mistake of glancing in the rear-view mirror, and caught Jess's expectant eye. Guilt overcame her. She turned off the main road towards Ravenscourt Park — not the park nearest to their home, but the most pleasant. Often Amanda would spend more time cruising for a parking space than walking Jess, but she came across one almost immediately, newly vacated, close to the park gates. This must be my lucky day, she thought; perhaps I should buy a lottery ticket.

Jess clamoured to be allowed out. Once they were safely inside the confines of the park, Amanda unclipped the dog's lead. Without a word of thanks, the labradoodle gambolled off, pausing repeatedly to catalogue the myriad new scents since their last visit. Amanda strolled on, compiling a mental note of the chores she still had to complete before going to work. Near the ornamental lake she looked back to check that Jess was within sight, and spotted her a short distance off, making the acquaintance of a St Bernard by shoving her nose up its arse. As a qualified vet, Amanda knew that canine anal glands secrete aromas that give other dogs important information about health, temperament and so on. Even so, she wondered whether Jess mightn't be a little more discreet, especially in public.

Jess loped over to Amanda's side, the St Bernard in pursuit, intent on exercising reciprocal rights and conducting its own internal examination. Amanda knelt down to pat her pet's new friend, but the dog pulled back, eyeing her dubiously.

"He's a little neurotic, I'm afraid."

Amanda turned at the sound of a male voice approaching.

"Always a bit suspicious of people he doesn't know."

"I'd call that sensible," Amanda replied, rising to her feet. "I thought perhaps he recognised me." The owner of the St Bernard frowned, not following her. "I'm a vet," she explained, "so not a dog's best friend."

The guy smiled, accentuating laugh lines framing his hazel eyes. He was in his late forties, Amanda estimated, dressed casually but expensively, like someone trying to give the impression they weren't hung up on fashion, it just came naturally. I bet he buys men's style mags, Amanda thought, and takes note of the ads. Well, it's working for him. He's attractive, even though he'd say so himself.

"Which practice are you with?" the man asked, striking up a conversation Amanda didn't particularly want.

"Alexandra House, off Askew Road."

"We go to Buxton Lodge."

Amanda nodded. "They're good," she said. "We're better."

Again the smile. Amanda couldn't blame the guy. He had a killer smile; it would be a waste not to use it.

"Perhaps we should switch," he said, fixing his eyes on Amanda's in a way that made her think he might be coming on to her.

"Our lists are full," she replied, which wasn't true, but best not encourage him. She turned to resume her walk.

"I'm Ben, by the way."

The tyranny of manners forced Amanda to stop and acknowledge him. "Amanda." She felt a little as though she'd been forced to give out this information against her will.

"Amanda," Ben repeated, rolling the sound around his mouth like a good Shiraz. "That's not a name you hear much nowadays."

Amanda shrugged. "My parents' choice."

"Did you know it comes from Greek?" She didn't. "It means 'divine beauty'. It suits you."

If Amanda had been in any doubt that this guy was flirting, she wasn't now. She thought it best to leave his remark alone, to run through, uncontested, to the keeper.

"I haven't seen you round here before," Ben continued, undaunted.

"And you won't again." The remark came out sounding more brusque than Amanda had intended. The guy meant no harm; it wasn't like he was a pest. She tried to soften the blow. "I mean, we don't come that often."

"That's a pity. Well, we'll just have to hope you do. We're here most days at about this time."

OK, that's enough, thought Amanda. She'd tried to be pleasant but now he was pushing it. Time to make something abundantly clear. "I'm really not interested in being chatted up," she said.

Ben was all innocence. "I just meant that my dog seems to have taken a shine to yours."

It was true. Jess and the St Bernard had progressed beyond the butt-sniffing stage and were playing canine tag, taking turns to chase each other.

Amanda felt herself flush. "Oh. Right. Sorry," she stammered, embarrassed at her presumption. "So you weren't coming on to me?"

"Well, yes. Guilty as charged," Ben confessed, unleashing that smile. "But, in my defence, you're an attractive woman who isn't wearing a wedding ring."

"And what? No ring means I'm there to be hit on?"

"No," Ben said quickly, before adding with a shrug and a little more honesty, "Well, possibly."

Amanda's irritation receded. In truth, she was flattered. She was conscious of being an attractive woman who could still turn the head of many a passing male, but since many a passing male most likely wasn't getting any, this didn't seem much of an accomplishment. At thirty-six, she did wonder for how much longer she would retain her allure. At what age would she become invisible, like her sister Geri, who, as a forty-one-year-old divorcee, had recently started online dating?

"Well, I'm spoken for," said Amanda, conscious of her antiquated choice of words. "We've just never seen the need to get married. We're very happy," she added, unnecessarily.

"And I'm very happy for you. Forgive me if I spoilt your walk." Ben tilted his head, a gesture of apology. If he'd been wearing a hat, perhaps he'd have doffed it. "Come on, Byron!"

The St Bernard leapt to Ben's heel. As they took their leave, the dog cast a wistful look at Jess.

"You didn't —" Amanda called after Ben — "spoil my walk!"

Ben waved an acknowledging hand without turning back. Amanda watched his broad-shouldered retreat. It was true: he hadn't spoilt her walk. Quite the opposite.

Returning to her VW Golf, Amanda googled her name and discovered it wasn't Greek, as Ben had claimed, but Latin. Nor did it mean "divine beauty" but "worthy of love". He had been making it up; it had been a line! She laughed out loud and thought of ringing Geri to share this story. But on reflection she realised that her sister, reduced to trawling the internet for love, might not see the humour. Greg, then. Except he probably wouldn't, either. Oh well, she would just have to cherish the memory for her own private amusement. And putting the car into gear, she did.

Sarah had expected her lunch date, at a chichi little bistro in Highgate village (is there any other kind?), to be a somewhat dry affair; she had failed to take into account her dining companion's voracious thirst for alcohol. Veronica was halfway through an initial glass of Pinot Grigio while Sarah was still perusing the starters. As the dishes were cleared for the arrival of their mains, Veronica emptied the bottle. The booze had not had the effect of loosening her tongue; no stimulant had been necessary. Veronica was naturally garrulous and kept

Sarah entertained with a slurry of unsubstantiated gossip. Miguel, the pro at their club, who was not in the least good-looking but was twenty-four and Spanish, was giving more than tennis lessons to Melissa White. A sixth-former at Russell's private school had been suspended for possession of drugs supplied by the art history teacher. And Pippa Scott's black eyes were not, as Pippa claimed, the result of cosmetic surgery but an abusive husband.

Sarah sat back as the waitress set down her chicken Caesar salad and Veronica complained about her twelve-year-old daughter's brutal periods. It came as something of a shock to Sarah to discover that menstruation was now common among pre-teen girls, but on reflection it had been at around the same age that Russell had started masturbating, judging by the telltale stains on his bedding. Because she felt she had to offer up some tittle-tattle of her own as quid pro quo, Sarah found herself telling Veronica about the internet sites she'd discovered Russell frequented.

"Darling! He's bound to be inquisitive," was Veronica's sanguine reaction. "Though, at his age, you'd hope he'd have a passion for football or *Game of Thrones*, not tying up women."

Sarah felt a maternal instinct to defend her son. "It was all very mild. There weren't even rope burns."

"Still," Veronica continued, not wanting to hear anything that devalued the salaciousness of this morsel, "you don't know what other sites he's been looking at. They may be worse."

Sarah nearly gagged on an anchovy. It had never occurred to her that a dominatrix from Santa Fe might be the least of it. And yet of course it was a distinct possibility.

"If I were you," Veronica sailed blithely on, "I'd keep an eye on him."

Veronica broke off the conversation to call the waitress and quiz her on the whereabouts of their second bottle of wine. Was it perhaps still on the vine? Chastened, the young woman withdrew.

"Keep an eye on him?" Sarah picked up where they'd left off. "How?"

"Oh, there's any number of ways. Hide a camera in his room."

"He's fifteen. I know he gets up to things I don't want to see; I've smelt the evidence."

Veronica's eyes lit up with glee. "Marijuana?"

"No!" Sarah replied without elaborating. Veronica knew what she meant. But that wasn't titillating; all boys did that.

"Then install a program on his computer that will monitor his activity," she said.

"He deletes his browsing history," Sarah protested.

"Of course he does, darling; that's the first thing they learn. No, it's called keylogging. It records every stroke made on the keyboard. And the beauty is the little bastards have no idea you're watching. We've done it with Ruby."

Ruby was Veronica's fourteen-year-old, the older of her two daughters. Sarah was shocked. "You think Ruby might be looking at porn?"

"I know she is, but it's very tame. Good job she's not keylogging me!" Veronica's braying laugh resonated around the restaurant, causing other diners to glance across. "No, we wanted to check that when she said she was in her room working on assignments, she wasn't spending all her time on Facebook."

"And is she?"

"On Facebook? Pretty much, yes. That, Snapchat, Tumblr and Instagram."

The waitress returned with their wine. Sarah still had half of her second glass to go, but accepted a top-up. She didn't want to be thought a killjoy, though she suspected Veronica preferred abstemious company — all the more for her.

"You can download keylogging software from the internet," Veronica continued; then, on seeing Sarah's doubtful expression, "Or get your husband to."

Sarah couldn't envisage either scenario. "I don't think Dan would approve," she said. "After all, it is snooping."

"In your child's best interest! I mean, ask yourself this, darling: would you allow your son to go to a sex club frequented by perverts and degenerates?"

"No, of course not."

"Well, that's what the internet is."

Sarah had never thought of it quite like that, but she could see Veronica's point. Who could imagine what sort of people Russell might meet online? Certainly not her naive son.

"Look," Veronica continued, draining her glass and pouring herself another, "if you don't feel confident installing the software, I'll have Tony pop round to do it for you. Dan doesn't even need to know."

Wasn't it Sarah's duty as a mother to keep Russell safe at all times?

Dan was feeling guilty. Earlier, he had told a lie and, even though it was a small one, white in complexion, he was riddled with regret. During the lunch break he'd considered telling Greg, casting him in the role of father confessor, seeking his absolution, but he suspected Greg would simply laugh and tell him it was no biggie. And even though Dan knew this to be true, it didn't make him feel any better.

The cause of his guilt wasn't the lie itself so much as the person he'd told it to: Lynda — with a "y" — the young woman in the earlier session with whom he'd exchanged a little-known but interesting personal fact. In the hours since, Dan had thought of any number of fascinating details about himself. Well, three. But at the time, when this task was sprung upon them, he had frozen. He could conjure no memories of his forty-one years that seemed noteworthy in any way. Just when his vacuity was beginning to embarrass them both, Dan had blurted out that, when he was eight years old, he had walked in on his parents having sex, and as a result had been so traumatised that he had not spoken for a year, and subsequently had developed a speech impediment. He had related all this with a lisp.

Like the best fictions, it had its basis in fact. Dan had indeed once caught his parents making love. But, far from being anguished, he'd been engrossed, and had hung at the door until his father's shuddering ejaculation. Why Dan had felt it necessary to embellish on what was a perfectly satisfactory story he had no idea. Had he been hoping to impress Lynda? If so, he had succeeded. As his narrative had reached its (and his father's) climax, her olive-green eyes had moistened. Their sympathetic mien had left no doubt that she could visualise the eight-year-old Danny struck dumb by the horror he was witnessing, and was at his side as he ran to hide under the kitchen table, his vocal cords already starting to spasm.

Lynda was an enchanting girl with a lovely nature and Dan felt that he had mocked her. He had seen her since, across the crowded hotel lobby; they'd exchanged smiles — hers, he'd thought, tinged with compassion. It didn't matter that they would never meet again. He had caused her distress. Small and soon to be forgotten, yes, but unjustified, based upon a lie, and for that Dan felt a shit.

Like Dan, who sat beside him in another stultifying lecture, Greg was present in body but not mind. His thoughts too had gone AWOL, revisiting the conference session of that morning. "When I'm sexually aroused, I purr like a cat" played on a loop in his head. Greg liked to think he had a knack for reading people — in part, it was what made him a good salesman — but he couldn't for the life of him work out why Liz would have said such a thing. Had she perhaps been coming on to him? His ego liked to think so. Or did she have Tourette's and was prone to inappropriate outbursts?

"When I'm sexually aroused, I purr like a cat." Greg replayed Liz's words, again and again, each time with a slightly different emphasis or intonation. But, however he phrased it, he couldn't escape the conclusion that she had been sending him an invitation, gauging whether he had any interest. Him! He couldn't deny it was flattering. "When I'm sexually aroused, I purr like a cat." This time the voice in his head sounded like Mariella Frostrup. Sexy. He shifted in his chair to release the pressure in his trousers, then resumed his pleasurable analysis.

Sarah was impressed by the speed with which she mastered the keylogging software that Veronica's husband, Tony, had installed on the family laptop. Perhaps she wasn't the technological dinosaur she'd imagined.

Tony leant in to show her a shortcut. Sarah reeled from the stench of his armpits. No wonder Veronica resorted to online porn. Not for the first time, Sarah was grateful for Dan's high standard of personal hygiene.

"It's really quite straightforward, isn't it?" she said, to give herself an excuse to lean back and look Tony in the eye, out of range of his BO. "And you're sure Russell won't have any idea that I'm checking up on him?"

"Not unless he's looking for it," replied Tony, thankfully standing. "Would it be something he might suspect? Or think you capable of?"

"I can't even download a photo to Facebook."

"That's 'upload'," Tony said, unsure whether she was joking. (She wasn't.)

Sarah rose quickly, as he threatened to bend down again. "So now there's just the computer in his room," she said.

"The motherlode!" The glint in Tony's eye was just a little disturbing.

As Sarah and Tony were climbing the stairs, Russell was on his way home from swimming practice. He loved swimming because of the sensation of being underwater. It was like a filter to the outside world. Light was diffused and sound suppressed. He felt cut off, unreachable. A few months earlier, while flicking through TV channels, he'd happened upon a rerun of *The Graduate*, joining the movie at the moment when Dustin Hoffman's character, Ben, was being quizzed by his parents' friends about his intentions, post-college. Ben had taken refuge in the family's swimming pool, sitting on the bottom, breathing through an oxygen tank. The beauty of the image had left a lasting impression on Russell. Never had he felt his own need for solitude so eloquently expressed. He'd subsequently downloaded the movie from the internet so he could watch it from the start, but five minutes in had been bored. God, those old films were so slow! Hadn't they heard of editing?

His mum and dad had been both surprised and delighted when Russell had announced his intention to try out for the swimming team. Their son and competitive sport? It had seemed an unlikely pairing.

But then they were unaware of the real reason for his interest. Josh Trelawney was a boy two years ahead of Russell, on whom he had a crush. In Russell's mind, Josh was perfect. Everything about him: his confidence, his smile, his swimmer's physique. Russell wasn't gay. He didn't think he was gay. He didn't want to think he was gay. He just wanted to be the older boy, or, if he couldn't be him, then be around him. Admittedly, when Russell masturbated, he increasingly (like, always) found himself thinking of Josh: Josh stretching before diving in; Josh hauling himself out of the pool, his triceps tensing; Josh towelling off after a shower. But that didn't make Russell gay, he told himself. And even if it did, so what? Who cares? Who fucking cares? Fuck you, if you do. Fuck you!

Such thoughts often occupied Russell, and they assailed him now as he let himself into the house. Distracted, he would not have noticed the figures on the landing had he not heard his mother's voice, betraying a hint of shame as she said, "I can't pretend it doesn't leave me feeling a little grubby."

Russell looked up, at the same moment as Sarah looked down.

"Russell!" she started. "I thought you had swimming."

"Cancelled. Turd in the shallow end."

Russell's gaze shifted to the middle-aged man with his mother. Sarah noticed her son's eyes settle on her partner-in-crime. Is this how the so-called "plumbers" felt when their break-in at the Watergate building was rumbled? she wondered.

"Oh, this is the plumber," she improvised. "I'm finally getting the shower looked at."

Russell regarded the man. He didn't look like a plumber. He wasn't wearing overalls, but suit trousers and a pale blue shirt that had dark blue patches under the arms.

"I'll email you our quote, Mrs Sinclair." The guy's performance was as unconvincing as Sarah's. Russell watched them descend the stairs. Their expressions were such studies in innocence, Russell was convinced of their guilt. And he could guess their crime. But how to be certain?

"Can I have some Frosties?" he casually asked his mother.

"Sure," Sarah replied, showing the "plumber" to the door. Bang to rights! His mum never let him have cereal after school.

It was the last night of the conference. Inebriated delegates, displaying all the discipline of a Beijing bus queue, stormed the hotel bar, baying their demands for immediate and copious amounts of alcohol. The two harassed bartenders, massively outnumbered, fought a rearguard action to hold the seething hordes at bay. It was carnage. Greg had managed to manoeuvre himself close to the battlefront. He stood at the thickset shoulder of a customer being served — a prop forward, judging by his girth. When the guy received his drinks and withdrew, Greg would insinuate himself into the gap and be next in line. He'd already laid the foundation, making eye contact with the barmaid and smiling in a sympathetic manner that said, "You're doing a great job. And you've clocked that I'm next, right?"

The rugby player paid for his round and pushed past Greg, slopping beer on the sleeve of Greg's jacket. But this was no time for recrimination, not when glory was his for the taking. Greg slid into the vacated space.

"Four pints of Directors, love."

Greg frowned. That didn't sound like his voice. And indeed it wasn't. The order had come from behind, shouted over his shoulder by a Young Turk in a sharp suit, seeking to jump the queue. Greg was outraged, doubly when the barmaid, *his* barmaid, acknowledged the request and started pulling pints, her eyes washing over Greg like he didn't exist. Greg's usurper, a handsome bastard a good ten years Greg's junior, eased his way to the bar like he belonged there and fobbed Greg off with a matey wink.

Greg wanted to hit him, but the bloke looked a bit handy so that wasn't going to happen. Protest then, rail against this breach of etiquette. But neither was that an option. Complaining would only emphasise his emasculation. Better he limp off into a quiet part of the jungle to die. Greg felt all of his thirty-eight years, and then some. He vowed that this would be the last time he attended this conference.

He remained at the bar. He wanted to glower at the barmaid, bore daggers into her soul, but all power lay with her. Greg only had injustice in his arsenal and, as the world's poor know all too well, that is an unloaded gun. Finally, having flirted with the queue jumper over his change, the barmaid deigned to look Greg's way.

"Four JD-and-cokes," Greg snapped coldly. Usually he'd have added, "please," but, like Elvis, politeness had left the building, taking the same route as the barmaid's tip.

"Hello again!"

Greg turned at the sound of a voice beside him.

"Liz!"

"You remember my name!" She beamed.

"No, you've still got your badge on."

Liz rolled her eyes — silly me! — shooting a hand to the name tag on her breast. It remained a very shapely breast, Greg noted.

"Let me get you a drink," he offered.

"Oh, I'm with someone." Just his luck. It was bound to be someone young, good-looking and male. He scored two out of three. Liz's companion was young and good-looking. And female. It was Lynda.

"Fantastic!" Greg said. "The more, the merrier!"

The barmaid returned carrying his drinks.

"Oh, and four more." The barmaid shot him a sour look. "Please," he added sickly sweetly, which had the desired effect of further pissing her off. Politeness may have returned, but she could still stick her tip.

While Greg was at the bar, Dan was on his mobile, hoping to turn a lead into a deal. Landing the contract would still leave daylight between him and this month's target, but at least he'd be in there fighting. As he always liked to say, and Sarah had tired of hearing, slim chance is better than fat chance. But this call seemed to offer neither, as it went straight to voicemail. Dan left a brief message that he hoped didn't betray his desperation, then punched off the phone.

"Look who I bumped into!"

Greg's voice drew Dan back to the here and now. He looked up to see Greg with Liz and . . . Oh, shit.

"You remember Lynda, don't you?" Greg pulled up chairs for the women.

"Yeth!" Dan lisped, attempting a welcoming smile and almost making it.

Amanda had finally succeeded in wrangling Molly and Lauren into bed. It was never an easy task, made harder because the girls shared a room. This was not due to a lack of space. The sisters did not regard sharing as a hardship; to them it was "bunking down together" — fun. The day would come when each would crave privacy and despise her sibling, but not just yet.

It was usually Greg who put the girls to bed. He had less opportunity to be with his daughters and therefore more patience with their delaying tactics. In his absence Amanda was nominally in charge. She was edging towards lights out, but slowly. The girls were double-teaming her, with Molly now taking the lead.

"Guess what happened today in science?" she asked as Amanda tucked her in.

"Tomorrow," Amanda said wearily, with no great hope of staunching her daughter's flow.

"Jason Livingstone asked me to be his girlfriend."

Amanda perked up. This augured to be a bit more interesting than your average classroom anecdote.

40

"What did you say?"

"That I'd think about it."

Amanda smiled. Although only ten, Molly was remarkably self-composed. Amanda was aware that a few of the girls in Year Five had boyfriends, but thankfully Molly had, as yet, shown little interest.

"Well, I think that's very wise," Amanda said. "You don't want to rush into these things." She kissed her daughter and moved towards the door, her hand reaching for the light switch.

"I don't think I want to be, but I'm not sure." Molly's voice was tinged with doubt.

Amanda sighed. Tomorrow was a school day. The girls should be asleep by now, but she remembered how perplexing playground romance could be. She returned to perch on the edge of Molly's bed.

"You're still young," she assured her. "I didn't have my first boyfriend till I was fourteen."

"Was that Daddy?" Lauren piped up from across the room.

"Go to sleep," Amanda ordered her younger daughter.

Lying on one elbow, Lauren raised a disdainful eyebrow to show what she thought of that command. Her mother accepted defeat.

"No. It wasn't Daddy. He came later." About seven blokes later, she didn't add.

"But if I say no to Jason," continued Molly, claiming the spotlight once more, "he might ask Tilly Reece."

"Is Jason the one with the ears?" Lauren chipped in. The others ignored her.

"Would that be so bad?" Amanda asked, apropos of Tilly Reece.

Molly was horrified. "She's my best friend!"

She's your best friend this week, thought Amanda, who suspected Tilly could kiss goodbye to being Molly's bestie should she and Jason hook up (whatever that actually meant).

"I don't know what to say to you," she told her older daughter, "except things will look a lot clearer in the morning."

Reflecting on what a useless piece of advice this was, Amanda gave Molly a kiss. "Now go to sleep, both of you!"

She switched off the light and almost pulled the door shut but remembered to leave it ajar by the prescribed amount. She was halfway along the landing when she heard Lauren's voice.

"I wouldn't be his girlfriend. Not with those ears."

"You're eight!" Molly castigated her sister. "What would you know about love?"

Amanda smiled and continued down the stairs.

CHAPTER
THREE

The moment Amanda had predicted had finally arrived: Greg was having a ball at the annual conference. So too, it seemed, was Dan, though Greg noticed he'd developed a peculiar lisp. Probably alcohol-induced, thought Greg; they'd both had a skinful. Liz and Lynda were great company, their knowledge of drinking games encyclopedic, not that Greg in his inebriated state could have hoped to spell that word, or even pronounce it. The squeals and laughter from their table cut through the tumult in the sweaty, teeming bar. The young buck who'd stolen Greg's place in the bar queue shot more than one envious glance his way, much to Greg's satisfaction.

As the night wore on, the lights were dimmed and the music cranked up. Beyoncé's "Single Ladies" came on; Liz whooped with glee and pulled Greg to his feet. He let her lead him to the dance floor. Amanda would not have recognised him. She knew Greg as a reluctant dancer, but tonight he'd reached the optimal level of intoxication. He'd gone beyond self-conscious but was still some way short of unconscious.

Dan barely looked up as Greg and Liz staggered off. He was showing Lynda a photo of Russell.

"He looks a really sweet kid," she said.

"He wath then," Dan lisped. "He'th thiftheen now."

Dan replaced the picture in his wallet.

"Look, I've a confession," he said. "I don't have a lisp."

"I know." Lynda smiled.

"You do?"

"My brother, James, has a lisp. You can tell when someone's putting it on."

Dan's face fell. "Oh, my God. I'm so sorry. If I'd had any idea . . ."

Lynda burst out laughing. "I'm winding you up."

Dan was confused. "You don't have a brother?"

"He doesn't have a lisp. But I could tell you didn't either. It kept coming and going."

Dan felt such a fool. "Why didn't you say anything?"

Lynda shrugged. "No skin off my nose. Besides, me and Liz had a bet on how long you'd keep it up." She checked her watch. "I've won."

Dan shook his head in awe. He thought he'd been having her on, while it was the other way round. What a great girl.

"So why'd you do it?" Lynda asked matter-of-factly, taking a swig of Jack Daniel's.

Dan bowed his head. They'd been getting on so well. And now she'd think he was an idiot. Unable to meet Lynda's eye, Dan described his dread of being thought dull. Even to his ears, it sounded pathetic. Lynda received this explanation in a stony silence. Or so it seemed to Dan. But a silence has no character, it's just an absence of words, the rest is our interpretation, and

Dan couldn't see the smile that spread across Lynda's face.

"That is so sweet," she said, dissolving into laughter. Her laugh, when she *really* laughed, as she did now, was more of a cackle, like a pantomime dame. It should have been unattractive but Dan found it just the opposite.

Greg was kicking up a storm on the dance floor. He and Liz *owned* it. One of Molly and Lauren's party tricks was to mimic, step for step, the video to "Single Ladies (Put A Ring On It)". Last Christmas, they'd insisted on teaching Greg the choreography so the three of them could perform the routine for Amanda. At the time, Greg had wondered why he was allowing himself to suffer such indignity. Was it for the kids' amusement, of which there had been plenty? Amanda's? No. He'd thought so at the time, but he understood now that it had all been in preparation for this moment, his apotheosis. It was uncanny. Greg *became* Beyoncé.

Bleary delegates formed a circle, hooting and hollering as Greg and Liz swivelled, thrust and generally bust a move. With perfect timing, they hit the end beat and held the pose, index finger on right hand assertively pointing at ring finger on left. The bar went wild, clapping and cheering. Greg, gasping a little but trying to play down his breathlessness, hugged Liz to him, like *Strictly* contestants awarded perfect tens. He leant to kiss her on her glistening cheek, but she turned her face so their lips met, then she murmured something in his ear. With the music cranked up to eleven, its meaning was lost on him. "What?" he shouted above the din. Liz grabbed his shirt, pulled him close and pressed her mouth against his earlobe. This Greg found a not altogether unpleasant sensation. She repeated what she'd said and this time he caught every word. Or thought he did. But surely not. He couldn't have. Between his eardrum and his brain, the message must have become garbled. He cocked his head enquiringly, like Jess the labradoodle on hearing her name called. Liz held his gaze and nodded. You heard right, the gesture said. Bloody hell!

"One minute," Greg said, buying himself some time. About sixty seconds' worth.

Dan was grateful for the volume of the music. It meant he and Lynda had to lean in close to each other as they made conversation. Their heads were almost touching; Dan could feel her breath upon his cheek. He almost swooned.

Lynda and Liz, he had learnt, worked for a London marketing agency that specialised in information technology; Dan had vaguely heard of it. Lynda rented a room in a two-bedroom flat in Willesden, a part of north London that local estate agents, with more imagination than optimism, describe as "up and coming". Her flatmate was an air hostess she barely knew and rarely saw. Dan was preparing a supplementary question when Greg arrived at their table, sweating and skittish like a Grand National runner spooked by the big occasion.

46

"Can I have a word?" he asked Dan, his voice an octave higher than usual.

"Now?" Dan wished Greg would go away. Instead of replying, Greg took Dan by the arm, hoisted him out of his seat and hauled him across the bar. Dan just had time to shoot a despairing look Lynda's way.

The door to the Gents' slammed against the wall as Greg lumbered in, dragging Dan with him. Greg paced agitatedly while Dan crossed unsteadily to a urinal; for the past half hour he'd been in urgent need of a pee. He unhitched himself, feeling the joyous relief as his stream cascaded against the steel splashback. He leant his free hand against the wall for balance; he was more pissed than he'd realised.

"You got any coins?" Greg loomed at Dan's shoulder.

"I think so. Hang on a sec."

Greg waited for Dan to finish up. And waited. And waited. Christ, this was one impressive spray, Greg thought. Finally, Dan zipped himself in and fumbled in his pocket for change.

"Great evening; nice girls," Dan said, slurring slightly.

"Yeah, yeah." Greg was impatient.

"You know Lynda used to be a gymnast?" Dan handed Greg some coins.

"Really?" Greg paused, processing this information. "Wow!"

He crossed to a device on the wall and drunkenly fumbled money into the slot. It took Dan a moment to register that it was a condom machine.

"What the hell are you doing?"

"Mate! We are on a promise! Liz just came on to me."

"What?"

"Invited herself back to my room. Made it pretty clear what she'd like to happen there."

"You're kidding!"

Greg pulled open the machine's tray and, at the second attempt, dug out a box of condoms.

"Are you out of your mind?" Dan cried.

"No. Off my face, perhaps." Greg grinned. Dan didn't.

"You're not seriously thinking . . . You can't . . ." Dan was struggling to form complete sentences. "You're gonna cheat on Amanda?"

"Whoa, whoa, whoa!" Greg recoiled in horror. "Who said anything about cheating?"

"You just did."

"Not *cheating*. This is just a bit of fun."

"*Fun?*"

"Yes, fun. You remember what that is?"

Greg prised the cellophane wrapper off the condom box.

Dan gawped at his friend in disbelief. He wondered whether he knew him at all. "Have you done this sort of thing before?" he asked.

Greg seemed almost offended. "No. Never."

"So why do it now?"

It was a fair question. Flirting was second nature to Greg, like a language in which he was fluent. But he had never been tempted to take it any further. Why should he? He and Amanda were happy. So what made tonight different? Not drink. He'd been pissed before, on many occasions. What else then? Greg could spend the rest of time mulling this question. Or he could have sex with Liz. Maybe that was it: opportunity, pure and simple. It wasn't every day, or indeed ever, that an attractive, younger woman propositioned him. Liz *wanted* him. In her eyes, he was desirable. He wasn't some clapped-out thirty-eight-year-old who couldn't get served at the bar. He was *virile*. He owed it to her, to himself, to all men on the cusp of obsolescence. Amanda wouldn't mind. She wouldn't know, and what you don't know can't hurt you. It was a victimless crime, not even a crime — conference sex, and everyone knows that doesn't count. He turned his attention back to Dan.

"Tell me, how often have you thought about cheating on Sarah?"

Dan's answer was immediate and unequivocal. "Me? Never!"

"Come off it. You must have fantasised about sex with another woman."

Dan looked uncomfortable. This time his denial wasn't as swift, or even voiced.

"Fantasies are harmless," he said, "so long as that's what they remain."

"So, what? You'd rather dream about life than live it? Cos I'll tell you this, Dan, if Liz is up for it, you can bet Lynda is, too."

Dan was assailed by conflicting emotions. He wanted to defend Lynda's reputation, deny that she was the kind of girl who'd sleep with a man she'd only just met. But, because that man was him, he also wanted to believe it possible.

Greg sensed his advantage, pressed it home. He tore open the box of condoms, extracted one, held out the foil wrapper to Dan. "Come on," he said, his eyes locked on Dan. "We're mates; we're in this together."

Dan recoiled to the other end of the Gents', putting a physical distance between him and his tempter.

"No! Even if she *were* interested, no!"

Greg took a step towards his friend. Dan raised a hand, defensively, as if it held a cross and a vampire was closing on him.

"I know what your game is," he shot at Greg. "You know what you're doing is wrong. And you think, if you can involve me, you won't be as culpable."

Greg stopped, considered what Dan said. He had no idea whether it was true, but it sounded plausible.

"Mate," he said, adopting a conciliatory tone, resuming his slow advance on Dan. "We have maybe thirty years of sexually active life ahead of us. That's a hell of a long time to spend with one woman, however much you love her. These girls," Greg jerked a thumb towards the bar, "they're giving us a chance to step off that treadmill, the last we might ever get. They're grown-ups; they know the score. They don't want a 'relationship'; they just want to have a bit of fun. With us!"

Greg reached Dan, pressed the condom into his hand. Dan stared at the wrapper's seductively shiny

50

surface, his mouth suddenly dry. He looked up at Greg. "No, I couldn't." He offered the condom back, but instead of taking it, Greg closed Dan's hand around the packet, pressing his fingers tight.

"Lynda's a great-looking girl," Greg insisted, "ten years younger than your wife. And a former gymnast, so *limber*."

Dan opened his fist and regarded the condom lying on his palm, as enticing as a siren's call. He thought about Sarah, how their sixteen-year marriage had become mired, stuck in a rut. He could count the times they'd made love in the last year on the fingers of one hand, not including the thumb. Or the pinky. He thought of Lynda. What a sweet girl. Could she really be attracted to him? It seemed unlikely — improbable, even.

Come on, come on, Greg silently urged, conscious of the passing minutes. Make your bloody mind up!

Dan envied Greg's confidence, and the ease with which he could override his conscience. But Dan was not like Greg. Not like him at all. Was it morality or fear of rejection that caused Dan to shake his head?

"I can't. Sarah would find out."

"She won't find out!"

"She'd know! Or I'd have to tell her. We tell each other everything!"

Greg sighed. He was very fond of Dan but there were times he found him exasperating. This was one of them. "Well, just don't fuck it up for me!"

Greg turned and strode out. Lingering, Dan caught sight of his reflection in the mirror above the washbasins. He thought he looked a little diminished. He trailed Greg out of the Gents'.

Amanda was watching a repeat of *Lewis* on ITV3. She thought she might have seen it before, but couldn't be sure. One episode was very much like another. Bicycles, Oxford quads and Kevin Whately's doleful expression. Was he the least charismatic leading man on television? she wondered. Greg had a theory that you could tell who the killer was by looking at the cast list. The murderer, he reckoned, was always the starriest name; it was only the chance to play the villain that persuaded them to sign on. It was annoying how often he was right.

Jess, snoozing stretched out on the floor at Amanda's feet, lifted her head as thunder grumbled in the distance. A storm was approaching. By now, most dogs would be whimpering under the table, but Jess had never been particularly bothered by loud noises, even fireworks. Amanda nevertheless gave her a reassuring stroke.

Lightning snuck under the curtains. A few seconds later, thunder rumbled, louder, moving closer. Jess stirred, the TV flickered, and from upstairs came two little voices.

"Mum?"

"It's nothing; go back to sleep," Amanda called, reluctant to miss the ending. She and Lewis had come this far together; she wanted to complete the journey.

The next lightning flash and thunder clap were almost simultaneous, the storm now overhead. The windows trembled in their frames. Jess barked at the same time as the girls screamed.

"*Mum!*"

Amanda sighed. She knew she would never discover who had murdered a retired professor, his housekeeper and a visiting American academic. But it was probably Simon Callow. Switching off the television, she headed for the stairs. Jess padded loyally along at her heel.

Greg returned to find the bar as he had left it: the music loud, the behaviour louche. Jackets had been discarded, as had inhibitions. On the dance floor was an overabundance of pale and flabby flesh. With Dan a couple of paces behind, like a wife in the Middle East, Greg forged a path through the mass of writhing, sweaty bodies. Liz and Lynda looked up on their approach.

"We thought you'd gone to bed." This from Liz.

"Without you?" Greg aimed for nonchalant and landed roughly in the same postcode.

Liz leant in to Lynda. She dropped her voice conspiratorially. "I'll see you at breakfast." Lynda nodded, her eyes flitting reflexively to Dan. Like him, she seemed uncomfortable, a reluctant witness to this brazen transaction.

Greg and Liz made, a little unsteadily, for the exit, Greg placing a solicitous and, Dan thought, proprietorial hand on Liz's elbow. Dan managed a wan smile at Lynda. He could think of no small talk; the night had progressed beyond that. They sat in an awkward silence, each conscious of the absence of the others and its reason. Dan swirled his glass of bourbon, as though hoping that a topic of conversation might be discerned among its depths. He came up empty. He stole a glance at Lynda just as she was glancing at him. They exchanged bashful smiles.

"Would you like another drink?" Dan asked, even though she still nursed half a Jackie D.

"No. Thank you. I thought I'd call it a night."

"I'll come with you," Dan said, rising; then he heard how those words must sound to her ears. Like presumption. He reddened. "I mean, I'll leave with you." That sounded almost as bad. "At the same time as you." Oh, shut up, Dan, he told himself.

Greg and Liz stepped out of the lift at Greg's floor. He had a momentary horror. Which room was he in? Was it 612? Or 621? The doors all looked the same. Why weren't key cards numbered? For security, obviously, but come on! How embarrassing it would be if he got the wrong room! Worse if it were occupied. 612 or 621? What if it were neither? How long would Liz stand there while he tried random doors along the corridor? Talk about a passion killer.

They arrived outside 621. Yes, this was it, he was almost sure. Unless it was 612, diagonally opposite. Greg felt like a bomb-disposal expert, poised to choose between two wires. Which to cut? Green or red? Red or green? He hoped Liz couldn't see the tremor in his hand as he fumbled the key card into its slot.

A red light appeared. Fuck, fuck, fuck! Stay calm, he told himself. It didn't always engage first time. He shot Liz a (he hoped) reassuring smile as he pulled the card out then eased it back in, like a solicitous lover, or a safe-cracker feeling for the right combination. A green light lit up and Greg heard the lock roll back, the sweet sound of success. He triumphantly pushed open the door and held it wide, his shoulder straining against its weight. Liz walked ahead of him into his room: fantasy made flesh.

Six floors below, Dan and Lynda found a lift standing open, waiting to bear them aloft. They entered. Dan pushed the button for the eighth floor. He turned to Lynda. "Which floor are you?"

"Fifteen." Was it Dan's imagination or did he sense a hint of let-down in her tone? His finger hovered over the button a moment before he pressed it.

"Hold it!" a drunken voice hollered. A ruddy-faced delegate fell into the lift, clutching his jacket, his tie and his sleeping partner for the night, a woman with sweat-smeared make-up and whisky breath. The guy, who looked to be in his mid-fifties but was actually ten years younger but fifteen kilos overweight, punched a floor button and leered at his conquest.

The lift ascended. The newly arrived and almost as newly formed couple began pawing each other like teenagers, slobbering kisses that aimed for the mouth but didn't always hit their target. Dan and Lynda stood mutely by, apparently engrossed in the illuminated numbers above the lift doors. Dan watched them change, marking off the floors one by one, counting down their time together. He desperately wanted to say something to Lynda.

"I think you're wonderful. You deserve to meet someone who'll make you happy."

That's what Dan wanted to say, but shyness prevented him. So instead he said nothing, just stood in rigid silence, doing his best to ignore the couple making out. With his neck craned upwards, he watched the numbers mount: six . . . seven . . . eight. The lift shuddered to a halt. Its doors parted with a sigh, as though to expel him for having failed to seize the day. Pussy, they seemed to jeer.

"Well, this is me," he said lamely. Lynda nodded and smiled shyly. Should he kiss her? On the cheek, just to say goodbye. But what if she misinterpreted his leaning in, and recoiled from his puckered lips? A handshake then. No, that would be ridiculously formal. Dan settled on a compromise, a wave, which really did look ridiculous. "It was nice meeting you," he said. "Perhaps I'll see you tomorrow."

Again Lynda smiled hesitantly. Was that another tinge of regret Dan sensed? Or did she just wish he'd hurry up and get the fuck out of the lift so she could go to bed? He had no idea, but of this he was sure: he didn't want to leave her.

"I had a lovely evening," he said.

"Me too," Lynda replied. Which, it struck Dan, is what you say when you're being polite. Except her eyes held his. Perhaps she meant it. Who knew? Not Dan.

He could think of nothing else to say. He stepped forward, colliding with the lift doors as they closed. Instead of springing back, the doors seemed insistent that they had the right of way. They buffeted him

56

repeatedly. Dan managed to force them ajar and slip through the gap, but it was a humiliating retreat. Fitting, really. Again his eyes found Lynda's, a second or so before the doors shut and the lift spirited her away.

It was! Regret! Dan was certain of it. That was the look he'd seen in Lynda's eyes.

"Piss! Shit! Wank! Fuck!" he exclaimed.

Sarah was luxuriating, there was no other word for it. All the boxes were ticked: a bubble bath, the water hot enough to discomfort a lobster; a large glass of South African Pinotage, both the glass and the measure large; candles, six of them, giving out a sepulchral glow that caused shadows to dance on the bathroom tiles; and the piéce de résistance, the storm still raging outside. Sarah had deliberately left the blinds open to admit the intermittent flashes of lightning, a *son et lumière* Nature had laid on for her private enjoyment. Sarah loved an electrical storm. She found its raw energy a visceral thrill. It was almost sexual.

A low rumble of thunder sent a shudder through her body. It was like listening to poetry read by James Earl Jones. She shifted the wine glass to her left hand and slipped her right under the waterline. Her breathing became heavy. She rarely masturbated; she was too self-conscious. She couldn't lose herself in the moment, but instead became a witness to it. It was like an out-of-body experience. She could see herself, her fingers lodged between her thighs, her hand quivering like a Parkinson's sufferer. The image always struck her as faintly absurd, as base as two dogs fucking. But tonight she had no such qualms. She took another mouthful of wine, allowing a little to spill over her chin and trickle down her neck. She strangled a cry; Russell might still be up. Her fingers probed deeper, to a faster tempo. The water lapped from one end of the bath to the other and over the side, spilling on to the travertine floor. Christ, this felt good! It was so long since she'd been fucked — *properly* fucked. As her orgasm broke like a wave over her, the first tear slid down her cheek.

The drunk couple had progressed beyond heavy petting by the time Lynda's lift approached her floor. Their proximity made her deeply uncomfortable; it was like having closer than front row seats at a live sex show. Thank God there wasn't audience participation. She idly wondered whether there was an elevator equivalent of the Mile High Club. The Mezzanine Floor Club, perhaps. It was with relief that Lynda alighted. She started towards her room, feeling in her bag for her key card.

It occurred just as she was passing the emergency stairs. She wasn't prepared, but why should she be? Who expects to be mugged in the corridor of a four-star hotel, even in Birmingham? But that's what Lynda thought was happening as the fire door crashed open and an assailant leapt out at her. She tried to scream but her vocal cords were paralysed by fear. She scrambled in her bag for her rape alarm. And then she recognised him.

"Dan!"

Dan couldn't speak.

"Are you all right?"

Doubled over, sucking in oxygen, Dan tried to raise a reassuring hand. He hadn't the energy, so settled for flapping a limp arm. It could just as easily have been a distress signal.

"You'd better come and sit down."

Lynda helped him along the corridor. Sprinting seven floors had brought Dan to the brink of a heart attack. And the threshold of Lynda's room. It was more than worth it.

In the thirteen years Greg had been with Amanda, he had not kissed another woman. Socially, of course, but not in earnest. Not like this, with tongues. It surprised him how dissimilar the experience could be. He'd assumed, for example, that the lips on one woman would feel very much like those on another (apart from Angelina Jolie, whose lips always reminded Greg of a bouncy castle). But Liz's mouth bore little comparison to Amanda's, though that didn't stop Greg making one. And she used it differently. Amanda liked to brush her lips against Greg's; Liz was more assertive. She mashed their mouths together, her tongue tracing the outline of his teeth, as though counting to ensure he had a full set.

Even through the protective layers of a bra and blouse, her breasts felt different too. Amanda's were petite (a word she preferred to "small"); Liz's were full, navel oranges to Amanda's imperial mandarins. No,

Greg corrected himself, mandarins tended to be a little saggy, their skin looser than the flesh within. Amanda's were more like cherry tomatoes. Christ, stop thinking about fruit! Greg admonished himself. And Amanda. Get in the moment, man!

Is there a more erotic act than removing a woman's blouse? Greg wondered, as he lingered over each button. The bra Liz was wearing was made of lace. It was not the sort Amanda would buy. Maybe in their early days, but now she tended to shop at M&S, practicality trumping sensuality. Greg slid a hand inside, his fingers brushing a nipple, which hardened at his touch. He wanted to take her breast in his mouth, and sent his free hand around Liz's back to separate hook and eye. It struck him that it was a while since he had undressed Amanda. Nowadays, they were generally naked before foreplay commenced. He was out of practice. He struggled to find the clasp and dispatched his other hand to assist. Was it at the front or back? He felt like an inexperienced adolescent, clumsily fumbling. Where was the bloody thing? He was in danger of fucking this up. Liz spared his embarrassment, reaching behind with one practised hand. Greg descended on a liberated nipple, flicking it with his tongue as his mouth encircled her areola. So different to Amanda's, he thought. Amanda's were much more . . . Christ! Will you shut the fuck up about Amanda?

Amanda lay in bed, wide awake. She had Molly pressed into one side of her, Lauren the other. The girls had begged to be allowed to sleep in their parents' room and, though the storm was already passing over, Amanda had acquiesced. When Greg was away, the three of them often ended up in the same bed. It never made for a restful night. Lauren, in particular, was a pain. In her sleep, she'd turn sideways and dig her feet into her mother's ribs, seeking to nudge Amanda over and claim more mattress for herself. Amanda didn't mind. It was a treat to have her children snuggled into her, to have this opportunity to gaze unobserved at their faces, so peaceful in repose. Careful not to disturb her, Amanda shunted Lauren across, so that the eight-year-old only occupied her third of the bed and then some. She stroked a strand of hair off Molly's face and replaced her favourite soft toy, a scruffy cat called Clarissa, in the crook of her arm. She wished Greg could see his daughters at this moment. They were so beautiful. She wondered whether he was sleeping any better than her.

Liz was naked, save for her knickers; Greg still wore his underpants and socks. As he lay on top of her, he attempted to peel off a sock with his opposite foot. The first time he missed, the second he scratched his calf and drew blood, the third he nearly dislocated a toe. Sod that, he thought. They can stay. But you can't make love in socks, not when they're all you're wearing, and now Liz was pawing at his underpants in an effort to remove them. Greg reached behind, flapping a hand towards his right foot, as though attempting an advanced yoga pose. He managed to grab hold of his sock in the same instant that he felt his hip buckle. He cried out in pain, but to Liz it must have sounded like rapture because she tightened her grip on his balls. It was no good. Greg had to get shot of the socks! He bucked away from Liz's grasp and ripped them off, flinging them across the room.

Now they were both down to their last item of clothing and Greg could fully enjoy himself. But as Liz sent an exploratory hand past his waistband, an image popped into Greg's head — of Amanda in bed, flanked by their daughters! Outside the bedroom window, lightning flashed. The girls squealed and burrowed into their mother's arms. What was this? A memory? A dream? Or a vision? Storms had been forecast for west London. Was Greg seeing what was happening at home at this very moment?

He shook his head, dislodging the unwelcome image, and with renewed vigour threw himself into the task at hand. Liz grabbed his wrist. Her strength surprised him, or maybe it was determination. She jabbed his hand between her legs. But just as his fingers were about to penetrate, Greg was assailed by another image — again of his family, but this time he was with them, and so was Jess. They were somewhere in the countryside, walking through a meadow, he and Amanda hand in hand, the girls excitedly pointing at a hot-air balloon drifting overhead. What the fuck is going on? Greg thought. I'm trying to have sex, here! Admittedly, with another woman.

But, of course! It was guilt. Guilt, the gatecrasher, intent on spoiling the party. Well, screw that! Guilt was no match for animal instinct. For lust! Greg allowed Liz's insistent hand to lead him. She gasped, arching her back and tearing out a small clump of his hair. It hurt, but not enough to make an issue of.

"I want you inside me," she rasped. Her voice brooked no dissent.

Greg was ready, his body primed. But his mind had other ideas. Into his head, unbidden, popped another image: Amanda — just Amanda — her face in close-up. Was she watching him in bed with this other woman? She couldn't be; she was smiling. And yet she was looking at him, directly at him, into his very soul, it seemed. And then a flicker of doubt appeared in her eyes, like the shadow cast by a cloud on a sunny day. Her expression said, "Is this who you are, Greg? Really? Because I don't think so."

Greg reared back, gasping for breath.

"I can't do this!"

What the fuck? thought Liz. She grabbed Greg's arse and pulled him towards her. "Yes, you can!" But, although she was strong, Greg was resolute.

"No! I mustn't." He slid off her. "I can't." He turned to sit on the edge of the bed, an abject figure. "I'm sorry," he said. And he was.

Liz lay on her back, panting. Now he gets an attack of conscience? she thought. Now? For a good half-minute, neither of them moved. Liz waited for Greg to explain himself, but he just sat there, staring into the darkness of the room. Finally, she broke the silence.

"Have you never cheated before?"

"No," he confessed in a small voice. "I thought it would be fun." Then, realising she might take that as a slight, "I mean, it was. But . . ."

"Pass me my bra," she instructed him.

Greg plucked the bra from where it lay on the floor and handed it to Liz. She turned away as she hooked the clasp, then climbed off the bed, careful to avoid any physical contact. Greg stood, adjusting his drooping cock in his underpants.

"I'm sorry," he said again, not looking at her. "I really am."

"Do me a favour, will you?"

Greg looked across, his eyes asking, What?

"Shut the fuck up."

Greg nodded. Fair enough, he thought. He'd be pissed off if he were rejected at the eleventh hour. Later than that. Four minutes to midnight.

He made no further attempt at conversation. He just stood there while she pulled on clothes, feeling guilty for what he'd almost done to Amanda, and what he hadn't done to Liz.

She finished dressing. With a final, eloquent flourish, she snatched up her bag from the floor and swept towards the door. Pulling it open, she paused. Greg stood miserably in the middle of the room. As a parting shot, she'd intended to tell him what a piece of shit she thought him, but realised that she didn't.

"What's your partner's name again?" she asked instead.

"Amanda."

"I envy her."

Well, isn't it ironic? Greg thought. Except Liz wasn't being facetious.

"I mean it. In your position, most men would cheat without a second thought. She's fortunate to have you."

Standing in his briefs, the last hint of his hard-on still visible, Greg doubted that Amanda would share that assessment. But he appreciated the sentiment. He turned to say as much, but the heavy clump of the closing door indicated that Liz had left.

Dan had never imagined he would find himself in bed with a woman other than Sarah. Even as Lynda had helped him into her room, he'd have said it was improbable. And yet, as they'd sat beside each other on her sofa, sipping coffee and talking, the odds had been cut, then narrowed further, until the moment when sleeping together had seemed not just likely but inevitable.

They did not have sex. They made love, like Dan wished he and Sarah were still able to. It was tender, two people taking comfort in each other. Afterwards, Dan held Lynda as she drifted off to sleep. He lay awake, thinking how wrong, yet how right, this felt. He knew he shouldn't have come to Lynda's room, but now he was here he didn't want to leave. He wanted to prolong this moment — all night, if possible — but, anaesthetised by alcohol and lulled by the calming effect of Lynda's regular breathing, he finally succumbed to exhaustion.

Dan woke first. His head was throbbing; his mouth was dry. Dawn light seeped into the room, and with it, realisation. There was no split second when Dan had to work out his surroundings, collate the memories of the night before. He knew exactly where he was, and why he was there. And he hated himself for it. The radio alarm's digital display illuminated a torn condom wrapper on the bedside table. Dan swung his legs out of bed, gently so as not to disturb Lynda. In the near darkness, he did not see the spent condom on the floor, shrivelled like an old man's penis. But his foot felt it. He leant down and picked it up, unsure whether its tacky texture was due to lubricant or seepage. Either way, it was disgusting — as, thought Dan, am I. Disgusting, vile and despicable.

Dan dressed in silence. He considered rousing Lynda to say goodbye, but only briefly. Let her sleep it off. She'd wake soon enough and, like him, regret the night before. That's presuming she was asleep now, and not feigning it, lying still, just wishing he would leave. Perhaps she'd even faked it last night. She hadn't seemed to, but that was the point, wasn't it? Men couldn't tell. Dan regarded her prone form. She was such a lovely person. What could she possibly see in him? Nothing. It was ridiculous to think that she might. She had been drunk and he had been there, it was as simple as that. Well, there was no hangover more painful than the sober reality of the following day. Despising himself, Dan picked his way across the room and went out, cushioning the impact as the door swung shut.

Lynda didn't stir. She slept on for another forty minutes and then, when she came to, she wondered where he'd gone and why he hadn't so much as left a note. And she felt hurt.

CHAPTER
FOUR

Greg was old enough to remember when hotels cooked breakfast individually, to order. Those were the days, he reminisced — a halcyon era before the bean counters (the baked-bean counters?) dictated that the bottom line was best served by the punters serving themselves from heated trays on to which the components of the full English were shovelled in industrial quantities. They called it a buffet but it was more like a trough, Greg thought, as he prodded a congealed slab of scrambled egg. He ladled a dollop on to his plate, accompaniment for two anaemic sausages, which looked like they'd begun life in a tin, a warmed-through tomato, the colour of which was a vague approximation of red, and three limp rashers of streaky bacon that were more streaky than bacon. Greg considered this unappetising spread, then discarded his plate and opted for toast.

The toast was cold but, slathered in raspberry-*flavoured* jam (from a plastic sachet, not the miniature jar Greg cherished from his childhood), was almost edible. Greg sighed, knowing that he couldn't blame the breakfast for his shitty mood.

He looked up from the table to see Dan approaching, balancing a yoghurt, a bowl of stewed prunes and a glass of grapefruit juice. Purging himself, the morning after the debauchery before. Greg brightened at his friend's arrival, affecting a happy, smiley face. Got to keep up appearances.

"Morning," Greg chirruped, receiving a gloomy nod in reply. Hangover, thought Greg with a liberal helping of schadenfreude.

Dan spooned the yoghurt over the prunes. Tasting the dish, he grimaced. He'd wanted natural yoghurt but apparently had picked strawberry. Christ! Strawberry yoghurt and prunes: not even the twisted imagination of Hugh Fearnley-Whittingstall would conjure such a perverse combination. But, hey ho. Dan couldn't be arsed to go back to the breakfast bar. He took another mouthful and found it wasn't quite as nauseating as the first. He would persevere.

"Good night, last night," Greg said breezily.

"Yeah, great," Dan felt forced to agree.

Greg waited for more, hoping for details of what passed between Dan and Lynda after he and Liz had left the bar, but Dan remained mute, silently chewing his prunes and . . . Was that *strawberry* yoghurt? Greg wondered. Weird.

"So . . .?" he probed. "Did you and Lynda . . .?" He described a circle with his spoon, flicked his eyebrows twice in quick succession and leered. Dan watched this dumb show. What a dickhead, he thought.

"What?" Dan asked blankly, playing the ball straight back to the bowler. If Greg wanted dirt, he could do some manual labour, digging.

"You know . . ." Greg indulged in more *Carry On*-style mugging.

"You mean, did I fuck her?" Dan asked levelly.

Greg was taken aback. It wasn't like Dan to be so vulgar. And frankly it wasn't called for.

"Yes," he admitted.

Dan weighed his response. To tell Greg the truth would be to make an anecdote of something that, at the time, had felt special, precious. It would reduce it to a yarn, a war story, a shared secret that Greg would embellish and, for years to come, trot out with nods and winks. He would cheapen it. And Dan felt cheap enough already.

"No," he told Greg. "We only stayed five minutes after you, then called it a night. Went our separate ways."

It was exactly what Greg had expected. Dan was such a wuss.

"How about you?" Dan asked. "Good time?"

Greg was tempted to tell Dan the truth. About how he'd had an epiphany, a realisation of the extent of his love for Amanda; not just love, but respect also. But he knew it would sound like bullshit, like he was trying to explain away his failure to seal the deal. He would come across as feeble, unmanly.

He leant into the table, gesturing for Dan to meet him halfway. He dropped his voice to a confidential whisper. "You know that thing I told you about Liz, the purring like a cat?" Greg cast quick glances about the restaurant. Thankfully, the women were nowhere to be seen. He smirked. "It was more like a leopard. Or a cheetah. Big game. You know, sort of, 'Grrrrrrrrrrrrrrrrrr!' "

Greg growled from deep in his throat, a guttural, animal sound.

Dan stared at him with an expression that Greg took to be awe but was actually distaste. Dan barely knew Amanda. They'd only met a couple of times, at industry functions, but what he'd seen he liked; she deserved better.

Unable to read minds, Greg sailed blithely on. "But, look, we don't breathe a word of this to anyone. What happens on tour, stays on tour, right? Our little secret."

"Sure," agreed Dan, who just wanted to forget the whole sordid experience.

The part of London in which Dan and Sarah resided was not blessed with an overabundance of good state secondary schools. Which meant it was no different to the rest of London. Muswell Hill, in fact, had more than most: one. Competition for places was fierce. The catchment area was constantly being redrawn, closer and closer to the school gates. The boundary was now within a stone's throw; soon you'd have to live in the bike sheds to be guaranteed admission. To buy within the hallowed zone, you wouldn't get change from a million quid. So much for fair and equitable access to education.

Dan and Sarah lived four streets from the Golden Triangle (as it was known locally); they may as well have had a Siberian postcode. When Russell turned twelve, the local authority offered him a place at a secondary school whose most celebrated alumni included a member of the gang responsible for the

Brink's-MAT robbery in 1983, a former kickboxing champion, who'd since died of an overdose, and the ex-girlfriend of a Premiership footballer. Russell had only attended this school once, when Sarah had taken him to an open day. She had been shocked by what she'd seen; even the graffiti was misspelt. Reluctantly — who wants to pay for something he'd expected to get for free? — Dan had agreed to send Russell to a public school. A private school. Confusing how words that are opposites are used to describe the same institution, but symptomatic, perhaps, of how wealthy schools snatch more than their fair share of resources.

Russell was happy enough at Widcombe College. Dan and Sarah were happy too. His reports suggested he was doing well and, unlike most fifteen-year-olds (boys and girls), Russell did not spend his weekends drinking to the point of oblivion. Dan did not think the private school system could claim any of the credit for his son's sobriety (most of his classmates were binge drinkers), but if it was in any way responsible, then Dan deemed the fees worth paying.

The fees, mind you, were only the half of it (or 85 per cent, to be actuarially accurate). On top were the extras: the uniform (summer and winter, and detention to any child who, on that rarest of occasions, a sweltering October day, dared to don the linen jacket only sanctioned for summer wear; better heatstroke than a violation of the dress code), the excursions (a French exchange, the annual ski trip to the Italian Alps) and transport. While travelling by public bus was not prohibited (public, in this context, meaning public), it was discouraged following a spate of incidents in which pupils were beaten up for being posh.

Russell was not a fan of the school bus. He would only catch it on the days his dad was unavailable to drive him, or he couldn't be arsed to walk. The school bus was a zoo, the kids upon it animals. As soon as they climbed aboard, out came the phones, passed from hand to hand as each year-group vied to be first to show off the latest viral video, or a new meme that had set the virtual world atwitter. Russell felt an affinity with the driver, who looked like he'd rather be somewhere else. This might explain why Russell didn't have many friends. He didn't mind. He was happy with his own company. And while there wasn't a gang of kids he hung out with — or "hung with", in their parlance — there were plenty he was happy to talk to, like his classmate, Ruby, who slid into the seat beside him now, as the bus pulled away from her stop.

"Hiya," she said.

Today, though, Russell was not in the mood for conversation. He was still processing the events of the previous evening, when he'd caught his mum upstairs with a man who was not his father. So he returned the greeting with a grunt, and resumed staring out of the window.

"What's up with you?" asked his neighbour.

"Nothing," Russell replied grumpily, his denial confirming the accusation.

Ruby shrugged — suit yourself — and left Russell to stew.

He cracked under the pressure of her indifference. "I think my mum's having an affair."

"Shut up!" squealed Ruby, which just happened to be one of Russell's least favourite expressions, along with "YOLO" and "totes". He swallowed his irritation and recounted the story of his arrival home the day before.

"Wait! Your mum said it made her feel grubby?" Ruby interjected. "Like, that was the word she used?"

Russell too had considered this a damning piece of evidence. Reluctantly he nodded.

"That's, like, as good as a confession." For Ruby, as for most girls her age, the world was black and white. "What are you going to do?"

"What can I do?" Russell had lain awake much of the night mulling this very question. He had failed to find a satisfactory answer.

"Like, tell your mum you know," Ruby said.

"Yeah, right!" Russell snorted sardonically.

"Or tell your dad."

He had considered this option. Didn't his dad have a right to know that his wife was cheating? But what would he do with this information? Russell would receive no thanks, that much was sure. All hell would break loose, his parents would fight, one of them would move out — probably his dad, though it was his mum who'd done wrong. They might even divorce — not immediately; in a year, maybe two. Either way, it would fuck up Russell's GCSEs. Thanks, Mum! Didn't think about that when you were screwing the "plumber", did you?

The other alternative was to do nothing. Say nothing. Pretend he had seen nothing. But didn't that make him complicit in her dirty little secret? Her perfidy? (Russell was this term studying *The Tempest*.)

"I don't know what to do," he admitted to Ruby, before adding, "You won't tell anyone, will you? You'll keep this to yourself?"

"Dude! Like, totes."

How Russell hated that expression. But he let it pass.

The train from Birmingham to London takes an hour and a half on a good day. This wasn't one. Track work outside Rugby slowed Greg and Dan's already sluggish progress. They travelled in silence, occasionally disturbed by the train manager's repeated, over-amplified apology about the lack of a buffet car. Each of them was happy to give the other the impression he was suffering a monumental hangover; in truth, both were wrapped in their own thoughts. That morning, they had largely managed to avoid Liz and Lynda, though there had been a close call as they checked out. Greg had drawn Dan's attention to the women at the other end of the lobby. Liz's gaze had washed over Greg like she didn't recognise him. Dan and Lynda's eyes had met but, at that moment, she was called upon for her credit card. Dan wasn't sure she'd seen the shy smile he'd sent her, but, anyway, it wasn't returned.

Greg couldn't wait to get home to Amanda. He pictured her leaning against the front door as he pulled into the drive, her arms crossed in front of her, her head tilted to one side in that slightly quizzical way she had. Knowing her, she'd run a hand through her bobbed hair, tucking a stray strand behind her ear. Could ears be attractive? Hers were. When Greg had first met Amanda, he'd rated her an eight and a half out of ten — higher than him, but not out of his league. But that had not done her justice. It had not taken into account her personality: her warmth, her humour, her goodness. Even her occasional furies were endearing, though never tell her that, Lord no, at least not while the storm was raging. Greg smiled at the memory of making that mistake once.

How he was missing her! He hoped she'd be in. Would she be at work today? He couldn't recall. He could phone and check but he didn't want to spoil the sweet torment of his anticipation. Nor would it be enough to hear her voice. He wanted to lay his eyes upon her, to take her in his arms, to kiss. Perhaps they'd make love; a little afternoon delight.

Dan was dreading his reunion with Sarah. She was bound to ask about the conference. She'd have in mind the sessions, the networking, but he would immediately think of his infidelity. And that's when he would crack, break down and tell all. He had no option. She would spot any lie the moment it left his mouth. He had to make a full confession and throw himself on her mercy. As the train idled outside Milton Keynes, delayed by a slower engine ahead, Dan came to the conclusion that this was his best course of action. His only course of action.

So far that morning, Amanda had treated a dachshund harbouring a tapeworm, a Persian cat that was vomiting and a cocker spaniel with a urinary tract infection. She longed for some more exotic patients. Where was the resident of Hammersmith and Fulham who kept a python as a pet? Surely someone locally had a baboon in their back garden? Even a stick insect would have served to break the monotony. Still, at least she hadn't had to spay any bitches. That was the worst part of the job. The look on those dogs' faces when they were brought in to be neutered — so accusatory, like they couldn't believe one woman would do this to another. Perhaps it was the foreign-sounding word — spay — but Amanda was always put in mind of Nazi concentration-camp doctors when preparing the instruments for an ovariohysterectomy.

At lunchtime, she headed home. She often worked half shifts, covering for the permanent staff when they were temporarily unavailable: on courses, at the dentist's, waiting in for the gasman. She preferred a full day, the money was better, but today she was glad to hang up her scrubs and clock off early. She was looking forward to seeing Greg. And she wanted to get the house halfway straight before his return. Molly and Lauren were good kids but were congenitally untidy. Computer games, clothes, DVDs, crayons, books — there was not a chair or tabletop that didn't become littered with their debris. It made no difference whether their mum lured them with inducements or threatened them with retribution. Intervention bought, at best, a day's respite before disorder was restored.

Amanda surveyed the tip that was the kitchen while Jess sat at her feet, head cocked, tail wagging, hopeful that this display of canine cuteness might entice her owner to reach for the lead. But before Amanda could be seduced, they both heard the sound of a key in the front door. Jess erupted in a paroxysm of barking that switched from antagonistic to ecstatic the moment she identified the intruder.

Greg had barely set down his bags before Jess was upon him, dancing on her hind legs, pawing and licking. You'd think he'd been to war, not away a couple of nights. He tousled the labradoodle's fur, then budged her aside as he spotted Amanda.

"God, I've missed you!" Greg crossed the distance between them in a couple of bounds, the equal to Jess in his enthusiasm. He swept Amanda into his arms. "Let's go to bed."

Amanda laughed. This was most unGreg-like. Not the desire for sex, but the spontaneity. He could go away more often.

If you're young, the chance to get laid is in and of itself enough to cause you to forget all your responsibilities. Amanda was no longer young. She made a quick mental list of her chores — cook the dinner, collect the girls, tidy the house — before just as quickly ticking each off — they'd get a takeaway, the girls had dance after school and weren't due to be picked up till six, stuff the house. She threw herself at Greg, wrapping her arms round his neck, her legs his waist. "Take me," she commanded, with more than one meaning in mind.

Greg didn't need to be told twice. With Jess leaping at their heels, keen to join in this game, Greg carried Amanda upstairs. She didn't feel anything like the sixty-one kilos she weighed, but that's testosterone for you.

Dan's taxi pulled up opposite a bay-fronted Victorian semi. He stared across the road at his home. Perhaps not his home for much longer, it occurred to him; that depended on Sarah's reaction to the news he had to break. He made no move to pay the driver or get out, seizing any and every opportunity to postpone his fate.

"This is where you wanted, yeah?" asked the cabby in a north London accent by way of Islamabad. In one way, yes; in another, no, thought Dan, reaching for his wallet. Even with his world about to implode, he was too much of a stickler to neglect office protocols. "I'll need a receipt," he said.

He remained standing on the pavement as the taxi pulled away, casting about in the hope he might engage a passing neighbour in conversation about the weather or the vexed issue of residents' parking permits. But the street was deserted. He could put it off no longer. He began the slow walk up his garden path to the gallows.

"Hello?" Immediately upon opening the front door, Dan sensed that no one was in. It was a weird thing with empty houses. Silence settled like dust. "Sarah? Russell?" No reply. There was nothing to do but wait.

So Dan waited. He sat. He stood. He tried in vain to settle. He made himself a cup of tea, then forgot to drink it. He found a bulb had gone in the lounge. He didn't change it. He thought about Sarah, the support she'd given him over the years, the belief she still retained in him. He thought about how he'd repaid her. He sat. He stood. He tried in vain to settle.

This must be what it's like to be on death row, he thought. Outside the prison walls there's feverish activity — candle-lit vigils, petitions, last-minute appeals — while, alone in his cell, the condemned man wishes they'd just get on with it. He doesn't care about the means of execution. He just wants it over. Anything is preferable to lingering uncertainty.

The silence was so deafening, Dan didn't hear Sarah's car in the drive. He leapt to his feet as she let herself into the house.

"Where have you been?" he asked urgently.

Struggling under the weight of her Waitrose bags, Sarah judged a reply redundant.

"There's more in the car," she said, continuing into the kitchen.

Dan followed. "I was worried about you."

Sarah couldn't imagine why. Muswell Hill Broadway was hardly South Central LA. She started unpacking the groceries, handing Dan a tub of Häagen-Dazs to stow in the freezer.

"How was the rest of the conference?"

Dan froze like the ice cream. Did Sarah suspect something? Else why was she asking? Calm down, he told himself. It's a perfectly innocent question. But his answer would reveal his guilt.

"There's something I have to tell you," he said.

The truth, the whole truth and nothing but the truth. No finessing, no sugar coating. He would accept whatever sentence she imposed.

I cheated on you. The words were forming in his head as Sarah began speaking.

"There's a light gone in the lounge. I tried changing the bulb but I think a fuse has blown."

"I'll look at it later," he said, wondering whether there would be a later. Sarah casually stacked shelves. Dan steeled himself. Come on, just four little words. I cheated on you. All they need are inverted commas. Say them out loud and your life can move on.

"You know the car boot's open?" Russell, who'd caught the school bus home, shuffled into the kitchen, dropping his rucksack on to a chair.

"Yes," said Sarah. "There's shopping to be brought in. Perhaps you'd like to bring it."

Russell fixed his mother with a six-feet-under glare, which he switched off as he acknowledged Dan.

"Hey, Dad."

Dan nodded, unwilling to trust his voice. He managed to summon an anguished smile.

Russell's heart went out to his cuckolded father. It seemed clear to him that he was suffering, and equally obvious that he didn't know why. Well, Russell could tell him. And, as he left the room to collect the rest of the shopping, he resolved to, at the earliest opportunity.

"I don't know what's got into him," Sarah said once Russell was out of earshot. "He's been foul the last day or so. Probably hormones. You said there was something you wanted to tell me."

Dan had played this scene over and over in his mind but in none of the permutations had Russell been present. He did not wish his son to witness his abasement. At least spare me that, he thought.

"Well?" Sarah pressed, a can of chickpeas in her hand.

Dan had to be quick. Any moment now, Russell would return with the rest of the shopping. It was now or never.

Or later on tonight.

"I think I might miss my sales target this month."

"That's the second time in a row, isn't it?"

"Yes," Dan admitted. "But I'm hopeful next month will be better." It wasn't true, but he didn't want her to worry unduly. He mustered a brave smile.

Sarah put the chickpeas in a cupboard. "Well, that's not the end of the world, is it?"

No, he thought, but what I'd intended to tell you is.

Russell returned, hauling the other shopping bags, talk turned to the evening meal and normal life was resumed. It was a stay of execution. But only temporarily.

The gibbet still loomed large, casting its shadow over Dan.

It was not the best sex Amanda and Greg had ever had, but it was up there. Casting his mind back, as Greg, lying in bed, now did, he speculated that it might even crack their all-time top ten. "A new entry this week, in at number seven —"

Amanda barged into Greg's train of thought, carrying his overnight bag into the room.

"I'm going to put a wash on," she said. "Have you any dirty laundry?"

Christ, if only she knew! "In my bag. The hotel wanted three quid just to wash a pair of socks. You can buy them for less."

"That's because you shop at Poundland."

Greg grinned. Poundland didn't do socks, did they? He lay back on the pillow, his hands behind his head. He felt a very fortunate man. When he considered how close he'd come to making the biggest mistake of his life . . . But that was behind him now, forgotten, never to be dredged up. He admired Amanda's figure as she sorted through his washing. She'd pulled on a T-shirt over a pair of undies. She was undeniably sexy. He was transported back to their early days, the first flat they'd shared, overlooking a cemetery in Stoke Newington. It seemed she'd always been in a state of undress then; him, too. Given the frequency with which they'd had sex, they likely had been. He smiled at the memory. He'd always found her T-shirt-and-knickers combo sexy — the more so if, like now, the T-shirt was one of his. He wondered whether there was something narcissistic in that. Or homoerotic. He didn't notice Amanda stiffen.

"What's this?" she asked in an innocent voice, her back to him.

"What?"

"This." She turned, her hand holding the box of condoms Greg had bought at the hotel.

Holy fuck! Greg thought. He must have packed it by mistake.

"They're condoms," he replied, stating the obvious in as casual a tone as if he were describing paperclips or stamps. "I thought we were out. I was wrong," he added with a mischievous grin, hoping a sly reference to the great sex they'd just had might distract her. It didn't.

"Why would you buy them from a vending machine? A two pack?" Amanda seemed genuinely puzzled, because she genuinely was.

"Because it was there. I was in the loo. I was drunk." Greg climbed out of bed. "Here, let me show you the presents I got the girls." He rummaged in his bag. "Look, aren't these cute?" He pulled out souvenirs of Birmingham, made in Beijing.

But Amanda wasn't interested. Clearly she did not consider the subject of the condoms closed. Please don't let her open the box, Greg silently implored a God he didn't believe in.

Amanda opened the box. That would teach Greg to be an atheist.

"There's one missing."

"Yeah," Greg agreed, stalling for time. He needed a good cover story, but the only thing he could think of was, Ohfuckohfuckohfuckohfuckohfuck.

"Well, where is it?" Amanda fixed him with a look.

"I gave it to Dan." It was only as he said this that Greg realised it was, in fact, the truth.

"Dan?" Perplexed.

What happens on tour, stays on tour? Screw that! Greg's neck was on the line here. If Dan had to be sacrificed, so be it.

"Yeah. I bought them for us, like I said. But Dan met this woman . . ."

"Dan?" Sceptical.

"In the bar." Just go with it, Greg's brain counselled. Believe in it and you'll sell it. "Him and Sarah, they're not happy, not like us. Anyway, he was drinking, they hit it off, one thing led to another."

Amanda considered this story. She weighed the box of condoms in her hand. Greg had to remind himself to keep breathing.

"Why didn't he buy his own?"

Shit! That was a good question. Greg felt like he was clinging to a cliff face and his fingers were beginning to lose purchase.

"It was late. The machine was out."

Amanda stared deep into his eyes. Greg found this unsettling.

"Bullshit!" she exclaimed.

"It's not! The machine was empty. Or broken. I don't know!"

"Not that! All of it! You cheated on me!"

"No!"

"There's one missing!" Amanda shook the condom box to illustrate her point.

"I gave it to Dan!"

"You slept with some woman!" Amanda flung the box at Greg. Its sharp corner caught him flush above the eye. It stung to a surprising degree.

"Amanda! Listen to me!"

But she wouldn't. She wasn't done talking.

"That's why you were like you were when you came in! All lovey-dovey!" As evidence went, it was pretty thin, but the prosecution seemed to find it compelling. "'Oh, Amanda,'" she mimicked his voice, making it whiny and wheedling, "'I've missed you so much!' You were feeling guilty!"

"I wasn't! I've nothing to feel guilty for!"

Greg felt exposed, and not just because of his nakedness. But that much, at least, he could control. He grabbed a pair of underpants as Amanda wildly began stuffing clothes back into his bag.

"Sweetheart! What are you doing?"

Greg never called Amanda sweetheart. This was not the best time to start.

She swung on him, breathing heavily. "You flirt. You always flirt! Which is fine. Until you take it too far!"

"I swear. I didn't!"

Amanda, unmoved, resumed her packing.

"You got drunk, and you shagged some woman. Some tart!"

She snatched up Greg's bag and swept past him towards the door. He gave chase.

"I'm telling you the truth! Dan was off his face. Out of control!"

Amanda flew down the stairs, Greg falling over himself as he tried to keep up.

"Look, slow down! Let's talk about this."

But Amanda had heard enough. The case was closed, the verdict in. Guilty! She sailed across the hall like an Antarctic icebreaker, wrenched open the front door —

"Amanda! I wouldn't cheat on you!"

— and hurled Greg's overnight bag into the garden. Shirts and dirty socks spilled out.

"I wouldn't!"

Jess leapt about, barking; she seemed to think this was another game. Amanda, her fury unquenched, seized Greg's work bag from where he'd left it by the door —

"I couldn't!"

— and flung it too out of the house.

"That's my laptop!"

Maybe Amanda's aim was improving with practice, or perhaps it was because, in size and weight, the case shared the aerodynamics of a discus; whatever the reason, the laptop cleared Greg's clothes by a good metre. It landed on the path with a leaden thud that was either satisfying or sickening, depending on whether you were Amanda or Greg.

"For Christ's sake, Amanda!"

Fearful for the health of his laptop (it had been weeks since he'd backed up his files), Greg took a step out of the house. A tactical blunder. With a triumphant flourish, Amanda threw the front door shut. Its slam sounded as though it were taking her side in the argument.

Greg was suddenly very aware that he was dressed only in a pair of underpants. He heard an idling lawn-mower and turned to see Mickey, his neighbour from two doors down, gawping in slack-jawed wonder at this domestic dispute. Mickey had a daughter in Molly's class. The two girls were occasionally friends, and their parents socialised at Christmas. Greg found him a smug prick. Why the fuck isn't he at work? he wondered, raising a hand in casual greeting. Perhaps he's lost his job. This thought gave Greg short-lived solace before he was headbutted by reality and recalled that he was standing half naked in his front garden, cast out of the marital home.

Amanda saw none of this. She was a woman on a mission. After checking that the doors were locked, she started up the stairs, ignoring Greg's entreaties through the letter box.

"Amanda, please! If you'd just listen to me . . ."

In their bedroom, Amanda found Greg's jumble of keys on top of the chest of drawers.

"Babe! People are looking."

She separated his house keys from the rest, then crossed to the window and pulled it open.

Greg heard the sash window rise. Thank God, he thought, she's calmed down a little. He looked up in time to see his keys hurtling towards him. He was barely able to flinch before the key ring struck him — in the same spot as the box of condoms. The slight discomfort that earlier assault had provoked was as nothing to the pain he now felt. The key ring, even shaved of two of its number, was an effective missile, cutting Greg above the eye, adding injury to insult. He heard the sash window glide smoothly shut. Well worth the four hundred quid it had recently cost to have them refurbished.

Greg had not expected to be checking into a hotel again so soon. He'd managed to cobble together an outfit from the clothes strewn on the lawn, though the socks didn't match. He'd waited patiently for Amanda to leave the house, since he knew at some point she would have to. And one hour and twenty-two minutes after his ejection (Greg still had his watch), she had duly emerged on her way to collect Molly and Lauren from their dance class. Greg, perched on the rockery, leapt to his feet. This was his chance to try and effect a reconciliation — at the very least, to have a conversation. And words were exchanged. Unfortunately for Greg, Amanda's contribution to the dialogue was confined to, "Just fuck off, Greg," spat out as she brushed him aside before driving away.

Greg did not want his daughters to see their parents bickering. It wasn't often that he and Amanda had rows, and they were always careful to try and shield the girls, lest they read into the animosity more than passing irritation. Given the mood Amanda was in, Greg thought it politic, for tonight at least, to make himself scarce.

North London boasts many fine hotels that rival the four-star splendour that Greg had enjoyed in Birmingham, but, as he was now paying out of his own pocket, he considered none of them. The Clifton Motor

Inn was a step down, and a star less. It was a three-storey structure — the word "building" evokes too homely an image — constructed in the 1970s to the architectural standards of that period. In other words, it was ugly. But, in its favour, it was close, affordable and not full.

"And how long will you be staying, sir?" the receptionist asked, tapping precisely at his keyboard, as though he feared breaking a nail.

"Just the one night." Greg slid his registration form across the counter. The receptionist, whose badge identified him as Howard, entered Greg's details.

"In town on business?"

Greg really wasn't interested in making small talk. The cut above his eye was beginning to throb. He just wanted to get to his room so he could neck a paracetamol or three.

"Yes," he replied curtly.

The receptionist looked up from his typing. "And yet you live within walking distance," he observed, one eyebrow raised archly. It was at this moment that Greg took against Howard. He met and held Howard's gaze, challenging him to make something of it.

Howard pursed his lips and looked away, his eyes taking the scenic route, flicking over Greg's wound before again settling on the computer screen. Another husband caught cheating, he thought wryly to himself. Haven't had one of those for, oh, must be a month.

Waiting to be allocated a room, Greg's headache intensified.

CHAPTER
FIVE

Stupid, stupid man! These three words (two if you want to be pernickety) had become Amanda's mantra, repeating in her head as she drove to collect the kids. Inwardly, she was seething. And outwardly too, as a Mercedes driver talking on his mobile phone discovered when he cut her up. Amanda accelerated alongside and unleashed a stream of invective. Even separated by two plates of glass and with his business partner loud in one ear, the man could have been left in no doubt as to her opinion of him. Especially if he could lip-read the word "cocksucker".

The other mums waiting to meet their daughters would have had no idea that anything was amiss. Amanda appeared her usual breezy self. She put her hand up to help make the dresses for the dance troupe's next showcase. And she gushed over Esmé Seabrook for passing Grade One clarinet, though the effect was somewhat spoilt as she got both the child's name and her instrument wrong.

Amanda drove home in silence. Molly had won the squabble for the front seat. She and Lauren bitched about their fellow dancers; typically, for girls their age, finding fault with each and every one. Amanda made a special effort to hide her ill humour, but needn't have. Her daughters would only have noticed her had she not been there.

Turning into the drive, Amanda was relieved to see no sign of Greg's car. Stupid, stupid man. It was only when Lauren asked what time he was coming home that Amanda realised she had to tell them something. She improvised, saying that the conference had been extended. She didn't say by how long. Their disappointment at their father's absence lasted as long as it took them to discover an old episode of *Friends* on TV, which is to say it lasted no time at all, as an old episode of *Friends* is always on TV. Breaking house rules, Amanda let them watch while she made their tea.

"I cheated on you."

Finally, *finally*, Dan had said it out loud. That wasn't so difficult, was it? he asked his reflection in the mirror. Now he just had to say it to Sarah.

He emerged from the cloakroom under the stairs to find Russell standing by the door. Dan took a step to one side, to let his son pass, but Russell didn't move. He just stood there, regarding his father oddly — and, as far as Dan was concerned, unnervingly.

"Did you want something?" Dan asked.

"Were you talking to yourself?"

Christ! Had Russell heard Dan's confession? Surely not. He had merely muttered.

"I was singing," he improvised, fashioning an apologetic shrug and a smile. "I'm happy."

Russell seemed knocked off balance by this pronouncement, as indeed he was. He'd been maintaining a vigil outside the cloakroom, waiting to grab his dad when he emerged. He'd planned to drag him up to his bedroom and there embark on a prepared speech: "Mum's cheating on you. I caught her upstairs with the plumber, except he wasn't." But to be told that his dad was happy! Russell's resolve deserted him. He didn't know how to proceed. Should he tell his dad regardless and ruin his mood? He tried to speak but no sound emerged.

"Did you want the loo?" Dan prodded.

"No." Russell met his father's eyes; he came to a decision. "Dad? I'm glad you're happy." Russell gave his father an awkward hug.

Dan watched his son climb the stairs. What a strange youth he was. Dan sighed. He had told another lie. This was becoming a habit. The truth was he wasn't happy. He was in turmoil and would be until he lanced the boil that plagued him. Well, now was the moment. Russell was in his room, doing whatever Russell did in his room (which did not include surfing bondage websites, Dan was pretty sure of that); Sarah was alone in the lounge. With a heavy hand and a heavier heart, Dan opened the door and went in.

Except the room was empty, the TV on. He sat on the sofa, sighed heavily. Unprompted, his thoughts returned to Lynda's hotel room. Had it really been just the night before? It felt like a lifetime ago. How despicably he'd acted. Cheating on his wife. He felt contempt.

But not just contempt. Contempt tempered with . . . exhilaration! Yes, despite knowing that what he'd done was wrong and beyond forgiveness, Dan couldn't help experiencing a blister of pride. Was it possible that two such contrasting emotions, contempt and pride, could go hand in hand? He reviewed his feelings and concluded that it was. What complex creatures we humans are.

Dan replayed in his mind the events of the night before, but less out of a need for self-flagellation and more in the interests of nostalgia. He indulged himself in reliving the moment he and Lynda had first kissed. She had poured them both drinks from the minibar, then, eschewing the chair opposite, had sat beside Dan on the sofa. With their knees close to touching, the electricity between them had been palpable. It had given Dan the confidence to behave completely out of character. Lynda had raised her glass for him to chink and he had taken it from her, assertively setting it aside with his. And then — he could barely believe this still — he had leant in and kissed her on the mouth. It was outrageous, really. He hadn't sought her permission or approval. He had just assumed it was what she wanted. And how she had! They never did finish those drinks. Or start them.

Dan smiled at the memory. In that moment on the couch in Lynda's room, he had become a different person. Someone more like Greg. Assured, decisive — a man of action. And he had liked it! He did not want to revert to his former self.

Suddenly he realised what he had to do. Or rather what he mustn't. He must not tell Sarah about last night. It would be his little secret, locked in a strongbox in his mind, occasionally to be taken out and dusted off, appreciated in private like a stolen old master unable to be sold on the open market. There was no benefit to Sarah knowing; none to her and certainly none to him. Wasn't it the case that men who admitted to adultery did so for *their* peace of mind, to salve *their* conscience? Confession was a selfish act, for the weak-willed. Not for men like Dan, the Dan he aspired to be.

But could he get away with it? He'd told Greg that he would have to confess, because he and Sarah had no secrets from each other. But that was bollocks. What about the website of Santa Fe's Sadie Servitude? If he was honest with himself (and as a rule Dan tried to be), he already had a history of dissembling. But an innocent penchant for bondage was small beer compared to his tawdry transgression with Lynda. Could he really hope to keep that quiet? Well, possibly. He hadn't cracked in the six hours since he'd returned home, even though he'd actively been *trying* to tell her. How much easier it should be if his aim was to say nothing!

Dan flicked the combination on his mental safe and removed the memory again. What was the word Greg had used to describe Lynda? Lissom? Lithe? Limber! That was it! Limber Lynda. Though she was lithe and lissom too. And sexy. God, she was sexy. Right down to her belly-button ring. For heaven's sake! Him, strait-laced Dan Sinclair, having carnal knowledge of a woman with a belly-button ring! Who'd o' thunk it? Dan had always found piercings distasteful, a form of self-mutilation. Not any more! His conversion had been as instantaneous as St Paul's U-turn on the road to Damascus. And as complete. He had fallen upon her belly, licking and nuzzling her silver band. Lynda, surprisingly ticklish, had squirmed and squealed as his tongue had probed her navel then traced a line south towards her —

"Dan!"

Dan lurched in his chair. Sarah was standing over him. He was conscious of the telltale mound in his trousers. And the guilty look on his face. He hoped the latter was a close enough cousin to his usual countenance that he might escape detection.

"Greg Beavis," Sarah said.

She knows something, Dan thought. She must do! Why else would she bring up Greg? Then he noticed the phone that she was holding out to him. She gestured: take it. He took it.

"Greg, mate." What could Greg want at this hour that was so urgent?

"Amanda's kicked me out."

"What? Why?"

Sarah, settling on to the sofa, heard the startled note in Dan's voice. She raised a querying eyebrow. Dan shook his head reassuringly: it's nothing. But she continued to look his way.

"You know, it's pretty late, fella," he said into the phone, affecting a casual tone.

"She found the condoms in my bag!" Greg exclaimed, so loudly Dan worried the words might leak past his ear into Sarah's hearing.

"I'm sure it's nothing. We'll talk about it tomorrow, OK?" Dan punched off the phone before Greg could respond.

"Problem?" Sarah asked from the sofa.

"No. No, work thing," Dan replied easily, relaxing into his chair. Sarah seemed satisfied by this explanation. Or uninterested. Either way, she turned her attention to the newspaper.

Dan feigned an interest in the TV, but it was difficult. And not only because of the dreary discussion of pensions reform on *Newsnight*. What the hell had happened to Greg? And what were the implications for Dan? It was too awful to think about. But that didn't stop him.

"Hello? Dan? Hello?"

Greg couldn't believe it. The bastard had hung up on him! What about mateship? What about, "We're in this together"?

Greg needed someone to talk to, someone who would listen, sympathise and offer reassurance that this was much ado about nothing, a fart in a pedal bin that, by tomorrow, would have all blown over. Dan had not been his first choice for this role. But Amanda wasn't picking up and, anyway, Greg had to admit that, under the circumstances, she was probably less than ideal casting.

He tossed his mobile beside him on the bed and leant back against the headboard, like scores of occupants had done before him, as the faint stain of hair grease testified. He took in his dismal surroundings. The walls were painted a hue that didn't exist in nature but which could best be described as "blah' — a muted magnolia chosen, no doubt, for its inoffensiveness and which, as a result, could not have been more offensive. Night-time reading was provided: a copy of the Gideons'" Bible. Lying next to it on the bedside table was the much more useful TV remote. Greg aimed and fired and found he had fifteen channels, all showing snow. Excellent, he thought.

Who to call? Amanda's sister, Geri? She'd always been fond of Greg; in fact, she'd seemed to prefer him to her ex-husband, even during their marriage, which, on reflection, might have been one of the reasons for its failure. Greg had a soft spot for Geri too, embarrassingly a little harder one particular Christmas some years ago when the drink had flowed and they'd been slow dancing to "Sitting On The Dock Of The Bay". Geri hadn't held it against him, even though he briefly had her. But would she be sympathetic to him now? She was first and foremost Amanda's sister and, while their sororal relationship was naturally volatile, on this occasion she might be expected to find in favour of the wronged woman, even though she was considerably less wronged than she imagined.

Upon whose shoulder could he cry? Into whose sympathetic ear could he pour his tale of woe?

Of course! Why hadn't he thought of her before? She was the one person who would understand this injustice. She'd said it herself: Amanda was fortunate to have such a great bloke. OK, maybe not in those exact words, but the sentiment had been vaguely akin.

Newly energised, Greg grabbed his computer bag and shook it out on to the bedspread. A fistful of business cards tumbled out along with Greg's laptop, which slid off the bed and fell to the floor. The screen, already wounded following its close encounter with the garden path, snapped off. I've just invented the tablet, Greg thought, as he kicked the moribund device aside and set to sifting through the business cards. He'd collected dozens. Most of the names meant nothing to him, but then Greg had been drunk and the people giving him cards dull. Ah, here she was: Liz Henderson, work and mobile numbers.

Greg waited for his call to be answered. It was late; perhaps she was asleep. If he woke her, she'd be pissed off. But then she shouldn't have left her phone on, should she?

"Liz's phone."

The use of the third person and the male baritone in which the words were delivered led Greg to conclude that Liz was not the speaker.

"Oh!" he said, taken aback. "Is she there?"

"Babe!" the voice called. "Your phone!"

Babe? Who the fuck is that? thought Greg. He heard feet padding towards the phone.

"Hello?"

"Who the fuck was that?" he asked.

There was a pause, then, evenly, "Who's this?"

"It's Greg. Greg Beavis. From the conference."

"Oh, no. No way." This in a tone of disbelief.

"I need to talk to you."

"Give me the waybill number, Peter."

What? What was she on about? Peter? Waybill number?

"It's Greg! You remember." She hadn't been that pissed, surely?

"I'll chase it up. First thing. No, no, you're welcome."

The line went dead.

"Hello? Liz? Hello?"

Fuck!

Amanda woke as per usual when the alarm roused her at six thirty. Seven minutes later, her mobile rang. Greg. He must have calculated that she'd need seven minutes to drag herself out of bed and take a pee, she thought as she rejected his call. He could leave a message. He was getting lots of practice, what with the six he'd left the night before. She'd listened to a few seconds of each before deleting them. The gist seemed to be that this was all a terrible misunderstanding and when Greg had a chance to explain, he'd convince Amanda. Well, good luck with that, she thought. She checked her mood. She'd gone to bed seething, and woken up . . .? Still seething. How could Greg have been so dumb? Dumb to let it happen, dumber yet not to destroy the evidence! Thinking about it incensed her.

Then she wouldn't think about it. She'd get Molly and Lauren up, as though nothing were untoward. She'd make them breakfast and take them to school.

And then she'd turn her mind to her fuckwitted partner.

Alighting the school bus with his earphones in, Russell was almost run down by a BMW sashaying past towards the drop zone. "My bad," he acknowledged with a wave.

"Isn't that Russell Sinclair?" the BMW's driver asked. "I had lunch with his mother the other day."

The speaker was Sarah's friend, Veronica, who was delivering her two daughters to school. The older happened to be Ruby, Russell's classmate and sometime bus companion.

"You know she's having an affair," Ruby said, matter-of-factly. "Russell caught them."

This titbit of gossip so excited Veronica that she leapt on the brake, almost causing a Volvo to rear-end her.

"Sarah is?" There was no mistaking her gleeful tone. Ruby was reminded that she'd promised Russell she wouldn't tell a soul. But since she doubted her mother had one, perhaps she hadn't broken her word.

"You won't tell anyone, will you?"

"No, of course not!" Veronica offered this guarantee with such conviction she almost believed it herself. "Well, isn't she a dark horse!" she added in a tone that blended wonder with respect.

Dan slumped at his desk, too tired to contemplate work. He'd tossed and turned all night, still torn between self-loathing (how could he have cheated on his wife?) and excitement (he had slept with another woman!). He wondered whether any of his colleagues would notice were he to close his eyes. He could lean on one hand. To anyone passing his workstation, it might look like he was thinking; not part of the job description of a sales rep, but not unprecedented either.

For the third time since he'd got in forty minutes earlier, Dan unlocked and pulled open his desk drawer. Within lay Lynda's business card. He should destroy it. Rip it up; toss it in the bin. What was the point of keeping it? He'd never phone her. Way too dangerous. Besides, she might not want to hear from him. Unless she did, was waiting for his call. Throw it out; destroy the evidence, he told himself. But he couldn't. It was a keepsake, a trophy — proof that his memories were real.

He rubbed his thumb over the embossed printing. Perhaps it would bring him luck. One way to find out. Shrugging off his tiredness, he snatched up the phone and punched out a number. Three weeks ago he'd quoted on a contract to supply a new computer system to a chain of private nursing homes — for the staff, not the residents, many of whom had Alzheimer's and, if they saw a computer, would sit in front of it waiting for *Antiques Roadshow* to come on. He'd heard nothing back and had been loath to call. He hated rejection, hated hearing the other party's discomfort as they delivered the bad news. And while you didn't know, you could live in hope.

Five minutes later, Dan had closed the deal. He'd had to shave a little off the price, but nonetheless it represented a worthwhile profit. He logged the figures in his sales file, then took Lynda's business card from his desk, running his finger over the sharp corner. My talisman, he thought. He smiled as he replaced it in his desk. What other leads can I follow up? he wondered with unfamiliar confidence.

Greg had had a worse night than Dan. He'd lain awake for hours, punishing himself with one nagging question: why hadn't he got rid of the spare condom? It wasn't like he and Amanda would use it; it wasn't their usual brand. Greg had next to no idea just how finely tuned a woman's nerve endings were down there, but he hadn't been about to risk Amanda sensing a difference. "Wait a minute, lover! This doesn't feel like it's double ribbed for a lady's pleasure!" So why hang on to the bloody thing? Was it possible that, deep within the sewers of his psyche, he had actually wanted to get caught? That Amanda's discovery had not been a disastrous accident but Greg's unconscious desire? Nah, that was crazy talk, the sort that had made Sigmund Freud a household name and still made many a charlatan a more than decent living. So why, then? Despite exhaustive analysis, Greg had failed to find the answer. Further speculation was futile; the damage was done. What was important now was thinking of a plausible excuse.

Howard was not on duty when Greg checked out. For this much, he was grateful. As he left the hotel, already late for work, Greg caught sight of himself in the chrome frame of the sliding doors. He looked like shit. He was bleary eyed and unshaven, with a bluish-yellow bruise supplementing the slash of red above his eye, completing the trifecta of primary colours. First stop, a chemist's. For plasters, not condoms.

"I hope you don't mind me calling," said Dan.

"No. No, I'm glad you have," replied Lynda. "I didn't think you would."

"Neither did I."

It was true. Dan had been on a roll. After his first sale that morning, he'd made a second and had been going for his hat-trick. He'd picked up the phone to call a building-supplies firm in Romford. In his other hand he was holding Lynda's business card, but only so he could rub it, like a rabbit's foot, for good luck. Somehow, as if acting independently of his brain, his fingers had dialled her number. He realised now that this had always been his intention. Just to hear her voice. Nothing more than that.

"So you got back from Birmingham all right?" he asked. As conversation went, it was pretty lame, but it beat the silence that would otherwise have ensued. Dan thought he could hear Lynda smile.

"Is that why you rang?" She had a way of cutting through the bullshit.

"No," he admitted. "I'd like to see you again."

Jesus Christ, he hadn't intended to say that! Now his mouth had gone rogue. Did his brain have no control over the rest of his body?

"I'd like that too."

It was as simple as that.

Having made an arrangement to meet, Dan replaced the phone and leant back in his swivel chair. He didn't need to search for his pulse to calculate his heart rate, he could count the beats pounding in his chest. Deep breaths, he told himself. Fuck, he thought, I have just arranged an assignation with another woman. A tryst. A rendezvous. I have crossed the Rubicon.

I won't go, he told himself.

You will, his brain sneered. And in that moment Dan realised. The rest of his body had not been acting independently at all. His brain had been behind this all the time, the evil mastermind orchestrating his every move. It now dictated that he make another call.

It struck Sarah that Russell's room didn't need cleaning so much as fumigating. She threw open the window to release the adolescent fug that made it difficult to breathe — a malodorous mixture of farts, stale sweat and semen, overlaid with Lynx body deodorant, by some distance the most noxious ingredient.

Her eyes alighted on Russell's laptop, sitting on his desk beside a little-thumbed copy of *Differential Calculus for GCSE*. She had not yet used the keylogging software installed by Veronica's husband. She hadn't had an opportunity. Either Russell or Dan had been around and neither must know of her clandestine surveillance — Russell because he was its target, Dan because he wouldn't approve.

She stood over the sleeping computer, nudging it awake with the mouse. The cursor blinked expectantly, demanding a password before allowing access. A month earlier, Russell had rung from school during recess (as break was now known, thanks to America's domination of global culture), in a panic over an English assignment (formerly "homework") that he had failed to hand in. He had given Sarah his password so she could email the project to his teacher. He hadn't expected her to remember the complex series of numbers and letters, lower and upper case. Why should he? Gfr5t83Xp hardly tripped off the tongue. But something (a mother's intuition?) had told Sarah to note down the sequence in her diary, just in case. In case of what, she hadn't known. All she had been sure of was that knowledge was power. And, in the unequal struggle between mum and son, she needed every weapon at her disposal. A week later, she'd discovered to her surprise that Russell, underestimating his mother's cunning, had not changed his password. A rookie error; not the sort of mistake you'd expect from the preternaturally distrustful younger generation.

Sarah settled herself at Russell's desk. She almost readjusted his chair to her height, then realised that this would be a dead giveaway the next time he sat down. She smiled, impressed by her talent for espionage, as she tapped in Gfr5t83Xp and the machine bade her welcome. She'd missed her calling; she could have had a career as a secret agent. And then it struck her that that's what she was: a spy, a snoop, a sneak.

Her index finger hovered over the keyboard. Did she really want to do this? Violate Russell's privacy? He was a good kid. Of course he had secrets, all teenagers did. And the one she'd so far discovered was hardly abhorrent. It was Veronica who had twisted Russell's idle curiosity into evidence of deeper depravity — Veronica, a self-confessed consumer of online porn. Who knew what kind of sexual antics she got up to with her fetid-breathed husband? Russell was a mere novice, skiing the nursery slopes of sexual discovery. Leave him be, she thought. But still her finger hovered.

And then the phone rang.

"So, yeah, I should be home by eight. Thirty. Nine at the latest."

Dan took no pleasure in lying to Sarah. He felt worse even than when he'd slept with Lynda. Because this deception was premeditated.

But, as he ended the call, Dan could feel his mood lifting, replaced by something else. Was it anticipation? Excitement? It had those flavours but there was more to it than that. It took him a moment to identify the emotion, because it wasn't one he had experienced in a while. And then he realised what it was. It was the sensation of feeling alive.

A hand clamped down on his shoulder. He nearly had an embolism. His first thought was that he was under arrest.

"Someone's jumpy!" said an accusatory voice.

Dan turned to find Greg gurning over him.

"What happened to your face?" Dan asked, indicating the gash above Greg's eyebrow, now hidden under a plaster but all the more conspicuous as a result.

"Amanda," Greg replied pointedly. He jerked his head: follow me.

Dan trailed Greg across the open-plan office. Finding the photocopying room unoccupied, Greg ushered his friend in, closing the door behind them. He related the catastrophe that had befallen him: Amanda finding the condoms and her refusal to accept Greg's explanation for the box being one short. He omitted from his account his attempt to implicate Dan. Unnecessary detail.

"Amanda thinks I used the missing condom." Greg summarised his dilemma.

"The one you gave me?"

"Precisely!"

Dan frowned. "How come you had any left?"

"What?"

"Condoms. There were two in the box. You gave me one . . ." Ergo, he was going to add, but doubted Greg's grasp of Latin.

Greg got the message nonetheless. He did the maths. Two minus one equalled him not using any. "Oh, we used hers," he improvised, adding with a conspiratorial wink, "All of them."

Dan felt a little stab of disgust.

Both men started as the door opened and a PA entered, bearing a document to be copied. She eyed them suspiciously; they feigned insouciance. The three stood in cramped silence as the photocopier churned interminably through the pages. Finally, after an age of glacial proportion, the PA collected her work and left, shooting the men a knowing look. Greg picked up his narrative.

"So, here's the thing. If you put your hand up to the missing condom, I'll be in the clear!"

Dan was horrified. "I can't do that!"

"Why not? You took it."

The door opened and the same PA re-entered. She hefted a larger document. At this rate, we're going to be here all week, thought Greg.

"Jemma? Do us a favour? Come back in five?"

Jemma was tempted to point out that the photocopying room was for photocopying and the meeting room for meetings (the clue was in their names), but Greg was one of the good guys in the office, always the first of the reps to stand a round in the pub.

"Mine's a vodka and tonic," she told him.

Greg nodded. "A double," he said. And, for that, Jemma did not leave the door open but closed it behind her.

Dan resumed his renunciation of Greg's plan.

"I can't tell Amanda I had it. What if Sarah finds out?"

"She won't! They're not friends."

"They've met! Amanda might phone her. You know, 'sisterhood' and all that bollocks."

Greg could not believe Dan was being so disobliging. "Mate! My relationship is on the line here!"

"My marriage would be over if Sarah thought I'd got up to anything."

"But you didn't!"

They were straying into territory that Dan found uncomfortable.

"She might think I did!"

Dan pulled open the door to signal an end to the discussion. Self-preservation came first, but he couldn't help feeling a little bad about leaving his friend to swing in the breeze. Greg looked so pathetic, beaten down as well as beaten up. Dan took pity on him.

"If there was some other way I could help . . ."

"You could come for a drink after work."

"Tonight?" Dan remembered his date with Lynda. "I can't tonight. Some other way?"

Greg's day did not improve. He tried to do some work, following up leads. Some he'd been certain were shoo-ins, just needed a gentle tickle to get them over the line, but one by one they fell over. Some days were like that. Your luck just wasn't in. Tomorrow would be better. It couldn't get any worse.

Tortuously slowly, the clock tiptoed towards five thirty, the earliest anyone could respectably leave the office. Greg phoned Amanda. She still wasn't picking up. He considered going home, but doubted she'd let him in. If only he had his house keys, he could walk into the kitchen like nothing had happened; the kids would leap up from their homework, overjoyed to see their dad, and, for their sake if no other reason, Amanda would be unable to cause a scene.

And then he remembered the spare set of keys in his desk drawer. Bingo!

They didn't fit. They were copies; maybe there's a knack, Greg thought. He put down the bouquet of flowers he was holding and tried each key in turn, jiggling it this way and that, feeling for the tumblers to fall. Nothing. Then he noticed the shiny newness of the chrome mechanism. Bugger me, she's changed the locks, he realised. Wow! She is seriously pissed off. He suspected that, despite having cost forty quid, the flowers weren't going to cut it.

He stood up. He could wait for Amanda to get home with the girls. That could be ugly. Or he could beat a tactical retreat. Clearly this was the wiser option. Perhaps surprisingly, given his recent track record, it was the one he chose to take. His neighbour, Mickey, was in his drive, washing his car while watching the latest developments two doors down. Does he never go indoors? Greg wondered. As he drove away, Greg waved and flashed Mickey a cheery smile. "Cunt," he muttered under his breath.

Greg returned to the Clifton Motor Inn. Standing behind the reception desk, Howard looked up with a smile of recognition. It wasn't Greg he recognised as much as his situation.

"Missed us, did you, Mr Beavis?" Howard asked, reaching for Greg's registration card, which he hadn't yet filed, suspecting it might still be active. In reply, Greg raised a sardonic eyebrow. Being the eye he'd recently gashed (or rather Amanda had), this hurt somewhat.

"And how long do you think you might be staying" — Howard paused for dramatic effect — "this time?" During his four years in the job, Howard had found that tormenting the guests made a monotonous shift pass that little bit faster.

"Let's take it one day at a time, shall we?" said Greg coolly.

Howard noticed with delight the muscle in Greg's jaw tighten. He buried himself in his computer screen while sharpening his next barb.

"And would you like your usual room?" he enquired innocently.

Howard stole a glance up to gauge Greg's reaction. The look on his face! Howard had to bite the inside of his cheek to keep himself from sniggering.

Dan hadn't felt this nervous since . . . well, since he'd phoned Lynda earlier in the day. Now he was in her shared flat on the top floor of a three-storey Victorian conversion somewhere in Willesden (thank God for his Sat Nav or he'd never have found it). Her flatmate was fortuitously away, on a short haul to Eindhoven, not due back till late. The bikes in the hallway, the IKEA furniture, the posters on the wall — it all reminded Dan of a student let, except the posters were framed, a sign, perhaps, of the occupants' maturity or greater disposable income. Standing in his business suit, Dan felt incongruous. He didn't belong here, he thought. Don't think, he told himself. Just live in the moment. He sought distraction in the photographs, also framed, arrayed on a sideboard. The bubbly brunette in the puce livery of a budget airline was presumably Lynda's flatmate, Dan forgot her name. The couple in their sixties were someone's parents. Lynda's or what's-her-face's? And who was this hunk: mid-twenties, his muscled arm round Lynda while they both beamed at the camera? Dan picked up the photograph for a closer look, scanning the handsome features for a family likeness.

Lynda entered bearing drinks and caught Dan with the photo in his hands.

He feigned casualness. "Brother?" he asked.

"Boyfriend," she replied, handing Dan his glass. Dan blinked; Lynda laughed. "Joke," she said.

"Good one," he replied without laughing. He replaced the frame on the sideboard.

They stood facing each other — somewhat uncomfortably. Neither could think of anything to say.

Dan fell back upon the photo of the couple in their sixties. "And whose parents are these?"

"Charlotte's."

So that was her name.

Again the uncomfortable silence.

"What are you doing here, Dan?"

What indeed? Dan exhaled, sat on the IKEA sofa. It wasn't particularly comfortable. Lynda sat beside him, awaiting his answer. Pensively, he sipped his whisky and water. More whisky than water. He made a mental note not to have a second. He didn't want to be breathalysed on his way home and have to explain to Sarah why he'd been in Willesden, which was in Greg's patch, not his. Huh, I'm already thinking like an adulterer, he observed wryly. How easily it comes.

"I don't know," he admitted. The truth was he hadn't considered the implications of this meeting; he'd just wanted to see Lynda again. He felt different in her company, not like the forty-one-year-old husband whose teenage son looked at him as though he were faintly ridiculous and whose wife didn't look at him much at all. In Birmingham he'd felt more like the man he'd hoped to grow into — good company, a man for whom everything was possible, someone other men admired.

He stood. "I should go."

Lynda remained seated. "Is that what you want to do?" She looked a little hurt, he thought.

"Oh, I don't know." He sat down again, took her hand, traced her fingers with his. "No," he said.

A small smile escaped her mouth. They sat in silence a moment. This time it didn't feel so uncomfortable.

"Would you like to see my bedroom?" she asked.

Yes, he thought. He would.

CHAPTER
SIX

Amanda had had a fuck-awful day. At work she'd been distracted, unable to concentrate. Just after lunch she'd prepared a lethal injection with which to euthanise a geriatric Burmese blue. Only at the last minute did she remember that he'd been brought in to have his teeth cleaned. Even so, she'd been tempted to continue. She was in the shittiest of moods, the cat was blind and incontinent, and, besides, she was more of a dog person.

Steeling herself, Amanda locked her Golf and crossed the car park to the Clifton Motor Inn. The hotel's glass doors slid open on her approach, whispering their welcome. From behind his desk, the receptionist looked up, standing erect as Amanda entered, pulling down his jacket sleeves in a fastidious manner.

"Madam?"

"Can you tell me which room Greg Beavis is staying in?" Amanda enquired.

Ah! thought Howard. The wronged wife. Unless, of course, she was the other woman.

"I can call him for you," he offered, picking up the phone.

"I'd rather go to his room."

Howard smiled tightly. "I'm afraid we don't give out that information."

Amanda sighed. This place wasn't the bloody Dorchester. "I'm not a prostitute, if that's what you're thinking."

"It hadn't crossed my mind," sniffed Howard. It was true. A hooker would make a lot more effort with her appearance. Either that or starve.

"Though I suppose you do get them," Amanda added, casting a disdainful eye about.

Oo, shnap! This one's feisty, thought Howard, warming to her. He was still holding the phone.

"Who shall I say is calling?"

Amanda held his gaze. She wondered how long it would take to drive to the surgery. In the fridge was the syringe she hadn't used on the Burmese blue.

"Amanda," she reluctantly conceded.

Howard's manicured fingers punched in Greg's number.

Shortly after, Greg appeared, sprinting down the corridor.

"Amanda!" he cried. "You came!"

Greg careered to a stop. Howard affected not to be watching this reunion, but not a detail escaped him. He saw Greg go to embrace her, then restrain himself when she flinched. The wronged wife, then, Howard thought. I was right the first time.

"Is there somewhere we can talk?" Amanda asked Greg, her eyes darting to Howard, who was suddenly terribly busy, meticulously rearranging tourist leaflets into alphabetical order.

* * *

Amanda knocked back Greg's first venue suggestion: his room. She favoured a neutral setting. Greg proposed Switzerland but Amanda didn't smile. They compromised on the nearest pub.

The Bricklayer's Arms had seen better days. At least Greg hoped it had, because it was a shit hole now. There was only one other occupant of the lounge bar: a balding middle-aged factory worker whose burgeoning beer belly branded him as a regular. He was feeding his take-home pay into a fruit machine. Its jingling chimes provided the pub's soundtrack. Greg doubted that there was a more depressing noise. The sound of despair, he thought.

Amanda looked up from shredding a beer mat as Greg brought over their drinks. He joined her, perched at a high table, setting down his pint.

"How are the girls?" he asked.

"They're fine. I've told them you're still away."

Greg nodded.

"Greg, what were you thinking?" The anger, upset and disillusion that Amanda had suppressed all day bubbled to the surface, vying for supremacy.

"I swear, I didn't cheat on you."

Anger won out. Amanda slammed her hands down on the tabletop. She took a deep breath. "I told myself I'd try not to lose it," she said.

"Do you think you could try a little harder?" Greg looked nervously around the pub. Happily, the barman was out the back and the fat regular appeared oblivious, engrossed in the fruit machine. His gaze returned to find Amanda skewering him with a look that warned him not to push her buttons — any further, that is.

Greg tasted his pint, weighing his words. He set down his glass and looked Amanda in the eye.

"OK, I admit something happened," he started, "but not what you think."

"Greg. Things don't just happen. You let them. Or you *don't*."

"I'm trying to explain . . ."

"Don't you think I have men come on to me?"

"Of course you do," he replied by rote, before hearing what she'd said. "Do you?"

"Just the other day. In Ravenscourt Park."

"The bastard!"

"It was nothing. Because I didn't let it become something."

She was right, of course.

"Look, hear me out," he said. "The truth, OK?"

Amanda weighed this request. It was, after all, the reason she'd come. She hugged her crossed arms to her for protection and leant back on her stool, ceding the stage to Greg. He considered his opening.

"I bought the condoms. The last night of the conference. You were right; I'd had too much to drink and I was flirting." Greg's eyes were fixed on Amanda, assessing how each word was being received. She sat immobile, impassive. So far, so good. "I know being drunk's no excuse," he admitted, before adding, in the hope it might excuse him, "but I was completely off my face."

Amanda's expression remained blank. Greg hesitated. He was coming to the difficult part.

"Dan and me got talking to these two women. They invited us back to their rooms. That's when I got the condoms. I gave Dan one — that part was true — I kept the other for myself."

"Go on."

During the day, Greg had practised this speech so many times he could see the scene as vividly as if it had actually happened.

"We split into pairs and left the bar. We got into separate lifts . . . I mean, Dan and his woman, me with mine. Mine had a room on the sixteenth floor, or something; it was high, anyway — I think that's what made the difference. It gave me time to think." Greg's eyes drifted off like he'd seen actors on television do when they were recounting a flashback. "There was a mirror on the control panel by the door. I caught sight of my reflection." He looked back at Amanda, attempting an expression of mystic wonder. "It was like I was seeing myself through your eyes. I suddenly saw what I was doing. To you and the kids." Greg smiled sadly — piteously, he hoped — a touch he'd refined during rehearsals. "When the lift arrived at her floor, she got out. And I didn't." Greg again broke eye contact, adding a hint of humility. "I couldn't. I couldn't do that to you." Eyes back to Amanda for the big emotional finish. "I respect you too much."

Greg was pretty pleased with his performance. He felt he'd struck the right tone, offered enough detail to make it sound authentic, but not so much that she'd think he was trying too hard. He'd buy it. But would Amanda? He could sense her deliberating.

"That's it?" she finally asked. "The best you could come up with in twenty-four hours?"

"It's the truth," he said earnestly.

"You just made your excuses and left?"

Put like that, it sounded a little thin.

"Yes!"

Greg willed Amanda to believe him. She regarded him for a long moment. He felt like it could go either way. He shifted uncomfortably under her penetrating gaze.

At last, she spoke.

"How attractive was this woman?" Offhand, like she was just making conversation.

Greg sensed danger, an unexploded bomb in the vicinity.

"Attractive?" He looked confused, which wasn't difficult.

"Yes. Just out of interest."

Greg didn't like it; Amanda was too calm.

She continued in the same casual tone, "I mean, if she was a dog, then what does that say about me, the fact you wanted to sleep with her? If, on the other hand, she was gorgeous," Amanda's eyes narrowed and bore gimlet-like into Greg, "then I don't believe for one second that you didn't shag her."

Greg was in a bind, torn between two lovers, a rock and a hard place.

"She was . . . somewhere in between?" he offered hopefully.

120

Amanda wasn't buying.

That faithful retainer, Howard, was still at his post when Greg returned to the hotel.

"Looks like I'll be staying a few more nights," Greg announced breezily.

Howard strangled a smirk; he'd have put money on it.

Crossing the lobby, the prospect of spending further hours in the cheerless confines of his room, with its sickening décor and too-bright illumination, hit Greg like a football to the testicles. He stopped dead in his tracks. Fuck, he thought. And then a heartening realisation: he had other options. It didn't have to be the Clifton Motor Inn. He turned back to the reception desk. "Actually, print my bill, will you? I'm checking out."

Greg went off to pack, the spring restored to his step. And Howard was surprised to realise that he'd miss him.

Amanda made a detour into Sainsbury's on her way home. She didn't so much need any shopping as an alibi, to back up the cover story she'd given her mum when she'd asked her to mind the girls.

Margaret was pouring herself a glass of wine as Amanda entered the kitchen. Her second, judging by the bottle.

"Was there a particularly long line at the checkout?" Margaret asked, gesturing with her glass at the toilet rolls and milk that were Amanda's sole purchases. "You gave the impression you'd need a Red Cross parcel if you didn't get to the shops. I had to cancel bridge."

"And I greatly appreciate it, Mum," Amanda said in the sickly sweet voice she increasingly found her mother provoked in her. "Still, at least you got to spend some time with your grandchildren." She busied herself putting the shopping away. It didn't take long.

Margaret sniffed. "So where have you been all this time?"

Not that it's any of your business, thought Amanda. She started stacking the dishwasher so she wouldn't have to look her mother in the face as she lied to her.

"I went to see a friend who's in hospital. Diane."

"Diane? Which one's that?"

Oh, for Christ's sake! Her mum didn't usually take this much interest in her life.

"She's a colleague. A vet."

"Oh. What's her problem? Dog bite?"

"Cancer. Terminal." That should shut her up, hoped Amanda. "Where are the girls?"

"After they had their tea, I said they could watch television."

"Mum! You know the rules."

"I thought they deserved a treat. They were upset."

"The girls were? Why?"

"Because you've kicked Greg out."

Amanda usually had a ready retort for anything her mother said, but not on this occasion.

"Do you even have a friend called Diane?" Margaret asked. "Does she have cancer?"

"Yes. And no. How do the girls know about Greg?"

122

"A child in Molly's class was teasing her. Apparently her father saw you tossing Greg's things out on to the street. Really, Amanda! I thought we'd brought you up to show a little more decorum."

Amanda felt her grip tighten around the knife she was holding. She forced her hand to relax.

"So what was it all about?" her mum pressed.

There were only a few people Amanda would choose to confide in. Her mother wasn't any of them.

"I don't want to discuss it," she said. "It's private."

"It sounded all too public to me."

"We had a disagreement, that's all."

"Well, thank goodness it wasn't a full-blown row or think what you might have done!"

Amanda was struck by how snug the knife felt in her grasp. Her sickly sweet voice returned for an encore.

"Mum, thanks for coming over, but I really need to talk to the girls, so you can go now."

"I haven't finished my drink," Margaret protested.

"Yes, you have," said Amanda, pouring her mother's glass down the sink. "You are driving."

Amanda always has been wilful, Margaret mused; she gets that from her father. Amanda's dad had died four years earlier, a decade after his marriage to Margaret had ended in divorce.

"Whatever's going on between you and Greg, you shouldn't inflict it on the children," Margaret sniffed, with a sanctimony that she found quite satisfying.

There was so much Amanda could say to that — a lifetime of precedents — and how she would have liked to vent. The words gathered on her tongue, like troops raring to be sent into battle. Cry havoc and let slip the dogs of war! But she bit them back. Now was not the time to open old wounds.

In silence, she walked her mother to the door, like a nightclub bouncer escorting a rowdy patron off the premises.

Dan paused before inserting his front door key. No telltale signs of where he'd been the last hour and a half? No lipstick on the collar, fly at half mast, look of sated lust upon his face? Check, check and check.

He let himself into the house, quietly congratulating himself on the composure with which he crossed the threshold into his other life. He was struck by his ability to be both in his skin and at the same time to stand apart, observing his performance. Not just observing, but assessing, and adjusting accordingly. It was as if he was being filmed for one of those fly-on-the-wall TV documentaries, conscious of how he was coming across to the cameras and keen to ensure that he presented the desired image. A weird sensation, but not unpleasant; an extra dimension he'd managed to unlock.

Sarah was coming out of the kitchen. She met him in the hall and offered her cheek to be kissed. Just a quick peck, Dan thought, in case Lynda's scent still clung to him.

"Sorry I'm late."

"Meeting run on?" Sarah asked with a solicitude that momentarily made Dan suspicious. But just because I'm being deceitful doesn't mean everyone is, he reminded himself.

124

"Yeah. Will dinner keep? I need a shower first."

He started towards the stairs.

"Well, make it quick," Sarah called after him, adding in a hissed undertone, "I'm running out of things to say to Greg."

Greg? Dan's leading foot, raised to ascend the stairs, froze in mid-air. His head swung towards Sarah as she turned for the kitchen.

"Greg?" he hissed in return.

"You might have warned me you'd invited him for dinner."

What the fuck? Dan scurried after Sarah. Sure enough, there was Greg, cradling a can of beer, his legs leisurely stretched out under the kitchen table while he pored over Russell's history homework. That's my job! thought Dan. Greg looked up at the sound of Dan's anxious footsteps.

"Ah! The hunter-gatherer! What was this meeting I missed?"

"What?" Dan was momentarily nonplussed. "Oh. Nothing. One of my accounts."

Dan waited for Sarah to turn her attention to the oven, then mugged at Greg, ordering him out of the room with his eyes. Dan bundled Greg into the lounge, closing the door behind them.

"What the hell are you doing here?"

"Amanda won't see reason."

"So?"

"So I couldn't spend another night in that hotel. I was going to open a vein!"

Dan saw with horrible clarity the plan Greg had in mind. "You can't stay here!"

"You've got a spare room, haven't you?"

Yes, but that wasn't the point.

Greg saw where Dan's mind was going. "Look, you've got nothing to fear."

"Guilt by association!"

Greg waved away this piffling concern. "Anyway, it's down to you I'm in this mess."

"*Me?*" That came out a little louder than Dan had intended, though it adequately expressed his incredulity.

"If you hadn't had the second condom, I'd be sweet."

"You forced it on me!"

Both men jumped as they heard the door open. Sarah's head appeared. She immediately sensed that something was amiss. Dan and Greg looked like schoolboys caught smoking out of bounds.

"Is everything all right?" she asked Dan.

"Fine," he assured her. "Problem at work. Not important."

Sarah wasn't sure she altogether believed him. She looked from Dan to Greg, who had the countenance of an unmolested choirboy. No, there was definitely something up.

"The meal will be ready in ten minutes," she said. Then, when Dan didn't react, "You were wanting a shower?"

"Yes! Thank you."

Sarah cast a final look at them both. Whatever their secret was, she'd find out soon enough. Dan would tell her. She went out, leaving the door ajar to see whether they closed it. Dan reached for the handle, but only to pull the door wider so he could follow.

Greg grabbed his arm to hold him back. "You are telling the truth, aren't you? About the meeting that kept you late?"

Fuck, he's guessed, thought Dan, until he noticed the beseeching look in Greg's eyes.

"I mean," Greg continued, "you would let me know — if it was something I should be aware of."

"Yes!" Dan shrugged off Greg's hand. "I told you! It was one of my accounts."

Dan seemed too earnest, too eager that Greg should believe him. And so, of course, Greg didn't. While Dan showered, Greg's mind ran riot. There was something afoot at work, and he was not in the loop. Jesus Christ, he thought, on top of all my other problems . . .

Amanda didn't immediately disturb the kids. She let them watch the rest of *The Simpsons* first. Why upset them more than was necessary? As the episode ended, and before another began, she reluctantly called them into the kitchen. They joined her at the kitchen table, turning their large, expectant eyes her way. Amanda considered where to begin.

"You know how me and Dad sometimes have arguments?"

Her daughters said nothing. They recognised a rhetorical question when they heard one, despite not knowing what a rhetorical question was.

"Well, as Jasmine's daddy saw, we had an argument yesterday that was a bit worse than usual."

"Why?" asked Molly, getting straight to the nub of it.

"Well," said Amanda tentatively, making it up as she went along, "because Daddy's done something very silly."

"Did he leave the shower curtain outside the bath again?" This from Lauren.

"No. No, it was a bit worse than that." Amanda shuddered at the thought of Greg with some other woman. "A lot worse. Anyway . . ."

"What was it?" Molly was not to be sidetracked.

"That doesn't matter. Something that grown-ups sometimes do. The thing is . . ."

"Like what?" Lauren asked; apparently she and Molly had formed a tag team.

"It's a grown-up thing; you don't need to know. Do you want an apple?" she asked, hoping to distract them. The children shook their heads. "No, thank you," Amanda said, since they hadn't. Christ, I sound like my mother, she thought. Decorum, etiquette. "The point is we had a big row . . . and Daddy's moved out for the time being."

Both girls stared at her.

"How long for?" Molly asked gravely.

"Well, we don't know."

"But he is coming back?" Lauren insisted.

Amanda opened her mouth but no sound issued. Was Greg coming back? That was up to her. She couldn't imagine it at the moment. But when might she? What if that moment never came? Lauren's mind was tending in the same direction.

"Are you getting divorced?" she asked, a trace of fear audible.

Molly rolled her eyes. "They're not married, stupid; they can't get divorced."

"Don't call your sister stupid."

For once, Lauren had greater concerns than her sibling's scorn. "Justin Pope's parents got divorced. His dad moved to Canada. Now he only sees him at Christmas."

"Your dad's not moving to Canada."

"But he will be coming home?" Molly pressed. Like her younger sister, her eyes were wide, begging for reassurance.

"Yes," Amanda heard herself say, before tacking on a rider, "to see you, take you to school . . ."

The girls were young but also bright. They knew when they were being fobbed off. They wanted certainty, not equivocation. They regarded their mother reproachfully.

"Look, I don't know what's going to happen," she admitted. "We'll have to wait and see. But Daddy loves you just as much as ever. And so do I."

"I want him to come home," Molly said in a tiny voice, climbing on to Amanda's lap.

"Me too," said Lauren, staring sadly at her hands.

Amanda reached for Lauren with her free arm, pulling her aboard her knee. Though their combined weight made it uncomfortable (how quickly they were growing), Amanda hugged the children to her.

"I know you do," she said.

She kissed them in turn. The girls remained where they were, taking comfort from their mother's embrace. Amanda hated herself for hurting them so. But she hated Greg even more for being the cause. Why can't he just admit that he fucked up? she asked herself for the umpteenth time. Why maintain this ridiculous fiction that he didn't cheat?

The sound of the doorbell hijacked her thoughts.

"Daddy!" the girls shouted in unison, Amanda instantly dismissed as they leapt off her lap and hurtled towards the front door. Amanda composed herself and slowly followed. She'd rather Greg had rung ahead, not used their daughters as a human shield, but she wasn't surprised he'd stoop to such tactics.

Except Greg hadn't. It was her older sister who stood on the doorstep.

"Geraldine!" Molly cried with delight, flinging herself into her aunt's arms.

"Daddy's left home," Lauren announced as Geraldine gathered her up.

"So Grandma tells me," Geraldine said, with a meaningful look over Lauren's head at Amanda.

Christ, that didn't take long, Amanda thought. Her mum must have been on her mobile before she'd backed out the drive. The bush telegraph, on speed dial. Exasperated, Amanda turned and headed for the kitchen — which Geraldine took as her cue to follow.

Dan and Sarah were trying to keep the conversation flowing over dinner but there were two impediments to their efforts: Russell and Greg. Both were morose and withdrawn. Russell had the excuse of being a teenager but Sarah could not fathom why Greg was glumly chasing his chicken chasseur round his plate. Sarah didn't know Greg well, but taciturn was not a word she would have used to describe him. Extrovert, brash, bumptious — these were more apt adjectives: the life and soul of the party. As someone more likely to be standing on the sidelines (keeping Dan company), Sarah found Greg's customary ebullience a bit much, but this dour demeanour was, if anything, worse. Why had Dan invited him over?

Each time she stole a glance Greg's way, Dan would leap in with a new conversational gambit, as much to distract her as Greg, it seemed to Sarah. She tested her theory, allowing her eyes to drift to Greg's melancholic countenance, and — boom! — in jumped Dan.

"Oh, I didn't tell you!" he said, drawing Sarah's attention back to him. "I've managed to get Macpherson Healthcare across the line. A tidy fifteen grand."

"That's wonderful!" Sarah enthused. "Does that mean you might make this month's target?"

"Well, it's still a long shot, but the bookies haven't stopped taking bets just yet." Dan said this with an optimism Sarah was unused to. She was almost persuaded to believe he could pull it off. She turned to involve Greg.

"And how are your sales going, Greg?"

The mention of his name stirred Greg from his reverie.

"Sorry?"

"We're just discussing this month's sales target," she prodded encouragingly.

"Oh, I'm not there yet," Greg offered.

Really? thought Dan. So I'm still in with a chance!

Maybe that's what's bugging Greg, thought Sarah, though he's certainly taking it badly.

Greg reached for the wine bottle in the middle of the table and poured himself an unhealthy measure. Sarah and Dan exchanged uneasy looks.

"I'm not sure you should have any more, Greg," Sarah said, "not if you're driving."

Russell looked up. His mum, admonishing a dinner guest for drinking too much? That didn't happen often — ever, in fact. This had the potential to get interesting. Like his parents, Russell watched Greg for his reaction. Greg languidly poked at his food, then glanced up to find all eyes on him.

"Oh, Dan said I could stay," he remarked casually.

This was news to Sarah! She shifted her attention to her husband, imperceptibly widening her eyes, silently shouting, You did what?!

Bastard! He's painted me into a corner and got me over a barrel, thought Dan, mixing his metaphors. His eyes met Greg's, and held them. I won't be dictated to in my own home, his expression said. Yes, you will, Greg's replied, unless you want to be dropped in it. Dan swallowed a morsel of chicken and with it his resistance.

"Just for the one night," he informed Sarah, but also negotiating a deal with Greg.

132

"I really appreciate it," Greg told his hostess, with a winning smile that failed to move her. "You're probably wondering why I can't go home," he added.

"Well . . . yes, I suppose I was," she admitted.

"Me and Amanda have had a bit of a falling out. She thinks I cheated on her."

Whoooa! Alarm bells clamoured in Dan's head. That was way more detail than was called for.

"It's really none of our business," he suggested to Sarah.

Russell was all ears. His parents' dinner parties were never this entertaining.

"At the conference," Greg added, by way of clarification.

"Like I said . . ." reiterated Dan, his eyes appealing for Greg to shut the fuck up.

"I see," said Sarah. This explained the covert chat she'd interrupted earlier. "And did you?"

"Sarah, darling." Dan frowned, hoping to warn her off.

"No," Greg told her. "I mean, I flirted. Lipstick on the collar stuff —"

"That's how she found out," Dan put in quickly before the conversation turned to condoms. But Sarah was concentrating on Greg.

"Nothing to justify turfing me out," he lamented.

"She obviously thought so," Sarah said in a voice that suggested she did too.

"It'll just be the one night," Dan reassured his wife.

"Or a couple." Greg was keen to keep his options open. "Till Amanda calms down."

"A couple," Sarah said coolly, her gaze flicking to Dan.

"Shouldn't be much more than that," Greg volunteered, before a disturbing thought struck him. "Unless she's premenstrual."

Sarah already had no sympathy for Greg but after that remark had even less.

CHAPTER
SEVEN

Amanda poured herself and Geraldine glasses of wine, then topped them up, making the adequate measures generous. Molly and Lauren were in the lounge. They'd wanted to stay with their aunt, but had been bribed with the offer of TV. They were easily bought.

"So, what's the story?" Geri asked. "You chuck Greg out of the house — it must be something big."

Amanda remained tight-lipped. Geraldine was unperturbed; she'd flush her out. She sipped her wine. Not bad, she thought; better than what she drank at home, but then Amanda and Greg probably didn't select their cellar from Aldi's three-for-a-tenner range.

"I'm guessing he got up to no good at the conference."

That was so typical of Geraldine — to think the worst of people. And be right.

"Is that it? He got pissed, shagged some tart?"

Amanda winced. "Like I told Mum, I don't want to talk about it."

"Well, that's a yes."

Amanda shot Geraldine a dirty look, warning her sister to leave well alone.

Fat chance.

"A one-off, was it?" Geri added casually.

Amanda was torn. On the one hand, she had no desire to discuss her falling-out with Greg; she didn't need people prying. On the other, she wanted someone to vent to, someone who would share her outrage and understand her fury. A sister, in other words. And who better for the role? It was this hand that won out.

"He claims it wasn't even a one-off. Says nothing happened."

"So what makes you think it did?"

"The smoking gun in his luggage."

Geraldine frowned; she didn't follow.

Amanda reluctantly spelt it out. "I found some condoms he'd bought. One was missing."

"Whoa! Bang to rights! And still he maintained his innocence?"

"He says he gave it to a friend."

"Sounds like he gave it to her, all right!" For which Geraldine earned herself another admonishing look. "Still," she carried blithely on, "it's not like you suspect him of having an affair."

Amanda stared at her sister in consternation. "Your point being . . . what, exactly?"

"Well, there's a world of difference. An affair's first-degree murder; a one-night stand's more GBH. Have you got any crisps?"

Amanda couldn't believe what she was hearing. Her sister seemed to regard this as a matter of little import. She was more concerned whether there was any food in the house. No wonder she's divorced, she thought.

"No wonder you're divorced," she said, because if there's one advantage to being sisters it's being able to say whatever's on your mind.

"Hey! Dave might have been a low-life, good-for-nothing, gambling drunk, but he always kept it trousered."

That's true, thought Amanda; you had to give Dave that.

"Crisps?" Geraldine reminded her.

Amanda climbed off her stool and ransacked the cupboards for snacks. She unearthed a packet of Bombay mix that wasn't wildly beyond its sell-by date and tipped the contents into a bowl. Geraldine dived in.

"I mean, I can understand you being upset, but it's not at the worst end of the spectrum."

"He cheated on me!" Amanda exclaimed, since the point seemed to be getting lost.

Geraldine was unmoved. "We've established that. At a conference. It's what men do."

"Not Greg."

"Well, yes, apparently Greg." Geraldine shrugged apologetically, sifting through the Bombay mix for her favourite bits. "So you've kicked him out. How long for? I mean, you are going to take him back?" She spotted the doubt clouding her sister's eyes. "You don't jeopardise your relationship over something like this!"

"He's the one jeopardising our relationship!" Amanda countered, her tone a little shrill. She regained a more controlled register as she continued, "Whatever punishment I choose to mete out, he deserves it."

"Well, yesssss," Geraldine agreed, but drawing out the word so its meaning sounded more like no. "But even so —"

Amanda had had enough. She spoke over Geraldine, her voice rising. "The first time Dad cheated, Mum forgave him. And the second. And the third. Till finally he left her. You can't blame him. I mean, who could live with someone they had so little respect for?"

Amanda hadn't meant to get so het up. She felt that somehow Geraldine had manoeuvred her into revealing more than she'd intended, more than she had even been aware of.

"So that's what this is really all about," her sister said, chewing a curried peanut.

God, Geraldine could be infuriating, especially when she had a point. Not that Amanda would acknowledge that. Setting her jaw, she rose from the breakfast bar.

"I've got to get the girls ready for bed," she said and walked out of the kitchen.

"He's having a bath," Dan announced, entering the lounge where Sarah was watching the ten o'clock news.

"No hot water for us, then," she said tartly, still annoyed with Dan for inviting Greg to stay.

Dan doubted Greg would use up the whole tank but could see no benefit in arguing the issue. Instead, he settled on to the sofa alongside Sarah and turned his attention to the news. Apparently tornadoes had ripped through the American Midwest. Funny how they always seem to zero in on trailer parks, Dan thought; almost as if God has something against mobile homes. Or their owners. Dan wondered which state had borne the brunt this time.

He wasn't to find out. Sarah muted the TV; she turned to face him.

"So, the conference . . . A little more interesting than you made it sound."

Dan regarded Sarah, trying not to blink more than usual.

"Don't you want to watch the news?" he asked.

Sarah made no move to increase the volume. She was still waiting for Dan to respond to her remark. He ran through a quick damage assessment and concluded that saying nothing was more likely to arouse her suspicion.

"Greg made a fool of himself," he said offhand, "had too much to drink." He returned his gaze to the TV, as though there was nothing more to add. A morbidly obese woman in a sequined T-shirt and too-tight pink leggings sobbed among the plywood splinters of her home.

"And what about you?"

"Me?"

"Did you have too much to drink?"

Dan turned to face Sarah, the better to assess the tone in which this question was asked. Her expression seemed innocent enough. It betrayed no hint that she suspected anything.

"You know what I'm like with hangovers," he said. "I could see the way things were headed — beginning to get out of control — so I called it a night, slipped off to my room." Dan shrugged as though apologising that he didn't have a more colourful tale to relate. Sarah regarded him a moment, her brow faintly corrugated in . . . it looked to Dan like disappointment.

And that's exactly what it was. Sarah was disappointed to discover that she believed every word Dan told her. She could imagine the scene: Greg, loud and pissed, accidentally spilling drinks over girls, provoking shrieks of laughter as he wiped at their breasts with a soggy cocktail napkin. And Dan, quietly disapproving of this debauchery, sidling towards the lobby without announcing his departure, then increasing his pace as he spotted an empty lift, his means of escape.

Sarah hadn't for a minute bought Greg's story about lipstick on the collar. Evidently there was more to it than that, and she could guess what. She'd be horrified if she thought that Dan had behaved similarly. But he could at least have considered it, been tempted. When, she wondered, had he become so middle-aged? And why had she not raged against this dying of the light? Why had she stood meekly by, complicit in his decline? She turned up the TV news. Footage of shanties in Brazil being washed away by floods. The weather again picking on the poverty-stricken.

Dan stole a glance in Sarah's direction. She clearly suspected nothing. She doesn't know me as well as she thinks she does, he thought. But then neither did he. He was a far better dissembler than he would ever have imagined. And not as nice a person as he'd hoped.

140

Greg took in his surroundings. He was in the spare room, though that was too grand a description — box room was more like it. Generally it was used for storage — toys of Russell's that he'd outgrown but which Sarah couldn't bring herself to give to charity; bin bags of winter clothes, inappropriate for the current season; a couple of tins of old paint that Dan kept for reference or touching up but which he wouldn't reopen until long after they'd congealed into an oily residue. There was so much clutter there was barely room for the single bed on which Greg now sat. Sarah clearly did not want him here — that much was clear. She'd made no effort to make him feel welcome. She could, for instance, have found him a more appropriate duvet cover than this one featuring characters from *Ben 10*, a kids' cartoon that once must have been Russell's favourite. She hadn't even offered him a towel, and when he'd asked for one, had reached deep within the airing cupboard for a fraying piece of cloth so coarse it looked and felt as though it had been used by generations of boarding-school pupils.

Greg sighed. That it had come to this! If he could only turn the clock back, have his time again, he wouldn't make the same mistake. How many men must have thought that over the years? But then they had cheated, he hadn't. All he was guilty of was fumbling. It was so unjust.

He moved some plastic figurines of American wrestlers with over-inflated muscles off the bedside table, making space for the framed photograph of his girls. God, he missed them. It was one thing to go away for a few days. That was respite, R & R. But not to know when he'd see their smiling faces again. That was hell. And Amanda — he missed her most of all. He'd once seen a blackboard outside a café on which was chalked, "A day without laughter is a day not lived". Greg didn't hold with the current fad for cafés to offer their clientele life training — he'd rather be informed of a great deal on bacon butties — but, walking away, munching his bacon butty, the truth of the aphorism had struck him. Though he would slightly amend the words. Because it was Amanda's laughter that Greg lived for. He felt a rush of fulfilment every time he induced a smile to light up her face, laugh-lines to punctuate her eyes. And he was good at it. It was his reward most days.

At least it had been in the past. It wasn't in the present. And as for the future? Who could say when he might make Amanda laugh again? The look of animosity she'd cast him as she left the pub that evening suggested Antarctica would have to freeze over to its pre-global-warming extent before she'd find him even remotely amusing. Christ, he'd been a fool. And all because his fragile ego had succumbed to the flattering attention of a young woman with succulent breasts.

Greg considered some self-administered hand relief. That usually helped him relax. But he couldn't summon the enthusiasm; his heart wasn't in it. He wouldn't be able to think of Amanda without seeing the look of disapproval on her face. And to fantasise about anyone else, even Jennifer Lawrence, felt like a betrayal.

I'm fucked! He thought. I might never have sex again, even with myself.

It was so unjust.

Dan had often wondered what it would feel like to have an affair. And now he knew. Because, let's be honest, he reflected as he lay in bed, his hands interlaced behind his head, that was what he and Lynda had embarked upon. As he'd left her flat that evening they'd made arrangements to see each other again.

It was not like he'd imagined. Being previously unversed in such matters, he'd assumed an affair would be agony, a constant struggle to keep your two lives separate. It must be mentally exhausting (he'd thought), ensuring the details of one existence didn't bleed into the other: a task that would require vigilance twenty-four/seven. He'd even heard of one guy who'd taken as his mistress a woman with the same name as his wife, to avoid the risk of uttering the wrong name during sex.

But maybe what they said was true, that men were good at compartmentalising. Already he felt there was little danger he'd say the wrong thing to Sarah. He was reminded of his youth. As a teenager he'd had two distinct vocabularies. At home he used a sanitised version, but when he was out with his friends his speech was peppered with "bloody" this and "fuck" that. He could switch between them at will. That's what this felt like — like being bilingual. Dan found it intriguing. Was it nature's way of giving the adulterer an even break?

Dan Sinclair: adulterer. He still found it hard to believe. As would anyone who knew him. That was, perhaps, his best cover. He wasn't proud of his accomplishment. It had been borne of weakness. But strength is overrated. Given the choice, who wouldn't prefer to be happy? And, on balance, Dan was.

The door to the darkened room opened and Sarah slipped in. She'd stayed up, ostensibly to watch some art-house flick on Film 4, though Dan suspected she was still pissed off at him. Feeling charitable (and guilty), Dan had settled in to watch with her. The film was a Vietnamese drama about an elderly rice farmer whose arthritis impeded him gathering his meagre crop. The movie had been about as exciting as watching rice grow, short on dialogue and even shorter on action. It had needed spicing up in some way — an explosion, say; a previously undetected Vietcong landmine blowing the rice cropper and his paddy to kingdom come. No such luck. Forty minutes in Dan had admitted defeat in his battle to keep his eyes open. Sarah had not objected when he'd proposed going to bed, but nor had she switched off the TV and joined him. Since then, of course, sleep had proved elusive; he'd lain awake, thinking about Lynda.

Dan felt the mattress shift as Sarah lay down, careful not to disturb him. In the darkness he sensed her settle to sleep, her back to him.

"How did the movie end?" he asked.

144

"The rains came and washed away the farmer's crop. Then he died."

Yep, that would be right. What a miserable bloody movie. Dan said nothing. A silence grew between them like a barbed-wire fence. He risked tearing his skin on its jagged spikes by extending a hand and resting it on Sarah's shoulder.

"I'm sorry about Greg," he said. And he was. He fervently wished his friend had not brought his problems under their roof.

"It's not your fault," Sarah replied, which Dan interpreted to mean, It is your fault, but I forgive you.

Dan could have left it at that. They would have gone to sleep with some semblance of cordial relations reestablished. But he didn't want to remove his hand; he liked the feel of her skin. It struck him that it had been an age since he had touched her in this way; weeks, certainly — possibly months. He gently caressed her arm, feeling the soft down, then, putting a slight pressure on her shoulder, pulled her over towards him. He was astounded. What the hell am I doing? he wondered. It's just a few hours since I made love to my mistress (how he relished the carnality of that word). But, of course, that was it. The experience of being with Lynda had made Sarah more attractive to him. He wanted her.

What the hell is he doing? Sarah asked herself with wonder. She was tired; she'd stayed up to watch that God-awful film that, had it been about a potato farmer from Cleethorpes, would never have seen the light of day. She really just wanted to go to sleep. The last thing she needed was Dan thrusting himself at her, just so they could tick off June and postpone confronting their sexless marriage for a few weeks yet.

But when Dan pressed his lips against hers, she was conscious of a different tenor to his embrace. He was kissing her like he meant it, not just going through the motions. She felt herself respond.

Sarah had an orgasm that night — her first for over a year that was neither faked nor DIY. Because it took her by surprise, she was quite unprepared for the ecstatic wave that surged up her body and burst forth from her lips like a prisoner released into the sunshine after years in a windowless cell. Fuck me, she thought. Where did that come from?

Lying awake under his *Ben 10* duvet, Greg heard Sarah's sharp climax. There's nothing that reinforces a sense of isolation more than the sound of other people having sex. Greg buried his head under his *Ben 10* pillow.

Salespeople fall into three types. There are those for whom the deal is everything. Paula "Strap-On" Stratton, Regional Sales Manager, north-west, was a member of this breed. She would go to any lengths to make a sale. When she smiled it was with her mouth only, her eyes alert for any advantage. Clients lived in awe of her. And slightly in fear. Her figures were always good but were heavily dependent on new business.

Greg was less hard-nosed. He fell into the second category. These reps rely on their charm and affability. When they smile it is with their whole being. They too are eager to sell, but also eager to please. They're popular and entertaining company, many of their deals forged over lunch. Customers often consider them friends.

Dan was a member of the third fraternity, the smallest of the trinity, what might be called "technical" reps. They know their products inside out and love them like they're children (in some cases like their children). If they can't provide the perfect solution to a client's needs, they'd rather not make the sale. They smile when they receive letters of appreciation. They find repeat business a cinch.

What the three types of sales rep have in common is that they are each only as good as their last deal. As a result, many suffer a nagging fear that their success is a fluke, based on luck. They face a daily battle to shore up their self-belief. The hours before dawn are the hardest. Feelings of insecurity, easily repressed during the day, creep out under cover of darkness and infect their vulnerable minds. Sandbags of self-confidence can build a levee against this storm surge of doubt. But when the dam breaks . . .

Greg was staring at another blank page in his ledger. Since the conference his sales had fallen off a cliff. He'd sold nothing. Zip, zero, zilch. Fuck all. Admittedly it had been only two days. Just a dry spell. But when does a dry spell become a drought? It sounds like the set-up for a punchline but Greg was in no mood to laugh. The joke was on him.

If he could just make one sale, he was sure he would be all right. He had to do something to change his luck, to lift him out of this trough. He'd already shifted his cactus plant to the other side of his desk. And played Candy Crush on his iPhone until he'd unlocked a new level. Both had worked in the past when he'd sensed a barren patch looming. Not this time. In despair he'd broken one of his own rules, discounting so heavily he was basically offering a deal at cost — anything to return him to the winners' circle — but the customer had thought the price too good to be true and had baulked, the asshole.

Of course, Greg knew what the real issue was: the problem with Amanda. It had disturbed his equilibrium, knocked him off balance. His aura of invincibility had gone, like an invisibility cloak torn from his shoulders to leave him exposed and vulnerable.

Greg sat at his desk, doodling while he pondered his dilemma. He drew a hangman, then lopped its head off. He could have done some work instead, followed up leads or sown some fresh ones, but he knew the effort would be futile — everything was until he sorted things with Amanda. But how? Even if he could get her to speak to him — she was still ducking his calls — how could he persuade her of his innocence when she was so convinced of his guilt?

Greg ripped the sheet off his A4 pad, balled it and threw it at his waste-paper bin. It missed. Let's be methodical about this, he thought. Suppose he'd been accused of a murder and all the evidence pointed his way. How could he escape conviction? Well, if he had an alibi, to prove he hadn't been at the scene at the time of the alleged crime. Except he had been there, front and centre.

But wait just a minute! No crime had been committed, that was the point. This was a murder case without a corpse. In fact, it was the corpse herself who could testify to his innocence!

Newly energised, Greg fumbled in his computer case — reminding himself that he still needed to replace his laptop — and found Liz's business card. He rang her work number.

"Buzz Marketing!"

What a wanky name, Greg had time to think, before the switchboard operator continued, "How may I direct your call?"

"Liz Henderson, please."

"One moment."

One moment turned out to be twenty seconds of ersatz music that made the wait seem longer. Then a perky female voice came on the line.

"Liz Henderson."

Given the last time they'd spoken, it occurred to Greg that Liz might be less than delighted to hear from him. He thought it possible — probable, even — that she might hang up on him again. He took a deep breath and launched into his prepared spiel.

"Liz? It's Greg. Please don't hang up, just listen! Amanda knows about what happened at the conference. She found my condoms. I tried to explain but she kicked me out. You have to help me!"

There was a prolonged silence on the other end of the line. But the office acoustic at least meant that she hadn't hung up. Good, Greg thought, she's weighing my SOS. Finally, she spoke. It wasn't the response Greg had expected.

"You must want the other Liz Henderson. We're always getting each other's calls. I'll just transfer you."

Oh shit, thought Greg, as he listened to another twenty seconds of ersatz music.

"Liz Henderson."

Less perky, but definitely her this time.

"Liz? It's Greg. Please don't hang up, just listen —"

"For fuck's sake! Stop calling me, will you?"

No office acoustic this time, just dead air.

"Hello? Liz? Hello?"

Bollocks!

What a difference a shag makes. Sarah felt a completely different woman. Catching sight of herself in the rear-view mirror as she drove to the shops, she could have sworn her hair looked like it had extra bounce. As usual, the supermarket car park resembled the centre of Milan during the heist in *The Italian Job* (the superior British original); demand for spaces far outstripped supply. Sarah cruised the car park on a forlorn quest. Rather than the irritation this inconvenience would normally provoke, she appreciated the opportunity to hear *Desert Island Discs* through to the end — whoever would have thought that Bill Bryson would choose a pool table as his luxury? Finally, a space opened up. Sarah nabbed it, narrowly ahead of a young woman in a beaten-up mini who flicked her the finger. Poor lamb probably hasn't got laid in a while, thought Sarah with satisfying condescension. She reverse parked in one fluid movement, which was quite unlike her. Could an orgasm improve your spatial awareness? she wondered.

Steering her trolley among the other shoppers, Sarah considered what to cook for dinner. How about steak? A juicy slab of lean meat to replenish Dan's stock of red blood cells. Sarah smiled, allowing herself a moment's self-indulgent recall of the great sex they'd recently enjoyed. Dan had ravished her! *Ravaged* her. Most unlike him. Not that she was complaining — far from it. More, please! Russell could do with some building up as well. She tossed a tray of grain-fed sirloin into her trolley. Enough for the three of them.

And then she remembered their house guest. Bloody Greg! He should be on the streets, not seeking refuge under her roof. It bothered Sarah that, by taking Greg in, they might seem to be excusing his behaviour, while all her sympathy was with Amanda. Well, one more night, then he could sling his hook. Resentfully, she threw another steak in — a piece of brisket approaching its sell-by date and reduced in price. She was damned if she was going to waste prime cuts on Greg.

In the fifteen minutes before the end of the school day, the playground slowly filled with arriving parents. Mums congregated in small gaggles, ostensibly showing an interest in each other's children, but merely awaiting an opportunity to speak of their own. A couple of dads, one unemployed and the other a house husband so within sight of each other on the social ladder, huddled together. A third father, set apart by his suit, stood by

151

himself. He caught the eye of Amanda, also standing by herself, and smiled, acknowledging their mutual isolation.

Amanda didn't want company; she preferred to be alone with her thoughts — of Greg, naturally. She could think of nothing else. Had he cheated before? she wondered. He'd had plenty of opportunity. Not just the computer industry's annual conference, but IT trade fairs, site meetings, away days. Did he have a girl in every USB port?

Not that it much mattered. Once was enough. Enough to destroy their most precious asset — the trust they'd built up over all these years. Trust wasn't something you could have in degrees; it was all or nothing. Its loss was pernicious; it destroyed not only your future, but your past too. Already Amanda was looking back over their thirteen years together, questioning whether the happiness she thought she'd enjoyed was nothing more than a myth, and she the victim of fraud. That's what really made her blood boil (she could feel it percolating now).

One of the mums detached herself from the group and started to make her way across. Short of walking away, which would appear incredibly rude, Amanda could not think of how to avoid a conversation. Still, she nearly chose this option, but Helen was one of those powers in the playground it was best not to cross. She knew all the gossip — she'd started most of it herself and spread the rest; you either played nice with Helen or got hurt.

"Helen," Amanda said brightly, evincing more enthusiasm than she felt.

Helen was a mother of four who'd made no effort to shed the weight she'd accumulated during each of her pregnancies. She carried the extra pounds like a war wound, a constant reminder to her husband of how she'd suffered for his benefit. A bangle-draped arm shot out from her garish muumuu; a solicitous hand settled on Amanda's wrist.

"How are you?" Helen's voice was double-dipped in compassion.

Amanda looked at her askance. Had she heard?

Helen tilted her head, adopted a pained, puppy-dog expression and pushed out her lower lip, like a bad actor doing "pity".

Yes, she's heard, Amanda thought. "All round the playground, is it?" she asked.

"Well, I don't think it's reached kindergarten yet."

Amanda sighed. "It will."

The solicitous hand shifted to Amanda's forearm. "I suppose it can't have come as a great surprise to you," Helen commiserated.

Amanda bristled at that. "I'm sure I don't know what you mean," she said primly, reminding herself of a character out of Jane Austen.

"Well, Greg's always been something of a charmer, hasn't he?"

"I would hope so." Amanda was surprised to find herself leaping to his defence. Old habits, eh? "But charming's not cheating."

153

"No," Helen agreed, less than wholeheartedly. "A cousin, perhaps; not too distant."

Amanda hadn't thought of it like that; maybe Helen was right. She was weighing her response when she became aware that she'd lost the other woman's attention. She swivelled to see what had so piqued Helen's interest. Greg was striding across the playground towards them. Amanda turned back to Helen, but she had taken her solicitous hand and was scuttling across to the other mums to alert them to this development.

"In all the playgrounds in all the world . . ." Greg affected a Bogart drawl as he reached Amanda.

She wasn't playing. "Fine," she snapped. "You pick up the kids."

Amanda made to leave, but Greg held her back.

"Please don't go."

Amanda shot a pointed look at Greg's hand. Sheepishly he removed it. Conscious of the many eyes upon them, Amanda stayed.

"Tell me what I have to do," Greg beseeched her.

"You've already done it, Greg," she said softly, though had she shouted, the words couldn't have hit home harder.

Greg hung his head. "I didn't cheat on you," he mumbled, as though he no longer hoped to convince her but, for appearances' sake, must maintain his innocence. "Can we talk a moment?"

Amanda checked her watch. There were still a few minutes before the girls were due out. She indicated a nearby bench that was out of range of prying ears. They

154

crossed and sat, a short distance and a massive gulf between them.

"I wish I could forgive you," Amanda started. "Geri tells me I should."

This was the first civil thing Amanda had said to Greg since his indiscretion. He held his breath, hoping for more — an olive branch of some kind.

"Maybe it's just a matter of time —" Amanda seemed to be talking to herself as much as to him — "till I can see you and it's not the first thing I think of; till I don't think of it at all."

It was a glimmer of hope; Greg fished for more. "How long do you think that might be? Weeks? Months?" He paused, giving her an opportunity to jump in that she didn't take. "Years?" In the hope she'd deny it.

"I don't know, Greg. I don't know whether I'll ever be able to forgive you." She met his eyes and held them.

He doubted he'd ever loved her more than in this moment. Well, that will teach you, you fucking idiot, he thought. It was a lesson he may have learnt too late. He wanted to take her hand, but feared the move would backfire.

"I do love you, you know." Greg had told her this many times in the past. Now he wished he hadn't, because repetition had robbed the words of their potency and, more than ever, he needed her to believe him.

She nodded, but only to acknowledge his remark, not accept it. "Will you do something for me?" she asked, knowing there was only one answer he could give.

"Anything." And he meant it. Anything within her imagination and his power.

"Stop phoning me. Give me some space, all right? To work out how I feel."

The twelve labours of Hercules would have been easier. Tell Greg to clean the Augean stables and, there and then, he'd have reached for the dustpan and brush. But Amanda was asking him to do nothing, to leave his fate in her hands. What choice did he have? He nodded dully.

A bell rang to indicate the end of school. Amanda leapt to her feet.

"I don't want the girls to see us together."

Greg stood as the first children began streaming out. "I'll go." He wondered whether she would allow him to brush her cheek with his but it was a moot point; she was already crossing the playground to intercept their daughters.

Lauren was out first; Lauren was always out first, hungry to devour the next slice of life. Amanda scooped her up into her arms. Lauren did not notice her father hastening towards the gates.

"Hey, you. How was your day?"

"Good." The usual response, which could mean anything from nondescript to best day ever.

"Have you got your lunch box?"

Lauren mugged "oops". She was still young enough for her absent-mindedness to be beguiling, but the clock was ticking. She scrambled out of her mother's arms and skipped back towards her classroom, passing Molly, who sauntered out with the assured air of a primary-school senior. Amanda snuck a glance in Greg's direction, but he had already disappeared from view.

Russell had been correct when he'd concluded that the man he'd seen upstairs with his mother was not a plumber. Tony (not that Russell knew his name) was an estate agent.

"I saw that friend of yours today, the one I loaded software for," Tony told his wife, Veronica, as they were stacking the dishwasher after dinner. "I'd just been showing that Edwardian in Wellington Street; you know, four beds, three baths, offers over one point two. She was coming out of Boots. I didn't recognise her at first. When we met, I thought she was quite dowdy, but today she looked positively glowing."

"Well, I can tell you the reason for that!" There was nothing Veronica loved more than a good gobbet of gossip. This statement is not hyperbole. There literally was nothing. Not even sex, especially not sex with Tony. He had certain idiosyncratic tastes. And BO. Over the years, Veronica had become inured to his distinctive smell (in much the same way that residents near Heathrow don't notice the thunder of departing aircraft), but during physical exertion his sweat became overpowering. As a consequence, she sought to avoid too much bodily contact, unless she had hay fever and her nose was blocked up. She hadn't had hay fever for weeks.

Veronica crossed to the door to check that their daughter, Ruby, wasn't within hearing. She wasn't. She was in her bedroom sending photos of her breasts to her ex-boyfriend on Snapchat, in a doomed attempt to persuade him to resume their relationship.

"She's having an affair!" Veronica announced triumphantly, feeling the thrill of the scoop.

"That woman is?"

"Sarah, yes. I don't know who with. She didn't breathe a word of it at lunch the other day. She doesn't give the impression she'd be the sort, does she? I suppose they're the ones that are, though."

Veronica continued in this vein for some time, but Tony only gave the impression of listening, a technique he'd perfected over the years. So Sarah was the type to have an affair, was she? How interesting! She really had looked quite attractive that day . . .

CHAPTER
EIGHT

Liz Henderson was a smoker. Not the Liz Greg had met at the conference, but the Liz he'd inadvertently spoken to on the phone. Like other nicotine addicts, this Liz Henderson was an outcast, a refugee from the office whenever her urge for tobacco proved irresistible. At just before one, the day after Greg's misdirected call, she shivered in the building's concrete shadow among a small cluster of smokers (a cancer cluster?) indulging their carcinogenic craving. She cupped her free hand over a flame as she fired up the Marlboro Light of a colleague. Beverley from Accounts nodded her thanks and inhaled deeply, flooding her lungs and reducing her life expectancy by a few precious minutes. Fellow workers fled the office block on their lunch hour, like convicts making a prison break. Among them was Liz — the one Greg had met at the conference. The other Liz's smoking companion nudged her.

"There's your namesake," she pointed out.

Liz Two nodded without much interest. It was tough being the less attractive Liz Henderson in the firm. But then she brightened as she remembered the curious phone call she'd received the day before.

"Want to hear some juicy gossip?" she asked Beverley. The face sucking on the Marlboro Light lit up with anticipation.

"Promise you won't tell a soul," Liz Two demanded, even as she knew such an undertaking was worthless. Beverley nodded frenetically, causing the smoke leaking from her nostrils to ripple in waves.

Sauntering across the forecourt, Liz was unaware that she was the object of any interest. And it wasn't just the other Liz Henderson and her fellow junkie whose eyes were fixed upon her. She had a stalker. He'd secreted himself behind a billboard advertising a healthy breakfast cereal that was chock-full of carbohydrates but which, it was true, could lead to weight loss as part of a calorie-controlled diet — if, for the rest of the day, you fasted. As Liz passed en route to the sandwich bar she frequented most days, her stalker materialised from his hiding place and fell into step alongside her. It took Liz a moment to realise she was being shadowed. And a moment more to recognise Greg.

"You! I've got nothing to say to you." She quickened her pace.

"Liz, please!" Greg scampered to keep abreast. "I have to talk to you. It will only take a minute."

Liz shot him a sideways glance. His hair was mussed, his wild eyes bloodshot and those parts of his chin that didn't sport outcrops of stubble were spotted with blood. What the hell had happened to him? Her resolve faltered, and with it, her step. She stopped. "A minute?" she asked, making it clear that was all she was offering.

Greg smiled his gratitude. Liz resumed walking, Greg now with her, not just alongside.

"My horoscope said to expect an unwelcome caller," she told him. "I'd figured telemarketing."

Greg didn't mind being the butt of her humour; at least they were talking.

The maître d', wearing a uniform as crisp as the linen tablecloth, pulled back Lynda's chair. She caught Dan's eye and suppressed a giggle as she sat. She wasn't used to such assiduous service. But then she was more accustomed to restaurants with names that included words like "pizza" or "express" or both. She reached for her napkin but the maître d' got there first. With a flourish, he threw it open, like the climax of a conjuring trick, though lacking a dove, then laid it gently in her lap before discreetly withdrawing.

"This is so fancy!" Lynda whispered, her eyes dancing. Le Crouton had recently been awarded two hats. Apparently, in foodie circles, this is enough to have them salivating.

Dan beamed. "It's cover. If anyone we know sees us, they'll think it's a business meeting."

Lynda gaped at the clientele, without exception wealthy and middle-aged. "I don't think anyone I know comes here."

In truth, Dan was also trying to impress her. He felt he had to, lest she see him for what he was — a middle-aged man whose best years were not only behind him but hadn't been that crash hot in the first place. If the gift you're giving is less than impressive,

161

then wrap it in shinier paper. Dan suggested champagne and oysters to start.

The sommelier discreetly uncorked the bottle then poured with a deftness born of years of practice. The champagne bubbled to the brim, looking certain to overflow, then receded as though obeying a silent command. Lynda did not hear the approach of the waiter, who set a dozen oysters with a tomato salsa and vodka dressing in front of them. She reached for her phone.

"Who are you calling?" Dan asked.

"No one," Lynda replied. "Just posting this to Facebook."

"Don't tag me," he joked, congratulating himself on his knowledge of the vernacular. He had Russell to thank for that. He watched while Lynda lined up the shot just so, framing her champagne flute against the plate of oysters. Part of him felt foolish. What was he doing with a woman young enough to be a member of the generation that routinely shares photos of food with friends? A larger part of him felt like a shit. He never took Sarah to such flash restaurants. He promised himself he would. She'd appreciate it almost as much as Lynda. Then Lynda looked up from the table and smiled at him — joyously. And Dan felt exultant. He tasted his champagne and his misgivings evaporated like the bubbles on his tongue. If you're going to do this, then enjoy it, he told himself. He returned Lynda's smile.

"I'll have what she's having."

It was partly a desire to quote the classic line from *When Harry Met Sally* that caused Greg to order the

162

same sandwich as Liz. But mostly he couldn't be arsed to choose among the countless options that spanned two blackboards above the counter. Mistake. Big mistake. (To quote another classic movie.) He'd ended up with white bean and avocado on rye.

"Who was that guy who answered your mobile the other night?" Greg asked as he paid for them both. There's no such thing as a free lunch — Liz would have to give Greg more than just a minute.

"Oh, that was Brad," she replied airily. "My fiancé."

Greg was so taken aback, he didn't think to count his change. Liz, engaged? She hadn't mentioned that at the conference; he was sure he would have remembered. She flashed him the ring she hadn't been wearing then either. It was suitably gaudy — a fuck-off big diamond that shouted to other women, "Eat your heart out, girls! I've snared me a man!"

"Wow!" Greg said, arranging his features into an appropriately enthusiastic expression. "Congratulations."

As they collected their order and moved outside, taking seats on a bench among cycle couriers and council workers also taking the (polluted) air, Greg tried to get his head around what he was hearing. Was it possible Liz had got engaged in the last couple of days?

"So when did this happen?" he asked.

"About four months ago."

Long before the conference then. So why had she hit on Greg? Suddenly it dawned on him.

"Oh, I get it! One last hurrah." He felt quite chuffed. Liz could have had her pick of the delegates. The young buck who'd stolen Greg's place in the bar queue even.

Yet she'd chosen him. It was quite an honour. She seemed to read his thoughts.

"It could have been anyone, to be honest. Well, under fifty with a full head of hair. His own."

Greg tried not to look affronted; he was only partly successful.

"The thing is," Liz confessed, "I've had my doubts about Brad."

"You think he might be gay?"

"No! No, about whether we're right for each other. I thought if I were to sleep with someone else it might make things clear. And it did. I picked you: the one guy who couldn't cheat! Well, it was a sign, wasn't it? That we're meant to be together."

Greg tried to follow her logic but got lost along the way.

"You don't think trying to sleep with me was a sign you're not?"

Liz's brow furrowed. "That makes no sense at all."

Greg stared at her but Liz seemed unaware of any contradiction. OK, she's a fruit loop, he thought, but she's still my best hope. Shifting tack, he quickly filled her in on the calamity that had befallen him.

"So here's what I was thinking: if you'd just talk to Amanda, tell her what happened — glossing over some of the detail — she might be prepared to forgive me. I mean, you said it yourself: she's fortunate to have a bloke that can't cheat."

"Yes . . ." Liz agreed doubtfully. "I was naked in your bed when I said that."

164

"Technically you were only half naked and, anyway, that's the sort of detail I thought you could gloss over. In fact, in the version I gave her, we never got as far as the room. Oh, and it was your room."

"Mine?"

"Makes me seem less of a villain."

Liz weighed this. "Well, marginally," she finally allowed. She tried to imagine the conversation. If she were Amanda, Liz's account, however sanitised, would make her see red. Blood. Greg's, certainly; possibly hers too. Greg sensed her scepticism.

"You think it's a crap idea, don't you?"

How could she put this? "Up there with vaginal deodorants."

Greg sighed. It had been his hope that Liz would embrace his plan, even offer to weave a fiction that would not just restore him in Amanda's eyes but perhaps raise his stock. Which just goes to show how delusional the desperate can be. "The thing is, I don't know what else to do."

"You could try telling her the truth."

Greg snorted. "Amanda's very Old Testament when it comes to fidelity. Her dad was a shagger. I'm not sure she's prepared to give second chances. It's one strike and you're out."

"Then what were you thinking?"

Greg had asked himself this question many times in the days since his fall. He hadn't been thinking — that was all he could come up with. But he doubted Amanda would accept thoughtlessness as an adequate defence.

"This morning I closed the deal that takes me above my monthly target," Dan told Lynda as the waiter refilled their glasses.

"That's wonderful!" Lynda raised her glass in a toast. "To your success!"

"To you," Dan countered. "It's down to you, you know."

"Me?" Lynda's nostrils twitched as the bubbles went up her nose. Dan found it charming.

"I'm a different person since I met you. I used to shrink from life. I expected to fail and, sure enough, I did. But now, everything feels possible. When I pick up the phone I know I'm going to make the sale. People listen to me in meetings. I've physically changed! I've had to adjust the rear-view mirror in my car because I'm sitting higher in the seat." He took a gulp of champagne then held the flute up for Lynda's inspection. "You see this glass? It's half full."

Lynda smiled. "And how are things at home?" she asked.

"Good," he said. "Much better." He left it at that. Having led Lynda to believe that his marriage was practically sexless, he thought she might not appreciate knowing that he'd recently resumed relations with Sarah. She might even take the view that Dan was cheating on her with his wife. Some things are best left unsaid.

His mobile pinged with an incoming email. Dan checked it; force of habit.

"Holy shit! My boss has quit."

"Really? Jumped or pushed?"

Dan scanned the email for clues. "He wants to spend more time with his family. So pushed then. There were rumours he'd been fiddling his expenses."

"Claiming for lunches that weren't legit?" Lynda raised an eloquent eyebrow.

Dan grinned. "You're in the business."

"Who'll get his job?"

"Greg, I suppose. He'd be considered the heir apparent."

"Why not you?"

Dan chuckled. It was a nice idea.

"I'm serious," Lynda said.

Was it so far-fetched? He'd hit his target for this month; as far as he was aware, Greg hadn't. And while it wouldn't be decided on the basis of one month's figures, they'd be taken into account. Momentum was with him. In sales, as in sport, that counted for a lot.

"You'll apply?" Lynda pressed him to agree.

"Yes." He surprised himself with his certainty.

Lynda beamed. Dan appreciated her confidence. With that sort of belief behind him, a man could really go places.

Liz swallowed the last of her sandwich. Greg was struggling to stomach his. He'd pick up some chips on his way back to the office.

"How come you and Amanda haven't got married?" Liz asked.

Greg considered the question. It was one he'd been posed before, by those who were themselves married. Or about to be. He raised his usual objection.

"Why the assumption that we should?"

"Well, because most people in long-term relation-ships do."

"Yeah, and forty per cent of them end up divorcing."

Liz turned this comment over in her mind.

"So it's fear of failure that's stopped you?"

"No." Greg laughed, a little defensively. "No; if something ain't broke, don't fix it. Besides, Amanda never wanted to. Her parents' marriage wasn't the best advertisement."

"So you discussed it then?"

"Yes." They had, hadn't they? Greg was fairly sure they had. They must have, at one time, surely. "I think so."

"But it's not like you ever proposed and she turned you down?"

Greg shifted uncomfortably. What was this? An interrogation? "I didn't need to. She'd made her feelings plain."

Liz nodded thoughtfully, like this confirmed a suspicion she had. Greg didn't know what, but sensed it didn't reflect well on him. He felt like a suspect whose alibi had turned out to be less than watertight. He felt he ought to say something more in his defence.

"If I'd ever thought she might accept, I would have."

"Really?"

Greg hesitated. Would he have? He wasn't sure. Amanda's apparent indifference had always suited him. The truth was he had never wanted to marry. On the rare occasions when he was asked to reveal his marital status — the census, for example — he liked to be able to tick the box marked "single". It didn't mean anything. He and Amanda were an item, as committed as two people could be — they had a joint bank account, a mortgage and two children — but it made him feel like a free man, who still had options. Husband sounded so . . . *final.*

"Maybe not," he admitted.

"So, possibly, she gave the impression she didn't want to marry because she knew you didn't —"

"No, no, it wasn't like that. Shouldn't you be getting back?"

Liz checked her watch. Christ, was that the time? She jumped to her feet.

"I'll walk you," Greg offered, relieved that he'd managed to shift the conversation. He rose from his seat, almost colliding with a Lycra-clad cycle courier who was hobbling past on shoes that looked unnecessary for cycling and unsuitable for anything else. Greg was struck, not for the first time, by just how unsexy Lycra was, although the tight material did show you exactly what you'd be getting.

"Maybe you should ask Amanda to marry you," Liz remarked. Apparently Greg had not succeeded in changing the subject after all.

"Yeah, right!" he scoffed. "I think she'd say my timing sucked. And then she'd say no."

"And, besides, you don't want to get married."

Greg shrugged: that too.

"Well, you need to find some way to convince her you love her."

"I've told her, but she won't listen."

"*Show* her. Actions speak louder than words."

Greg thought it over. The bouquet he'd bought Amanda the other day was still on the back seat of his car. Past its prime — he really should have put it in water — but not quite dead.

"And not flowers." Liz knew the way men's minds worked: unimaginatively. "Something that will take her breath away."

"Like a punch to the solar plexus?"

"Yes, but romantic."

Ah, the big romantic gesture. It worked in the movies every time. Greg thought back to some of the mushier films he'd seen with Amanda. Maybe he should light hundreds of candles in their back garden. That always looked good. No, it would take forever and, besides, they'd go out. Funny how Hollywood always overlooked that detail; perhaps there was no breeze in LA. Still, it gave him the germ of an idea . . .

When Amanda was young, she'd been a Girl Guide. That had been the sum total of her after-school activities. She'd spent the rest of her childhood hanging around the rec, wondering when her life was going to start. Kids nowadays barely had a spare space on their dance card. If it wasn't poetry it was pottery, if not figurative art then a martial art. Greg and Amanda had tried not to saddle their daughters with too many of these other "interests" (the term used loosely since the participants often had no interest whatsoever). They wanted to leave room for their children simply to be children. But it was difficult to withstand the pressure

170

of the Sunday supplements, which preached that unless you signed your child up for t'ai chi or tae kwon do, you were denying them the best start in life. And so Molly and Lauren had dance one day, clarinet (which they both hated and never practised) another, and drama tonight.

Drama. That made it sound grand; visions of Shakespeare and Chekhov. As far as Amanda could tell, the class consisted of the girls pretending to be tigers or balloons or lost in a forest — in other words, games of make-believe. Not much for ninety pounds a term (each), but at least it kept them off their iPods.

Amanda handed Molly and Lauren into the care of their drama instructor, the highlight of whose career had been playing a burns victim in an episode of *Casualty*. While this had not led to any starring roles on the West End stage, it had seemingly qualified her to teach acting to others. And, to be fair, Amanda would acknowledge that Molly's impersonation of a tree was uncannily realistic. As Greg had commented when forced to watch her performance, you could almost hear the wind rustling through the leaves. Sitting beside him on the sofa, Amanda had considered this an inspired and inspiring critique, but Molly had been less than impressed — apparently it was midwinter and her branches were bare. To which Greg had quipped, "Good God! Already doing nudity!" Amanda smiled at the memory before she remembered it concerned Greg and she frowned instead.

The drama studio was a short drive from Amanda's sister's flat. This was located off Kensal Rise, among a huddle of streets where you were never more than a few espadrille-clad footsteps from a health food store or second-hand-clothes shop. The rent was relatively cheap and Geri had grown to love the shabby-chic character of the area and its inhabitants. Kensal Rise was laid-back but also had an edge; it felt like a community, the streets of which a woman could walk at night without fear (well, before 9p.m.).

Their mother liked to describe Geraldine's one-bedroom flat as an apartment, but Amanda doubted that even the most brazen lettings agent would possess that much gall. It was situated above a taxi firm, which was handy, although the sweet smell of marijuana that permeated the walls suggested the drivers' acuity might be somewhat compromised.

Geraldine opened the door to her sister's knock.

"I don't want to talk about Greg," Amanda said before Geri had the chance to say anything.

"How is he?" Geri asked as she let her sister in, earning a sardonic look.

Amanda ignored the question. She followed Geraldine into her cramped and chaotic bedroom. It looked like a dressing room at the Moulin Rouge. Clothes were everywhere except on hangers. A feather boa hung from the mirror of a dressing table, at which Geraldine now took a seat; she began applying make-up.

"You'll have to talk to me while I get ready. Fix yourself a drink if you like."

"Are you going out?" Amanda asked unnecessarily.

"No — housework, but I like to look my best." Geri pulled a face in the mirror, a look she'd first given her younger sister more than thirty years before and which she'd perfected in the interim.

"A date, is it? Who's the victim this time? Anyone I know?"

Geri paused mid-mascara-stroke and regarded Amanda, as though weighing whether to tell her. "You said you didn't want to talk about him."

"Who?"

"Greg." Geri shrugged apologetically.

Amanda blinked, almost sure her sister was joking, but not quite.

Geraldine sensed her uncertainty. "You don't mind, do you? I wondered whether I should check with you but that seemed like it'd be making a thing out of it. I think he just wants to talk."

Amanda didn't like the sound of this at all. "Then why are you getting all glammed up?"

"You mean this old thing?" Geri looked down at the dress she was wearing. It was one of her best, an Alexander McQueen, albeit second hand. She allowed Amanda a moment's more discomfort.

"Of course I'm not seeing Greg!" She resumed applying her make-up. "But I gather from that, you haven't taken him back yet."

Amanda sank on to Geraldine's unmade bed, annoyed and relieved. "I still haven't forgiven him for cheating, if that's what you mean."

"Then maybe I should ask him out. He's a good catch and, if I don't, some other woman will."

"Well, if he's in the least sincere about wanting to come home then hopefully he'll turn them down."

A good return of serve, Geraldine granted her sister that.

"So who are you seeing?" Amanda persevered.

"His name's Trevor. You introduced us actually."

"I did?"

"At that fundraiser you dragged me to."

Amanda cast her mind back a couple of months. "The one you left after ten minutes?"

"Well, it was hellish. Children everywhere."

"It was a school fete!"

"They should make older kids attend. That would cut the rate of teen pregnancy. Anyway, I did my bit — entered the raffle. You don't think I might have won, do you? I could do with a new telly."

"How many tickets did you buy?"

"One."

"No. Who's Trevor? I don't know anyone by that name."

"Married to Moira."

Amanda's eyes widened in surprise. "Chair of the PTA? You're going on a date with Moira's husband?"

"Trevor, yes."

Amanda felt Geraldine was missing her point. "Moira's *husband*, Trevor."

"They're separated." Geraldine said airily, pausing for effect. "Like you and Greg."

Amanda didn't want to get sucked into that again. "Oh, God, I remember! You were sounding off about

174

how horrendous the fete was. A fete worse than death, you called it. Very loudly."

"I wasn't that loud."

"You were shouting."

"Well, I had to. The PA system was deafening; I had tinnitus for days afterwards."

Amanda recalled it all too well. She'd turned to agree with Geri's assessment, only to notice Moira standing beside them. "You were right next to the Chair of the organising committee. I thought I'd better make you aware of that."

"And how did you do that? By introducing us. Which, considering she'd heard every word I'd said, was hardly doing me a favour. Except, as it turns out, you were. Because while you two were chatting, I got talking to Trevor, who quietly agreed that it was one of the inner circles of hell. Though not quietly enough, judging by the look Moira gave him. Then last week I happened to see him in the gym. And he told me that they'd separated."

"Because of what he'd said about the fete?"

"No!" Geri said scornfully before she frowned, reconsidering. "Actually, I don't know. Could be. I'll ask him."

She stood up, her warpaint on, primed for action.

"How do I look?"

"Predatory."

Geraldine's reaction suggested this was the correct answer. Amanda hadn't intended it to be.

"Do you think I should take condoms?" Geri asked.

"No!"

Geraldine thought it over. "You're right; he should provide them."

"I mean, you're not going to sleep with him on a first date!"

"God, you're out of touch! It's a buyer's market. I've got to be prepared to, or he might not call again. At least, that's my experience."

Amanda was appalled. "Seriously? The first date?"

Geraldine shrugged. "If you meet through the internet, yeah. Well, not *Guardian Soulmates*; there, the going rate's three. That's cos the guys feel they've got to be 'sensitive'."

How the world had changed since it went online, Amanda thought. "Well, call me old-fashioned, but I think you should only sleep with him if you want to."

Geraldine deliberated. "I wouldn't mind. I mean, I've been going through the AA batteries like nobody's business. And Trevor's quite hot — all that working out. We'll see."

She plucked a bolero jacket from a pile of clothes on the floor and made for the door. Amanda trailed after her.

"How are my nieces?" Geri asked, checking in her bag for her car keys. "Coping all right?"

Back to the thing with Greg; it was all anyone thought she had to think about. It did tend to overshadow all else. "They're doing fine. Waiting to see what happens. It's like they're holding their breath."

Geraldine grunted. "I know Lauren's got a pair of lungs on her — I've heard her throw a tantrum — but a week's a long time for a kid to hold their breath." She let them out of the flat. The aroma of marijuana that drifted from below encouraged them to inhale.

"It hasn't been a week," Amanda said, splitting hairs.

"Getting there," Geraldine pointed out, pulling the door shut like a full stop.

With the budding thespians not due to be picked up for another hour and a quarter, Amanda decided to swing by home and get the dinner on. She was surprised to find a flatbed lorry parked outside the house, two planks propped against its open back making a ramp. Odd. One of the neighbours must be having some work done. Even odder was the trail of mud that crossed the pavement and weaved in parallel but haphazard lines over the lawn and around the side of their house. The tracks were spaced a few feet apart and seemed, judging by the width of the grass that had been flattened, to have been caused by a miniature tank. As Amanda, channelling Miss Marple, examined the evidence and tried to work out what the hell was going on, she heard the throaty growl of a diesel-driven machine coming from their back garden.

She immediately sensed what had occurred. Their next-door neighbour, Mrs Lucas, was having a conservatory installed. A notorious cheapskate who refused to give to charity on the grounds that that's what she paid her taxes for, the wealthy pensioner must have employed a gang of builders so cowboy that they'd got the wrong address and started digging foundations before learning of their error. Either that or the police had discovered that, years ago, Amanda and Greg's home had been owned by Fred West.

Neither scenario was encouraging. Amanda ran through the open gate at the side of the house, unsure whether she'd be greeted by Bulgarian navvies or police incident tape. Instead she saw Greg sitting on a miniature excavator — a baby Bobcat, as they're known — gouging inexpertly at the turf with its mechanical bucket. She had to shout his name four times, finally bellowing with vein-haemorrhaging ferocity, before he became aware of her. He killed the engine and hopped out of the driver's cab.

"Hello, love!" he greeted her cheerfully, not at all like they were currently estranged.

"What the *fuck* are you doing?" Amanda yelled, dispensing with niceties.

Far from denting Greg's jollity, this abrupt enquiry merely caused his smile to broaden.

"A makeover," he announced, sweeping his gaze over the full extent of the damaged lawn.

"A *what?*" Amanda asked. She knew the concept, of course, but couldn't equate it with the devastation that met her eye.

"You've always complained about the garden."

She had, with good reason. It was their home's worst feature: a patch of scratchy lawn pockmarked by knot-grass, bordered on three sides by flower beds that resisted all attempts at cultivation. The fourth side was laid unevenly to slabs, of fifty shades of grey. The gaps between these lumps of discoloured concrete were the only parts of the garden that supported plant life. And how resilient these weeds were, laughing in the face of defoliants that had more than proved their efficacy during the Vietnam War. Amanda had often shared with Greg her vision of a rockery (with water feature), a soft-play zone and sand pit, a barbecue area and — the crowning glory, she'd murmur in a come-hither tone, hugging Greg to her as she laid out her plans — a hot tub where they'd sip mulled wine under the stars after the kids had gone to bed, the steam billowing up into a crisp, clear winter's night. Never mind that London tended to be blanketed in cloud from November to March.

Amanda was the gardener, not Greg, but she didn't have the time, and so her dream had remained just that — visible only in her mind. Until now, when Greg had taken it upon himself to make this project his labour of love, his own modest version of the Taj Mahal, the shrine the Mughal Emperor, Shah Jahan, had built to commemorate his Queen. But Greg's was an even greater act of devotion (or so he believed), because he had no army of indentured labour; he would get his own hands dirty. And how! Greg's eyes burned with a messianic zeal as he walked Amanda through his plan. She watched in mute incredulity as he pranced from one mound of earth to the next, caring nothing for the soil that clung to his trousers. Over here would be the sand pit; there, the rockery, its water feature providing a soothing accompaniment as they luxuriated in the hot tub. It hadn't occurred to Greg that the din of the spa would drown its tranquil melody. But don't rain on his parade! He was a visionary — passionate and determined.

"It's what you've always wanted," he triumphantly declared, turning back to Amanda, confident that her heart would melt at such overwhelming evidence of his love.

He was to be sorely disappointed. Where he could see the Gardens of Babylon, she saw a hole in the ground that Greg would come to regard as a chore, tire of and abandon.

"No," she said evenly. "What I always wanted was for you not to cheat on me."

Why couldn't she share his faith? There had been a time.

"But it's my big romantic gesture," he said, his voice sounding pathetic to his own ears.

"To carpet-bomb the back garden?"

Greg's shoulders sagged. They were already somewhere around his knees.

"Just go, Greg. Before you make any more of a mess."

He got the impression that it wasn't just the garden she was referring to.

Amanda turned and stalked towards the house, leaving Greg among the earthen ruins of his ambition. What had he been thinking? Yes, the lawn had been less than pristine but it more than served when the girls played Pony Club. Now their imaginary parade ring lay violated, shredded by the tank tracks of the baby Bobcat. Unless the girls developed a sudden passion for motocross, it would lie forsaken, unused and unloved.

180

It began to rain. Earth liquified into mud. Greg's shoes were ruined. Wearily, he hauled himself into the driver's cab of the mini-excavator. Crashing the gears, he found reverse and ignominiously withdrew from the scene of his humiliation, slithering towards the garden gate, like Napoleon's troops retreating from Moscow. He hadn't fully mastered the digger's controls. This little mattered when he'd been tearing up the garden, but precision was paramount when loading the machine on to the flatbed truck. It took him three attempts and two dents, which he optimistically thought added character and hoped the hire company wouldn't notice.

By the time the baby Bobcat was secured, Greg was drenched and disconsolate. And the back garden was a quagmire. So much for big romantic gestures.

At first Sarah had been adamant that Greg should not stay more than two nights. She didn't like him and she didn't like having him around. It was his own fault that Amanda had kicked him out (in the circumstances, she'd have done the same), and Sarah couldn't see why she should be punished too by being inflicted with his company.

Early on the morning of day three, while showering, Sarah had decided that enough was enough. She'd emerged from the en suite, brusquely shaken Dan awake and told him straight. If he didn't subtly suggest to Greg that it was time he moved on, then she would, but without the subtlety. Dan's reaction had surprised her. He'd kissed her with ardour, then kissed her again ardour still. They had had sex, for the second time in a week. And as before it was *good*. Sarah put Dan's unexpected vitality down to his improved performance at work, not realising that though the two were linked, she had muddled cause and effect.

After another shower Sarah had floated down to breakfast, where not even Greg's presence at the kitchen table could puncture her serenity. He had shot her a meaningfully arched eyebrow over his bowl of muesli, with an accompanying smirk. Ordinarily this would have pissed Sarah off, but experiencing an aftershudder of bliss as she was, it had instead prompted in her a beatific smile. She was feeling goodwill towards all men, Greg included. She'd even offered to boil him an egg, though he'd declined, wanting to get to the office early in the vain hope of resuscitating his flagging sales. Sarah had not mentioned him moving out. In that moment, it hadn't seemed particularly important.

Nor had it since. Days had passed. With Dan's success requiring him to work longer hours, Sarah and Greg often found themselves thrown together. Familiarity ousted contempt. Sarah discovered that the Greg she thought she knew, and whom she'd met at a handful of social functions in the past, had been a construct for public consumption. Party Greg, she'd named this version. The real him was softer, less abrasive and, thank God, less overbearing. To her surprise Sarah went from enduring Greg's company to enjoying it. When he could be stirred from the doldrums of his melancholy, he was fun to be around.

182

Russell liked him too. Perhaps it was because Greg still seemed something of an adolescent himself — not fully formed — but the two had struck up an unlikely camaraderie. Greg seemed genuinely interested in the youth's opinions and encouraged him to express them — on everything from *I'm A Celebrity* . . . to the conditions for textile workers in Bangladesh. Greg helped Russell with his homework. And he made him laugh — imagine, her fifteen-year-old son *laughing*! To Sarah's ears it was a sound as rare as a politician's apology and worth much more. For that alone Sarah would be grateful to Greg.

Subsequently Sarah again asked Dan whether he had yet had a word with Greg about moving on. When her husband sheepishly admitted that he hadn't, she told him not to. One way or another Greg and Amanda would shortly sort out their future; in the meantime it was no hardship to have one more mouth to feed.

Now, fully a week since Greg's arrival, Sarah was cooking the evening meal. Russell was sitting at the kitchen table, doing his homework without having to be threatened or cajoled. Sarah heard the front door. She stole a look at the clock: twenty-five past six. Most likely Greg, she thought (they'd given him a key). She was wrong.

"Evening, all!" Dan said cheerily as he strode into the kitchen, clutching flowers in one hand and a couple of shopping bags in the other. He made straight for Sarah, kissed her like they were young or Italian, and offered her the bouquet.

"Dan, they're beautiful! Thank you." Azaleas — her favourite. "Is that a new suit?" she asked as she hunted in a cupboard for a vase.

Dan did a twirl. "Well, if I'm going to be the new Regional Sales Manager, I'd better look the part."

"You've been offered a promotion? Darling, that's wonderful!"

Dan raised his hands to rein in her enthusiasm. "Not quite," he explained. "The job's become available; I'm going to apply. And you have to dress for success."

"Well, you certainly are." She fingered his lapel, felt the quality of the cloth. "You didn't get this from M&S, did you?"

No. The suit had come not from a chain but a high-end menswear store, the sort Dan found intimidating even to walk past. Wild horses could not have dragged him within its superior walls — but Lynda had managed. She'd taken him shopping after lunch.

Dan flourished the bags he was holding. "Shirts as well. And a couple of ties. The ones I wear are a bit sober." Lynda's opinion, not his.

"You mean the ones I buy for you?"

Oops.

Sarah smiled at his embarrassment. She took the new ties out of their bag. "I like them. You've got good taste." Yes, Lynda did.

"Want to shoot some hoops, Russell?" Dan asked his son.

"What about your suit?" Sarah interjected.

"You'll treat me gently, won't you, Russ?"

184

"Sure, old man," said Russell. Father and son proceeded out to the back patio, Dan's arm round Russell's shoulder. The scene would not have looked out of place in a feel-good television drama. Sarah watched them with affection, thinking, not for the first time, how good life was lately. She turned her attention to the flowers, trimming their stems. The front door banged shut. Greg. Sarah waited for him to enter and was surprised to find that she was looking forward to seeing him, hearing about his day.

Greg lingered in the hall, removing his shoes. Caked in mud, they were beyond salvation, beyond the Salvation Army even — only good for the bin. Holding them in one hand, he padded into the kitchen. Sarah looked up from her flower arranging. Her face fell at the sight of him — drenched and mud-splattered.

"Good God!" she exclaimed. "Have you been mugged?"

"Kind of," he volunteered. "I went to apologise to Amanda."

"By grovelling?" Sarah was only half joking; Greg looked like he'd crawled on his hands and knees.

"I might have had more joy," he said dolefully. He managed to rustle up a smile but it sat like an imposter on his dejected face.

It would have taken a woman of steely resolve — Amanda perhaps — not to feel a degree of sympathy for him. He'd caught Sarah in one of her more charitable moments.

"Have you got another suit?" she asked.

"Yes," he said, before, crestfallen, he remembered. "At home."

Sarah reached under the sink for the washing powder. She nodded at Greg's trousers. "Take them off," she ordered, assuming control of the situation. Greg began unbuckling his belt, before Sarah's voice pulled him up.

"Greg?"

He looked up to find her regarding him.

"Not in here," she said.

"Oh. Right. Sorry."

Greg slunk into the hall and pulled the kitchen door closed behind him. Sarah shook her head in the manner she had when scolding Russell for some misdemeanour such as leaving wet towels on the bathroom floor. And, just like when she chided her son, she found a smile nudging her mouth.

CHAPTER
NINE

Amanda couldn't sleep, hadn't slept properly since she'd kicked Greg out. She knew there were a couple of Valium in the bathroom cabinet that she'd filched from her mum's stash some time ago. She'd intended to save them until the next time she had a long-haul flight, or deserved a treat. That was the extent of her recreational drug use these days. Perhaps she should pop one now. It might help her to drop off — or at least not to care.

She pulled on the bathroom light and filled a glass under the tap. There was a full moon, she noticed. Perhaps that was the reason for her insomnia. Yeah, as if! It was so bright outside that, at first, she thought the security light had come on, triggered by one of the urban foxes that were everywhere nowadays. But the bulb had gone months ago and Greg still hadn't replaced it. She gazed out over the cratered back lawn. With its humps and hollows it resembled a diorama of a First World War battlefield. If ever she felt her anger towards Greg dissipate, all she needed to do to be reminded of his folly was look out of the window. Nice one, Greg.

Amanda swallowed a pill and returned to bed. She lay down and waited for to the drug to work its magic and bear her off to oblivion. Which it duly did.

But that's the trouble with sleeping pills — they just give the illusion of a good night's rest. In the morning Amanda felt like shit. She had a hangover, without having had the benefit of getting smashed the night before.

On rising she returned to the bathroom cabinet and swallowed a couple of Nurofen with paracetamol chasers. My God, she thought. Self-medicating before breakfast; I really am turning into my mother.

Sitting at his desk, Greg stared at the words on his computer screen. So Dan hadn't been making it up. The previous night over dinner he'd brought up the job vacancy. It had been news to Greg. He hadn't seen the company-wide email announcing their boss's departure — or, lately, any others. Unlike most of his colleagues, and Dan in particular, Greg didn't believe in religiously checking his inbox. Experience had taught him that those emails that weren't irrelevant or dull were rarely pressing and easily ignored. Not this one. He read the memo again: "A desire to spend more time with his family." Greg could relate to that. He'd like to spend any time with his family. But Amanda had warned him off and he felt his only hope was to comply.

Regional Sales Manager, south-east. Greg knew he'd be considered the leading candidate — a shoo-in, in most people's eyes. He was the company's leading salesman, had been the last three years. Dan was his closest competitor. But while Dan was respected, considered dependable, a safe pair of hands, he was hardly a leader of men. At least he hadn't been. He'd lately acquired a certain aura, which Greg found a little disconcerting. He cut quite a dash in his new suit. And was he wearing lifts in his shoes? Greg wasn't sure, but Dan seemed to be walking a little taller these days.

The only other serious candidate was Paula Stratton, the north-west Regional Sales Manager. Strap-On was making her irresistible rise to the top of the company by trampling anyone who stood in her way. Those above her in the hierarchy admired her zeal. With each promotion, the ranks of those below her swelled, and so too did the number of her detractors. Greg was sure she'd love to return to the capital, the better to launch her assault on the summit. But distance was to her disadvantage. She was in a far-flung corner of the empire, while Greg was at the centre of power. It was the difference between Mongolia and Peking. But hadn't Genghis Khan been a Mongol? Hmmm, it was a point worth bearing in mind.

Still, the job was Greg's to lose. He turned the barren pages of his order book. Their virginal whiteness hurt his eyes. He needed a big score to return him to the top of his game — and soon, to reassure management that he wasn't a burnt-out case.

His smartphone chimed the arrival of a text. It was from Amanda. Oh, joy of joys! His banishment was over. She'd initiated contact and was holding out an olive branch!

Perhaps.

The grls r asking 2 c u. Does 2moro suit?

Greg was not a fan of abbreviations in texts. It was like a code the recipient had to break. He translated Amanda's message into plain English, then read it through twice, trying to draw encouragement from its meaning. It was, at least, a start — the opening of a line of communication; a dialogue even, since a reply was invited. But no kiss, he noticed.

Sure. Shall I pick them up from home? What time would you like me to come? X

He hit send. The world stood still while he waited for a response.

Ping!
His thumb fumbled for the *open* button.

6. Don't be 18

Still no kiss, but what the hell? Amanda was talking to him again! Or texting at least, which, in the modern world, was practically equivalent. And her tone was civil — no shouty capitals. For a man prepared to clutch at the most anorexic of straws, it was encouragement indeed. Tomorrow Greg would see his daughters — Amanda too. And the process of reconciliation would gather pace. He felt sure that his days in the wilderness were numbered.

190

Riding this wave of good fortune, Greg snatched up his office phone and called one of his regular clients, the Purchasing Manager of a haulage company. The guy explained that he didn't need anything right now. But Greg was deaf to the word "no". He laid out some of the great discounts he was in a position to offer favoured clients, if they would only commit today. And, in less time than it takes an Intel i7 processor to warm up, the deal was sealed. Greg recorded the details in his ledger, breaking the hymen of that week. The figure wasn't huge, but it was a sale. More importantly, he'd ended his drought.

He was back, baby. He was back!

Sarah had finally decided to act on her vow to get into shape. It was resuming her sex life with Dan that had provided the catalyst. She wanted to be attractive for him. And while recent evidence suggested she was, a touch of firming and toning wouldn't go amiss. Nor would more stamina.

She was just pulling on her leotard, a little more snug than she remembered, when the doorbell rang. She checked she looked respectable in the mirror — not bad, she had to admit — then went downstairs.

"Hello, Sarah." It was Veronica's husband, Tony of the body odour. Sarah took a step back, out of range. He took in a full view of her. "You look fantastic!" he said, a little too enthusiastically for her comfort.

"Well, thank you," she replied, because that's what you say to a compliment, however unwelcome.

"No, really!" he stressed.

Sarah felt no further gratitude was necessary. She waited for Tony to explain why he'd called round. Or is he just going to stand there ogling my tits? she wondered.

The latter, apparently.

"Is there something you want?" she asked lightly, crossing her arms in front of her chest in the hope of shifting his eyes from her cleavage.

It had the desired effect. He looked up. "Something I want?" He swallowed nervously, causing his Adam's apple to flinch unattractively. "I just thought I'd check how you were going with the keylogging."

She'd forgotten all about that. She'd resolved not to use it. Now would be a good time to get the software removed. Except that would require inviting Tony in.

"It's fine, thank you. No problems."

He looked disappointed, she thought. He seemed disinclined to leave.

"Was there anything else?" she asked. "It's just I'm due somewhere."

Tony swallowed again. Sarah was put in mind of a fairground "test your strength" machine, Tony's Adam's apple like the puck that ascends towards the bell.

"Veronica doesn't understand me," he said.

"I'm sorry?" Sarah replied, not understanding him either.

"We hardly ever make love."

"Oh." She couldn't think what else to say.

"You're a very attractive woman, Sarah."

Oh, Christ, she thought, as she saw where this was going.

"I'd like to make love to you."

"I think you should go now."

But this far in, Tony could only press on. "What sort of things do you like?"

"Tony, stop."

"I like to be spanked."

"Stop!" Sarah cried.

Tony stopped.

"Veronica is my friend. And anyway . . ." Her lip curled in distaste. "No!" She slammed the door in his face, her heart racing. What on earth had got into the man? Poor Veronica!

Tony lingered a moment, in the hope she might be reconsidering. After all, he knew for a fact she put out. But the door remained resolutely shut. Wasn't he good enough for her? "Stuck-up bitch," he muttered, revealing the misogyny that festered just beneath his skin. Feeling aggrieved, he drove back to his office and jerked off in the Gents'.

Amanda had felt lethargic all day, a side effect of the Valium she'd taken the night before. After an unusually busy shift at the surgery, walking Jess, collecting the kids from school, supervising homework, making tea and washing up, and finally ordering the girls to get ready for bed (an instruction the chatter from upstairs suggested was only nominally being followed), she poured herself a glass of wine. She'd been looking forward to it for about twelve hours — no, hang on, she'd woken early — fourteen. She was about to raise the glass to her lips when the doorbell rang. Jess began barking. Amanda sighed. Should she allow herself a quick swig of Merlot before answering the door? Or postpone the pleasure, and savour the moment fully when the unwelcome visitor had been dispatched? Instant gratification versus delayed but arguably greater reward. The doorbell sounded again.

Amanda opened the door to her mother and sister: a double whammy. She instantly regretted not tasting the wine — to the bottom of the glass.

"Your sister and I would like a word," Margaret said without preamble.

Amanda looked at Geraldine.

"It was her idea," Geri offered apologetically, making a fuss of Jess.

"Coward," Amanda said, an assessment Geraldine didn't contest.

Margaret pushed the door wider (since Amanda hadn't) and stepped into the hall; Geraldine followed like a brigade of troops reluctantly tailing their commanding officer over the top of the trench. Amanda closed the front door but made no move further into the house.

"You could at least offer us a drink," Margaret said.

"But then you might stay." Amanda held her ground.

"Fine," Margaret replied, the "have it your way" unspoken but audible. "Your sister and I would like to know when you're going to forgive Greg."

It was what Amanda had expected when she'd seen them on the doorstep, but, even so she was annoyed.

"And what business is that of yours?" she demanded, flicking her eyes across to include Geraldine.

"We're family," said her mother righteously. "That gives us certain rights. And responsibilities."

"OK, we'll take a vote, then," announced Amanda dramatically. "All those who think I should allow Greg home?" Neither Margaret not Geraldine reacted, but Amanda cast their ballots for them. "Two. All those against?" Amanda raised her hand. "One. And, since mine is the only vote that counts, the motion is defeated. Thank you for your time."

"What about the children?" This from Margaret too.

"They're not of voting age."

"Don't their opinions matter?" Margaret pressed.

Geraldine, Amanda noted, was being remarkably reserved. She wasn't usually slow to offer her opinion, but she seemed content to let their mother stand point. Maybe they were doing bad cop, silent cop, or perhaps Geri just couldn't get a word in.

Margaret was speaking again: "I'm sure they'd like to have their daddy home."

Margaret's use of the diminutive incensed Amanda. How dare her mother employ that tactic? Tugging at the emotional heartstrings, like she ever took into account anyone's feelings but her own.

The trepidation that creased Geri's brow suggested she knew their mum had gone too far. She could see the storm brewing in Amanda. If Margaret saw it too, she gave no hint or, more likely, didn't care. She ploughed on: "No one's condoning what Greg did. But you've made your point and, for the good of your family, it's time you forgave him."

"You'd like that, wouldn't you?" Amanda's eyes were locked on her mother now, dangerously so. "If I were to be just like you?"

"Sis . . ." Geraldine cautioned from the periphery of their mother's force field. But, with the blood roaring in her ears, Amanda couldn't hear.

"This has got nothing to do with me," Margaret said piously, finding the moral high ground and setting up camp there.

"Well, that much we agree on!" Amanda turned on her heel and marched towards the kitchen. It wasn't that she considered the subject closed and expected her relatives to take the hint and leave, she just needed that glass of wine. She was taking a large draught when Margaret swept into the kitchen, Geraldine trailing by a couple of paces.

"You know what your problem is, don't you?" The question Margaret posed was rhetorical, but Amanda pounced.

"Yes, Mum! The fact Greg cheated on me."

"Pride! You get that from your father."

Amanda had a glint in her eye, like a centre forward in front of an open goal. She shoots; she scores.

"Well, no one could say I get it from you."

Geraldine grimaced. "Oh, boy."

"You know nothing about my marriage." Margaret fixed Amanda with a look as stony as her tone, which contained an implicit warning to Amanda to put the gun down and step away now. But that's the problem with shared DNA: Amanda was no more likely to shrink from a fight than her mum.

"Oh, excuse me!" Amanda snorted histrionically, in a manner that, had she been party to this scene, eight-year-old Lauren would have admired and no doubt later mimicked. "I was there! I may have been in bed, but I still heard the rows, the doors slam, his car drive away! And each and every time, I never knew whether he'd be coming back!"

"He always did," her mother sniffed, casually finding a glass and, uninvited, pouring herself some wine.

Amanda spoke quieter, but loud enough for her mother to hear the knife sinking deep. "Until the time he didn't."

Margaret waved away this detail. "You'd left home by then."

"So — what? You stayed together for the sake of the children? You didn't do us any favours." Amanda pointed an accusatory finger at Geraldine. "She grew up with no expectations of men, and still managed to find one who fell short of them —"

"That's true," Geraldine acknowledged, though neither Amanda nor Margaret was paying her any attention.

"— while I dreamt of meeting a prince, only to have him turn into a frog!"

"Oh, don't be so melodramatic —" Margaret resented anyone stealing her role — "and naïve! You know it's not all happy ever after. You have to work at a relationship."

"Tell that to Greg!"

"I can't! He's not here!" Margaret proclaimed gleefully, relishing her equaliser.

197

"Grandma! Geraldine!"

Before Amanda could riposte, or think of one, Molly and Lauren bundled into the kitchen and the arms of their relatives. They were blithely unaware of any atmosphere between the adults, but their childish innocence demanded that it dissipate. Hostilities were suspended.

"Have you grown?" Geraldine teased Lauren as she lifted her up.

"No! But I've got a loose tooth," Lauren declared proudly, waggling the wobbly molar for her aunt to inspect.

"I hope the tooth fairy's got lots of change handy. What's the going rate now?"

"A two-pound coin."

"Two pounds!" Geri mimed amazement. "In my day it was ten pence."

"Inflation," explained Amanda.

"Indulgence," muttered Margaret into her glass of wine.

Amanda shot her mum a cool look that confirmed the truce was a ceasefire, not a cessation of their conflict.

Geraldine put Lauren down and drew Molly in. She addressed both children: "Listen, I'm going to take your mum out for the evening."

"What? No!" This from Amanda, not her daughters.

Geraldine ignored her. "It's what she needs. Let her hair down a bit. How would you like Grandma to babysit?"

"Yay!" This from the girls, not their mother.

"I don't want to go out," Amanda protested. "I've got things to do." She looked about for support, but not even Jess was offering any.

"Get your coat," Geraldine ordered, proving she could do bad cop just as well as their mum.

Dan was working late.

No, really, he was. He'd been out in the field most of the day, had paperwork he needed to catch up on. And with interviews for the post of Regional Sales Manager, south-east, set for the following week, there was no harm in letting his bosses see him burning the midnight oil. The seven o'clock oil. Except the lazy sods had already pissed off home — one of the perks of senior management, he supposed. He'd find out soon enough.

Dan smiled to himself. He was already imagining himself in the job. But that was one of the secrets of success, according to the audio book he'd started listening to in the car. All top sportsmen, it said, visualise a successful outcome to their efforts. Jonny Wilkinson, standing over a conversion, sees his kick sailing over the posts; Tiger Woods, lining up a putt, sees the ball drop into the hole (the CD was a few years out of date). It was good advice, though not a particularly entertaining listen; Russell had begged Dan to switch to FM, even Radio 2.

Dan stretched, leaning back in his swivel chair, which squeaked in protest. He'd get a new one when he was promoted, ergonomically designed with lumbar support. Install it behind the aircraft-carrier-sized desk in his corner office. What other changes would he make? A new car, of course. A new house?

A new wife?

It's what men of a certain age did, wasn't it? Trade in their wives for a younger model — who, if the men were rich enough, often was a model.

Lynda and Dan. They sounded like one of those Hollywood power couples. Brad and Angelina. Brangelina. Lyndan.

He wondered how Lynda would react were he to announce he intended to leave Sarah. Sceptically, if she had any sense, and Dan knew she had plenty. It's what men promised their mistresses all the time, but hardly any followed through. He could understand why. It was the monotony of marriage that caused men to cheat. Why would you replace one wife with another? It had failure built in.

And yet Dan couldn't deny the appeal. No skulking around, stealing moments in private, wearing a mask in public. Out and proud. Free to see Lynda whenever he wanted — to stay as long as he liked, not to have to be home in time for dinner.

Dan checked his watch. He really should be getting back. Sarah would be expecting him.

He tried to envisage life without his wife of sixteen years. He couldn't. He and Sarah were like two plants — a hawthorn and a blackthorn, say — that had become so entwined they were grafted the one on to the other. Indivisible and indistinguishable. That was the benevolent interpretation. There had been times he'd suspected one of them was bindweed. Strangling.

Suffocating. But not recently. Not since he'd started seeing Lynda.

Dan did not want to give up Sarah. He would be lost without her, adrift without anchor or compass. But he didn't want to give up Lynda either. Thankfully, it was not a choice he was being called upon to make. One day perhaps. But not now.

He logged off his computer, took his jacket from the back of his chair and returned home to the embrace of his family.

Sarah, balancing a large pile of laundered clothes, knocked on Russell's bedroom door. She thought he was having a bath, but it was always best to check. No answer as expected. Sarah shouldered the door wide and entered. The usual aroma of spent semen assailed her nostrils. When Russell wasn't on his Xbox, did he spend all his time wanking? It really was the most unpleasant odour.

She cast an eye around the room. Good. No claggy tissues curdling on Russell's bedside table or coagulating on the floor. He'd gone through a spate of omitting to dispose of them. His mother's subtle enquiry as to whether he'd started with a cold had been enough to send him scuttling to clear up his room, albeit only of the offending and offensive Kleenex.

Sarah plonked the washing down on Russell's bed and began sorting it into the correct drawers (Russell wouldn't). She became aware of his laptop blinking from his desk, beckoning her. Veronica's reptilian husband, Tony, had reminded her of the keylogging software he'd installed. Sarah had decided that she wouldn't use it, but happening to nudge the computer awake and see what was on the screen could hardly be considered a violation of Russell's privacy. With a pair of his clean underpants in hand, she crossed to the dozing computer. She bumped the desk with her hip. Nothing. She did it again, harder, causing a scale model of the Starship Enterprise to topple over and a snow globe to unleash an improbable blizzard over Hawaii.

The laptop stirred and Russell's Facebook page popped up on screen. Russell had been Sarah's first Facebook friend when she had joined three years ago (she now had forty-two) and the only one to subsequently block her. He'd imposed this sanction after Sarah had replied to one of his posts by correcting it's grammar (it had been an inappropriate apostrophe that had drawn her ire). She had appealed against the punishment, but Russell had declared that it wasn't cool to be Facebook friends with your mum and the ban remained in place.

Sarah leant in to read Russell's newsfeed. His friend, Bugsy, had accumulated forty-four likes for asserting that Mr Kettridge (Russell's science teacher) was the gayest member of staff. This contention had generated a lively debate ("Kettridge must be a lesbo cos he's a gay cunt!") but, thankfully, Russell had not contributed. A girl Sarah didn't know, called Dixy Meverall, had changed her profile picture, an apparently popular move since 116 people approved. A boy Sarah didn't know (why didn't she know any of these kids?) had posted a video in which a youth skateboarding while holding on to the back of a speeding truck got "like, totally creamed, LOL". For the boy's mother's sake, Sarah hoped the clip had been faked.

"Mum! What are you doing?"

Sarah jerked upright. She hadn't heard Russell's approach.

With one hand clutching at the towel round his waist, he grabbed the laptop from his desk and hugged it to his hairless chest, shielding it from her view.

"I was just sorting out the clothes I've washed for you," Sarah said huffily, as though she were the injured party. She resumed the task, seeking to provide herself with an alibi, albeit after the fact.

"I've asked you not to look at my laptop."

"I was trying to turn it off. I nudged it by mistake."

Russell wasn't listening. He was intent on closing the computer down. Stacking socks in his cupboard, Sarah noticed her son's cheeks flush and the tips of his ears redden. Interesting, she thought. Something of an overreaction if all he had to hide was a skateboarding clip of dubious taste.

A lingering whiff of spermatozoa wafted up her nose. Oh no, she thought. Earlier, he must have been looking at porn. If she'd only pressed the back button, she'd have found the sites he'd visited. Some sort of sadomasochism, she suspected. But how extreme?

Thank goodness for the keylogging program. Tomorrow she'd find out just how broad her son's sexual tastes were.

CHAPTER
TEN

It was only reluctantly that Amanda had agreed to accompany her sister on this excursion, but now that they were in the West End, she was glad she'd allowed herself to be bullied. Apart from her cheerless drink with Greg in the Bricklayer's Arms, she hadn't been out in the past week; she deserved to have some fun. She'd been all for walking to her local, but Geraldine had insisted on driving into town. Luck was on their side — doubly so; not only had they found a parking space, it still had a couple of quid on the meter. Geraldine pointed her key fob to lock the dilapidated Saab (it was one of the few features that still worked reliably), then took Amanda's arm in hers as they walked. The bright lights of Shaftesbury Avenue provided an illusion of glamour.

"Hey, how did your date with Trevor go?" it occurred to Amanda to ask.

"Interesting," Geraldine said, in a tone that suggested she wasn't exaggerating.

"I want every gory detail!" Amanda exclaimed gleefully. God, how she craved some good girly gossip! For the last week, she'd only had one subject on her mind. What a welcome change, not to be reminded of

Greg and his crass stupidity, Amanda thought, inadvertently reminding herself of Greg and his crass stupidity.

"OK, so we started off at Vibe for cocktails."

"Classy."

"Well, it seemed to be the thing to do. You know, to get us in the mood. Trevor had a sexual craving and I had a need to get laid."

"Jesus, Geri! Since your divorce, you've been like a greyhound on heat."

Geraldine fixed her sister with a level stare. "That's what our cocktails were called."

"Right. Yes. Of course," said Amanda. Oops, she might have added.

"A greyhound on heat, am I?" Geraldine wasn't about to let it lie.

"What about this place?" Amanda said, stopping outside a pub, grateful for the chance to change the subject.

"No." Geraldine curtly dismissed Amanda's suggestion and continued up the street.

Not wishing to antagonise her further, Amanda meekly followed. "So what did you do after Vibe?" she ventured in a mollifying tone as she caught her sister up.

"I'm not sure I want to tell you now — if you're going to be all judgemental."

Amanda hastened to reassure her. "I'm not!"

"Well, we had a curry, and then we went back to his place."

"Okayyyyy." Amanda wasn't sure she'd be able to keep her pledge of moments earlier. They reached an inviting-looking bar, all neon and pumping music, but Geraldine carried straight on past.

"What's wrong with there?" Amanda enquired as Rihanna's "Diamonds" receded behind them.

Geri cast a glance back, as though only now noticing the place. "You tell me; I've never been in." She didn't break stride.

"Well, isn't there a first time for everything?"

"Which brings us back to Trevor," said Geraldine, leaping on the segue. "So, anyway, he had a sexual craving and I had a need to get laid."

"We've done that bit."

"I'm not talking cocktails now."

"You know, when I said I wanted every gory detail . . ."

"Do you think this is weird?" Geri continued. "When Moira moved out, she left some of her clothes in a wardrobe; Trevor insisted on showing me them."

"Yes, I'd say that was weird."

"No, that's not it. He wanted me to wear one of his wife's dresses while we had sex."

"He didn't!"

"He did."

A more horrifying thought struck Amanda. "You didn't!"

Geri at least had the grace to exhibit a hint of embarrassment. "I did."

"Geraldine!" Amanda couldn't believe what she was hearing. "Why would you do that?"

"She had some nice stuff! Nicole Farhi."

Amanda's voiced oozed sarcasm: "Oh, well! If we're talking *designer labels* . . ." She added, a tad sorrowfully, "What happened to your self-esteem?"

"Dave got it in the settlement." Geraldine's eyes flashed with defiance. "Look, I'm forty-one years old. I haven't had sex for months — well, not with another human being. And if I'm honest . . . the idea turned me on."

"Oh, my God!" Amanda was appalled, then disconcerted to discover her moral outrage surpassed by idle curiosity. "So what was it like?"

"It was liberating. Like wearing a mask, you know? I mean, I felt a bit guilty at first — like I was betraying the sisterhood, or something. Trevor wanted me to abuse him, verbally, like he said Moira does. 'You worthless piece of shit!' That sort of thing. 'Call yourself a man?' I felt a bit self-conscious at first, but I warmed to it. Vented all I felt about Dave. And Trevor *really* got off on it!"

Amanda had to ask: "But was he making love to you or her?"

"Me, as a way of getting at her. He hates Moira! Says when she walked out, she took part of his manhood with him. I tell you, Mand, he must have had a hell of a lot to begin with, cos there's plenty left!"

"That is depraved!" Amanda said, almost admiringly.

"I know!" Geraldine grinned. "It was great."

"Are you going to see him again?"

"Hell, yeah! I've got my eye on a Vivienne Westwood for next time."

The two sisters collapsed in giggles, leaning against each other for support. God, it felt good to laugh. I haven't laughed in so long, thought Amanda. Ever since . . . Enough.

They arrived outside a nightclub called The Forge. Geri stopped. "This is the place," she said.

Amanda took in the nondescript building. As far as she could see, it had little to distinguish it from the bars and clubs they'd passed, and certainly nothing to recommend it, unless Geri was attracted by the two-hour-long happy hour. No, Amanda concluded, it couldn't be that; cheap drinks had ended at 7p.m.

"You'll see," Geraldine said, reading Amanda's thoughts.

She led the way past the two bouncers on duty at the entrance. One was a bodybuilder and the other a Polynesian. Both would have to turn sideways to pass through the double doors. They looked bored. Amanda tried to brighten their evening with a cheery smile. It fell like seed on stony ground. Clearly, making punters feel welcome was not within their brief, mused Amanda, as she followed Geraldine into the club's murky depths.

Crossing to the bar Amanda took in the ambience. The club was reasonably well populated for a week night. Men outnumbered women by maybe two to one. Most significant, everyone seemed, if not necessarily old (though there were a few that description fitted), then mature. There was no one who looked younger than forty. Not your usual crowd, Amanda supposed, though perhaps the scene had changed. It was years since she and Greg had been clubbing.

"What are you drinking?" Geri asked.

"Oh, I'll get these," Amanda said, reaching for her purse. "You drove."

"Put that away," Geri admonished. "We don't use money in here."

Amanda didn't understand what her sister meant, but let it go. Perhaps there was some kind of promotion on. "A vodka and tonic then," she said.

Geraldine nodded and turned to the barman. "Two glasses of champagne."

Amanda frowned. Hadn't Geri heard? The music, a silky Barry White ballad from the seventies, wasn't that loud. Still, who says no to champagne? Not Amanda.

"May I get these?"

Amanda turned to see a suave man she estimated to be in his mid-fifties smiling at Geraldine. At his side stood his friend, a portly guy of roughly the same vintage. It was difficult to tell his precise age in the low light, though Amanda caught the leer he gave her.

"That's extremely generous of you," Geraldine purred at her would-be benefactor, as he handed the barman thirty quid and received no change. Geri passed Amanda a glass of champagne with a smirk.

Oh, for fuck's sake, thought Amanda, as it finally dawned that Geraldine had brought her to a singles night for the over-the-hill.

"Four nil!"

Russell was giving Greg a hammering at Fifa 15 on the Xbox. Greg only had himself to blame. He'd chosen to be Scotland against the might of Russell's Spain. How times have changed, Greg thought. When he was a kid, no one wanted to be Spain. Mind you, back then it was Subbuteo. What a shit game that was! Nostalgia was so overrated.

The door to the lounge opened and Dan stuck his head in.

"Could I have a word?" he asked Greg.

"Sure," Greg replied, rising to his feet. "Call it a draw, shall we, Russ? Game called off before full time."

"It's OK," Russell replied. "I can pause it."

Great, thought Greg, as he followed Dan into the kitchen.

Dan handed him a beer from the fridge. "So, look, I thought we ought to have a chat," he started.

Oh, no, thought Greg. He's going to tell me it's time I moved out. Please don't send me back to the Clifton Motor Inn and Howard's sneering disdain.

"I really appreciate you and Sarah putting me up," Greg said in a pre-emptive strike. "It shouldn't be for much longer. I'm seeing Amanda tomorrow; I think she's coming round."

"That's great," said Dan, taking a swig of Peroni, "but that's not what I wanted to talk to you about. It's the job: Regional Sales Manager, south-east." Dan loved the sound of that title. He'd been saying it out loud on his drive home, till it rolled off the tongue: "Dan Sinclair, Regional Sales Manager, south-east."

Greg was feeling fairly chipper. Buoyed by the texts from Amanda, he'd made another small sale that afternoon; still whitebait, when he should be trawling for tuna, but he could reasonably claim to be on something of a roll. The month was young; like the successful salesman that he usually was, Greg had every confidence that he'd be able to make up the lost ground. The trickle of sales would shortly become a flood. He'd hit his target. And then some.

"What about the job?" Greg asked.

"Well, I've applied," Dan told him.

Greg nodded. "And you'll be a very good candidate," he said, managing to sound only a little patronising.

"As will you," Dan tried to sound patronising in return but, annoyingly, Greg seemed to take the compliment at face value. As he might, Dan privately acknowledged. "I just thought we should agree to keep it clean and above board," he persevered. "I mean, we are mates after all."

"Hell, yeah! We won't let this come between us. In fact, I pledge full and open disclosure. If I hear anything to my advantage, I'll pass it on to you."

"Likewise." Dan assessed that, as the horse likely running second, he had the more to gain from this agreement.

"So have you?" asked Greg. "Heard anything? In these meetings that have been keeping you in the office late?"

Dan blinked. "No. But if I do . . . Full disclosure."

"May the best man win," toasted Greg.

"So long as it's not Strap-On, I don't mind which of us gets it."

Oh, I do, thought Greg.

Geraldine was giving Amanda a masterclass in flirting. Their new friends, Graham and Gavin, as they'd learnt, hung on her every coquettish gesture. Amanda looked on, torn between awe and horror. It seemed to be tacitly understood by all that Geraldine was paired with Graham and Amanda with his overweight friend. Amanda had no idea how this agreement had been settled, she'd just suddenly found Gavin by her side while Graham directed all his attention to her older sister.

"You're a dentist!" Geri gushed, her eyes widening in admiration. This was apparently the right reaction. Graham beamed, revealing a set of perfectly aligned incisors. "You'll make me self-conscious," she continued, coyly raising a hand to cover her mouth. "I'm going to have to talk like this."

"No, you've got good teeth," Graham opined, lowering her hand and holding on to her wrist a moment longer than was called for. "A slight overbite, but nothing that can't be corrected."

Amanda watched, mesmerised. It was like an episode of *Blind Date* for the superannuated.

Graham leant in to Geraldine and confided in a conspiratorial tone, "Of course, with closer inspection, I could give you a more definitive assessment." He waggled his eyebrows, a gesture clearly intended to be seductive, but which came across as sleazy. The smile

Geraldine had frozen to her face slipped, revealing a hint of repugnance beneath. Graham sensed he'd blown it and scrambled to save the situation. "Did I mention I drive a Porsche?"

"Could I have a word?" Amanda interposed, seizing Geraldine by the arm and dragging her off without waiting for a response.

A sexagenarian with implausibly black hair breathed in deeply as Amanda passed. "Ugh!" She recoiled. "That man just inhaled my hair!"

"It happens," Geraldine said, matter-of-factly.

A short but safe distance from their new friends, Amanda turned to confront Geraldine.

"What the hell are we doing here?" she enquired.

"Enjoying a night out." Geraldine sipped her champagne and flashed goo-goo eyes at Graham.

"You might be," Amanda said, though she found it hard to believe. "I'd have been happier down our local."

"But that's not where you'll go."

Amanda frowned. "When? What do you mean?"

Geraldine waved to Graham with just the tips of her fingers, reminding Amanda of Jack Lemmon in *Some Like It Hot*. As Geri turned to face Amanda, she switched off her smile. She eyed her sister with steely severity. "You won't listen to Mum, so now it's my turn." Grandly, Geraldine swept a hand around the bar, like an MC introducing the band. "Welcome to your future — if you're daft enough to ditch Greg."

"Oh, for fuck's sake —"

"And I know you; you *are*." Geraldine's lip curled. "You've got 'standards', 'principles'."

"You say that like it's a bad thing."

"They won't keep you warm in later life. Look around you, Mand. It's ugly out there. No place for a middle-aged woman who's on the shelf."

"I'm not middle-aged. My oldest daughter's only ten."

"You will be, sooner than you expect. But that's another thing: don't mention you've got kids. Not until you've got a man hooked. Oh, I know you think I'm exaggerating. You think, 'I'll be fine; I've got friends.' Yeah, they'll be sympathetic for a while — a month, maybe — and then they'll come to look at you differently. At best, you'll be an odd number; at worst, a threat. Your friends will drop you. Your world will implode. Till it's a toss-up between eHarmony and this place — Club Climax, as it's colloquially known."

Amanda felt the heat rising. It wasn't just the temperature in the airless club.

"So — what? — Greg screws around and I have to swallow it?"

"Swallow. Spit. No. You kick him in the balls so fucking hard it'll look like he's got mumps. And then you move on."

"He still gets away scot-free."

Geraldine looked doubtful. "I was serious about the kicking," she said. "Look, Greg made a mistake. He won't do it again."

"How can you know that?"

"Because I know Greg!"

"I thought I did."

"He loves you — and the girls. He won't want to risk losing you."

"If that were true, he wouldn't have cheated in the first place."

Geraldine had to admit Amanda had a point there. She tried a different tack. "You know, I used to think that men fall into two categories: those that cheat, and those that just think about it. But there are two types of men that cheat. Those like Dad, who never stop, and those like Greg, who do it once, wish they hadn't, and will never do it again."

Amanda nodded, apparently concurring with her sister's analysis. "And do you know how you can tell which type a guy is?"

"No. How?"

"You can't. But all the guys like Dad start out like Greg, by cheating once. And their wives forgive them. And the men think, 'Wow! I can get away with this.' So, after a while, they do it again. And when they get caught, they're just as sorry as the first time. And the wives, who swore blind they'd never be made fools of twice, find that, actually, it's not so difficult to forgive them this time, because it's not like they have as much to lose. Not their dignity, or self-respect. That's already gone."

Geraldine looked at Amanda like it was only now she realised something.

"You blame Mum more than Dad."

Amanda stopped. She'd never considered this before; she hadn't seen it as a competition. But Geraldine was right. Her late father she exonerated to a degree because he couldn't be held fully responsible for his actions. He had been a human being of flawed design — a man, whose brain was no match for his cock. But her mother had *chosen* to forgive him. When Margaret had discovered his first infidelity and turned a blind eye, she'd become an accomplice after the fact. But, by so doing, she was complicit in all his subsequent cheating. Yes, Amanda blamed her mum more, because Margaret hadn't only let herself down, but all women.

"I blame them both," she fudged, "but I'll tell you this: if you behave like a doormat, you deserve to get walked all over."

"More champagne, ladies?"

The women turned. Graham and Gavin held four flutes of champagne (sixty quid's worth, by Amanda's quick calculation). Graham handed one to Geraldine, and Gavin held one out to Amanda.

"Oh, boys, you shouldn't have," Geraldine cooed as she swapped glasses with Graham, giving him an empty to dispose of.

"No, really. You shouldn't have," Amanda agreed, declining Gavin's offer.

Gavin was thrown. He'd thought they were following a time-honoured mating ritual, the form of which was as prescribed as a cotillion of Regency England. But his dance partner had misstepped. She had performed a cross and go below when a chassé was called for. He didn't know which way to turn. He looked to his more worldly friend for guidance, but Graham was equally perplexed by Amanda's apparent rebuff.

Geraldine stepped in. "Don't worry about my friend," she said. (She hadn't admitted to Amanda being her sister; as the older, she didn't want to invite any speculation about their difference in age.) "She just thinks we should buy this round."

Amanda looked askance. No, I don't, she thought.

"Oh! One of those feminists, are you?" smirked Graham at Amanda, before returning his gaze to Geraldine and winking. "I hope that doesn't make you lesbians."

No, but you could, thought Amanda.

"It's our pleasure," Graham continued. "It's not every night we get the opportunity to enjoy the company of two such beautiful young ladies."

Gavin nodded in overeager agreement. Geraldine took the champagne flute from his grasp and passed it to Amanda.

"Well then, gentlemen, we accept," she declared on Amanda's behalf, "because I'm afraid we couldn't reciprocate. Bubbly is beyond our budget."

Graham waved away this trifling concern. "Money is no object."

"You drive a Porsche," Geraldine pointed out.

Graham beamed, comforted that this carelessly inserted detail had counted in his favour.

"The thing is, though," Geraldine persisted, holding her glass up and watching the bubbles dance on the surface, "some guys think that if they buy a woman a couple of drinks, she's in their debt, owes them something, if you know what I mean."

"Not us." Graham looked to Gavin for confirmation, which he enthusiastically supplied. "We merely seek to slake your thirst."

Geraldine smiled sweetly. "Would you give us a moment to confer?"

Graham, fully expecting to benefit from said confab, drew Gavin back to the bar.

"I'm not joking, Mand," Geraldine said, picking up on their earlier conversation. "This is what awaits you if you won't get off your high horse: Graham the Porsche-driving dentist and his nodding-dog of a friend. And they're better than most; I speak from bitter experience. That's why you need to forgive Greg. Not for him. Or the girls. For *you*."

Geraldine held her sister's gaze, to impress upon her how serious she was. This is a bit like an intervention, she thought, having once tried to persuade a friend to give up drugs. But, as on that occasion, it ultimately came down to whether the person you were seeking to help was willing to help themselves, was capable of acting in their best interest but against every instinct.

"Can we go home now, please?" Amanda asked in a small voice.

"Sure." Geraldine took a last swig of champagne, then crossed to Graham and Gavin at the bar. They looked up expectantly.

"Sorry, boys; it's not going to work tonight. My friend's not ready. You know, recent break-up, the wounds still raw. You do understand, don't you?"

Graham could hardly protest. He would have liked to (he'd dropped ninety quid on the deal, though he'd

218

later touch up Gavin for half), but it was just such insensitive outbursts that had cost him his first marriage. Until his second, he was resolved to be on his best behaviour.

Geraldine laid a consoling hand on his arm. "But it was a real pleasure meeting you. Maybe next time." Her eyes promised what her words only intimated.

Amanda apologetically handed Gavin her untouched champagne and followed Geraldine. She caught up with her as they passed the doormen, who shot them the same indifferent look that had been their greeting.

"That was nice of you," Amanda said, as they retraced their steps to Geri's car, "letting him down lightly."

"Oh, I meant it," Geraldine replied. "Once I've exhausted Moira's wardrobe, I'm going to be on the lookout. And Graham drives a Porsche. Besides, you never know when some cheap dentistry might come in handy."

Geraldine grinned. Amanda couldn't tell whether she was joking.

Sarah sat down at Russell's laptop and nervously typed in his password. Although she knew she was alone in the house, she had to force herself to take measured breaths; she didn't need her son returning home for his maths textbook to find her hyperventilating on the floor of his bedroom. She opened his internet browser. She'd decided that checking his viewing history would be less of an intrusion than using the keylogging software hidden on the computer. She wasn't sure quite how, it just felt like it. But, as she'd expected, the history had been wiped. Still, that confirmed that Russell had something to hide. Sarah felt vindicated in her need to know. Marginally.

When that creep Tony had installed the keylogger, he'd been at pains to hide its presence from casual view; there was no handy icon on the desktop screen or shortcut on the start menu. Either would have been like leaving a Post-it note that screamed, Hey, Russell! You're bugged! The upside of this was that Russell should have no idea she'd been snooping; the downside was that Sarah had forgotten how to access the program. She knew she had to press a combination of keys: control, shift, alt and one other, but which? She went round the keyboard. At the twelfth attempt, control, shift, alt and K did the trick. Like a genie emerging from a bottle, or Flash Harry from the bushes of St Trinian's, the spyware company's logo filled the screen as the program opened. Sarah found herself checking over her shoulder to make sure she wasn't being observed. There's no one as paranoid as a spook.

The software offered a number of ways to track usage. The first was "keystrokes typed". This gave Sarah a directory of the websites Russell had visited. Topping the list was something called www.football365.com, which sounded harmless enough but Sarah felt she ought to check. She double-clicked on the heading and was presented with the following message:

[DOWN] [DOWN] [DOWN] [DOWN] [Left mouse-click] Jose Mouri [RIGHT] [Enter] [DOWN]

[DOWN] [Left mouse-click] [DOWN] [DOWN]
[UP] [UP] [UP] [UP] [UP] [UP] [UP] [UP] [UP]

Not only was this unfathomable, but boring. She retreated to the main menu. The second category was "screenshots": pictures not words; grabs of webpages Russell had visited. Much more promising. She opened this file and clicked through its contents: football news, TV gossip, photos of swimmers in revealing Speedos. Sarah paused; she enlarged this last image. Russell must be wanting some new trunks, she thought. Well, he's not getting any like this! They left hardly anything to the imagination. Presumably they were designed to reduce water resistance, but Sarah couldn't see them being sanctioned for use in the Olympics, at least not by any countries ruled by mullahs.

Good-looking models, she noted. Nice bods. She allowed herself a moment to appreciate their lithe physiques before moving on, and then, like the image, she froze. In the next screenshot, the swimmers had towels draped over their broad shoulders. Sarah desperately wanted to believe that this was what had piqued Russell's interest — he was shopping for towels — but the most striking aspect of the photographs was the models' nudity. They were stark bollock naked. Like anyone else who viewed these pictures (Russell included, Sarah didn't doubt), her eyes were drawn to the mounds of pubic hair, and the impressive cocks that made one wonder how their trunks could ever contain them. She forced herself to look elsewhere, at the grain-fed preppy faces, but, try as she might (and really, she did try), she felt her focus drawn inexorably down, sliding over the athletes' dripping torsos, the pronounced V of their pelvic bones like an arrow guiding her gaze.

Sarah was confused. Had Russell arrived here by accident? That must be it. He'd been looking at the previous page, which was innocuous, even if the Speedos were somewhat skimpy, and, like her, he'd clicked through without knowing what to expect. Yes, that was it. Sarah relaxed.

But this charade only lasted as long as it took her to review the rest of the screenshots: a parade of naked young men, like an Abercrombie and Fitch catalogue but without the clothes; an orgy of buff beefcake, many of the shots worthy of the porn equivalent of Standard and Poor's AAA rating — XXX, perhaps. There was no question of Russell happening upon this material by chance. This was by design — or, rather, desire.

Sarah closed the keylogging program and turned off the computer. She continued to sit at Russell's desk, paralysed, incapable of movement. She felt . . . She didn't know how she felt. Empty. Bereft. But, most of all, sickened. Not by the images she'd seen, nor by Russell wanting to see them, but with herself — for looking. She was a voyeur, beneath contempt. But still she managed to despise herself.

She went into the bathroom and ran herself a shower. Stripping off, she stood under the powerful jets, hoping the water might cleanse her of her shame. It didn't. Afterwards, she still felt dirty.

CHAPTER
ELEVEN

Mindful of Liz's advice to eschew flowers, Greg had bought Amanda a box of chocolates. It sat on the passenger seat as he drew into the drive and parked. He didn't immediately get out, taking a moment to sit, observing his house. His "home". During the last week, inverted commas had crept in and settled around that word. Greg wondered when they might be removed — if ever.

In the darkness before dawn, self-propagating seeds of doubt had taken root in Greg's mind. He'd begun to doubt whether Amanda's text had been, as he'd dared to hope, a goodwill gesture, the beginning of a rapprochement. Perhaps it was the opening salvo of a formal separation. And Greg, blithely arriving to see his daughters, was walking into a trap, tacitly acceding to terms on which future contact with the girls would be permitted. Greg could imagine the scene now: a family court; a world-weary judge, struggling to bring a fresh ear to arguments she's heard ad nauseam; and Amanda's lawyer, looking and sounding a lot like David Cameron, though in better shape, wearing a bespoke suit that Greg is paying for, oleaginously cross-examining him in the dock. (Why he's in the dock,

Greg doesn't know, but it seems right.) "Is it not true, Mr Beavis, that, since your separation, you have seen your daughters once a week and every other weekend, without complaint? I put it to you that you have no grounds upon which to contest access." And, while Greg flails about, claiming he wasn't even aware they were separated, the pompous brief lowers his exquisitely tailored arse on to the bench, with a disdainful, "No further questions, Your Honour!" Oh, and Amanda's gloating smile as she sees Greg's dawning realisation that she's duped him.

Greg didn't want to believe this scenario, wanted to dismiss it as spawned by the night terrors, but the man who underestimates the fury of a woman scorned is a fool who very rarely gets to see his daughters and then only at a family contact centre with some middle-aged do-gooder acting as chaperone to ensure he doesn't . . . what? Interfere with them? Say bad things about their mother? Cry?

Greg heard footsteps approaching in response to his ringing the bell. He hoped Amanda would return his smile, not flay him with dead eyes.

The door opened and Jess, barking, leapt out at Greg, more delirious than ever to see him. Fussing the dog, Greg extended the box of chocolates. Milk Tray. They looked a slightly pathetic offering now. Perhaps he should have gone for the bigger size.

"Oh, Greg! You shouldn't have!"

Right reaction, wrong speaker. It was Geraldine.

"I didn't," said Greg on looking up. "They're for Amanda."

Geri smiled, not without sympathy. "I figured." She shrugged apologetically. "She's not here."

Greg nodded. "Well, she knew I was coming."

Geraldine ushered him in. "Come on. I'll put those in water," she joked.

Being invited into his own house by his de facto sister-in-law . . . This all felt fucked up. But Greg didn't say anything, just followed Geri through to the kitchen, Jess leaping about adoringly.

"The girls will be down in a minute. They're just getting changed."

"Amanda avoiding me, is she?" Greg couldn't help asking.

Geraldine flicked on the kettle. "She's at work. Someone asked to swap shifts." She didn't let on that that someone was Amanda. "How have you been?" she continued, changing the subject.

"Oh, you know." He managed a brave smile, which gave a vague approximation of the hell he was living.

"Well, that's what you get for being a fucking idiot." Geraldine said matter-of-factly.

One of the things Greg liked about Geri was her no-nonsense manner. On this occasion, he'd have preferred it leavened with a sprinkling of tact.

"I didn't cheat on her, you know."

Geraldine regarded him a moment, as though weighing whether to give him the benefit of the doubt. Not that it made much difference. "Well, you may as well have," she finally said.

Ain't that the truth, he thought disconsolately.

225

"I'm making a brew. You want one?" she asked. He shook his head. Geri waited for the water to boil then poured it into a mug. Greg, leaning against a kitchen cabinet, watched listlessly, like all the energy had been sucked out of him. Which, Geraldine reflected, perhaps it has.

"Just give her time," she said. "She'll come round."

Greg looked up. "Do you think so?"

Geri considered this. "My honest opinion? I don't know. She's that stubborn. You remember our dad."

Greg nodded. Amanda's father had been a rogue; the word might have been invented to describe him. Greg had been a little in awe of him: a man who seemed to live life by his rules with scant regard for the opinion of others. Amanda had been less enamoured, for the same reason.

Geraldine flicked her tea bag into the sink, where it landed with a wet thud that sounded a little like Greg's hopes.

"Actually, I was just seeking reassurance," he said.

Geraldine smiled. "Well, then, yeah, I'm sure it'll work."

Greg didn't believe it either.

Geri crossed to the door and shouted to the girls that their dad had arrived. She returned to Greg. "I've put in a good word for you," she said. "For what it's worth."

"Thanks. It's worth a lot to me."

Greg's eyes met Geri's. She could smack her sister for being such a mug. So her bloke had dipped his wick where he shouldn't — allegedly; he still denied it —

but, either way, so what? He remained a good man, better than the vast majority. Better than Amanda had a chance of meeting again. Or Geraldine, for that matter.

"Daddy!"

Two small force fields exploded into the kitchen. Geri saw Greg's eyes light up, a smile leap to his face a second ahead of Molly and Lauren launching themselves at him.

Greg swept his daughters into his arms and hugged them to him. He hadn't seen them for more than a week. Christ, how he'd missed them! He hadn't realised till this moment. Or perhaps he had, he just hadn't allowed himself to feel it. A survival instinct, he supposed.

"Oh, it's good to see you!" he told them each in turn. "So, what do you want to do? Go to McDonald's?"

"Can we get a Happy Meal?" This from Lauren — as ever, the one with the angle.

It only took Greg a heartbeat to cave. "So long as you eat it; not just for the toy."

"Yayyyyy!"

Geraldine walked them to the front door.

"I'll tell Amanda to collect them from Macca's about eight," she said.

"I can drop them home," Greg offered. But then he imagined the girls wanting him to come in to say good night. And Amanda wanting him not to. Best avoid the potential for a scene, he thought. "Yeah, no, get her to swing by. Saves me going out of my way."

Geraldine nodded — out of sympathy, Greg felt.

Amanda had indeed been keen to avoid seeing Greg. She was concerned that she would still feel angry with him, more concerned that she wouldn't. This was what she was protecting herself from: the fear that time heals all wounds. She would not allow that to happen, to permit the passage of time to attenuate the gravity of his offence. He had cheated. It didn't matter whether it was once, twice or a dozen times.

There were moments, often when she was with the girls, mostly when she was alone in bed, that she found herself missing Greg: his buffoonish antics to make them all laugh, the way Jess would go berserk whenever he walked in the door, just the space he took up. But as soon as she felt any warm feelings encroaching, dissipating the anger, she stamped on them. She could not afford to weaken, to allow the granite encasing her heart to be chipped away. Because if she no longer hated Greg for what he had done, then she would hate herself instead. And so she forced herself to envisage Greg at the conference. She saw him with this other woman — in Amanda's fantasy, the woman was always young, blonde and vivacious; nothing like Amanda imagined herself to be — Greg was in her room, taking the lead, removing her bra with practised ease. Then they were on her bed, writhing in the sweat-dampened sheets, Greg going down on her — he rarely performed oral sex on Amanda any more; it helped to stoke the fire of her anger to think that he willingly indulged complete strangers.

228

Amanda knew that this was ridiculous, that, in seeking to punish Greg, she was also punishing herself — and their daughters, of course, as Margaret and Geraldine were so keen to remind her. She suspected that her sister was right, that there were no happy endings for single women, no longer young. Some found new partners, of course, but you always had the sense that, rather than true love, it was a marriage of convenience — two shipwreck survivors clinging to the same floating debris. Despite all these arguments, still she could not forgive him. This was her mother's legacy.

There was a knock at the consulting room door. Amanda tore herself away from her thoughts. They served no purpose anyway — she just walked them endlessly, like circuits of a prison exercise yard. Quickly, she scanned her appointment sheet: Byron, St Bernard. Byron? She thought she knew that name from somewhere, but couldn't place it.

"Come in!" she called.

The door opened and a skittish dog entered, followed by a killer smile on the face of the good-looking guy who'd hit on her when she'd been walking Jess.

"You . . ." she said, because she couldn't think of anything else.

"Hi." He lifted his dog on to the examination table, where it shivered like Lauren after she'd been in the sea too long. "Turns out your lists weren't full." He managed to convey the impression that he'd caught her in a lie, which, of course, he had.

"We've had some spaces open up," she said, perjuring herself further. "A couple of clients that died."

"Nothing you did, I hope." He smiled.

Oh, God, he's flirting again, Amanda thought. Just be professional, she told herself. With only a shuddering St Bernard on a narrow examination table between them, she was treated to a close-up view of his almond eyes. The irises had flecks of grey in them. Mesmerising. Just look at the dog, she ordered herself, at the same moment recalling that the guy's name was Ben.

"So, what seems to be the problem?" she asked in a voice she didn't recognise as her own.

"I don't know. He's been off his food, which isn't like him."

"And why didn't you take him to your own vet?" She looked at him when she said this. It was a mistake. He held her gaze; his grip was strong.

"You said you were better."

Amanda broke eye contact, before it could mean something, though she wasn't sure what. She turned her attention to Byron as Ben continued.

"Also, he knows their surgery too well; he gets really upset within a hundred yards of it; I thought a change might calm him."

"It doesn't seem to be working," Amanda observed. The St Bernard was shaking off the Richter scale. "Perhaps you should put him on the floor."

"You think that will help?" Ben lifted Byron down.

"I doubt it, but at least he won't pee on my table."

Amanda knelt down to the St Bernard and stroked his chest. "Let's have a look at you, fella," she said, revealing a liver treat in her palm that Byron seized upon. She found no discolouration in the dog's eyes; his teeth were healthy. Byron licked her hand.

"You've won him over," Ben observed.

"That's because I haven't done anything yet," she replied.

Ben knelt down beside her, an action that seemed somehow intimate. "I wondered about this lump," he said.

Amanda probed in the region Ben indicated. "I can't feel anything out of place," she said.

"Let me show you." Ben took her hand and ran it through Byron's fur.

Oh, for God's sake, this is like a scene out of *Ghost*, Amanda thought. Not that she was complaining. She liked the sensation of his fingers on hers. She felt her temperature rise a degree.

"There," he said.

There, what? thought Amanda, having momentarily forgotten why Ben was holding her hand. Oh, yes, I'm examining his dog. She prised apart the matted fur. "That looks like a blocked sweat gland to me. Nothing to worry about."

She continued her examination, Ben no longer touching her but still distractingly close.

"How's Jess?" he asked by way of conversation.

He remembers her name, Amanda noted. "Fine. We haven't been to Ravenscourt Park lately."

"I thought we hadn't seen you," he said. "Not that we've been looking. Well, I haven't; I can't speak for Byron." A thought seemed to occur to him. "You don't think that might be his problem, do you? He's missing Jess?"

"No," Amanda said flatly.

"They did get on well," he pressed. "I think he'd like to have seen more of her."

Amanda had the impression that it was not Byron and Jess than Ben was talking about.

"So you don't believe in love at first sight?" he said. "Among dogs, I mean."

Suddenly uncomfortable with his proximity, Amanda rose to her feet; Ben followed suit. Byron looked up, a little put out that he was no longer the centre of attention.

"Among dogs or humans," she said. "Tell me, do you always flirt like this?"

Ben looked genuinely surprised. "I wasn't aware I was flirting."

"Oh."

"Do you always imagine that people are?"

Somehow the conversation had strayed from the professional. Amanda felt awkward; she bent down to Byron again, slipping him another liver treat. Thankfully, Ben did not follow her to the floor.

"I mean, I don't deny I find you attractive," Ben explained, "but the last time we met you made it clear you weren't interested. Happily married, you said."

"Not married," she replied out of habit, adding, "and not happy at the moment." She tried to steer the

232

conversation back to Byron. "Have you changed his diet recently?"

"No. No, he always has the same thing."

Amanda cocked her head on one side and peered pensively at Byron, who cocked his head on the other and peered pensively back, which made Amanda smile.

"Hang on," Ben cut in. "The pet shop were out of his usual biscuits. I had to buy a different brand. Do you think that could be it?"

Well, durrr! Amanda thought, but did not say, though she raised an eyebrow that expressed the same opinion.

"I'm an idiot, aren't I?" Ben asked, happily.

Amanda stood up. "Well, I'm a vet, not a psychologist, but . . ." She left the sentence hanging. "I may be wrong, but try him on his old biscuits; if he still seems off colour, then bring him in again; I can run some blood tests."

Ben nodded. "Sorry if I wasted your time," he said.

"I get paid either way." She shrugged, opening a record for Byron on the computer. "And no one likes to see their dog unhappy." She turned back to Ben. "I'm sorry I accused you of flirting."

"It's a bad habit I have. But hopefully harmless."

"Mmm." Amanda couldn't help thinking about Greg. Time was she'd considered his flirting harmless. Past tense.

Ben noticed her distraction. "You mentioned you're not happy at the moment . . ." he ventured. "None of my business, I know, but perhaps I could help."

"Not unless you're a relationship counsellor."

"Actually, I am." Ben shrugged apologetically.

"Seriously?"

"Seriously is the only way to do it."

Amanda laughed. What were the chances? she thought.

"Do you flirt with your clients?" she asked.

"Only the women."

Amanda could find that all too believable.

Seeing her dubious expression, Ben grinned. "I'm joking. No, you have to be really careful. You get a lot of very vulnerable people. Offer a weeping woman a box of tissues, eight times out of ten she'll fall in love with you."

"You've researched this, have you?" Amanda asked.

Ben plucked a business card from his wallet and handed it to her. Byron lay down on the floor and rested his head on his paws. He sensed they wouldn't be departing any time soon.

Amanda scanned Ben's card. He had an impressive array of letters after his name. "What's your success rate, do you reckon?" she asked. "How many relationships do you save?"

"That's the wrong way of looking at it," Ben replied. "A success might be in helping a couple to split up amicably."

Amanda nodded, though she was sceptical. Ben took his card from her and scribbled his mobile number on the reverse.

"Look, if you want to talk anytime, just as a friend, then, you know, we could go for a drink, a bite to eat.

234

And, before you accuse me again, I'm not flirting, OK?"

It occurred to Amanda that she didn't have any male friends, not of her own. They tended to be the husbands or boyfriends of women she was friendly with, or they were mates of Greg's. She quite liked the idea of her own male pal. The possibility had never arisen before — and might have looked suspicious. Greg certainly would not have been happy. But he was not in any position to complain. It was harmless enough. It wasn't like there was a risk of any lines being crossed. Even if Ben might be keen for that to happen (and Amanda didn't fully trust his "no flirting" pledge), she wouldn't allow it. She was in control. And it would show Greg that men and women could be friends without it having to become sexual. Hmm, the more she thought about it, the more the idea appealed. It might even be beneficial to have a male perspective on the issues she was facing — with the added bonus that Ben was a trained counsellor. She'd be getting expert advice for free. And, last but not least, she liked him. Yeah, why not?

Was there a corporate mascot creepier than Ronald McDonald? Greg pondered as he munched on a string fry. No, not munched. The reconstituted potato was too lukewarm and limp to deserve any epithet redolent of crunchiness. "Sucked" was more accurate. Why appoint as the face of your company, Greg's internal monologue continued, not just a clown, when everyone knows kids are terrified of clowns, but one who looks as though he has a string of prior convictions? Unfathomable.

Greg dragged his attention back to Molly and Lauren. He'd intended this trip to be a treat, but it had the atmosphere of a wake. Neither of the girls would meet his eye. Molly was stirring the gloop that passed for a chocolate milkshake. And Lauren was peeling the slice of dill pickle off her hamburger patty.

"So, how have you been?" he asked cheerily, hoping with his gusto to stir or shock his daughters out of their lethargy. He beamed at each of them in turn, willing them to answer and hence launch a dialogue. He didn't mind which one, but one of you, please, he silently begged. Molly shrugged in a manner that Greg presumed was intended to convey "fine". Lauren stared out of the window at the playground. Greg wracked his brain for another opening — in vain.

"Why won't you come home?" Molly finally cut in, in an accusing tone. Lauren swivelled her head to face her dad. This she was interested in. Two pairs of eyes pinned Greg to his plastic seat.

He considered his answer carefully. "Well, it's not up to me," he said.

"Told you!" Molly affirmed to her sister.

"Hey! It's not your mum's fault," he said. Yes, it is, he thought. Their table lapsed into another uncomfortable silence. Greg helped himself to a chip from the paper bag between them — with instant regret. It sagged in his grasp, rather like his spirits.

"So, come on!" He brightened. "You must have some news. How's school?"

236

"Good." Molly shrugged.

"Fine." Lauren's shrug was identical.

Greg waited for more, arranging his face into a look of eager anticipation, an expression he hoped might encourage further detail. It didn't.

"Well, what sort of things have you been doing?"

The girls stared at him, like young offenders exercising their right to silence. Greg sighed. He didn't know whether their intention was to make him feel lousy, but that was their achievement. How to break through this wall of silence? Divide and conquer. He turned to Molly.

"Are you still playing modball?" he asked, awarding himself a point for remembering the version of softball that ten-year-olds played.

"The season's finished," Molly said, in a tone that suggested he should know this. And, had he still been living at home, he would have. He nodded, silently acknowledging his error, and docked himself the point.

"Can we go in the playground now?" Lauren asked.

"No; we're talking." Greg struggled to keep a note of frustration out of his voice. "How was your swimming lesson yesterday?" he asked his younger daughter.

"Good."

Of course it was. Good or fine, one or the other.

"What did you do?"

Lauren regarded him a moment like she suspected this was a trick question.

"Swim," she finally offered. There was no insolence in her tone; it was just a statement of fact.

"Guys, help me out, here!" Greg implored. "Give me something to work with."

The two blank faces that stared at Greg betrayed no hint of comprehension.

"Can we go in the playground now?" Molly asked.

"Yes." Greg conceded defeat.

The girls were off their chairs and out to the playground before Greg could change his mind. He watched them kick off their shoes, making a mental note of where Lauren's landed — she wouldn't think to fetch them. They scrambled on to the climbing equipment, each shouting for her sister to follow and both ignoring the other's instructions. Greg envied their ability to live in the moment. A minute ago their spirits had been low, depressed by the weight of their parents' problems. And now they hadn't a care in the world, except that their sibling should bend to their will.

Greg became conscious of another pair of eyes upon him. He turned to see a father and son sitting quietly at a nearby table, conspicuous among the raucous clamour of families and teenagers. The boy had his back to Greg, so he couldn't be sure of his age — seven or eight, he guessed; the adult looked to be in his late twenties. A divorced dad, Greg assumed. The man nodded at Greg, in acknowledgement and recognition. He thinks we're in the same boat, Greg thought. He was suddenly possessed of a need to go over and put the guy straight, explain that his story was quite different. And then it struck him that perhaps it wasn't.

So he stayed where he was, pasted to his plastic seat, reaching for a French fry that had long since gone cold.

It's a small world. Liz's fiancé, Brad, played in the same cricket team as the boyfriend of Beverley, the woman from Accounts who was the smoking companion of the other Liz Henderson. One evening, after nets, Beverley's boyfriend sought Brad out for a quiet word over beers in the club bar.

"Mate," he started, "I wasn't sure whether to tell you this, but I figured, in your position, I'd want to know."

Brad's form lately had been patchy. He'd been half expecting to be dropped. "Go on," he said.

Despite this invitation, Beverley's boyfriend hesitated. "The word around your fiancée's firm is that she's cheated on you," he finally ventured.

Brad had braced himself for bad news, but not this.

"Liz?" he asked incredulously, as though he might have more than one fiancée.

Beverley's boyfriend filled Brad in on the details of the phone call the other Liz Henderson had inadvertently received.

Brad was still reeling when the club captain called him aside and dropped him from the team. Shit night, huh?

Greg retrieved Lauren's shoes from where she'd flung them. As he stood up, he saw the divorced dad leave the restaurant, his arm round his son's shoulder.

"Mum's here!" Lauren announced.

Greg followed her gaze. Amanda had pulled up at the entrance. She did not get out of the car.

"Are you coming out?" Molly asked, retrieving from their table the toy that had come with her Happy Meal. Given the meal's cost, Greg shuddered to think how cheap the ingredients must be — or nutritious.

"No, I'll say goodbye to you here." He knelt down and hugged his daughters in turn. "Say hi to Mum for me. And be good for her, yeah?"

"Bye, Dad."

The word had a dreadful finality to it. Greg managed a brave smile. Molly kissed him.

"Can we do night nights?" Lauren asked.

"Sure."

"Night, night, sleep tight, see you in the morning light. Night night."

They kissed and rubbed noses three times.

"Come on; Mum's waiting!" Molly instructed her younger sister.

Lauren lingered. She didn't want to leave her dad. And he didn't want her to, either. But he gently pushed her away.

"Off you go. I'll see you soon."

Lauren jabbed another quick kiss at Greg, then scampered towards the door with Molly. Each clutched the free toy, which would remain their most prized possession for the duration of the journey home and then be discarded and forgotten. Greg eased back on to his seat. The detritus of their meal still littered the tabletop. Through the restaurant window, he caught

Amanda's eye. They exchanged neutral nods, neither apparently wanting to give too much away.

Amanda watched the girls look both ways before running to the car. Good; they'd taught them well. For once, there was no argument over who would have the front seat — Molly accepted that it was Lauren's turn. When Amanda heard the click of their seat belts, she put the car into gear and drove off. They rode in silence. Amanda wasn't sure whether this was because the girls were uncommunicative or upset.

"How was it?" she gently probed. "Did you have a nice time?"

Her daughters clearly considered it the other's responsibility to answer. Neither said anything. Amanda decided to leave it at that.

"Daddy bought me a new lunch box." Lauren finally spoke up. "I left it behind. Can we go back?"

"Not now, Lauren."

Greg remained in the restaurant. He sat, unmoving, unconsciously fiddling with a sachet of sugar.

"Are these finished with?" a teenage waitress enquired of the remains of their meals. She cleared the trays, sprayed the tabletop with an astringent cleaning agent and wiped the surface clean. Throughout this operation, Greg barely moved a muscle. The girl withdrew but, a moment later, returned and gently laid a couple of paper napkins on the table. Greg stared at them a moment, wondering why she'd done that. And then he became aware of the tears streaking his cheek.

CHAPTER
TWELVE

"You know, they say a third of divorced dads lose touch with their kids within two years."

When Greg had returned from seeing his daughters, Sarah had been happy to provide him with a shoulder to cry on. Listening to his woes distracted her from her own. She hadn't seen Russell since she'd rumbled his secret. Her head kept turning to the door, thinking she'd heard him enter; each time, it was a false alarm. Greg didn't notice; he was wrapped in his own gloom.

"A *third*. I could never understand that," Greg continued. "I mean, who wouldn't want to see their kids? I thought the men must be deadbeats, you know, the sort who'd never cared in the first place. And that explained why their relationships had failed." He took a swig from the bottle of beer Sarah had given him. "But I get it now; it's not that at all." His eyes met Sarah's just as hers returned from another journey to the door. "It's not because they can't be arsed. It's because it's too painful. You forget how to be with your kids. It's like visiting someone in hospital. You can't think of a thing to say." Greg was conscious of wallowing in self-pity. "Sorry," he finished.

242

Sarah laid a hand on his and gave it a squeeze. He appreciated the gesture far more than any empty reassurance she might have offered.

This time, there was no doubt: that was the sound of the front door. Sarah was already on her feet when Russell slouched into the kitchen, dropping his rucksack on the floor.

"Hello, son," she said, crossing to him, wanting to give him a hug but reminding herself how he hated it. "How was your day?"

"Yeah, good."

Greg looked up from the beer bottle label he was picking at. "Have you had your history essay back?" he asked. "About the causes of the First World War?"

"I got a B plus plus." Russell grinned at Greg. "'A marked improvement,' my teacher said."

"Russell, that's marvellous!" Sarah burst out.

Russell turned to look at Sarah, making her feel like she'd just gatecrashed their private conversation. Cheater, he thought resentfully. "Most of the class got the same," he said.

"Even so!" Sarah wasn't about to let him piss on his own parade.

Russell turned back to Greg. "Thanks for your help."

Greg shrugged. "All I did was read it," he said. They both knew that wasn't true. Greg had suggested several changes that Russell had subsequently made. But Greg wanted the lad to feel like he'd earned the mark himself.

And, in truth, Russell had. The words had all been his. "Good work," Greg said, raising a hand in the air.

Russell grinned and slapped Greg's palm. Sarah watched in awe. Her teenage son would shrivel with embarrassment if she tried to high five him. He'd leave her hanging, her outstretched hand like an appeal for people to notice her humiliation. She'd learnt that Russell regarded as the depth of naffness any attempt by Dan or her to be down with the kids (including the use of such phrases as "down with the kids"). Maybe Greg could get away with it because he wasn't Russell's parent. Or perhaps he was just cool. Talking to Russell like an equal did seem to come naturally to him.

"I'm going to do some work in my room," Russell told his mum. She didn't for a moment believe him. He'd be Snapchatting his mates before his door was shut. Or maybe he'd close it first, then cruise gay websites. Whatever, it was none of her business. And besides, a B plus plus buys a lot of credit.

"Sure," she said.

They heard him take the stairs two at a time.

"What the hell is a B plus *plus*?" Greg asked Sarah.

"One below an A minus minus," she dead-panned.

Greg shook his head in wonder. "I don't suppose anyone gets an F any more."

"I should hope not, the amount we're paying."

Greg smiled. "He's a great kid," he said, partly because it's what parents like to hear about their children, but mainly because it was true. He resumed picking at the label on his beer bottle. There was one

244

corner that his close-cut fingernail couldn't prise away. He didn't notice Sarah regarding him intently.

"Do you think Russell might be gay?" she asked.

Greg looked up, surprised by the question. "I don't know. I haven't given it any thought. Why?"

If Greg hadn't asked this question, Sarah might have let it lie. But he had, and she couldn't. She needed to unburden herself. She felt she could tell Greg, without him judging her, or Russell. She was half right. It didn't change Greg's view of Russell. But he was appalled to discover that Sarah had been snooping on her son. Appalled, yet, at the same time, more than a little impressed.

"My God! You're Mata Hari!" he teased. He cast his gaze furtively about the room as though searching for hidden cameras. "Are you recording this conversation?" he whispered.

"No, of course not." Sarah couldn't help smiling, though she felt contemptible.

"Have you told Dan?" Greg asked, more seriously.

"About the keylogging?"

"Any of it."

"No. Do you think I should?"

Greg weighed his response. "About the keylogger? No. About Russell? Well, that's up to you. Would it make any difference to him?"

"To Dan? I hope not. I don't think so."

"You know, it doesn't necessarily mean anything. Russell could be just exploring. It's what boys do at his age."

"Do you really think that?"

Greg hesitated. "No," he admitted.

Sarah nodded. She'd thought as much. "You know," she said, taking Greg's beer bottle from him and working her sharpened nail under the edge of the label before handing it back, "it's never your wish that your child be gay, but I really don't mind if he is. I mean, a little part of me does — the part that had hoped he might be a father one day."

"It hasn't stopped Elton John."

Sarah smiled: fair point. "I just think it will make life so much more complicated for him. You know, the agony of coming out."

"Well, then, it's good you know. You can help him."

"You think I should let him know I'm aware?"

"Hell, no! Let him tell you, when he's ready. And then just offer him all the love and support he'll need."

Sarah knew Greg was right. She'd tried to imagine a conversation with Russell in which they discussed his sexuality. She couldn't see it — apart from the look of pure horror on her son's face.

"I don't think I will tell Dan," she continued after a moment. "I shouldn't know myself. And, while I'm glad I do, there's no need to saddle him with the same knowledge. He'll find out in good time."

Greg nodded. He thought this the best approach but hadn't considered it his place to say.

They sat in silence a moment. Greg succeeded in removing the last trace of the label from his bottle of beer. He felt a small sense of achievement, and ridiculous for feeling it.

"Can I ask you a favour?" Sarah said.

Greg had anticipated this. "I won't tell a soul," he replied.

"That, too. But, no — the keylogging software. It makes me sick to think of it lurking. Would you remove it for me?"

"From Russell's laptop?"

"And the home computer," she confessed.

Her surveillance had certainly been comprehensive. A grin creased Greg's face; Sarah swatted him with a tea towel.

"Sure," he said.

They jumped as Dan came into the kitchen. They hadn't heard him enter. If Dan was aware of their awkwardness, he gave no sign. In fact, he wasn't. He was too concerned with hiding his own.

"Sorry, I'm late," he said, kissing Sarah. "The traffic lights were out on the North Circular."

He was fairly sure he hadn't used this excuse before.

After the double blow that Liz's fiancé, Brad, had received that evening, discovering her unfaithfulness and his demotion from the cricket team, he had sought to drown his sorrows. These had proved remarkably resilient. It had taken the best part of a gallon of beer to stop them resurfacing. He staggered home to the flat he shared with Liz.

"You fucked some bloke!" he spat at her, spittle spraying.

"No!" Liz chased after him as he lurched into the kitchen and more than filled a pint glass under the tap. "Where have you got that from?"

"Some bloke down the cricket club," he slurred, "heard it from his girlfriend —" he chugged the glass of water — "who heard it from someone else."

"It's all bullshit!" Liz cried. "Look, you're pissed —"

Brad swung on her. "You'd be pissed if you found out your fiancée had been sharing it around." He stamped towards the door. "I'm going to bed!" he shouted over his shoulder, as a result veering off course and colliding with the fridge, dislodging a magnet, a souvenir of a weekend break they'd spent in Barcelona. It fell to the floor and shattered.

Liz was left to pick up the pieces. She fetched a dustpan and brush. Her mind swirled. How had the news leaked? And how could she persuade Brad it wasn't true? On both scores, she came up empty.

The theme tune to *Mission Impossible* played in Greg's head as, the next morning, while Russell was downstairs eating a bowl of Frosties, he slipped into the boy's bedroom. A noxious fog slapped him in the face. Ah, the fragrance of adolescence, Greg remembered with nostalgia. Quite revolting. Armed with the password that Sarah had given him, it took Greg barely a minute to remove the keylogging software from Russell's laptop.

The lounge was his next port of call, the family PC his next target. Dan was safely out of the way, upstairs, changing into his suit. And, should he happen to lumber in, Greg had his cover story ready: the Wi-Fi on his phone was dropping out; Sarah had said to use their laptop to check his emails.

Greg stroked the mousepad, moving the cursor over "uninstall". His right index finger hovered above the keyboard and was jabbing down on "enter" when his brain suddenly screamed "ABORT! ABORT!" and Greg froze, his digit mere millimetres above the unpressed button.

Emails! Dan must occasionally use this laptop to check his emails from work. He'd have a password, of course. Everyone in the office did. You had to, or you'd leave your desk for just a moment and return to find a colleague perched like a vulture, making notes of the jobs you were quoting on, the deals you'd offered, anything they might use to their advantage. Sales reps were like Murdoch journalists in their attitude to hacking: everyone was fair game. Greg himself had had more than one go at cracking Dan's password, but all his attempts had failed. It wasn't as easy as they made it look on *NCIS*. Once he'd tried "Sarah", "Russell" and "password", Greg had conceded defeat.

What a boon it would be, with the interviews for Regional Sales Manager, south-east just days away, for Greg to know who Dan was talking to and about what. And the keylogging program would tell him. All he needed to do was access the keystroke files which recorded everything that had been typed into the machine, including, Greg could only surmise, the password to Dan's work email.

It was hugely unethical, of course. A betrayal not only of Dan but also of Sarah, who'd entrusted to Greg the task of cleaning up the computers. Had Greg felt more confident of his chances of promotion, he'd have had no hesitation in pressing "uninstall". But his recent sales revival had spluttered, then stalled, and Greg was feeling vulnerable, like the seasoned champion who knows his rivals are edging ever closer — like Roger Federer, say.

Greg set to work. What was the usual combination of keys to access a hidden program? Control, shift, alt and K? Boom! First time! Too easy. Greg went straight to the keystroke log. He ran a practised eye over the code, trying to discern the hidden meaning among the [UP]s, [DOWN]s and [Left mouse-click]s. He felt like Indiana Jones, unravelling the secrets of a Sanskrit scroll. In among the dross was the nugget Greg was seeking — the password to Dan's work email: lImBeR1YnDa

No wonder Greg hadn't guessed it. What the hell did it mean? It read like a random selection of letters. Greg made a mental note to change his password from "AmandalovesGreg" to something way more obscure.

He heard Dan on the stairs, calling Russell to hurry up. Greg should wait till they left, but then Sarah might want to see what he was doing. No — do it now; get it done.

Greg logged into Dan's email. There was little in Dan's inbox to excite his interest. Nor in his sent mail. Try the trash, he thought. This was where emails went once they'd been deleted. If you wanted to get rid of them completely, you had to remove them from this file, but it was ridiculous how many people forgot. Too busy, or, if you were Greg, too slack. His eyes scanned the list of co-respondents. One name kept recurring:

Lynda Bates. It rang a vague bell, but Greg couldn't remember why. He opened an email to her from Dan.

> I've told Sarah I have to go down to Kent to see a client. Perfect cover; no way could I be home before eight. And better than saying I'll be in the office late — Greg's stressing about these meetings he knows nothing about! I can be at your place by 5.30p.m. Tell me your flatmate's away . . .

Holy shit! lImBeR1YnDa. Limber Lynda — Liz's friend from the conference! The one nothing happened with. Like hell it didn't! And, by the sounds of it, it had gone on not happening ever since.

Greg quickly scanned other emails, confirming his suspicions. Dan was having an affair. Right under his nose!

He heard Dan and Russell in the hall, saying goodbye to Sarah. In a flurry of keystrokes, Greg logged off the computer. He hared for the door and wrenched it open, causing Dan to leap back in alarm.

"Give me a lift, will you?"

"Don't you need your car?" Dan replied.

Yes, but Greg could borrow one. "I'm in the office today. No point taking two. You'll be coming straight home, won't you?"

If he hadn't been looking out for it, he wouldn't have noticed Dan's slight hesitation. But, to Greg, it was like a chasm into which he could have shouted, "Cheat! Cheat! Cheat!" and had time to wait for the echo.

"Sure," said Dan casually, his lying eyes flicking to Sarah and away again.

"I'll just get my bag; meet you in the car." Greg made for the kitchen. As he passed Sarah, he nodded reassuringly, his eyes confirming that he'd removed the software. He made a mental note to do it that evening.

The sound of the radio masked the silence of the car's inhabitants. Each was immersed in his own thoughts. Dan was wondering what excuse he could make that would allow him to see Lynda after work. Greg was marvelling at the enormity of the lie his friend was living. And Russell, sitting in the back, was pondering why you never heard a working-class accent on the *Today* programme.

You had to hand it to Dan, Greg reflected, he'd done a masterful job of hiding his deceit. Greg now grasped why Dan always seemed to be visiting a far-flung client at the end of the day, flouting the convention that you start at the extremity of your patch and work your way home. He finally comprehended the reason for Dan's cocksure manner — with the emphasis on "cock". And it dawned on him that Dan's recently acquired fashion sense wasn't his at all, but Lynda's, and she the intended beneficiary. With hindsight, the clues were all there but even Sherlock would have been hard-pressed to spot them. Dan? A ladies' man? It seemed far-fetched. Greg shook his head in awe.

But admiration quickly turned to anger. When Greg cast his mind back to the conference. Supercilious Dan with his holier-than-thou sanctity. Hypocrisy, more like!

Dan had flat-out lied when he'd maintained he hadn't slept with Lynda. OK, so had Greg when he'd claimed to have shagged Liz. But there was no comparison! Greg was guilty of a little embellishment, Dan of a complete fabrication. An *affair*? Greg stole a glance at the face of the dissembler beside him, a mask of concentration as he waited to join a roundabout. Weren't they supposed to be mates? Hadn't Greg trusted Dan, poured out his troubles to him? Greg felt like Dan had cheated on *him*.

The car pulled up in the drop zone outside Russell's school. With a grunt that could have been a thank you or a goodbye, Russell was swallowed into the tide of kids trudging forlornly through the school gates, like orphans entering a Victorian workhouse.

"You sly bastard!"

The accusation spat at Dan caused him to swing round. He found Greg facing him with menacing eyes. "Gotcha!" they shouted. The driver of an Audi SUV behind them stood on her horn. There's no time for patience in a school drop-off zone.

"Start driving," Greg ordered, like he'd commandeered the car.

Was it Greg's tone, Dan's accommodating manner or Audi woman's bolshiness? Whatever the reason, Dan did as he was told, put the car in gear and pulled away. He shot a hesitant glance Greg's way, wondering what had brought this on.

Greg waited until they were safely back in traffic. "You're having an affair," he said — a statement of fact, not conjecture.

253

Shocked horror flooded Dan's face before he hosed it down and substituted a mask of incredulity. He checked his mirrors, pretending it was business as usual, but Greg wasn't fooled. No one who's passed their driving test pays that much regard to the Highway Code.

"What on earth gives you that idea?" Dan scoffed, feigning bewilderment.

"Your reaction, if nothing else."

Damn! thought Dan; should have gone with a denial.

"Now I get why you didn't want me around. 'Guilt by association.' You're the guilty one!"

So it's out there, Dan thought. As soon as one person knows, it's no longer a secret — especially if that person is Greg. He felt oddly relieved. Living a lie, while thrilling, was also quite tiring.

"How did you find out?" he asked neutrally, and thereby confirming his guilt.

"You little shit! You swore blind nothing happened at the conference."

Dan felt his anger spark. "It wouldn't have! If not for you — whispering in my ear."

Greg stared in disbelief. "You're saying it's my fault?"

"Yes. Yes!" Dan yanked the car to the kerb and stamped on the brakes, forcing the driver behind to swerve and lose her place in the text she was composing. He threw open the door and leapt out. Greg followed suit. They faced off across the roof of the car, like boxers at a weigh-in, kept at arm's length by their cornermen.

254

"It's *all* your fault!" Dan shouted, jabbing an accusing finger in Greg's direction. And it was. If not for Greg, Dan would still be living his unfulfilled existence. A lorry passed uncomfortably close, the trucker unleashing a stream of expletives at the cunt standing in the middle of the road. Dan made for the safety of the kerb, where Greg was waiting for him.

"I've been thrown out of my home. Amanda hates me. My kids are becoming strangers. I'm the victim here!"

"You fucked another woman!"

A passing pensioner, whose sight was failing but whose hearing remained sharp, tutted her disapproval of Dan's language. Greg and Dan didn't even notice her, but, being old, she was used to that.

"No, I didn't," Greg conceded, "fuck her. I couldn't."

Dan was thrown. What was Greg saying? And then he realised. "Jesus! You couldn't get it up?"

"It wasn't that! I couldn't go through with it. When push came to shove — as it were — I couldn't cheat on Amanda."

Dan shook his head in wonder. Talk about male pride. Greg would rather give the impression of cheating than be accused of sentimentality. "You fucking idiot," he said.

Greg felt his anger reignite. To be patronised by Dan! "Me? You're the one having an affair!"

"You think I wanted it to happen? I couldn't help myself. After the first time, I had to see her again. And, after the second, I couldn't stop."

"Just like eating Pringles." Dan could hear the contempt in Greg's voice. "Jesus, Dan! You've seen what's happened to me! What if Sarah were to find out?"

"She won't. We've been very careful not to get caught."

Which planet was Dan living on? "You have been caught!"

Oh, yeah. "How did you rumble us?" Dan asked.

Greg nearly answered, then realised that to do so would land Sarah in it. He cast around for an alternative explanation. "Liz told me."

Dan looked taken aback. "You're seeing Liz?"

"I have done, yeah."

Now who was the hypocrite? Greg had just claimed nothing happened with Liz. Now he'd fessed up that he was still seeing her.

"Not like that!" Greg said, reading Dan's mind. "Not like *you*. As a friend."

It struck Dan that Lynda must have told Liz about their affair. She'd promised not to. But clearly she'd been unable to keep it to herself. She'd wanted to tell her friend about the two of them. Rather than being annoyed, Dan found he was quietly chuffed.

"You won't tell Sarah, will you?" he asked Greg, his mind reverting to thoughts of self-preservation.

"I should. We've become friends."

"No, you haven't."

"How would you know? You haven't been there."

"Well, OK, but not friends like we're friends."

"That's true. She tells me stuff; you don't."

"What kind of stuff?" Dan was genuinely perplexed.

Like your son is gay, Greg thought but managed to stop himself from saying. "She lets me talk about Amanda. She's been very supportive."

Dan could just imagine Sarah providing a shoulder to cry on. She was good like that. He felt another pang of remorse for his betrayal. But not enough to cause him to reconsider.

"I'm not going to lie to her," Greg said.

"You don't have to. Just say nothing."

"We're living under the same roof!"

"Then move out! It's time you did."

"Oh, thanks! First you won't help me; now you want to make me homeless — just so you can carry on seeing your bit on the side!"

Dan didn't like Greg making Lynda sound cheap. "Hey! She's more than that," he said.

Greg saw the defiance in Dan's eyes. "Oh, Christ! Don't tell me you think you two have a future?"

"Would that be so ridiculous?"

"Yes! Yes, it would be. And, if you're even halfway serious, you're a bigger twat than I imagined."

Dan strode up to Greg. For a moment, Greg thought he was going to take a swing at him. But Dan merely poked a finger in his chest. "Word of warning: don't piss off your future boss."

Greg didn't flinch. "Good advice," he said. "You might want to follow it."

Damn, Dan thought, he always gets the last word. Well, we'll see.

Dan rounded the car, narrowly avoiding being side-swiped by another articulated lorry. He and Greg climbed in and resumed their journey to work. No further conversation was exchanged. The battle lines had been drawn.

The first thing Dan did on reaching the office was to phone Lynda. No, that's not right. He checked his emails — old habits die hard. Then he rang Lynda and brought her up to speed. Liz had told Greg about their affair. But this, he reported, was as far as word had spread. The contagion was contained. He'd have to go straight home tonight, to make sure Greg was on side, but he'd see her soon.

Replacing the receiver, Lynda wondered how Liz had rumbled them. They'd been so discreet. Still, she'd find out soon enough because, speak of the devil, here was Liz now, steaming across the office, in a lather about something. What's Brad done this time? Lynda wondered. He and Liz were always having spats, mostly, she suspected, so they could have the make-up sex after. Lynda was the one who suffered most — she had to hear all about it. But that's the price of friendship, she reminded herself.

"Fuck you very much!" Liz was three desks away when she opened up with both barrels. Lynda was completely taken aback. "Brad knows about what happened at the conference!" Liz accused. "You must have blabbed!"

"What? No! I didn't."

"Bitch!"

258

The best form of defence is retaliation. Lynda returned fire. "You told Greg about me and Dan!"

This wrong-footed Liz. She thought she was playing the role of the accuser. "What? What are you talking about?"

"Greg knows Dan and I are having an affair."

"Since when?"

"This morning. He told Dan on the way to work."

"No — since when have you been having an affair?"

"Since the conference. You know that!"

"I didn't. I do now."

"How did you find out?"

"You told me."

"When?"

Liz was confused. "Just now."

Lynda was even more confused.

Grade-A gossip though the disclosure of Lynda and Dan's affair was, it wasn't about Liz. She seized this opportunity to wrench the conversation back. "Brad's called off our wedding."

"What? Because of you and Greg?"

"It's all round the office." The accusation, although implicit, was plain.

"I swear it wasn't me!"

Liz took Lynda's vehement disavowal as confirmation of her guilt. She shot her a look that, could looks kill, would have brought gravediggers running.

"You're no longer my friend," she pronounced. "Or my bridesmaid."

Lynda didn't like to point out that, since the wedding was off, this last sanction seemed redundant.

Liz tipped over the pot of pens Lynda kept on her desk, which was less satisfying than she had hoped it would be. She flounced back across the office, causing heads to turn.

Lynda sat, stunned. She cast her mind back. Could she have spread the gossip? She'd certainly been tempted, but had resisted. But if not her, then who?

"It's not a date!" Amanda declared over the noise of the hairdryer.

"Sounds like a date to me," Geri observed from her position lying on Amanda's bed.

That had been Amanda's initial reaction, too, when Ben had called the surgery that afternoon, ostensibly to tell her that, since he'd sourced an alternative supply of Byron's dog biscuits, the St Bernard had rediscovered his appetite and was his usual rambunctious self. Ben had invited Amanda out for dinner by way of a thank you. No hidden agenda, he'd assured her.

"Well, it's not," Amanda reiterated to Geri, flicking off the dryer and crossing to the wardrobe to choose something to wear that would make her look attractive, yet not make her look available. It was a delicate balance. "It's just two friends, sharing a bite . . . at Neruda's."

"Neruda's?" Geri sat up. "*That's* a date."

OK, so Neruda's wasn't exactly a greasy spoon. The restaurant regularly made the "top ten" lists, which suggested they must be doing something right — their PR if nothing else. Known for its intimate atmosphere, it was a popular choice for special occasions: an anniversary, say, or an engagement, or a first date. But some people simply went for the food, Amanda was fairly sure, and she would be one of them. If Ben had an appetite for something more, he'd go hungry. Good company was all Amanda was bringing to the table.

Still, she wanted to look her best. From her wardrobe she selected a black tube dress, cut low in front, but modestly, so that it hinted at her breasts without screaming, "Hey boys, look at these gazungas!" She doubted the Taliban would approve. But then they were such grouches, those guys.

"What about Greg?" Geri asked.

"No. No, it's just me." In the mirror, Amanda caught sight of her sister's unamused expression. "I'm not thinking about Greg at the moment," she said, insinuating herself into the dress. "Like he didn't think about me."

Geraldine pushed herself off the bed and crossed to Amanda. "So, what? That's it? One casual shag, and ten years together, two kids — *phhhhht* — it's over?"

"It's thirteen years," Amanda corrected her. "But suppose I'd been the one to have a 'casual shag'? Would you disregard it so readily? Would Mum? Would Greg?"

"Well, that would be different." Even as she said it, Geraldine knew she could be had up on a charge of double standards.

"Why?" asked Amanda, giving her sister just enough rope with which to hang herself.

"Because you're not the sort of person to have a casual shag," Geri was pleased with the elegant way she managed to slip her head out of the noose.

"And Greg is?"

Geri realised she'd sidestepped one trap only to put her foot in another.

"No," she said, but she knew her defence sounded hollow. "Well . . . once."

Amanda snorted her disdain and flounced out of the bedroom.

Geraldine dragged herself off the bed and pursued her sister along the landing. "Look, he really regrets it. You should see him. He's a mess! He wouldn't cheat on you a second time."

Halfway down the stairs, Amanda rounded on her. "Well, there's a glowing testimonial! 'Won't cheat twice.'" She checked her watch. "So you'll pick the kids up from clarinet?"

Geraldine raised her chin in a gesture of defiance. "What would you do if I said I can't?"

"Accuse you of lying. You were going to stay the evening anyway."

"Yes. With you! That's before you got asked out on a date."

"It's *not* a date!"

The doorbell rang: Amanda's date. Not that it was.

"I expect I'll be home about ten," she said, turning to leave, but Geraldine was quicker and got to the front door first, throwing herself against it.

"Mand, don't do this. You and Greg can still work things out, but not if you start seeing other men."

Amanda regarded Geraldine blocking her exit. She considered wrestling her out of the way, but her older sister had always won their fights when they were young and, besides, Amanda didn't want to risk mussing her hair. "Don't you think I'm capable of having a male friend without it being about *sex?*" she asked instead. Geraldine was unmoved and unmoving. Amanda persevered, "I know what's appropriate behaviour. I know where the boundaries lie. I'm not Greg. Now, are you going to get out the way, or do I have to use the back door?"

Geraldine had forgotten the other exit.

"Look, I'm not going to do anything stupid," Amanda reassured her. "I just want to have a nice time, that's all."

Geraldine considered her. Her little sister. Of the two of them, Amanda had always been the more sensible. She stepped aside. "You look very nice," she allowed.

Amanda smiled, appreciative of the olive branch and grateful for the compliment. She let herself out of the house.

From the lounge window, Geraldine saw Ben open the passenger door for Amanda. Handsome, she thought. I wouldn't mind a piece of him myself. Amanda hesitated before getting into his car. Was she having second thoughts? Geri wondered.

Amanda wasn't. She was just a little taken aback to find Byron panting on the back seat.

"I didn't know we were a threesome," she said as she greeted Byron, ruffling his fur. "Hello, boy." Byron lifted his head so Amanda could tickle his chest. Typical male, she thought.

Ben slid into the driver's seat of the Range Rover. Relationship counselling must pay well, Amanda thought, but then you'd never run out of clients.

"You don't mind him coming along, do you?" Ben asked. "The neighbours say he howls if I leave him on his own."

"No, it's fine," Amanda replied as Byron panted heavily in her ear. Fine, but just a little weird, she thought.

CHAPTER
THIRTEEN

Sarah was conscious of an atmosphere over dinner. Being good mates, Greg and Dan usually revelled in taking the piss out of each other, but tonight they were all politeness. It was like a Wild West town that was too quiet. Sarah knew they had both applied for the promotion; she ascribed their diffidence to this. The date for interviews was drawing close.

Greg acted no differently around her, but Dan did. He felt self-conscious, aware of Greg's knowing eyes upon them. He overcompensated, was too hearty in his appreciation of Sarah's cooking, too enthusiastic to hear an account of Russell's day. He sounded fake to his own ears. For the first time since the start of his affair with Lynda, Dan felt at risk of giving himself away.

After dinner, while Russell and Greg stacked the dishwasher, Dan suggested to Sarah that they go to the cinema. There was a French film on that he knew she was keen to see. He hadn't a clue what it was about — the title was in French — but most French films were about infidelity, so it was probably that. That could make for uncomfortable viewing, though it was preferable to a night on the sofa, watching TV under Greg's judgemental gaze.

Dan was horrified when Sarah invited Greg to join them. What is this? he thought. *Jules et Jim?*

To Greg's credit, and Dan's relief, he declined. "You need some 'you' time," he told them, his eyes not shifting from Dan.

And you need to move out, Dan thought. He checked the screening times in the *Evening Standard*, then handed the paper to Greg, open at the rental listings. In case Greg failed to get the message, Dan had drawn a circle round them — in red.

Left alone, Greg and Russell settled in to watch the football on TV: England versus Croatia. Or, rather, they had the TV on. Greg, taking the hint, was running his eye over flats to let, while Russell was messing with his phone. The football commentator's voice leapt an octave. Greg looked up, but it was only a corner, nothing to merit such excitement. Still, I suppose they have to whip up the viewers, Greg thought, lest we realise how fundamentally dull football actually is.

He picked up his phone and dialled home. He was breaking Amanda's embargo, but wanted to let her know that he was flat hunting. Hopefully it might persuade her to allow him back.

"Hello?"

Greg experienced a little flutter of excitement on hearing Amanda's voice. As if sensing this, the football commentator's rose in pitch. Another corner. Greg muted the TV.

"Amanda!"

"Greg, it's Geri. Sorry to disappoint. Again."

"Is everything all right?" His first thought was of the girls.

"Fine. I'm babysitting."

"Where's Amanda?"

There was the briefest pause before Geraldine answered. "Out with some mums from school."

"Oh." Fair enough, he thought; I wonder what she'll tell them about us. "I thought she ought to know that I'm looking for a flat to rent."

"Right," Geraldine said flatly.

"There's not much on the market, and what there is is expensive," he said, to fill the vacuum.

"I could come and look at some places with you, if you like."

"You think I need to, then?" The poor mobile reception distorted Greg's voice, but could not disguise the anguish in his tone.

"Oh, Greg, I don't know." Geraldine hesitated. It wasn't her business to interfere. On the other hand, didn't he have a right to know? "Look, I don't want to give you false hope. Amanda's not with any school mums. Some bloke asked her out for dinner."

Jesus fuck! thought Greg, and not because England had just conceded a goal.

Byron peered out from the back seat of Ben's car. He checked that his master was still sitting at a window table in a nearby restaurant. Reassured, the dog curled up and went back to sleep.

267

Inside Neruda's, Ben held up a bottle of Merlot. "Another glass of wine," he suggested. "It might help you to relax."

"Don't you think I'm relaxed?" Amanda laughed, trying to be nonchalant but conscious of what a poor attempt she made.

"No," Ben said, though he didn't appear to hold it against her. He filled her glass.

"I'm sorry. I'm not used to this," Amanda conceded.

"If you prefer, I can take you home."

For a moment, Ben was concerned she might accept this insincere offer. For the same length of time, Amanda considered it. And then she drank deep of her wine.

"No. No, really. It's a night out, that's all."

"That's all," Ben agreed, topping up her wine again. "So, where were we?"

"You asked me about Greg."

"Ah, yes." That was why she'd tensed.

"But I don't want to talk about him. Out of sight, out of mind."

Had Amanda had eyes in the back of her head, Greg would not have been out of sight. He was standing just inside the entrance, Russell at his side, waiting to be seated. The teenager had no idea why they were here. They'd already eaten: macaroni cheese. Not his mum's finest culinary effort, a bit stodgy, really, though his dad had been enthusiastic. But at half-time in the footy, Greg had announced that he was still hungry, in need of further sustenance, and had insisted on dragging Russell along for company. In truth, Russell didn't much mind. The game had been boring and, generally, Greg wasn't; Russell considered him the acceptable face of adulthood.

A waitress led them towards the back of the restaurant.

"I'd prefer a table nearer the window," said Greg, spotting Amanda with some bloke who appeared to be hanging on her every word, ready to catch them should they spill. "Over there, perhaps."

"I'm afraid that table's booked, sir."

"Under what name?"

The waitress consulted her list of reservations. "A Mr Fazackerly."

Greg clicked his heels and bowed low like a dragoon of the Austro-Hungarian Empire. "At your service." He treated the waitress to his most charming smile.

Russell was in awe of this consummate bullshitting; Greg rose even higher in his estimation.

"Oh, Mr Fazackerly, I do apologise," the waitress blushed. "I didn't realise."

"No reason why you should," Greg replied magnanimously.

He and Russell took their seats at Mr Fazackerly's table, accepting the proffered menus. These were the size of small billboards. They disappeared behind them.

"Choose anything you'd like, Rusty," Greg boomed.

"I'm not really that hungry," Russell admitted, wondering why Greg was shouting.

"A dessert, then. You must like desserts."

Amanda was unable to concentrate on what Ben was saying. The diner at the next table had one of those voices that carried. Disconcertingly, it also sounded a lot like Greg. She snuck a look across, just as the man lowered his menu.

"Amanda!" Greg rearranged his features into a look of complete surprise. It would not have won him a BAFTA. Or even a nomination.

"What are you doing here?" Amanda asked, somewhere between an enquiry and an accusation.

"What a coincidence! My young friend, Russell, here, had a yearning for a banana split, and I thought to myself, Where does the best banana splits in all of London?"

"Actually, I'm allergic to bananas," Russell put in, but no one seemed to be listening.

Greg was already out of his chair and had crossed the short distance to the neighbouring table. "I'm Greg," he said to Ben, "Amanda's partner, the father of her children." Good-looking bastard, he thought, but mostly bastard.

Ben shot an amused glance Amanda's way. "We were just not talking about you."

"And you would be . . . ?" Greg enquired cordially. A little too cordially.

"Geri!" Amanda said as the penny dropped. "I should have known."

"I didn't quite catch that," Greg said to Ben. He wouldn't have; Ben hadn't said anything.

"Ben."

"*Ben.*" Greg rolled the name around his mouth, like chewing tobacco you'd spit out. He offered Ben his right hand to shake and, when Ben took it, Greg hit him with his left. It wasn't his best punch — it was his weaker side — but it caught Ben unawares and sent him sprawling to the floor, pulling the table down with him.

Amanda leapt to her feet. "Oh, for Christ's sake!" she cried.

It's a tough ask to maintain one's cool, lying on one's back draped in a tablecloth surrounded by spilled cutlery. It was a challenge that was beyond Ben, Greg noted with satisfaction. This, in itself, made his aggression worthwhile. Waiters came running, attracted by the ruckus, as Amanda helped Ben up. Greg readied himself for a counter-attack. Out of the corner of his eye, he was aware of Russell taking a position at his shoulder, feet firmly planted, fists balled. He shot Greg a nod that said, "Got your back, man," and in that moment Greg wanted to hug him.

"What the hell are you playing at?" Amanda snapped at Greg.

"He's trying to get in your knickers!" Greg pointed an accusing finger at Ben, who had regained his feet and was massaging his jaw.

"Oh, like you did hers?" Amanda countered.

"Outside, pal!" Greg challenged Ben, fancying his chances one on one, and knowing he had Russell for backup if things went south. Waiters scurried among the putative combatants, righting and resetting the table.

"Don't like it when the boot's on the other foot, do you?" Amanda glowered at Greg.

Ben decided to take the moral high ground, since it appeared unoccupied. "Come on, Amanda, let's go," he said.

"No!" Amanda stood her ground. "We've done nothing wrong."

The manager arrived, stopping just outside Greg's reach. "I think you had better leave, sir."

Greg fixed Amanda with a glare. "You've got two daughters at home who miss their dad."

Amanda blinked. "Using them, now, are you?" she asked Greg in a quiet voice that was far more menacing than had she shouted. "How low can you go?"

Greg sensed he'd blown it. Never play the children card, he reminded himself too late. Until this moment, he'd thought there was a chance, slim but breathing, that he could win Amanda back. But the contemptuous look in her eyes gave the lie to that. One careless remark, prompted by the sight of another man in his seat, had put paid to hope. Vanity, eh? How many unnecessary wars has that started?

The fight went out of Greg. He turned to his wingman. "Come on, Russell," he said. There was no clinking of cutlery as they beat a tactical retreat to the door. No one was eating; all eyes were on them. Even the kitchen staff had gathered to watch Greg's ignominious exit.

As he and Russell passed Ben's car, Byron went berserk. The St Bernard had seen the dastardly attack on his master and wanted a piece of his assailant. Greg was too preoccupied with beating himself up to notice.

Russell bounced on the balls of his feet, juiced on adrenaline. This had been the most exciting night of his life. He'd been in a fight! OK, not much of one — only one punch was thrown and not by him — but it had felt real enough. It could have really kicked off in there. And he hadn't shrunk from the action. He'd stepped up — like a man.

He stole an admiring glance at Greg, brooding beside him. Russell thought him the coolest dude he knew. He suddenly felt very hungry. Maybe that's the heat of battle, he thought.

"Do you think we could have some ice cream?" he asked.

Greg turned to look at him.

"*Now* you want dessert?" he chided, before breaking into a forlorn grin and tousling Russell's hair.

Russell was so happy he thought he might pee.

The movie was crap, but then most movies were nowadays. Studios no longer seemed interested in making a work of art but merely a profit. Although hadn't that always been their motivation? Perhaps it was just that in the past it had been possible to do both. Dan wondered whether he'd have enjoyed the film more in the company of Lynda.

"What's your favourite movie of all time?" he asked Sarah as they were driving home. They'd had this discussion before, of course, but so long ago that Dan had forgotten Sarah's response.

"Oh, I don't know," she replied now. "*The English Patient?*"

The English Patient! Dreary bollocks. Lynda's was *Legally Blonde*. Dan knew this because he and Lynda had had the same conversation the last time they'd been lying in bed together. *The English Patient* versus *Legally Blonde*. Or, as Russell would say, verse. Dan knew which of the two he'd rather see again. And it didn't star Juliette Binoche, despite her being gorgeous.

Sarah, gazing out of the window, noticed her friend Veronica's house as they passed. It reminded her of Tony's recent visit.

"Tell me," she said, "if you thought the husband of a friend of yours was having an affair, would you tell them? Your friend, I mean."

Jesus Christ! thought Dan, almost driving through a T-junction. Where the fuck has that come from? Had Greg said something after all? The unreliable bastard!

"Or maybe not having an affair," Sarah continued, "but giving the impression he'd like to."

Hang on! thought Dan. Maybe it's not me she's talking about.

"Who do you mean?" he asked, betraying only a little trepidation.

"My friend, Veronica. Her husband called round the other day on some pretext. Made it more than plain that he'd be up for it, if I was."

"Seriously?" asked Dan, taking his eyes off the road for longer than was advisable, but for a way shorter time than actors in movies do.

"I'm not trying to make you jealous." Sarah laughed, placing her hand on Dan's lap. "I just wonder whether I should mention it to Veronica."

274

"No," said Dan categorically. "I'd leave well alone, if I were you. She wouldn't thank you for it."

That's true, thought Sarah. She left her hand in Dan's lap. Although the movie they'd seen had been mindless dreck, there had been a sex scene that was quite well filmed. It had put her in the mood. She gently stroked Dan's thigh.

On two evenings already this week, Dan had made love to Lynda. He'd been thinking how he could do with a good night's rest, a chance to recharge his batteries for the next time they saw each other. But, as Sarah dug her fingernails into his flesh, he felt the familiar stirring. And he gently nudged the accelerator.

Greg and Russell sat in Greg's car outside a late-night Ben & Jerry's ice-cream parlour. Greg had chosen a Clusterfluff on the basis of the name. Russell had gone for a Triple Caramel Chunk.

"Thanks for your help back there," Greg said, harking back to the rumble in the restaurant.

Russell acknowledged Greg's gratitude with a brief nod, playing it cool, one guy to another. Ah bless, thought Greg.

They ate in silence, savouring the ice creams and the camaraderie. A drunk reeled past clutching half a bottle of cheap vodka as if it were his most prized possession, which, it struck Greg, it likely was. A respectable-looking man in his early sixties emerged from a dimly lit doorway that Greg had already determined was either a crack den or a brothel. Or both. The man guiltily glimpsed left and right before merging into the passing crowd. Either a Methodist minister or a bank chief, Greg reasoned. Or both. Two men approached, hand in hand, stopping a short distance ahead to exchange a deep-throated kiss. Greg glanced at Russell, who was pretending not to notice while watching avidly.

"My best friend when I was growing up was gay," Greg said.

If Russell considered this a non sequitur, he gave no indication, perhaps because he didn't know what a non sequitur was.

"Yeah?" Russell feigned disinterest.

"Yeah. Julius Coetzee, his name was." Greg smiled. "Crazy name, crazy guy. His parents came from South Africa." Greg left a subtle gap before adding, as an afterthought, "I often find myself thinking about him."

Greg left the bait dangling. After a few moments, Russell bit.

"Why?"

Greg looked at Russell as though he hadn't been expecting the question. "Because of what happened," he admitted. He paused, thinking back to that period of his life. The innocence of youth — and the cruelty. "I didn't know he was gay at the time. None of us did. At that age, in those days, you didn't admit to it. It was a name you got called by other kids. You know, poof, queer, homo."

"Faggot," Russell offered.

Greg nodded. They watched the gay couple pass the car, unselfconscious, happy, out. Greg bit into his Clusterfluff; not bad at all.

"So how did you find out he was gay?" Russell asked, like they were just making conversation.

Greg considered how much to say, and how to say it. "From his suicide note."

Russell stared at Greg, his eyes wide.

"He took sleeping pills. He survived, just slept for a bloody long time. But here's the thing: he was my best friend. Had been since we were six. Ten years and I didn't know the single most important thing about him. I didn't know him at all." Greg shook his head, still uncomprehending after all these years.

Russell said nothing. The car had assumed the air of a confessional.

"I just can't help thinking how lonely he must have been," Greg continued, "how hard he must have found it. And he hadn't even felt he could tell me — his best friend."

"Did it make you feel differently about him?" Russell asked.

"Did I care that he was gay?" Greg shook his head. "I loved him. Not in that way. What I mean is, no. Not in the slightest. Russ!" Greg jerked his head, drawing Russell's attention to his ice cream, which was melting down his hand. Russell jumped to it, licked the rivulet off his fingers. In that moment, he looked incredibly young.

"He was fine afterwards, but when I think how close he came . . . I just wish he'd felt he could tell someone; it didn't have to be me." Greg paused a moment, before adding, "Anyone your age who thinks they might be gay, I just hope they have someone they can confide in. They shouldn't have to keep it to themselves."

They lapsed into silence again. Greg bit the end off his cone and sucked the ice cream through, like he used to do as a kid. He swallowed the last of the cone and wiped his hands together.

"Greg?" Russell asked tentatively.

"Yes?" Here it comes, thought Greg.

"I've got some ice cream on your upholstery."

Greg turned to Russell, who looked genuinely worried that Greg would be upset. "Don't worry." He shrugged. "I'll be getting a new car in a few weeks." He switched on the engine. "Home?"

Russell nodded. He didn't say anything on the ride home. And Greg wondered whether he'd overdone it, making up that story about his schoolmate.

Ben seemed almost relieved when Amanda declined the dessert menu. They did order coffees. To not do so would have seemed like indecent haste, an acknowledgement that tonight had been a disaster. Neither wanted to grant that victory to Greg. Even after his eviction from the restaurant, he remained present, casting a pall like Banquo's ghost.

Over coffee, with the end of the meal in sight, Ben and Amanda managed to relax. She recounted how a childhood love of animals had drawn her towards veterinary science. And he revealed that he'd been a town planner in a previous life, but an acrimonious divorce had inspired him to become a counsellor, to help others avoid the same pitfalls. Amanda teased him

— was he suggesting that his ineptitude at relationships better qualified him to offer advice? Ben took the ribbing in good part. His eyes creased into that smile of his. Amanda warmed to him. She liked a man who didn't take himself too seriously. It was one of the traits that had first endeared Greg to her.

The waiter brought Ben the bill. This was partly due to centuries of tradition, but mainly because he'd asked for it. Amanda insisted they go Dutch. She was keen to avoid any impression that this was a date. But Ben was obdurate. He had invited her; next time it could be her turn. Amanda considered this. How did she feel about the prospect of seeing him again? Greg wouldn't like it. And that, in itself, was enough for her to agree; she allowed Ben to pay.

Byron was ecstatic to have his master restored to him. Judging by the enthusiastic greeting he gave Amanda, the St Bernard held her responsible for this joyful reunion. Ben drove Amanda home. He pulled into the kerb outside the house and switched off the engine.

The awkward goodbye: Amanda wasn't sure how to play it. She tried out different sentences in her head before settling on a tentative, "I'd invite you in . . ."

"OK." Ben had his door open before Amanda could get to the "but".

"Only we might wake the kids."

Ben pulled closed the door. "Sure," he said. "Some other time."

Notwithstanding Amanda's resolve that this was not a date, that was precisely how it felt. There was an electricity in the Range Rover. Was that inevitable when you had two sexually active adults in a confined space? she wondered. She realised that she should have got out of the car, but she seemed to have missed her moment. And now she couldn't think of an exit line. Ben interpreted her delayed departure as a cue for him to lean in towards her. At first she thought he was reaching for the hand brake but he kept on coming, moving in for a kiss. Would he aim for mouth or cheek? The former, Amanda was fairly sure; she didn't wait to find out.

"Ben —" gently but firmly — "please don't."

"Is it Byron?" he asked.

The St Bernard was resting his head on the back of Amanda's seat. She turned to regard him; his tongue was lolling as he panted heavily.

"Well, he doesn't help," she admitted.

"I could tie him to a tree if you like."

Amanda had an image of Byron suspended from a high branch. "No! No, it's not Byron." She left the rest unsaid, hoping Ben would work it out for himself. Despite his being a relationship counsellor, it still took him a moment. "Just good friends, yeah?" he asked.

"Please."

Ben nodded. He leant in quickly, before Amanda could protest, and landed a peck on her cheek. "Thanks for a lovely evening," he said.

"Was it?" she asked sceptically.

His eyes crinkled. "It had its moments."

That would serve as an exit line. Amanda opened her door.

"I would like to see you again," Ben said.

Amanda caught sight of Geraldine, peeking out from behind the lounge curtains. In the half-light she reminded Amanda of their mother. It's like I'm seventeen again, she thought. It was not an age she had ever considered she would want to revisit. This scene reminded her why.

Liz had every confidence she'd talk Brad round. She always had in the past. Generally, a blow job would suffice. And perhaps it would do the trick this time, if he'd only allow her to go down on him. But her fiancé — ex-fiancé, she reminded herself — was proving to be more than usually intractable, refusing to speak to her, to even acknowledge her, which, given the limited dimensions of their studio flat, was something of an achievement. She'd spent a second solitary night on their double futon, Brad's snores reverberating distantly from the sofa at the other end of the room, like a whaling trawler's mournful horn looming through the fog.

Bloody Lynda! This is all her fault, Liz seethed as she arrived at work, stabbing a finger at the lift like she was accusing it of something. Cow just couldn't keep her trap shut, could she? Well, she'll get hers! Liz had a plan.

Reaching her desk, she booted up her computer. She went straight to the website of Greg and Dan's firm, where a moment's research revealed Dan's surname: Sinclair. Next, a Google image search brought up a photo of Dan at an awards ceremony with his wife,

Sarah. From there it was just a few keystrokes to Facebook, where, after weeding out all the Sarah Sinclairs who were American, or young, or both, Liz found her quarry. Judging by the infrequency of her posts, this Sarah Sinclair was not an inveterate Facebook user. Still — no worries — intermittent was good enough.

Liz smiled to herself and wrote Dan's wife a message:

Hi! You don't know me. I work with Lynda Bates at Buzz Marketing. You might be interested to know that she and your hubsand

Oops. She backspaced to remove her typo. Take your time, she told herself. Revenge is a dish best typed slowly.

"And this is the lounge!"

Even without the estate agent's commentary, Greg thought he would have guessed that. The sofa, coffee table and ginormous TV kind of gave the game away. What exactly did an estate agent bring to the party? he wondered. All they did was state the bleeding obvious. He took in the room. It was difficult to see beyond the television, literally, as it took up most of one wall. At least it distracted attention from the shabby carpet and frayed curtains, which looked like they'd been salvaged from a seedy motel in the American south. A truck rumbled past, intruding on Greg's thoughts, the container it was carrying briefly dousing the light from the street. Greg felt his spirits sink further — something he hadn't thought possible after the two flats he and Geraldine had already visited. This two-bedder was probably the best of the bunch. It was habitable, albeit barely; that, in itself, was an improvement.

Geraldine entered from the hall. She was determined to stay positive. "Molly and Lauren could both fit in the second bedroom. So long as they're in bunks."

Greg was more of a realist. "There wouldn't be room to swing a cat."

"Oh, pets aren't allowed," the estate agent put in.

"One thing in its favour —" Geri persevered — "it's in a popular area."

"You mean the traffic," Greg said glumly.

The agent's mobile rang, barely audible as another articulated lorry lumbered past. "Excuse me," she said, as she left the room in search of a moderately quieter spot.

Greg slumped against a wall. Even on his way to meet Geri at the first of their viewings this lunchtime, he'd been hopeful of a stay of execution. He'd presumed that when Amanda got wind that he was looking for a flat, she'd be straight on the phone to tell him not to bother. He hadn't expected her to forgive him — not yet, anyway — but he thought she might allow him to serve the rest of his sentence at home. Under house arrest. But, although he'd checked his phone every couple of minutes, it had remained resolutely mute. No voicemails, no texts. He'd clutched at the straw that maybe Geri hadn't told Amanda of their mission, but she'd admitted that she had. So

Amanda knew and hadn't intervened. What more evidence did Greg need that they were drifting further apart, towards separation, away from reconciliation?

"Thanks for coming to look with me," he told Geri. He was sincerely grateful. He'd have hated to do this by himself. But he couldn't ask Amanda and he wouldn't ask Dan, so that had left Geri. She'd been on her own for six years now, but, until recently, it had not occurred to Greg how difficult a period that must have been. She didn't have kids to serve as a distraction, a smokescreen behind which she could hide the paucity of her own life. She deserved better. It was ridiculous. So many people were lonely — Greg was about to enlist in their ranks — yet an attractive, outgoing woman like Geraldine couldn't find a man. He stole a sideways glance, appraising her. OK, maybe she could do with losing a couple of kilos, but no more; in your forties, it's a fine line between trim and gaunt. But surely guys weren't so shallow that they couldn't see beyond a little cushioning? A bloke could do a lot worse than Geri, a hell of a lot worse.

She caught him looking at her, and cocked her head quizzically.

"Are you seeing anyone?" he asked, for the sake of something to say.

Geraldine regarded him a moment, perhaps wondering why he was asking. "I was. It fizzled. His wife came back for the rest of her clothes."

Greg nodded like this made perfect sense, though it did anything but. Geraldine didn't volunteer any more details.

"I'm sorry," he said. "You deserve to be happy."

Geraldine searched his face for signs of irony, but couldn't discern any. "So do you," she allowed.

Greg smiled sadly. Right now, he was living in a place that was as far from happy as it was possible to get, and the towns weren't twinned. He made a conscious effort to shift his attitude into a higher gear. He tried to see the flat in a more favourable light than the dull illumination given out by the bare bulb hanging from the ceiling like a suicide. He found his imagination wasn't up to the task.

"Christ! This reminds me of the hovels I lived in as a student," he said.

Geraldine slid on to the floor beside him, careful not to get any mould from the wall on her jacket. "Well, think of the parties you can have. And the landlord shouldn't mind if you trash the place — may not even notice."

Greg couldn't see it. Not the landlord's indifference — you had to think he wasn't house-proud — no, the parties. "I don't know enough people to throw a party. Most of them are Amanda's friends."

"I'd come."

Greg smiled ruefully. "Great. You and me dancing to 'Walking On Sunshine'."

"We could put a slow one on," Geraldine said. She leant her head against Greg's shoulder.

Greg felt his sphincter contract. What the hell was his de facto sister-in-law doing? He'd enquired whether she was dating out of casual curiosity, not personal interest! He should have realised though; in Geri's position, as soon as you got the whiff of an eligible man, you had to jump. It was the same with property. A "des res" got snapped up before it reached the open market. Only dumps like this flat hung around for any length of time. In Geraldine's eyes, he was fair game and she was making her move.

"Oh, shit, Geri! No," Greg stammered, clambering to his feet.

"What?"

"Don't get me wrong, I like you, always have. If I hadn't met Amanda, then maybe things would be different. But . . . I did."

Geri stared at him, doing a very good impersonation of utter disbelief. "You think I'm coming on to you? I was just being a mate!"

Greg gave her a look that suggested they both knew better than that. But apparently Geraldine didn't, and it occurred to Greg that perhaps he had been a little premature in connecting the dots. After all, she'd only suggested they dance to a ballad, not take it next door into the bedroom. But this realisation came too late. Geri was on her feet, brushing down her jacket.

"Fuck this!" she announced. "I've got better ways to waste a lunch hour." She snatched up her bag from the ratty sofa.

Greg went into damage control. "Don't go! Please. We'll pretend it never happened."

"It never did! For Christ's sake, Greg, I'm Amanda's sister."

"My point exactly!"

Geraldine shook her head. "You are such a prat." She swept past him and out of the flat. Greg briefly heard the traffic on the main road before the front door slammed.

A moment later, the estate agent reappeared in the doorway, punching off her mobile. "Sorry about that," she said in a tone that conveyed no sorrow whatsoever. She cast her eyes around the room and asked brightly, "So, what do you think?"

Greg considered this. "That I couldn't fuck things up any more than I do."

He followed Geri's path towards the door.

"I'll mull it over, get back to you."

Bugger, thought the estate agent, resolving never again to allow a phone call from her boyfriend to come between her and closing a deal.

When Amanda suggested a walk to Jess, the labradoodle did not question her motives, but simply burst forth with canine whoops of excitement. Amanda would have maintained that the purpose of the exercise was precisely that — exercise. She was being disingenuous of course. Were that the reason, she could have walked Jess round the local streets or in Wendell Park at the end of their road. But instead she went to the unnecessary bother of driving to Ravenscourt Park, scene of her first encounter with Ben. If by coincidence he happened to be there today walking Byron, all well and good. Their meeting would appear to be by chance, not design. Amanda wanted to apologise again for Greg's boorish behaviour the night before, but casually, so that Ben wouldn't read too much into it — or even anything. She didn't want to validate Greg's suspicion that she and Ben were more than just good friends. They weren't even that yet, she told herself.

School had not yet finished for the day and so the park was relatively quiet. A few joggers loped round, eyeing up the more attractive women pushing buggies. Some were mums, but most were nannies; Polish would literally be the first language of many of the babies. The women gave a wide berth to the down-and-outs huddled over a shared bottle of cider. They steered clear too of the smattering of pensioners, tottering on spindly legs that might snap if they came into even superficial contact with a Maclaren stroller. A typical weekday afternoon in an inner-London park.

Amanda unleashed Jess, who bolted off to sniff a steaming dog turd that a Jack Russell and its socially unconscious owner had recently abandoned. She ambled past the tennis courts towards the ornamental lake, casting glances back to ensure that Jess was not rolling in the excrement, as she was wont to do with sheep shit, Lord alone knew why — Amanda's veterinary training hadn't covered that. As she stood at the edge of the lake, speculating about the domestic arrangements of a group of mallards, two male and one female (did ducks do threesomes?), she felt a nose nudge the back of her knee.

"Byron!" she exclaimed. She knelt down to make a fuss of the St Bernard, who truffled in her pocket in search of treats. Amanda laughed. She'd come empty-handed; Byron eyed her like a father disappointed with his child's school report.

"I'm sorry. Is my dog bothering you?"

Amanda looked up to find an elegant woman in her mid-forties approaching. The woman's refined accent tagged her as English, though her hauteur suggested French.

"Your dog?" Amanda rose to her feet.

"He's usually wary of people he doesn't know."

As she said this, the woman seemed to understand its implication. Her warmth evaporated. She looked Amanda up and down, as though she now recognised her — not personally, but the type she represented.

"Byron," the woman snapped, "heel!" Byron obeyed without hesitation, as Amanda would have done in his position; the woman was quite intimidating.

The woman fixed Amanda with a hostile stare. She seemed on the point of saying something further but instead turned and strode away, Byron at her side not even daring to cast a backward glance of farewell. Amanda was tempted to follow, to ask about the woman's relationship to Byron and, more to the point, Ben. But her frosty demeanour had not encouraged conversation.

Jess gambolled up and sat beside Amanda, watching Byron accompany the woman out of the park. The labradoodle cocked her head at her owner, as if to enquire, "Who was that with Byron?"

"Who, indeed?" Amanda muttered. She resolved to find out.

CHAPTER
FOURTEEN

A long line of empty buses loitered at the school gates, looking like they'd just disgorged participants in a civil-rights march. Of course, they hadn't. Young people today don't protest; if they care enough to want to change the world, they do it by signing online petitions. Which suits those in authority just fine.

The bell rang to signal the end of classes, bringing salvation to pupils and teachers alike. A fire alarm could not have prompted a quicker evacuation. Kids spilled out on to the waiting coaches. A handful acknowledged the driver; most already had their heads buried in their phones, texting mates they'd been speaking to only seconds earlier.

Russell hadn't caught the bus for a couple of days now, preferring to walk. He was still burdened with the knowledge of his mother's affair. He'd decided to pretend he didn't know, but this policy would be untenable were he to catch his mother with her lover. Today though, he had a different reason for seeking to postpone his return home. He wanted to be alone with his thoughts. All day he'd been unable to concentrate on his lessons, turning over in his mind what Greg had said the night before about his childhood friend — the one it turned out was gay.

Russell's classmate, Ruby, fell into step beside him. She was avoiding her ex, Nate, who it was rumoured had been seen pashing Sunita Navaratnam in TK Maxx. "Hi," she said.

Russell barely acknowledged her. But she didn't seem to mind. She was comfortable with silence. It was a rare quality among their generation, and one of the things Russell liked about her.

He resumed his cogitating. Why had Greg told him that story? Did he think Russell was gay? Why would he think that? Russell wasn't gay. Maybe Greg hadn't meant anything by it. Maybe it was just an anecdote — about a kid who tried to top himself because he couldn't come to terms with his sexuality. That gave Russell pause.

What was it Greg had said? He hoped any young person who thought they might be gay had someone they could talk to. Russell shot a glance at Ruby. How would she react were he to confide in her? But confide what? That he wasn't a homosexual?

Ruby became aware of Russell regarding her. She turned to face him. "What?" she asked.

Russell hesitated; then, like a contestant on the celebrity diving show *Splash* — which he'd thought was crap and wouldn't have watched, except he liked Tom Daley — Russell forced himself to the edge of the high board, closed his eyes and jumped . . .

"I'm gay," he said. He exhaled, and felt the weight on his shoulders depart through his mouth. It was out there. He was out there. And, Christ, what a relief it felt!

"Yeah?" asked Ruby, as matter of fact as had he announced he was taking geography as one of his electives next year.

"Yes," he confirmed, surprising himself with his certainty.

"Cool." Ruby shrugged.

Was it as simple as that? Russell couldn't believe it. And, of course, it wasn't.

"No one else knows," he said. "And they mustn't."

Ruby nodded. She understood. There were a handful of girls in her year who claimed to be lesbians. One or two of them might be, but most were suspected of just craving attention. For girls, homosexuality felt like a dress they could try on for size and take back to the store when it no longer fitted or styles changed. For boys it was different. Once you crossed that line, there was no going back. You could be bisexual, of course, but you'd get tagged in the same way. No one ever described Barack Obama as white.

"Do you want to be my boyfriend?" Ruby asked.

Not for the first time in his life, Russell had the feeling that people didn't listen to a word he said.

"It's not like you'd have to do anything," Ruby explained. "But we're friends, anyway. People would leave you alone. And I'd get to say a big 'Fuck you' to Nate."

Russell thought it over. He'd never had a girlfriend before. Ironic that he received his first offer moments after coming out.

292

"OK." He shrugged.

Ruby smiled. She reached out a hand and took Russell's in hers. It felt good — for Russell too. He liked the warmth, the feeling of intimacy. They walked home in a companionable silence.

It had not required much detective work for Amanda to ascertain where Ben lived. En route to collect the girls from school, she'd swung by the surgery and checked Byron's records. It was unethical, of course — client confidentiality and all that — but then Amanda wasn't sure such protection extended to dogs.

Now she was stationed in a leafy street in Hampstead, a discreet distance from the target address. Number fifty-seven was a large Victorian villa. Amanda doubted you'd get change from two million quid at today's prices. Ben's Range Rover sat on the gravel drive, looking suitably inappropriate in this suburban setting. So this was indeed his house. But who did he share it with? Byron, fo shizzle, as the girls would say. But what about the mystery woman who had claimed to be his owner? Was there an innocent explanation? Perhaps she was Ben's ex-wife, and had visitation rights. Unlikely. Ben had got divorced ten years ago; a St Bernard's gestation period is nine weeks; Byron was six — the maths didn't add up. Ben's dog-walker then? Except she'd been immaculately dressed. Still, this was Hampstead. Or maybe she was a patient. Yes! Some delusional woman whose relationship had failed, who had sought counselling and fallen in love with her therapist. Even now, Ben might be a prisoner in his own home, trussed up while some nutter acted out her fantasy that she and Ben were married. It must happen all the time.

"Can we go home yet?" asked Molly.

Amanda had momentarily forgotten that her daughters were in the back, unwitting and unwilling accomplices in this stake-out. She'd tried to bribe them with chocolate and comics, but their patience was wearing thin.

As Amanda was trying to concoct another excuse to buy a few more minutes of the girls' cooperation, the door to Ben's house opened. Amanda tensed.

"I'm hungry!" Lauren whined. Without looking, Amanda tossed a packet of crisps into the back. It hit Lauren in the face, but she didn't complain; she was too busy shielding the packet from Molly.

Amanda watched as Ben and Byron emerged from their home, followed a moment later by the woman. She climbed into the front of the Range Rover while Ben let Byron into the back, then took the driver's seat. Amanda peered closely as Ben leant across to kiss the woman. She didn't seem to welcome the attention, but nor did she object.

There was no further denying it: the two were an item. Ben had given Amanda the impression he was on his own. He'd lied — about how much she couldn't say. Perhaps his whole life was a fabrication. His business card looked real, but it was simple enough to get some printed. Easy too to pose as a relationship counsellor. Any fool could do that; Amanda's mother, Margaret, considered herself an expert.

Amanda thought back to her encounter in the park — how Byron had greeted her; the look of surprise on the woman's face, rapidly replaced by dawning recognition. Ben's wife — girlfriend, whatever she was — she'd been in this situation before, of encountering someone she assumed to be his lover. Amanda felt almost sick. Ben had duped her, spun her a line about wanting to be friends, all the while hoping to add her to his tally of conquests. Greg had been right about him. What an arse-hole! Ben, that is — not Greg. On this occasion.

The Range Rover backed out of the drive. Rather than heading up the hill towards Hampstead Village, as Amanda had expected, the car was facing her and any moment would pass within inches. She panicked, ducked under the steering wheel and huddled in the footwell of the Golf. She heard the Range Rover's four-litre engine surge past and fade into the distance, but she stayed put, curled in the foetal position; it made her feel secure. And then she became aware of two small faces peering down at her from between the front-seat headrests.

"What are you doing?" Molly asked.

Amanda thought about it. "Playing hide and seek," she said.

"Not very well," Lauren pointed out.

Amanda saw herself as her children did, squashed under the dashboard of her car while stalking her suitor. The nutter wasn't the woman with Ben, she realised. It was her.

"Let's go home," she told the girls while she tried to extricate herself from her hiding place. Getting out proved to be a lot trickier than getting in. She opened the door and managed to decant herself into the gutter. Excellent, she thought. Abject humiliation. How fitting.

Greg was locking his car as Dan pulled into the drive. Their Cold War chill persisted; they'd avoided each other at work, sitting apart in the one meeting they'd both attended. Greg checked his watch: 6.18p.m. Dan hadn't been round to Lynda's then; he'd come straight home. Perhaps he'd also come to his senses. Greg waited for him to catch up.

"Not working late?" he asked, failing in his attempt to sound casual.

Dan regarded him coolly, checked around to ensure no one else was within hearing. "She has yoga. I'll see her tomorrow."

A Pilgrim Father could not have looked more disapproving than Greg. His censure was not lost on Dan.

"How's your flat hunt coming?" Dan asked as he let them into the house.

"Slowly," Greg admitted. He hoped Dan might tell him there was no rush.

"Well, speed it up, will you?" Dan said.

So much for that hope then.

They entered the kitchen. Sarah was sitting stock still at the table. In front of her was the laptop. Greg had the impression she'd been like this for some time. He noticed there was no evidence of an evening meal on the go.

"Russell home?" Dan asked, oblivious to his wife's abnormal demeanour.

"No."

Still Sarah didn't move. Something was definitely up. Greg shot a glance at Dan. He too seemed to have noticed her spectral calm.

"Is everything all right?" Dan asked.

In response Sarah turned the laptop round, inviting them to take a look.

Dan and Greg leant in. The screen showed Sarah's Facebook feed. It wasn't immediately obvious why. The page featured posts Sarah's "friends" had left, the usual blend of narcissism, sentimentality and weak humour. Greg saw it a moment after Dan: a small pop-up box featuring a message from Liz Henderson.

> Hi! You don't know me. I work with Lynda Bates at Buzz Marketing. You might be interested to know that she and your husband are having an affair. It started at Infotech 2014 at the Graveney Hotel in Birmingham. It's still going on.

Dan was the first to react.

"Jesus Christ!"

Sarah said nothing.

"But it's not true!" Dan spluttered.

Finally Sarah turned to face him. "She names the conference you were at — the hotel even."

"Yes, but . . . it's a lie!"

Having found her voice, Sarah gave full rein to it. "This explains everything," she said, rising to her feet. "The late hours . . ."

"I've been working!"

"The new clothes . . ."

"My job interview!"

"The sex . . ."

Ah. Dan didn't have an immediate reply to that. But Greg did.

"I think I can explain, Sarah."

"You can?" Dan's voice betrayed a trace of desperation; his eyes admitted to far more. But Sarah didn't see; she was looking at Greg.

"I owe you an apology," Greg told her calmly. "I haven't been completely honest with you."

Dan held his breath. Where was Greg going with this?

"I should have told you from the start what really happened at the conference."

Dan felt the blood drain from his face. "Greg, mate —"

"Let me, Dan." Greg silenced Dan with a look, turned his attention back to Sarah. "I told you I'd met someone in the hotel bar, flirted a bit. What I didn't tell you was that we had sex that night. And we've been having an affair ever since."

"*What?*" This from Dan; Sarah listened impassively.

"It was meant to be just a bit of fun, a one-off. After that first night I never intended to see her again. And I didn't want her contacting me. So I used a false name, the first one that came to mind."

"Mine," Dan said in wonder, as he cottoned on to the yarn Greg was spinning. He hoped that Sarah could not hear the voice in his head that was screaming, "Go, Greg, Go!" He ventured a glance her way, but her eyes were riveted on Greg.

"We were all wearing name badges," Greg explained to Sarah, "on our jackets, which we'd removed earlier in the evening. When things started getting messy in the bar, Dan decided to take himself off to bed. He picked up his jacket but dislodged his badge." Greg turned to Dan. "I noticed it on the floor after you'd left. I'd already led Lynda to believe my name was Dan. Wearing your badge she'd never suspect it wasn't. So I switched mine for yours. As far as she knew, she left the bar that night with Dan Sinclair."

"That's why I couldn't find my badge the next morning!" Dan exclaimed. "I searched high and low for that. Had to ask the registration desk for a new one!"

Settle, Greg's eyes cautioned; let's not overcook it. He resumed the narrative before Dan could.

"I didn't think I'd see her again. But then Amanda kicked me out and I realised I wanted to. Except, of course, I couldn't fess up to my deception. She might not have taken it well."

"I'm sure she wouldn't," Dan put in, indignantly.

Shut up, Greg silently yelled at him. "So I've continued being Dan Sinclair." Greg nodded to the laptop. "That poison pen post is correct; this —" Greg leant in again to check the supposedly unfamiliar name — "Liz Henderson has just got the wrong guy."

Greg had finished. Dan felt like giving him a standing ovation, but restrained himself. Instead, like Greg, he awaited Sarah's verdict. His future hung in the balance. He felt like a contestant forced to sing-off on a TV talent show. The votes were in; would he survive?

Sarah read the Facebook message once more — unnecessarily, since the words were seared into her memory. She turned to look at Greg.

"So all the while you've been saying you want to get back with Amanda, you've been carrying on with this Lynda woman?"

Greg hung his head in shame. "I'm sorry, Sarah. I'll go and pack my bags." He turned and walked out of the kitchen.

An image sprang to Dan's mind of Captain Oates leaving his tent during Scott's ill-fated expedition to the South Pole.

Howard, the receptionist at the Clifton Motor Inn, had lost twenty pounds on online poker and was contemplating risking another ten when he heard the entrance doors swoosh apart. He looked up to see a familiar face. The name escaped him though.

"Mr . . ."

"Beavis," Greg completed for him. "Just the one night."

"Of course." Howard reached for a registration form. He smoothed out its creased edge before sliding it across the counter for Greg to fill out. How satisfying it felt. "As a repeat guest, you qualify for our 5 per cent loyalty discount."

Greg paused in his writing. "I've been needing some good news, Howard," he told him, "but, frankly, that isn't it." Greg resumed filling in his details, only hesitating briefly when he reached home address.

Howard smiled to himself. It was good to have him back. Just like old times.

When Greg arrived at work the next morning, he placed two calls. The first was to an estate agent.

"You showed me a flat yesterday — on Askew Road."

"The one you described as foul, fetid and flea ridden?"

"I'll take it."

The second was to Liz.

"Liz Henderson!" a perky voice announced.

"It's Greg. Why on earth did you tell Dan's wife about his affair with your colleague, Lynda?"

There was a pause at the other end of the line.

Oh shit, thought Greg; I've got the wrong Liz Henderson. Again. But, on this occasion, he hadn't.

"Because the bitch told the whole office about me and you!"

"Lynda did?" Greg was sceptical; that didn't fit with Dan's description of her.

"How else would word have got around?"

Liz had a point. Who else knew about him and her? The two of them, of course, but Liz certainly hadn't told anyone. And nor had Greg.

Oh, hang on. Greg remembered his abortive phone call to the other Liz Henderson. "Erm, it's possible I might have had something to do with that . . ." he confessed.

Since travelling in the United States the year before, Ruby's mum, Veronica, had got (or rather gotten) into the habit of stopping on the way to school to pick up a skinny latte from Starbucks. Driving with a takeaway coffee in hand made her feel sophisticated and cosmopolitan, a little like a Kardashian, though sophisticated and Kardashian were two words rarely found in each other's company.

She took a sip of her latte now, as, with one hand, she expertly steered her BMW SUV into the kerb. Her younger daughter leapt out before Veronica had applied the handbrake. Eager to join her friends, Veronica thought, or fearful that they're plotting against her. It could go either way with twelve-year-old girls.

"I'll pick you up after school," Veronica announced, as Ruby, her elder child, climbed out of the car with studied casualness.

"No need," Ruby replied. "I'll walk home with my boyfriend."

This was news to Veronica. She'd thought it was over between Ruby and Nate. "Your boyfriend?" Her surprise was muffled by the sound of the closing door, but not enough that Ruby didn't hear the question. She ignored it anyway.

God forbid that they're back together, thought Veronica. In her view Nate was the main reason Ruby's school had slipped down the rankings. It wasn't dyslexia or dyspraxia or any of those other -*xias* that only seem to afflict the well off; the boy was just thick. Veronica had once caught him in Ruby's room with a compass, the sort used for drawing circles. She'd been surprised and, frankly, impressed. Nate revising maths? It seemed unlikely. And it was. He was using the compass needle to carve "Ruby forever" into his forearm. A week later, while the scabs of this self-inflicted tattoo were still livid, he'd dumped her.

But there was Nate over there, with his tongue probing the tonsils of Sunita Navaratnam. So where was Ruby? Ah, standing talking to Russell, the son of Veronica's friend, Sarah.

Veronica raised her latte to her lips, then watched as Ruby slipped her palm into Russell's and walked hand in hand with him into the school. Veronica's jaw fell open in horror. Her cup missed her mouth, spilling coffee down her chin and on to her Hermes silk blouse.

"Fuckity fuck!" she cried.

Her daughter's new boyfriend was Russell Sinclair. The bondage fetishist!

Lynda looked up from her desk to find Liz holding out a coffee to her.

"A peace offering," Liz declared. "I know you didn't spread the gossip about me and Greg."

Lynda regarded her. She considered making Liz suffer, but she missed having her as a friend. Besides, the coffee was from the deli, not the machine. Liz must be really feeling guilty.

"You're forgiven," Lynda said, reaching for the cup.

Liz pulled a face. "You haven't heard what I did yet."

At which point Lynda's phone rang. Dan. Liz sat, squirming, as Dan told Lynda about Liz's Facebook message to Sarah. Lynda's eyes grew wide, then wider still, and Liz increasingly uncomfortable. But no harm done. Greg's heroic sacrifice meant that Sarah was none the wiser and Dan and Lynda were in the clear. And, as a result, Liz too.

Liz reinstated Lynda as her bridesmaid. Even though, technically, the wedding was still off.

The erstwhile friends were pals once more. If only nations could settle their differences as easily, then it would indeed all have been over by Christmas.

Greg had never considered himself a traditionalist but he missed the days when estate agencies were named after their founders. Renfrew and Bagshaw — you knew where you were with them. But this mob . . . Blancmange? What the fuck did that mean?

He was roused from his reverie by the sound of the estate agent replacing her phone. "So, have you had a chance to look over the lease?" she asked, turning her attention his way.

In the twenty minutes I was waiting for you to finish your call? Greg was tempted to say. "Yes, I have," he instead replied. He'd had the time but not the inclination. Who ever actually reads one of these things? he wondered; not even the lawyers who draft them. Greg had not progressed as far as the small print. He'd got no further than the headlines: the length of the lease — six months, and the rent — five hundred pounds a week. No way I'm going to be able to afford that, he thought. Unless I get a promotion . . .

"If you just sign here." The agent pointed a manicured finger at the bottom of the third page. She offered Greg a Blancmange biro. He wondered whether he'd be allowed to keep it.

Five hundred pounds a week for six months: that was thirteen thousand pounds — one hell of a fine for a crime he didn't commit. He'd happily shell out that amount if it meant he could have his old life back. But that wasn't what was on offer. It was a thirteen-grand fine and life in exile. He stalled putting ballpoint to paper. Perhaps he should phone Amanda one more time, beg her to reconsider. But they hadn't spoken since Greg had lamped Ben. He suspected that his best hope of winning her back now was to give the impression he'd accepted his fate. He signed on the dotted line.

"And here," the estate agent said. "And here." Each flourish of the pen felt like another nail in Greg's coffin.

"Congratulations!" trilled the agent, though Greg wasn't sure who this sentiment was directed at. Herself, probably, for shifting another piece of overpriced real estate. "And here are your keys." She pushed a key ring across the desk, a fried-egg-shaped piece of plastic emblazoned with the word "Blancmange". So it wasn't just a free pen then; this deal was looking increasingly attractive. Greg felt the weight of the keys in his hand. Home sweet home, he thought morosely.

He stepped on to the street and contemplated his next move. Buy something to sleep on, he supposed. His spirits sagged like a poorly sprung mattress as he realised he'd have to furnish the whole flat. Not that it would take long; it wasn't large. But the emotional effort . . . He thought back to past IKEA trips with Amanda. When they'd first moved in together, they'd spent a joyful afternoon choosing all kinds of cheap shit with which to line their nest: a foam sofa bed — a steal, being two items of furniture for less than the price of one; plastic kitchen chairs that had shouted "hip" in store but "crap" once they got them home; a framed print of New York construction workers taking their lunch on the girders of a half-completed skyscraper in the pre-Health-and-Safety era. In the run up to the birth of Molly, Greg and Amanda had made the journey out to Wembley again. Although the reason for their visit had been even more joyous, they were less festive, already too tired, in training for the exhaustion a baby brings. They'd chosen a cot, which had taken Greg days to assemble, introducing part A to part B in the quaintly translated diction of the instruction manual; more plastic, this time storage buckets for the Sylvanian Families their child would inevitably collect; and, optimistically, given that their foetus had not yet entered the story, a blackboard and easel to encourage the artistic talents they were certain their offspring would exhibit. And now Greg would be making the trek north once more, but this time alone, for the bare essentials of a mid-life bachelor existence.

He couldn't face it.

"Looks like I'll be staying one more night," he announced to Howard as he checked back into the Clifton Motor Inn, giving each of them a sense of déjà vu.

"You know you're always welcome," Howard said.

Greg suspected him of irony, but the receptionist looked sincere. And indeed was. Howard felt for Greg the way one does for friends.

"Thanks, Howard," Greg said.

The receptionist smiled shyly.

Greg's mobile rang. Geraldine. Probably calling to give him another earful about misinterpreting her intentions the previous day.

"Geraldine, hi. Look, I'm really sorry about yesterday —"

"That's not why I'm ringing."

"It's not?"

"No. Though, since we're on the subject, you were a complete knob. Thinking that I was coming on to you! What does that say about me? That I'll jump at the first passing man that might be available?" She paused. "Well, OK, I might, but not if he's my sister's bloke. And what does it say about you, Greg? That you think you're God's gift to women? Were you ever? Cos, I'll tell you this, pushing forty with an inflated opinion of yourself won't attract many bids on eBay."

Greg waited till she'd blown herself out. He had to; he'd only provoke her otherwise. When he was satisfied she'd finished and wasn't just getting her breath back for a second salvo, he gently enquired, "So what were you calling about?"

"Oh, yeah, I forgot."

"My fault," Greg put in, before Geri could.

"Yes," she agreed. "So here's the thing: that date that Amanda went on?"

"With *Ben*," Greg said bitterly.

"Five'll get you ten there's no repeat performance."

Greg hesitated. "I've never understood betting. Does that mean you think she will see him again or not?"

"Not, you knob!" Clearly this was Geraldine's word of the day. "She wouldn't say why, but she thinks he's a complete tosser."

Which was worse, tosser or knob? It didn't matter; either way, it was great news.

"I got the impression she'd like to have punched him herself," Geraldine continued. "So kudos to you that you did."

"Really? You think it might have worked in my favour?"

"I dunno. But in terms of competition, you haven't got any. I thought you'd like to know."

"Geri! If you weren't on the phone, or Amanda's sister, I'd kiss you! Thanks for the heads-up."

"You're welcome," Geri said, punching off her phone, "you bastard," she added to herself. She hoped Greg could win Amanda back. Not just for his sake, or her sister's, but for Geri's, as well. Because, if a couple as sound as Greg and Amanda couldn't make it work, what hope did the likes of her have of ever finding happiness?

So Amanda had flicked Ben! Greg analysed the implications. Having tried the alternative and found it wanting, perhaps Amanda was better disposed to the original? It was a bit of a stretch, but Greg was feeling flexible. There was one way to find out.

As Howard had once noted, Greg lived within walking distance of the hotel. He ran home, pausing at the end of the road to collect his breath, which arrived a few paces behind. It wouldn't do to turn up gasping; it would give the impression he was overly eager. He sauntered along the street, ready, if necessary, to exchange greetings with the other residents. But he saw no one, not even his next-door-but-one neighbour, Mickey, who'd recently witnessed his humiliation. Twice. Perhaps Mickey's absence was a good omen.

Greg rang the doorbell. He heard Jess bark and expected one of his daughters to come running. But it was Amanda who opened the door.

"Hi," Greg said, making as much fuss of Jess as the labradoodle did of him. "I apologise for turning up unannounced."

It was breaking their unspoken agreement, but Amanda overlooked it. "The girls aren't here. Geraldine insisted on taking them out."

Geri must have had the girls with her when she'd rung. She'd known Greg would be straight round to Amanda; she was giving him a free run. Good old Geri, he thought. If it weren't for the fact he was in love with her sister . . . but best not go there again.

"It was you I wanted to see. I came to say sorry."

Amanda shrugged. "I doubt I'll be seeing him again."

"Not about *Ben*. My only regret there is using my left hand."

Amanda considered this. "You could have dropped a knee as well."

Good, so Geri was right: Ben no longer featured. The coast was clear. Greg sensed this was his opportunity. He'd thought the game was over, the final whistle blown, but there were still a couple of minutes of added time to be played — enough for one last-ditch assault. This was it. Leave nothing in reserve! Greg called every player into the opposition penalty area, goalie included. He took a deep breath. And hoofed the ball upfield.

"I want to tell you the truth," he said.

"I thought you had. Twice, at least."

"The true truth."

Amanda considered this request. Evincing no confidence that it would make a blind bit of difference, she stood aside to let Greg in. Might as well hear what he had to say.

Greg was unsure whether he was expected to go through to the kitchen or the lounge. Neither, it turned out. Amanda stood in the hall, arms crossed against her chest, waiting to see what airbrushed version of history he was peddling today.

"The truth is we went to *my* room. She came inside. Even in the bar, when I was just thinking about it, I was guilty of betrayal. By the time she was in my room, I was way over the line. I disrespected you, Amanda, and I am truly sorry. It was unforgivable." Greg paused. "That said, if you could see your way to forgiving me, then I promise I will never let you down again. I will

310

never seek to deceive you. I will never tell you another lie."

"Then, once and for all, did you have sex with that woman?"

Famously, when President Bill Clinton was asked that question, he had marched, head held high, through the green channel: Nothing To Declare. Back then, apparently, a blow job didn't count. Well, ever since Bill's denial, it had. But Liz and Greg hadn't even gone that far. They'd fondled, or, more accurately, fumbled. Third base, but no home run. Considered gynaecologically, Greg had not had sex with that woman. But wasn't this to split pubic hairs? They'd been about as intimate as two people could be without an exchange of bodily fluids.

Amanda was waiting for his answer. And Greg knew that there was only one she would accept. But he had just promised to be honest. So what should he do? Tell her the truth? Or lie?

Or find a form of words that would serve?

"I cheated on you, yes." Greg braced for the slap, but none was forthcoming.

Amanda sighed. "Finally," she said with what sounded like relief.

Greg felt in his pocket for the Blancmange key ring. "I'm moving into a flat," he said. "Askew Road. You'd be very welcome, if you're ever passing. There's a second bedroom for the girls." He detached the spare set of keys from the ring. "I don't suppose you'd consider holding these for me, would you? I'd leave them with one of my neighbours but, well, this is London — I doubt we'll ever meet."

"Of course." Amanda accepted the keys.

Greg felt like it should be her line next, but it seemed they were working from different scripts, because Amanda offered nothing. Greg broke the silence.

"I've got an interview tomorrow," he said. "Regional Sales Manager. Dan's going for it too. And the woman who's already doing that job in Manchester." It felt good to be talking with Amanda about normal stuff again, even if it were a soliloquy. "Before all this, I'd have felt confident of getting it. I'm less sure now. But I'm going to give it my best shot."

"I'll keep my fingers crossed for you," Amanda said. And then she felt churlish, for not being more effusive. Because she hoped Greg got the job. She had a vested interest, of course; it was bound to involve a pay rise. But, more than that, he deserved it. "I'll be thinking of you," she added.

It was as though she had pulled ajar a door, revealing a glimpse of light within, not the darkness Greg had feared. He could have wept.

"Thank you," he said. He didn't add how much her support meant to him. He didn't feel it necessary; she'd surely know.

His eyes held hers. He hoped she could read the message written in them. "I love you," it whispered.

The moment was building to something, Greg felt certain. Amanda seemed to sense it too. That would explain why she appeared uncomfortable, as though slightly fearful.

And then a phone started ringing. That's the trouble with technology — no sensitivity.

"I should get that," Amanda said.

Was it Greg's imagination? Wishful thinking perhaps? Amanda seemed reluctant to break away. But the phone refused to shut up, crying out for attention.

"Sure." He pulled open the front door.

"Greg?" He turned back. "Thanks for telling me the truth."

He nodded and left.

Amanda answered the insistent phone.

"Hello?"

"Amanda? This is Sarah, Dan Sinclair's wife. I was wondering whether you might be free for coffee tomorrow? A chance for us to catch up."

CHAPTER
FIFTEEN

Greg resolved to dedicate that evening to preparing for his job interview. He'd have ordered dinner in his room, had the Clifton Motor Inn offered that service, but since their catering facilities extended no further than a vending machine in the corridor, and that was broken, he'd had to make do with a takeaway pizza. This he ate lying on his bed in his underwear, while watching *Tattoo Nightmares*, a magnificently trashy reality show in which redneck Americans sought to have unsightly inkings concealed under more aesthetically pleasing body art. It was compelling — addictive even. In the episode Greg was watching, a gnarly-looking biker in his sixties, who you'd guess would still be handy in a fight, wanted shot of a pair of enormous breasts stencilled on his right bicep. He considered them inappropriate for a grandfather. The tattooist was endeavouring to incorporate the magnificent mammaries into a Hawaiian sunset. Greg did not rate his chances.

Greg licked the last of the pepperoni pizza off his fingers. He'd just watch to the end of the show, finish his beer then work on his strategy for the next day. If he got the job — strike that; *when* he got the job — he'd have five sales reps under his command, including Dan.

To impress the interview board he needed to research their markets, pinpoint the weaknesses, identify the opportunities. He also needed to build a case justifying his own poor performance this quarter. A couple of hours homework and he'd be sweet.

That was the scheme, but, as has been noted somewhere before, the best laid schemes o' mice an' men gang aft agley. The tattoo removal was a triumph, the Hawaiian sunset with which it was replaced a work of art, the blubbering delight of the old dude moving to behold. Even though he was alone, Greg was embarrassed to feel a tear spike his eye. Perhaps he was allergic to the dust in the room. Or maybe he was just feeling soft, the emotional turmoil of the last couple of weeks catching up on him.

The credits rolled and *Tattoo Nightmares* ended. But then another episode began. It was a marathon. Oh, praise to the crappy cable station that thought nothing of basing a whole night's programming on one show! Greg uncapped another beer and settled in for the duration.

He awoke around dawn, roused from a drunken stupor by the clinking of empty bottles as he rolled over in bed. He'd downed the whole six-pack. He found himself lying on the pizza carton, a piece of crust that he hadn't consumed the night before adhering to his stomach. He ate it now. Not for the first time, Greg marvelled at the way pizza, great when served hot, tasted even better the morning after. Like revenge, it was a dish best served cold. He squinted at his watch. Five a.m. He could get up and cram for his interview or set the bedside alarm and crash till seven thirty. No contest.

At nine twenty-five, Greg was sitting outside the conference room, waiting to be called. He chugged a couple of Nurofen Plus. A couple more that is; he'd already taken two. Double the recommended dose, but what the hell? If he didn't get this job, perhaps he'd swallow the rest of the packet and have done with it. He felt like shit, but at least he looked the part, thanks to the Corby trouser press that, along with the Gideons' Bible, was a staple in every room of the Clifton Motor Inn.

The door to the conference room opened and Paula Stratton emerged, thanking the interview board for their time. She was wearing a tight, flame-red skirt and matching jacket. It was a good look, sexy but businesslike, a combination of "fuck me" and "fuck with me at your peril". Greg could just imagine the reaction of the male-dominated board: horny. Paula shimmied on her stiletto heels over to Greg.

"Morning, Paula," he said. "You're looking good."

"Well, I can't say the same for you. You look like crap."

"But immaculately turned out, I'm sure you'll agree."

Paula sniffed, as though even that were open to debate.

"So how did it go in there?" Greg asked, keen to shift the conversation from his appearance.

"Very well," Paula confided confidently. "I could tell they were impressed with my presentation."

316

"You prepared a presentation?"

"You mean you haven't?"

Greg didn't like to admit that he'd planned to, but had instead watched eight episodes of *Tattoo Nightmares*. He tapped his forehead. "All the information I need's up here."

"Well, you're a better man than me, Gunga Din, if you can remember quarterly sales breakdowns for all five territories."

Greg, who was already pale, blanched.

"I see your own figures have tailed off recently," Paula continued. "I hope you don't mind, I felt it my duty to point that out to the board. I've got some ideas about how it might be addressed. We'll discuss them sometime."

You had to hand it to Strap-On, Greg thought, she had balls. He'd hate to work under her.

A receptionist took a brief phone call, then addressed Greg. "They'll see you now," she said as she replaced the phone. Just like on *The Apprentice*.

Greg rose, smoothed down his jacket pockets. "Wish me luck," he said to Paula.

She cocked an eyebrow instead. "May the best woman win," she said. "Oh, by the way," she added, as Greg started for the conference room, "they asked me who I'd give the job to if I wasn't in the running. I said you, Greg."

He nodded. "Thanks." He understood that she was looking for a quid pro quo, but he wasn't ready to give it; he'd wait and see if he got asked the same question first.

317

He entered the conference room and closed the door.

Amanda and Sarah met in Notting Hill, at an achingly hip café favoured by celebrities when they were playing at being ordinary. Amanda thought she recognised a moderately successful actress sitting in the corner. The woman was hiding behind a large pair of dark glasses, just in case anyone should fail to notice her.

"There's a free table," Sarah indicated, after they'd ordered coffees at the counter — and cake; they'd decided to treat themselves. But, being modern women programmed to feel shame if they weren't trying to lose weight, just the one slice, to share.

Sarah led the way across the room. On the phone she'd been evasive about the purpose of this meeting. But Amanda sensed it wasn't purely social. There was a point to it, though how long it would take Sarah to get there, Amanda had no idea.

"Thanks for putting Greg up," she said, for the sake of something to say. "And for putting up with him."

"It was about Greg I wanted to see you."

Ah, that didn't take long at all, Amanda thought, as she settled on to an ergonomically designed, yet uncomfortable, stool.

Sarah pulled her phone out of her bag. "I think you ought to see this," she declared. "A message I was sent on Facebook, from a woman I don't know." She handed Amanda her phone.

Amanda read through the post Liz had left, alleging Dan's affair with Lynda. She read through it a second

318

time, unable quite to believe what she was seeing. And nonplussed as to why Sarah would share it with her.

"Jesus!" Amanda said, "Dan?"

"It seems a little out of character, doesn't it?"

In more ways than one. From the little Amanda knew of Dan, mostly based on what Greg had told her, he seemed to have too many ethics and not enough balls to cheat on his wife.

"He denies it, of course," Sarah continued. "And, as it turns out, it's a misunderstanding, a case of mistaken identity. Apparently, the man this woman thought was Dan . . . is actually Greg."

Amanda was so stunned she didn't at first notice the waitress, standing at their table, looking to set down their order. "Sorry," she said to the girl, making room. While the waitress unloaded her tray, Amanda tried to marshal her thoughts.

"Will there be anything else?" the waitress asked.

"A second fork," Sarah said. The girl withdrew in search of cutlery.

"Is that what Dan told you?" Amanda turned her attention back to Sarah. "That it's not him, but Greg."

"It's what Greg told me," Sarah replied, watching Amanda for her reaction. "He made a full confession."

The return of the waitress gave Amanda another much-needed moment to regain her balance.

"An affair?" she finally said. "He swore blind it was a one-off. I believed him."

Sarah was already tucking into the cake. "I think he's lying," she said. "Not to you — about having an affair."

Amanda was bemused. "Why would he do that?"

"To save his mate's skin. He gave me some story about switching his name tag with Dan's. Just far-fetched enough to be plausible. I might even have believed it, had Dan not been so eager that I should."

Amanda glanced at the Facebook message again, then back at Sarah. "So you think they both cheated?"

"That's my guess. Greg had a one-night stand. And Dan has been having an affair. Still is, I would imagine." A slight tightness at the corner of her mouth betrayed the pain this admission caused her.

"Sarah, I am so sorry." Amanda leant forward to grasp Sarah's hand, but she withdrew it out of reach, spearing a chunk of cake with her fork.

"Umm, this really is very good," she said. "Do have some or I'll scoff the lot and hate myself for it."

Amanda took up her fork. She was staggered by the other woman's apparent indifference to her husband's adultery — until it struck her that it was merely a front, a mask to hide her true feelings, a coping mechanism.

"This will all be Greg's fault," Amanda offered as a sop. "You can bet he was the ring leader."

"Yes," Sarah agreed. "I doubt Dan would have had the nerve on his own."

Amanda stiffened slightly. Although she'd delivered Greg up as a scapegoat, she hadn't expected Sarah to be quite so willing to accept his sacrifice. "Still," she said, surprised to find herself appearing as a witness in Greg's defence, "Greg can't be blamed for Dan carrying on an affair."

"No," Sarah acknowledged bitterly. "He deserves the credit for that himself."

320

This point conceded, Amanda didn't know where to take the conversation. So, instead, she picked at the cake, grateful for its value as a diversion.

"What are you going to do?" she finally asked.

Sarah inhaled deeply, then slowly let the air out of her lungs. "I've no idea," she admitted. "We've been married sixteen years. You don't just throw that away on a whim."

Amanda was tempted to make the argument that that was what Dan had done. She was searching for a tactful way of putting this when Sarah spoke again.

"The stupid thing is, I thought our marriage was improving." She smiled bitterly. "Before Dan went to the conference, we were in something of a rut. We'd grown stale. I found him boring, and I dare say he did me, too. Then he went to Birmingham and, when he came home, things changed. *He* had changed. He was more confident and dynamic. And I found him more attractive . . . Of course, now I know the reason."

Amanda said nothing. She felt that Sarah wasn't done yet. And she was right. Sarah chased a piece of cake around the plate in a vain attempt to shovel it on to her fork, then laid the utensil aside. She looked up and Amanda saw in her face the effort required to retain her composure.

"You know," Sarah mused, a tad forlornly, "I always used to wonder whether the French didn't have it right."

"The French?" Amanda asked, wondering whether she'd briefly tuned out and missed a turn in the conversation.

Sarah nodded. "They take a much more relaxed view of infidelity — dismiss it with a Gallic shrug. They fail to see why we get so worked up about it."

Amanda suspected that this was a stereotype unrepresentative of most French women, the wife of Dominique Strauss Kahn aside, but this didn't seem the moment to debate the issue.

"Of course," Sarah added, "that was a view I subscribed to *before* I found out my husband was cheating."

"And since?" Amanda prodded.

"I'm less sure." Sarah shrugged. "Although I would have to accept that I benefited too — while I was in the dark."

"But you're not in the dark now."

"No. And I can't feign ignorance for much longer. That would quickly become pathetic."

Amanda was reminded of her mother. "As would you," she said.

Sarah was a little stung, but, on reflection, this rebuke seemed justified. "Quite."

They sat in silence a moment. Sarah weighed her options.

"I can't do nothing," she reflected.

Amanda thought of her own dilemma. "I'm the opposite; I can't do anything. I always maintained that, if Greg ever cheated, that was it — it would be over between us. Easy to say; harder to act upon. If I don't forgive him, who am I really hurting? The children, most of all. And, if I do forgive him, then he's got carte blanche to do it again."

"Do you really think so?" Sarah asked.

"I know so." Amanda told Sarah about her mother's chequered history. "That's my greatest fear," she confessed with a shy laugh, "that I turn into my mum."

"None of us want that."

"You've met her then?"

Sarah smiled. There was one morsel of cake left. "That's yours," she said to Amanda.

"You have it," Amanda replied.

"How very English of us. Shall we go back and forth, or leave it on the plate because neither of us wants to be so rude as to take the last mouthful?"

Amanda considered this conundrum, then reached out and swiped the cake. As she popped it in her mouth, she shrugged apologetically. "I've some German in me," she said.

Sarah laughed. She'd never had the chance to get to know Amanda. They'd previously only met at industry dinners, where talk was small and manners stiff. She found her candour refreshing.

"You and Greg have never married, have you?" she asked the younger woman.

"I was never keen. My parents weren't exactly role models. Greg didn't seem to mind. I wonder now whether there wasn't always a part of him holding back, unable to commit."

"I don't think there's any doubt about his commitment," Sarah said.

Amanda nodded. "Yeah, he has just cheated."

"No, I don't mean that." Sarah paused, weighing her words. "If I'm honest, I used not to like Greg. I didn't know him well, but the little I'd seen didn't impress me. He struck me as brash, shallow, immature."

"Seems to me you've got him to a T."

Sarah smiled. "The Greg I've come to know is a caring family man. He has his faults — which man doesn't? — but whatever mistake he's made, I know he regrets. I think he's learnt from it. There's a reason it was a one-off. He never wants to repeat it."

Amanda seemed less than swayed. Sarah opened a second front.

"You know, the main difference between a one-night stand and an affair isn't the frequency of the offence, it's the nature of the betrayal. Dan's is emotional; Greg's was purely physical."

"You think that makes it any less serious?"

"I know it does," Sarah said.

Amanda wasn't ready to concede the point. "It's a question of trust, Sarah."

"Yes, it is," she agreed. "Before the conference, you couldn't fully trust Greg to commit."

"And what happened in Birmingham proves I was right."

"You could say that. Or you could argue that it cured Greg of any subconscious misgivings he might have had."

Amanda sighed. "So, you're like my sister and my mum. You think I should just forgive him."

"No, I don't. You clearly can't do that — not if you want to retain any self-respect."

"So what do you recommend?"

"That, I don't know. You'll think of something. I hope you do. That's why I wanted to have this conversation — to impress upon you how much Greg loves you. He does love you, Amanda. So much . . . Well, so much it makes me envious." Sarah smiled sadly.

The waitress reappeared to clear their coffee cups. "Would you like anything else?" she asked.

Sarah looked at Amanda. "Shall we have another slice of that cake?" she asked.

"We shouldn't," Amanda said, tempted.

"You're right." Sarah turned to the waitress. "Another slice of cake, and two more coffees."

Sarah smiled at Amanda, who grinned back. And that's how friendships start.

Greg was pretty pleased with how the interview had gone. He'd winged it, but then that was how he'd approached his whole career and he hadn't come unstuck yet. The board had quizzed him on his recent dismal sales figures. He'd considered bullshitting, giving them some crap about how he'd chosen to focus on one major deal, which he was expecting to be able to announce within days. But instead he opted to tell the truth, confessing to problems at home. He did lie to an extent, by claiming that these were now resolved and he expected an immediate return to his usual form. "I'm Alex Ferguson, not David Moyes," he'd told them to appreciative chuckles from most and blank incomprehension from the two Directors who didn't follow football.

"Well, I think we've heard all we need to, Greg," the Chairman said, casting a glance round the table for dissent. He found none. "One final question. Should we choose not to offer you the job, which of the other candidates would you recommend?"

Greg knew the correct answer to this: that he couldn't look beyond himself, that none of the other candidates came close. He was sure it was the response Paula Stratton had given.

"Dan Sinclair," he said without hesitation.

"Really?" said the Chairman. "And why is that?"

"Because there's no one with greater technical knowledge. When charm and bluster and discounts aren't enough to get a client over the line, when they can't quite commit, Dan's your go-to guy. I've used him myself. You wheel him in and he answers all their concerns, soothes their nerves, rids them of anxiety. He's a safe pair of hands. I'd go over the top of the trenches for him." I did, Greg reminded himself.

"Well, that's a very generous testimonial, Greg." Other members of the Board nodded in agreement. "I'm sure we'll take it into consideration."

Bollocks, thought Greg. I may have just talked myself out of a promotion.

Dan waited outside the conference room, checking one last time the Powerpoint presentation he intended to show the Board. He wondered whether two of the slides wouldn't have greater impact in reverse order. He was about to swap them round when he instructed himself to stop. It won't be the difference between you getting this job and not, he told himself, and chances are you'll be halfway through making the change when they call you in, and then you'll be stuffed. Better to just sit here and do some breathing exercises. Except Dan didn't know any. So, instead, he took slow, exaggerated breaths. In and out. In and out. The receptionist looked up in alarm and considered calling the company medic.

On the brink of hyperventilation, Dan gave that up as a bad job and went through his presentation once more. Maybe it wasn't the order of slides six and seven that was the issue, but the transition between them. He'd used a wipe when perhaps a split would be better. Or a fracture! That could look cool. Or naff. It was so difficult to know. Think about something else, he told himself.

He still couldn't believe how close Sarah had come to finding out about him and Lynda. When Greg had spoken up, promising Sarah the truth, Dan had nearly shat himself, convinced that Greg was about to blow his cover. He should have had more faith. For all their recent differences, Greg was a true friend. He'd come through for Dan, sacrificing himself to save Dan's marriage — and Dan's affair.

He hesitated. Perhaps he should end it with Lynda. He could get out now, no harm done. Become a devoted husband again. But he wasn't ready to. He'd miss his stolen hours with Lynda. Miss her, too. Why give that up when he didn't have to? Still, it might be wise for them to cool it for a bit. He'd see her tonight, then suggest a short break, resume once he was promoted and on the road even more.

A dissolve! That's what the transition between slides six and seven needed. Do it! Do it now! Dan told himself. This was the sort of decisiveness that showed he deserved elevation to the ranks of senior management. He was about to effect the change when the conference room doors opened and spat out Greg. Phew, that was close, thought Dan, leaving his presentation as it was. A wipe was probably best anyway.

Greg made his way over. Didn't he sleep last night? Dan wondered. Must be nerves; he knows I'm coming after him.

"Hey, mate," Dan greeted him. "How'd you go?"

Greg shrugged. "We'll see."

None of his usual bravado, Dan noted. Either he fucked it up or blitzed it.

"You feeling confident?" Greg asked.

"Well, I could have done with a bit longer to finesse my Powerpoint," Dan conceded. "I had a vote of confidence earlier though."

"How's that?"

"Strap-On. She was waiting when I arrived. Said she'd recommended me for the job, should she not get it."

Greg broke into a grin. "She told me the same thing."

"That she'd back me?"

"No."

It took Dan a moment, but he got there. "Ah. Of course she did." He rolled his eyes. You had to admire Paula.

"Maybe that's the kind of duplicity that marks one out for high office," Greg said.

"Except she got caught."

Greg nodded: good point.

The receptionist reprised her *Apprentice* role. "If you'd like to go in," she called to Dan.

Greg stuck out his hand. "Good luck, mate."

Dan shook. "Thanks, fella. You too."

Greg watched Dan collect up his laptop and briefing notes, marvelling at how many he had. Dan crossed to the conference room. I wonder whether I should have mentioned that his fly's undone, Greg pondered, as he strolled towards the lift.

Amanda had not seen her mum for over a week. Nor had they spoken; Amanda had neither taken nor returned her mother's calls. She was therefore unsure what reception she would receive when she called round to her flat in Putney. Margaret opened the front door and blinked at her visitor, as though trying to place her.

"Don't tell me! It'll come to me. *Amanda*, isn't it?"

Amanda rolled her eyes as her mother stood aside to admit her. "Very droll, Mum," she said. "You missed your calling. You should have been an unemployed actor."

"Well, if I were, it wouldn't be my fault. They just don't write parts for mature women any more."

"Oh, I don't know," Amanda countered, unable to resist any opportunity to take issue with her mum. "Helen Mirren. Judi Dench. They're always in work."

"And the fact they're the only two you can name rather proves my point," Margaret said, smugly. God, she could be annoying!

She led Amanda through to the kitchen and flicked on the kettle. "Do you have time for coffee?"

Amanda remembered the two she'd just had with Sarah. "Sure," she said. A caffeine overdose was the best way to cope with her mother.

"So, how are my granddaughters?" Margaret asked. "Have they started university yet?"

"Yes, all right, Mum, I got the message. I'm a bad daughter."

"I never said that," Margaret protested. "An *absentee* daughter, yes."

"They're fine. Missing Greg, before you point it out. I think they want things resolved."

"I'm sure they do."

"So do I."

Margaret spooned coffee granules into two mugs. Living on her own she couldn't be having with the palaver of beans or filters. Top of the range instant was just as good, she maintained. And tasting it, Amanda agreed, though she'd never admit that to her mum.

"Why did you always take Dad back?" Amanda asked, once they were installed at her mother's breakfast bar. They had never previously discussed Margaret's marriage. It was Sarah who, as they'd parted earlier, had recommended that Amanda broach

330

this topic. The look on Margaret's face suggested she hadn't received advance warning of the agenda.

"Would you like a biscuit?" she asked, rising.

Amanda smiled to herself. Food as a diversion again.

"I need to understand," Amanda said, "if I'm going to do the same thing."

Margaret dispensed with the biscuits, resumed her seat. "Are you?" she asked. "Going to take Greg back?"

"I'm thinking about it," was all Amanda would allow.

Margaret threw her hands wide like a Baptist preacher. "Well, praise the Lord! She's come to her senses!"

"Although comments like that might cause me to reconsider."

Margaret put the crowing on hold. She sipped her coffee, well behaved.

"So, tell me about Dad. How many affairs did he have?"

"Oh, Amanda. I don't want to talk about that!"

"I need you to."

"It's not something I choose to discuss."

"Please."

Margaret sighed. She could continue to refuse, claiming it was none of Amanda's business . . . Except that she knew it was. Family: a curse as much as a blessing.

"Six," Margaret conceded. So Amanda was right. It was worse than her father had admitted to.

"Six that you know of," she said.

"Oh, rest assured, I knew of them all — some even before he did. I could recognise the signs."

"Then didn't you try to stop him?"

"How? You could have castrated your father and it wouldn't have slowed him down."

"So how did you feel, each time he cheated on you?"

"How do you think I felt?" Margaret snapped, before she remembered why they were having this conversation. "Probably like you. Hurt, disrespected . . ."

Amanda nodded; she empathised.

"Unloved," her mother concluded. Amanda caught herself; she couldn't say she felt that.

"Why didn't you leave him?" The big question.

"Because I loved him."

"Despite his faults."

"In some ways, I think it was because of. Well, who could bear being married to a saint? Always being found wanting by comparison. Your father was a deeply flawed character. But he was not without his merits. You just remember the bad times. But for me they were far outweighed by the good. He was funny, caring and, most of the time, sensitive."

"Apart from when he was sleeping around."

Margaret smiled. "What a quaint expression! Your father didn't sleep around. He was always faithful to his mistress."

Amanda had not expected her mother to condemn her dad — she never had before — but to appear as a witness for the defence was too much.

Margaret spotted the dismay in her daughter's eyes. "I cannot blame your father. Each time he had an affair, I was hurt, of course I was. The idea that he was sharing with some other woman the intimacy that should have been mine alone . . ." Margaret hesitated. "But I drove him to it."

Amanda had no idea what her mother meant. And Margaret did not appear eager to explain. But she was simply trying to find the courage to put into words memories that were both painful and personal. She'd grown up in a generation that did not tweet for all the world to share.

"You were a difficult birth."

It was a horror story Amanda had been told before. "I was breeched."

"Yes. Nowadays, they'd just perform a caesarean. But back then some doctors still favoured a vaginal delivery. Of course, they weren't the ones having the baby. I almost lost you. You were becoming distressed." Margaret's voice caught as she recalled the terror of those hours. Amanda reached out a hand and laid it gently on her mother's. "They had to scramble to get you out. And, in so doing, they made something of a mess of my . . . my undercarriage. In time, I made a complete recovery. Physically. But, emotionally, I carried scars. I completely lost any sexual desire. More than that. I couldn't abide any sexual contact. We thought it would be temporary. Your father was understanding — initially. But as the months passed and I rebuffed any overture, I could see his patience wearing increasingly thin. He gave me a year — generous, some might say — but when I still could not conceive of him —" Margaret sought to find an appropriate euphemism, then decided that her hesitation had probably done the job itself — "he announced that, if I could no longer satisfy him, he reserved the right to look elsewhere to address those needs. He spoke in that formal language."

"What about oral sex?" Amanda asked.

"Amanda, please! This is difficult for me to talk about as it is. I do not propose to stray into areas where I do not feel comfortable."

So no blow jobs, then, Amanda thought. "Did you give him your blessing?" she asked.

"No. I understood. But I resented him for it. 'For better or worse' — those were our vows. I took them seriously; he took other women to bed."

"Because of my birth."

Margaret rolled her eyes. "I know the fashion nowadays is to think that everything's about you, but I don't think you should consider yourself to blame."

Amanda smiled. Fair enough.

"I don't think I would have minded very much had he chosen to make use of prostitutes — like *his* father," Margaret said, before remembering that this was a characteristic of Amanda's grandfather that she was most likely unacquainted with. She moved quickly on. "But your father was always something of a romantic. He couldn't just have sex; he had to convince himself he was falling in love. It was the emotional betrayal I struggled with, because I understood that the day might come when I would lose him. As it ultimately did. But that was the risk I ran. Except, of course, I had no choice."

Amanda took a sip of her coffee. It had gone cold. She had underestimated her mother. Or not given her enough credit. Her story was more complex than she'd imagined. And her mother less of a victim than Amanda had chosen to believe. It would not be a stretch for Amanda to see her mother as, in some ways, heroic. But what of herself? Greg had not been guilty of emotional betrayal, even Amanda could see that. Was physical betrayal worthy of the same punishment? Maybe not, but it still deserved retribution in some form. And unless Amanda could impose a penalty that satisfied her, then their relationship could not recover — or long term perhaps even survive.

Her mother's voice cut into her thoughts. "I've never told Geraldine this, never told anyone." Margaret climbed down from her stool and put their coffee mugs in the dishwasher. "Given your situation I think you have a right to know. But I'd rather you kept it to yourself. I don't like gossip."

"Of course," Amanda assured her. "I appreciate you telling me." She tried to give her mother a hug, but Margaret was never comfortable with pity. Amanda felt her stiffen. She hugged her nonetheless, then freed her from the torture. "I think I may have judged you harshly in the past," she said, offering her mother a sop.

"Well, that's what daughters do," said Margaret, rejecting it.

Amanda smiled. Normal service was resumed.

"So," Margaret continued, as though the soul searching of the last few minutes was already ancient history, and with a hint of disapproval appearing in her tone, "Geraldine tells me you're seeing someone."

Apparently Margaret's embargo was confined to gossip about her.

"I wasn't seeing him," Amanda said, "and I'm not seeing him again."

And then she had an idea — for the sanction she could impose on Greg. It was an unusual punishment, some might even say cruel, which would be in contravention of the Geneva Convention. But Amanda wasn't a signatory. The more she considered it, the more she found it fitting — if she could enforce it. If: a small word, but a big ask. Still, were she to pull it off then maybe, just maybe, she and Greg might put this whole sorry saga behind them and be able, finally, to move on. It had to be worth a try.

CHAPTER
SIXTEEN

It was Liz who took the message.

"There's someone to see you in reception," she told Lynda.

"Me?" Lynda never received visitors at work. Unless . . . She broke into a grin. "James. His last email said he was due some leave."

Lynda's kid brother was in the Marines. For the past six months, he'd been serving in Afghanistan. He'd told his family Cyprus; he didn't want them worrying that he was going somewhere dangerous. Clearly he didn't know Ayia Napa on a Saturday night.

Lynda headed to the lift. She was surprised to find Liz falling into step beside her. "I'll just say hello," Liz said, adding with a shrug, "Well, he is sex on legs." From which comment Lynda concluded that Liz had still not managed to talk Brad round.

But there was no strapping squaddie waiting in reception — just a proud-looking middle-aged woman. Stepping out of the lift, Liz noticed her first. And she recognised the similarity to a Facebook photo she'd seen only a couple of days earlier.

"Oh, my God!" She stopped in her tracks and grabbed Lynda's arm. "That's Dan's wife!" she whispered.

"What?" Lynda was aghast. But it was too late. Sarah had already spotted them.

"Lynda Bates?" she asked. The question was directed at them both.

"Yes," Lynda replied, unapologetically, and only a friend as close as Liz would notice the slight tremor in her voice.

Lynda took a pace towards Sarah. Liz wondered if she should linger, to offer moral support, then concluded that she'd already done enough damage. She stepped back into the lift. Annoyingly, the doors closed immediately.

Sarah waited for Lynda to cross the lobby to her. Lynda may have home advantage, but Sarah was determined to make this her turf as far as possible. Lynda stopped, the distance of a Persian rug between them. They eyed each other across its length, like two gunslingers waiting to see who would draw first.

"I'm Sarah Sinclair." Sarah laid a slight stress on her surname.

"I know who you are," Lynda replied.

"I understand you know my husband too. Intimately."

Fuck, she's a cool one, Lynda thought, not without admiration. But then she wasn't close enough to see Sarah shaking.

"You're prettier than I expected," Sarah said. It could be a compliment. Or a put-down of Dan. Lynda suspected the latter.

"What is it you want?" Lynda asked.

Sarah smiled, as though amused by the situation in which they found themselves. "That's a coincidence," she said. "I came here to ask you the same thing."

With one hand Amanda attached an earring; with the other she opened the front door to her sister. Jess welcomed Geri into the house.

"Thanks for agreeing to babysit at such short notice," Amanda said.

"Available at no notice, me," Geraldine replied, tousling Jess's coat. "That's one of the advantages of being a middle-aged single woman."

"There are others?"

Geri grinned. It was good to see her kid sister back to her usual acerbic self.

"Girls! Geraldine's here!" Amanda shouted. Molly and Lauren suspended their discussion regarding the break-up of Jason Livingstone's romance with Molly's best friend, Tilly, and its implications for Molly's relationship with each, and came flying down the stairs.

Geraldine greeted them with equal enthusiasm. Her greatest regret was not having children. Technically there was still time, but you had to be an optimist or a fantasist to think it likely, and Geri was neither. Still, her nieces almost made up for her lack. After catching up on their news (the Molly/Jason/Tilly love triangle), Geraldine joined Amanda in her bedroom. The younger sibling did a twirl in the outfit she'd bought earlier that afternoon.

"How do I look?" she asked, fishing for compliments.

"I'd do you," Geri replied. "If we weren't sisters. And I was gay." She flopped down on the queen-sized bed that Amanda used to share with Greg — and which she shortly would again, Geraldine was quietly confident.

She congratulated herself on her role in effecting this rapprochement.

"So your talk with Greg last night went well, did it?" she asked. Amanda had been coy about the details when Geraldine had returned home with two ice-cream-bespattered children.

Amanda pondered. "Yes," she finally owned. "I think it really did."

"So where's he taking you for dinner?"

"Who?"

"Greg!"

Amanda regarded Geraldine, a puzzled expression on her face. "I'm not going out with Greg."

It was Geraldine's turn to look puzzled. Bewildered even. "Who, then?"

From downstairs came the sound of the doorbell, and the girls running to answer it.

"That'll be him now."

Amanda made a dash for the stairs, hoping to get a head start on Geraldine. And she did, but not for long. Geri was quickly on her tail, and her case.

"Please don't tell me that's who I think it is!"

There was no need. As they reached the bottom of the stairs, they saw Ben trying to use his fabled smile to bewitch Amanda's daughters. Apparently its power only worked on women beyond a certain age; the girls were having none of it. They stood shoulder to shoulder, silent and suspicious. A good judge of character, kids.

"All set!" Amanda declared breezily.

Geraldine arrived at Amanda's shoulder. "Just one moment," she said to Ben. Good-looking bastard, she noted, not for the first time, before shutting the door in his face.

Amanda just had a chance to see his winning smile lose something of its brilliance before it disappeared from view. "What do you think you're doing?" Amanda shot at her sister.

"What do you think *you're* doing? He's married!"

Amanda forced herself to remain calm. She turned to her daughters. "Go and watch television." They usually didn't need encouragement — or telling twice. "Now!" Amanda barked. The girls sloped off, not even the prospect of *Friends* adequate compensation for what they'd be missing. Amanda waited till they were out of earshot.

"So what, if he's married?"

Geraldine stared at Amanda in disbelief. "Well, talk about double standards!" she said.

"It's completely different," Amanda hissed, mindful that the front door wasn't that thick and Ben might have his ear to it. "His wife knows exactly what's going on. How she chooses to deal with that is up to her. Their marriage is her problem. Not mine."

With that, Amanda pulled open the front door.

"Sorry about that," she said, stepping out with Ben, leaving Geraldine to wonder what the hell her game was.

Ben escorted Amanda towards his car. He's had it cleaned, she noted. She wondered whether that was for her benefit.

"Ben?" she asked, as he pulled open the passenger door for her and she smelt the pine-fresh upholstery

341

within. "Would you mind if we skipped dinner? Went straight to dessert?" Her eyes suggested she wasn't meaning tiramisu.

"Sure," Ben tried to sound magnanimous. In truth, he couldn't believe his luck. Sex without the preamble!

"But let's not go to your place," Amanda added, as though she weren't fully aware that this wasn't an option anyway. "Somewhere neutral."

This was getting better and better! Ben hadn't yet come up with an excuse, should the evening go to plan and an after-dinner venue was called for. He'd thought he'd busk it, tell her he had his mother staying, or some crap like that. But she'd just spared him the trouble of concocting a lie. "No problem," he said aloud. Thank you, God, he said silently.

Amanda climbed into the Range Rover. "Evening, Byron." The St Bernard panted his welcome from the back seat, a bead of drool spilling from his jowls on to the leather.

Dan was on a high. All day he'd been looking forward to giving Lynda a blow-by-blow account of his interview. It had gone well, he'd concluded, perhaps even really well.

"So I was the last to be interviewed," he said as she opened the door, picking up a conversation they hadn't actually started, but which Dan had been conducting in his head on the drive over. "I'd thought that might be a disadvantage, but I reckoned it played into my hands, allowed me to leave the lasting impression."

342

"I had a visit from your wife earlier," Lynda said levelly as they entered the lounge.

Dan forgot all about his interview. "Sarah?" he asked incredulously. Then he relaxed. "Oh, I get it." He chuckled. "Joke, Dan."

"No joke, Dan," Lynda said, settling on to the sofa. "She came by the office."

Dan fell on to a chair. So this is what it feels like to be in shock, he thought. "But she seemed to accept that it was Greg having the affair."

"Apparently not. Not for a moment, is my guess. I suspect she was biding her time while she weighed her options."

"What did she want?"

"To know what my intentions are. I think that's the phrase. Am I trying to break up your marriage? Do I want you for myself?"

Dan tried to picture this scene, but he couldn't, it was too surreal. "What did you say?"

"No."

As baldly as that. Dan felt a tinge of hurt. He'd have liked to think that Lynda might be just a little torn.

"That seemed to reassure her," Lynda continued. "She gave us her blessing."

"She *what*?"

Lynda spelt it out for him very deliberately. "Sarah, your wife, has no objection to you and me conducting an affair. She told me so, in as many words."

Dan had known Sarah for nineteen years. He hadn't thought it possible for her to surprise him any more.

But she had stunned him like a mullet plucked from the Thames to have its brains dashed against a rock.

Lynda cut into his thoughts. "It kind of puts a different spin on things, don't you think?"

Dan wasn't sure he followed.

"Thanks for walking me home," Ruby told Russell as they arrived outside her house.

They'd been on a date — their first since they'd officially started dating (Russell kept using the word in his mind, trying it on for size). A trip to the movies, like real courting couples do. They'd seen the latest instalment in a blockbuster franchise, the fourth of what was originally planned as a trilogy, but which had proved to be so successful the studio had been unable to resist returning to the well at least one more time.

"Sorry the movie was shite," Russell said.

"I enjoyed being with you," Ruby divulged, a slight blush pricking her cheeks.

It had been fun. At a moment of high drama, Ruby had been moved to grip Russell's hand, digging her nails into his flesh. The crisis had passed, but Ruby had left her palm resting in his, and Russell hadn't objected. He'd enjoyed the sensation of their touching skin. He found himself hoping that her jagged nails had left an indentation for him to treasure in bed tonight.

He felt himself reddening too. Fortunately it was dark. "I should be getting home," he said self-consciously.

"Sure." Ruby reached up to give Russell a farewell kiss. She had been meaning to aim for his cheek, but

344

having to stand on tiptoe (he was a good head taller than her), she stumbled and missed. Her mouth landed on his. Russell's eyes widened in surprise, partly because he thought Ruby knew the rules, but more because he found he liked it. When Ruby sheepishly pulled back, realising she might have embarrassed him, Russell pushed forward and pressed his lips against hers. Now it was Ruby's eyes that widened, and then closed as she gave herself up to the kiss, slipping her tongue into Russell's mouth with a practised ease that would have horrified her mum. Russell was a little horrified too — at first. He'd never kissed a girl before, not like he meant it. And mean it he discovered he did. If Russell had been confused about his sexuality before, he was utterly confounded now.

Watching unseen from an upstairs window, Ruby's mother, Veronica, glowered down at them. That sex-fiend son of Sarah's was leading her daughter astray. Who knew what depravity he was contemplating in his degenerate little mind?

It was a very quiet night at the Clifton Motor Inn. Standing at reception, Howard had played so many games of hearts on the hotel computer, he was almost cured of his addiction. Almost, but not quite. He'd lost the last hand. He couldn't retire on a loss. He'd chalk up one more victory and then uninstall the program. He listened to the satisfying flutter as the computer dealt out the cards. He surveyed his hand. Promising. It was possible he might even shoot the moon.

Howard looked up as he heard the hotel's doors glide apart. A man he didn't recognise entered, accompanied by a woman he did. It took him a moment to place her. He'd only seen her once before, he was pretty sure of that. When had it been? She hadn't stayed; he prided himself on never forgetting a former guest. And then it came to him. Good God! She'd been with Greg Beavis. She was his wife! What was she doing here? And who was the bloke she was with?

"Hi. We'd like a room, please," the man said as he reached the counter.

Good-looking bastard, Howard noted. "Certainly, sir," he replied, turning to include Amanda. "'Madam'." Howard managed to make the inverted commas audible. Amanda didn't flinch, just held his gaze, challenging him to make an issue of it. Howard was reminded of why he'd warmed to her. He referred to his computer screen, ostensibly searching for an available room. Frankly they could have a floor to themselves, business was so quiet.

"And do you have any luggage?" he enquired, not waiting for a reply. "No, I thought not."

Dan did not stay long at Lynda's. But he was in no hurry to get home. Who knew what reception awaited him there? He rang Greg.

"Fancy a beer?" he asked.

"Probably more than George Best ever did; I'm queuing at the checkout in IKEA."

"Jesus."

"Tell you what, do me a solid," Greg said, employing one of his least-favourite phrases. "Meet me at my new flat and help me unload."

It wasn't exactly Dan's idea of a night out, but it beat the alternative.

Dan was standing on the street when Greg pulled the Bedford van he'd hired into the kerb. Dan had already given him a heads-up on what had transpired at Lynda's flat. Greg hopped down from the driver's cab. "It shouldn't take us long to get this lot upstairs," he said, "then you can fill me in."

It took them longer than Greg had predicted. Two single mattresses for the kids, a double (a little optimistically, Dan thought) for Greg; a double-bed frame; three tables: bedside, kitchen and coffee; four chairs: three for the kitchen, one for the lounge; an assortment of bedding and kitchen utensils; and, for old times' sake, a framed print of the New York skyline. What he still needed was just as long a list, but there was a limit to Greg's patience and IKEA had exceeded it. When his defence mechanisms were restored, he would contemplate another assault on the big blue box in north Wembley. Until then his daughters' mattresses would have to lie on the floor, as would their clothes when the girls came to stay.

Greg hadn't yet acquired a fridge. That was on a separate list, of white goods. He needed a fridge so he had something to pin all his lists to. And to cool his milk, which was currently standing in a bucket of cold water, jostling for space with a six-pack of Heineken lager. Make that a four-pack — Greg had removed two cans; he tossed one to Dan and popped the other. Foam spurted over the rim. The makeshift fridge wasn't proving particularly effective. Perhaps if he added some ice . . . But to make ice he needed a fridge. Catch-22. Now, there was a good book.

Greg sat down on his bed. As this was still flat-packed into three different boxes, it wasn't particularly comfortable, but he'd offered his guest the sole lounge chair.

Dan surveyed the abundance of boxes on the floor.

"Do you have a drill?" he asked.

"At home," Greg replied. Where the heart is. Where he wasn't. But best not dwell on that. "So Sarah didn't buy our little subterfuge, huh?" He wasn't altogether surprised; she was an intelligent woman.

"I can't believe she went to see Lynda, gave our affair her blessing. What do you think her game is?"

"Maybe she isn't playing one. Maybe she really doesn't mind."

Dan considered this. It didn't take him long to dismiss it out of hand. "No, not Sarah." A dreadful thought struck him. "My God! Perhaps she's planning to divorce me! Fuck!"

"You don't know that! You don't know anything till you talk to her."

"I don't want to go home," Dan admitted. He cast a glance around his friend's flat. "You've got a second bedroom, haven't you?"

"You're not staying here!"

"Just for tonight."

Greg heard an echo of an earlier conversation, though they were speaking each other's lines. "You've made your bed, you lie in it," he said, before he was reminded of the boxes on which he was sitting. "Speaking of which, I need to make mine. You must have a drill . . ."

"At home," Dan said glumly, making no offer to nip round and fetch it.

They sat in silence a moment, sipping their beers.

"We really fucked things up, didn't we?" Dan said finally.

"Yeah," Greg agreed. "Sorry."

"Ah, it's not your fault. I didn't have to go along with it."

Greg took in his new abode: the traffic noise, the tired carpet, the discolouration on the wall where a former occupant had hung a now absent painting. God, it was depressing. Softly, ironically, he began to sing: "*Moi, je ne regrette rien . . .*" The signature tune of Édith Piaf. "*Moi, je ne regrette rien . . .*" That's as far as he got; he didn't know any more.

Dan ruminated. He had regrets. Prime among them was the grief he'd caused Sarah. Was her pain worth the boost his ego had received? The cheap thrill of a secret attraction? Of course not. There was no comparison. And he'd known there wouldn't be, even while he'd been with Lynda. But that hadn't stopped him. Oh, he'd considered ending their affair — every time he left her flat. But not once did he retrace his steps, or call her to say it was over. It was almost like an addiction. No, Dan would not allow himself that excuse. It would be a cop-out to suggest that he had been in the grip of a power beyond his control. The truth was he had just been weak.

Shortly, he would have to go home and face Sarah's wrath. The reckoning. He felt like a man who's dined at an expensive restaurant and is about to be presented with the bill. He doesn't know how much the damage will be, just that it's going to hurt. And that it's only fair he pay.

Greg, too, harboured regrets: inviting Liz to his room; packing the box of condoms in his overnight bag (how could he have been so fucking stupid?); not telling Amanda the truth from the start. A litany of errors, all stemming from a fear of growing old, his terror that, at the age of thirty-eight, he might never again know the exhilaration of a completely new sexual experience. Well, asshole, he chided himself, that's all you've got to look forward to now — one new experience after another, a series of increasingly desperate encounters with increasingly desperate women. It had taken this episode, this catastrophe, for him to realise just how much he loved Amanda. And that was his greatest regret of all — that, though he now knew the full extent of his love for her, she didn't. And she never would because, try as he might to tell her (and how he'd tried), she refused to be swayed.

"I should go," Dan said, rising to his feet.

"Yep," Greg nodded. He didn't get up.

Dan took a last slug of Heineken — Dutch courage — and stepped over the boxes as he made his way towards the door.

"Mate," Greg called after him. "Good luck."

Dan nodded his thanks. Fuck, he was going to need it.

CHAPTER
SEVENTEEN

It had seemed like a good idea at the time. Don't get mad, get even. If Amanda could level the score, square the match, notch one up for the girls, then perhaps she could forgive Greg and they could move on.

Hence her decision to sleep with Ben. Not sleep with — Amanda didn't intend to hang around that long, and she doubted their congress would contain any hint of romance. Shag Ben: that's what she had determined to do. She didn't want to; she needed to. It helped that he was a good-looking bastard. And married. As she'd said to Geraldine, she felt no responsibility, no sisterhood, towards Ben's wife; the woman clearly knew what her husband was like — she was an accessory after the fact. No, Ben being married made it easier because it cast him as an even bigger rat. He had lied to try to get Amanda between the sheets. Well, he'd succeed, but it was him who was being used, not her.

Now that they were in the bedroom, Amanda felt her confidence seeping away like semen through a split condom. Fuck! she thought. Contraception. She'd assumed that Ben would have some. She berated herself for her negligence and made a mental note to ensure in later years that her daughters carried protection — when they turned twenty-one, say. Or eighteen. Oh, Christ — sixteen most likely. She glanced at Ben. She was fairly confident he'd come prepared. A burglar doesn't go out at night without a lock pick about his person.

She surveyed the room. Howard, in the hope he might prick her conscience and cause her to reconsider, had assigned her the very room, the very bed in which Greg had slept. The gesture was wasted — Amanda hadn't been to Greg's room. She had no way of knowing that he was responsible for the beer stain on the carpet that she was now eyeing with distaste.

"I think I might need something from the minibar," she announced to Ben. Like about a dozen miniatures.

He pulled open the fridge. "They've got whisky, vodka, gin and bourbon."

That would do for starters; they could always send out for more. "Let's go alphabetically. Bourbon."

Ben passed her the tiny bottle. By the time he fetched her a glass, she'd consumed its contents.

"Another?" he enquired, a little nervously, she thought. Was he concerned she'd be shit-faced? Or that he'd be cleaned out?

"No," she said. "Let's do this."

She wasn't exactly entering the spirit. But Ben didn't complain; he didn't want to say anything that might blow his chances. So, instead, he crossed to her, took the empty miniature from her hand and gently kissed her.

It wasn't so bad. Not objectionable. Not exactly a turn-on, either. Just . . . odd, really. Oh! He's bringing his hands into play, Amanda noted as she felt his palm land deftly on her arm, then wend its way upwards, rounding her shoulder before diverting south towards her chest. Amanda braced. This was getting personal.

From outside the window, she heard a long, drawn-out moan, an expression of grief and loss that brought to mind the widows of Cape Cod mourning their husbands, lost whaling off Nantucket Sound. Ben's fingers expertly described her breast. Amanda tried to concentrate, but the prolonged keening continued. She pulled her mouth away from Ben's.

"Is that Byron?" she asked.

Ben nodded ruefully. "He gets withdrawal symptoms if I'm out of his sight."

Amanda rolled her eyes. Fucking brilliant.

Outside, Byron kept up his vigil and his dirge.

"This isn't going to work," Amanda declared. She should have known it was a stupid idea. Men can have sex on command — some women too. Good luck to them. She wasn't wired like that.

"Wait," Ben pleaded, as he saw his prospects diminish. "We can fix this."

Greg tore open the first of two boxes that contained the elements of his bed frame. He sifted through the requisite nuts and bolts, sorting them into small piles. There were twenty-four screws alone. With a drill this would be the work of moments, Greg thought. Without, it could take all night, which would rather defeat the purpose.

354

He'd phone Amanda and ask to pop round for his toolbox. What would she be doing at this hour? The kids would have finished their tea. She'd be hollering at them to have a bath. She might even be pleased to hear from him; she'd been practically civil the last time they'd spoken.

He picked up his phone and scrolled through to Amanda's mobile number. On the other hand, she might think that he was trying to take advantage, using moving into his flat as a sob story to manoeuvre her towards forgiveness. He didn't want that mark against his name; it was blackened enough already.

He put his phone aside, picked up the tools he had at his disposal and set to work. Sweating, with twenty-three screws still in a neat pile, he gave it up as a bad job. Sod it. His mattress could rest on the floor like the girls'.

He pulled the ring on another can of lager. Perhaps *Tattoo Nightmares* was on. Not that it made much difference. He didn't have cable. Or a television. He added "TV" to his list.

Amanda kept Howard occupied while Ben went out to the car. She heard Ben's faint whistle, the signal that he was ready to smuggle Byron into the hotel.

"Do you have any tourist information?" Amanda asked Howard.

Unless you have glaucoma, you know I do; you can see the rack of leaflets, Howard thought. "What did you have in mind?" he asked.

"Legoland?" she offered.

Howard regarded her. He didn't know what was going on, only that something was. Mr and Mrs Drake, as Ben had written on their registration form, did not look like the theme park's typical clientele. They didn't look like they'd leave their room, to be honest. Still, if that's what she wanted . . . Howard turned to locate the Legoland brochure. He'd arranged them in alphabetical order, but receptionists on other shifts had paid scant regard and all the leaflets were jumbled up. Legoland, Legoland . . . Howard didn't spot Amanda frantically waving at Ben, or Ben scooting Byron through the lobby. Ah, Legoland, there it was!

"And perhaps Alton Towers, while you're there."

Was that feet Howard heard scurrying across the tiled floor? He started to turn. He got halfway.

"Wait! What's that?" Amanda cried, pointing behind him like she'd just seen a gecko. Howard followed her finger. "Next to Alton Towers! Madame Tussaud's? I'll have that as well."

Howard collected the crop of leaflets and handed them to Amanda. He had no doubt the Somali chambermaid would find them discarded the following morning.

"Thank you," Amanda chirped, waltzing off down the corridor.

Howard watched her go. And then he noticed what looked like a trail of muddy paw prints he was sure hadn't been there before. Odd. But, thankfully, housekeeping's problem, not his.

Liz was sitting on the sofa, idly flicking through bridal mags, when Brad stumbled in from cricket practice. He was in a good mood; he'd been celebrating his recall to the first team.

"I've been thinking," he said, only slightly slurring. "Whose word am I gonna believe? A bunch of office gossips, or the woman I want to spend the rest of my life with?" Liz wondered whether she was supposed to choose, but apparently it was a rhetorical question, because Brad continued, "If you say nothing happened at this conference, I believe you. And we get married. To hell with all the doubters."

Liz just stared at him. Brad had been expecting a little more enthusiasm.

"This is where you leap up and hug me," he prompted.

Liz stood, but didn't move to embrace him. She'd known it was only a matter of time till he came round. But now that he had, she didn't feel a sense of triumph. Or relief. She felt certainty. Suddenly everything became clear. She found herself speaking words she hadn't prepared but which, as they left her mouth, just felt right.

"The truth is, Brad, I went to the conference intending to cheat. It was meant to be a test — of us. But the bloke I picked couldn't. I took that as a sign. You were never supposed to find out. But the fact that word got round, that you did, *that* was the sign. We're not meant to be together."

Brad listened, but found he didn't understand. Being pissed didn't help.

"Are you saying you did fuck someone?" This seemed to him to be the crucial question. Most men might agree.

Liz broke into a slow smile. "No."

Brad frowned. He didn't get it.

"I'm sorry, Brad. I don't love you. Or, anyway, not enough."

Liz tugged off her engagement ring and handed it to Brad as she left the room. He considered it in dismay, thinking perhaps he shouldn't have had that fifth pint of bitter. He felt sure he must have missed something.

Sarah was at the sink, scrubbing pots and pans. It was how she'd decided she wanted to play this scene. Dan apparently regarded her as the little housewife, so let him return home from work to find her acting that role. Trouble was, he was late. She'd been standing there for a good twenty minutes, the suds slowly dissolving in the cooling water. She squirted some more detergent into the sink, then opened the hot tap hard, causing bubbles to froth. That looked better.

She heard the front door close, heard Dan put down his briefcase, shrug off his coat. She didn't turn around; her Marigold-clad hands resumed their scouring. Dan's footsteps entered the kitchen. Finally, Sarah acknowledged him, flicking a smile over her shoulder.

"There you are!" she said brightly, returning her attention to the sink. "I was about to send out a search party." A nice touch, she thought, the insertion of the bland cliché. It reinforced this picture of domestic harmony, as painted by Norman Rockwell.

Dan didn't speak. Even with her back turned, Sarah could sense his uncertainty.

"Russell and I have already eaten, couldn't wait for you any longer." She pulled the plug out and peeled off her gloves; they made a satisfyingly rubbery sound. "Have you had anything? I can easily heat something up."

Dan still said nothing. Sarah filled the silence with her voice.

"Will lasagne do?" She took a Pyrex dish from the depths of the fridge and straightened; at last she locked eyes with him.

Here it comes, he thought.

Sarah smiled pleasantly. "You've time for a shower if you like."

Why is she behaving like a Stepford Wife? Dan wondered.

Sarah adjusted the controls on the cooker. "How did your interview go?" she asked, her back to him.

"Fine," he replied automatically. "Should hear something tomorrow."

"Fingers crossed, then." She removed the clingfilm covering the lasagne, placed the dish on the middle shelf.

"Don't you want to know where I've been?" Dan asked.

Sarah clicked shut the oven door and stood. "Not particularly. I imagine you went to see Greg's new flat."

"I did, at is happens."

Sarah crossed to the fridge and busied herself inspecting its contents. "Russell's revising for a test," she continued chattily. "Maths, I think he said it was."

"Sarah. Stop it."

Sarah stopped, turned to regard him. "What?" she asked, a picture of innocence.

"This pretence that everything's normal."

She blinked. "Everything is normal, Dan," she said in an overly normal voice. She turned back to the fridge. "Do you want chips or salad?"

Dan was determined to have this out. "I know you went to see Lynda." There! Let her try and ignore that!

Sarah had not been sure how her strategy would play out. That afternoon and early evening, she'd weighed the various scenarios. If Dan came home and said nothing, it meant one of two things: that Lynda had not told Dan about Sarah's visit, and intended to continue their affair with Dan in the dark about his wife's knowledge and apparent approval, or that she had told Dan but he had decided not to let on that he knew, just one further deception to add to his growing list. Either way, Sarah would bide her time while mulling her next move. She'd considered both scenarios possible but improbable. More likely was that Lynda would tell Dan and Dan would want to confront the issue. And so it had proved.

She closed the fridge door and again turned, meeting his gaze. His eyes held a challenge, and Sarah felt her anger surge. But she was damned if she was going to allow him to dictate her mood. Or reaction. So he wants this out, does he? Well, who says he gets to set the agenda?

"Chips? Or salad?" she asked levelly.

"For fuck's sake, Sarah! I'm trying to talk about our marriage, here!"

Just then, Russell shambled into the room, exhibiting the adolescent's innate ability to pick precisely the wrong moment.

"Hi, Dad," he said, oblivious of his father's tense demeanour. "The Wi-Fi's down again."

"I'll look at it later," Dan said. "Give us a moment, will you, son?"

"But I need to print out a worksheet."

"I said I'll look at it later," Dan repeated, measuring each word carefully.

A sensitive person would recognise Dan's inflexible tone. Russell was a sensitive person — most of the time. The rest of the time he was a self-absorbed fifteen-year-old.

"But I need it now."

"I'll do it when I'm ready!" Dan snapped. "Now go to your room!"

Stunned by this uncharacteristic outburst, Russell obeyed without further demur. As he climbed the stairs, Sarah crossed to the door. Dan thought she was following their son, perhaps to offer him reassurance that everything was all right. But she stopped at the door, and closed it. Then she swung on Dan, her eyes ablaze.

"Don't you dare take this out on him," she threatened with cold fury.

"Then talk to me, for God's sake!"

Sarah regarded him. Her tone was controlled. "All right. If that's what you want." She inhaled, taking in oxygen to stoke the fire in her eyes. And then she unleashed, venting all the hurt, anger and bile: "Fuck

361

you! Fuck you for all the years our marriage has been dead! Fuck you for your sordid little affair! And fuck you most for making me a party to it!"

Dan leant against the kitchen cabinets, reflexively crossing his arms in front of him.

"My God," he said calmly. "So there is blood coursing through your veins."

"Fuck you, Dan." Sarah regarded him with loathing.

"Why do you think I've been having an affair?" he threw at her.

Sarah knew the answer to that one. "Because it's what men of very little imagination do."

"Because you haven't excited me in years."

"Oh, and you think you've done it for me?" Sarah topped up her anger with disdain. "I stopped making love to you long ago. It was always someone else: Russell Brand; one of the builders doing the Chambers' loft conversion; our son's maths teacher. *He's* particularly dirty, more than Russell Brand, surprisingly enough."

Dan had grown so accustomed to Sarah's even temper, he'd forgotten that she was capable of such passion. Its absence had led him to cheat. His cheating had led to its return. *This* was the woman he had fallen in love with. Like millions of men before him and countless more still to come, he arrived at this realisation just at the moment when she was most distant. There are many words to describe such men. "Dick" will do.

Dan sighed. No, he deflated. And as the air went out of him, so too did the fight.

"I won't be seeing Lynda again," he said.

Sarah took in this information. "Is that your decision or hers?"

It only took Dan a moment to choose to tell the truth. Candour felt cathartic.

"Hers," he admitted. "She says it's not the same now."

A small smile escaped to the corner of Sarah's mouth. And suddenly Dan understood what he had previously found baffling.

"That's why you went to see her! Gave us your blessing. You knew she'd end it."

"You give me too much credit," Sarah said. "I hoped she might; I had no idea whether she would. I just presumed that the fact it was illicit must be some of the appeal for her — or all. You're not that great a catch."

The jibe stung, but Dan had to admit it had the ring of truth.

"I'm sorry," he said.

"Yes," she simply replied. They both were.

"Would you like me to move out?"

"No." This said categorically.

The certainty in Sarah's voice gave Dan cause for hope, quickly dashed by the cold look in her eyes.

"That woman will not determine the future of our marriage. For now, we shall proceed as though everything is fine. Only you and I will know how far that is from the truth. Russell is to be unaware. I do not want him drawn into this. You can move into the spare room. We'll say it's on account of your snoring."

Dan nodded, accepting this interim banishment. It was Siberia, but at least within the confines of his home.

"Now," Sarah continued, "you never answered my question."

Dan looked at her doubtfully. What question was that?

"Chips or salad?"

Dan considered — not what to have with his lasagne, but whether it could be that simple to maintain the pretence of a happy, loving relationship. And then it struck him that that's probably what most married couples do.

"Salad. I can make it."

"No, you go and apologise to Russell for biting his head off. You could put it down to having to work late. It's a plausible excuse." The bitterness in her voice was not lost on Dan.

He went out. And life went on. Sarah made a balsamic dressing, resisting the temptation to be overgenerous with the vinegar.

She had seen off the immediate threat posed by Lynda. But Sarah took scant satisfaction in that. She still had a devastated marriage. She stood among its ruins, wondering whether it would be worth the effort to rebuild.

Amanda shuddered as she allowed Ben to unclasp her bra. She was finding it difficult to relax, and not just because of a panting Byron watching them blearily from the end of the bed. Once she'd accepted the idea of sleeping with another man, she'd imagined it would be easy, especially if he were attractive. A matter of mechanics. But when you've been faithful to your partner of thirteen years, it's difficult to be otherwise. Unless you're Greg, Amanda thought ruefully; he'd found it all too easy.

You can do this, she told herself as Ben nuzzled a nipple and she felt herself tense. You *need* to do this. Not just for you, but for Greg, Molly and Lauren. Unless you can overcome your inhibitions, you won't be able to accept Greg back on equal terms. Your partnership will be ruined irrevocably.

She felt Ben's hand on her inner thigh, gliding north. Reflexively she snapped her legs shut, stirring memories of her sixteen-year-old self. Fifteen, she corrected herself. Ben had the good sense not to force the issue, but instead use his experience to seduce her. It appeared he'd accumulated plenty. He bit and nibbled her earlobe, a zone she'd always found especially erogenous. Amanda felt her rigidity begin to dissolve. That felt good! Sensing her defrost, Ben moved to her neck. Oooo, yes, that was even better!

Amanda knew a woman once, a former receptionist at the surgery, who had used the services of a male escort. She'd been quite unabashed about it. Her husband had left her, she had had needs, and a gigolo had satisfied them. And her. The sex, she'd said, had been fantastic — worth all £250. "I didn't have to consider him at all," she'd said. "Can you imagine how liberating that is?" At the time, Amanda couldn't. Part of the joy of sex was that it was a shared experience, she and Greg finding pleasure in and with each other. But now she understood. She didn't care about Ben. Didn't even like him. This was all about her. So she may as well make the most of it. She dug her nails into his broad shoulder blades — hard. He emitted a moan, mostly but not exclusively of pleasure.

He rolled off her. She thought she'd gone too far, hurt him perhaps. But he tore at the belt of his trousers. She got the idea. She shrugged off her skirt (she'd dressed with ease of removal in mind), then lay back, wearing only her knickers. Ben's socks followed his trousers on to the floor where his shirt already lay. He went to pull down his boxers. "Not yet," she said, enjoying being in control. He smiled and fell upon her. She could feel his erection pressing through the cotton polyester blend of his underpants.

He kissed her — expertly — pulling at her lower lip with his teeth, darting his tongue into her mouth. She tasted Listerine; he must have been feeling quietly confident when he'd arrived to take her out for dinner. He slipped a hand into the waistband of her knickers, cupping her buttocks, pressing his hard-on against her. She grabbed a handful of his hair and yanked his head back, enjoying inflicting a little pain on the cheating bastard. He slid his hand into her bush, curling her wiry pubic hair between his fingers. She felt herself moisten. He sensed it, too, darting a finger to her vagina, probing towards her clitoris.

Amanda gasped. She wanted him to enter her — or thought she did. But then an image popped into her head — of Greg, at breakfast with the girls, Molly and

Lauren squealing with delight at the silly voices their dad was affecting, Jess barking, wanting to be in on the joke. That's what Amanda really wanted: to be with her family. But that was the reason she was here. Ben pulled off his boxers. They snagged on his erection, till it sprang urgently free, slapping against her thigh. She had another image of Greg, lying on one arm in bed, wiping a strand of hair out of her eyes as he bent to kiss her eyelid. Ben's cock nudged her insistently; his hand clawed to remove her knickers. A further image elbowed its way into her subconscious — of when she'd asked Greg, finally and definitively, "Then, once and for all, did you have sex with that woman?" How he, knowing she'd only accept an unequivocal yes but having sworn to tell the truth, fudged his reply: "I cheated on you, yes." And suddenly she suspected she knew exactly what had occurred at the conference in Birmingham. Because the same thing was happening to her.

"I can't do this!" She pushed Ben's hips away from her.

"What?"

"I'm sorry! I can't."

Ben was primed. The boosters had fired, the countdown was close to zero, lift-off was imminent. Could he be blamed if he felt the launch procedure was too far advanced to abort? Well, yes. Amanda could not have made her wishes any clearer.

"I want you to stop."

And, to his credit, although Ben was a cheating bastard who disrespected his wife at any opportunity, he was not a rapist. Admittedly, not much of a testimonial. Amanda wriggled out from under him and off the bed. She began pulling on clothes, abruptly embarrassed by her state of undress.

"I'm sorry," she repeated. "I just . . . I love my partner." Though she hated that word: partner. So functional, soulless, inexpressive of their feelings for each other.

Ben was not used to setbacks. But that's how he saw this rejection: not as a defeat, just as a greater challenge. Which, of course, made the prize all the more alluring.

"I understand," he said, already plotting his strategy. "We went too fast. Let's take a step back. Dinner next week."

Amanda smiled. Sweet, she thought, he thinks this is a courtship. She shook her head. "No. I won't be seeing you again."

"Why?" he asked, shocked. Women always wanted to see him again.

"Because you're married. And I'm spoken for."

So she'd found out about his wife. Yet she'd still come. "Then what was this?" he asked.

Amanda, doing up her blouse, paused to consider her answer. "Payback," she shrugged. "Bye, Byron," she said. She gave the St Bernard a final pat before letting herself out of the room.

Greg did not wish to develop a drink problem. He was determined not to finish the six-pack of lager he'd brought back to his flat — five-and-a-half-pack, since

368

Dan's visit. He'd allowed himself three cans. No more tonight, he'd pledged. But in the absence of anything else to keep him amused — he had no TV, no Wi-Fi, or, quaintly, no book — he was finding abstinence a struggle. And so, at just after nine, he went to bed.

Which is where he was now, lying on a mattress on the floor of the larger bedroom. He was listening to the sounds on the street. His flat was near a bus stop. Already, he quite enjoyed being able to identify the buses pulling up outside — every fifteen minutes or so. Occasionally the gap would be longer and he'd imagine the passengers beginning to get antsy, peering up the road for a number 266 that refused to materialise. He knew he'd have trouble sleeping tonight. Not because he was thinking of Amanda and the girls, although he was. Nor the anticipation of hearing the outcome of his job interview. No, the cause of his insomnia was more prosaic: a streetlamp was situated directly outside his window. He could have read a book by its illumination. He found a pen and added "curtains" to his shopping list. Then he added "book".

A buzzing sound came from the hall, long, low and persistent, like a mosquito on steroids. Fuck! thought Greg. He should have realised that, living on a main road, there'd be any number of drunken yobs who considered it the height of wit to press random doorbells. He ignored the intrusion, resumed listening out for the next bus; it should be due about now. The buzzer sounded again — little staccato bursts. Double fuck! Perhaps the previous tenant was a crack dealer who had failed to send out change of address cards. Or a prostitute and, even now, a queue was forming outside his door of sad, middle-aged men looking to get a load off.

Narrrrrrrrrrrrrrrrrrrrrr! The buzzer sounded annoyed at being ignored.

"Jesus fuck!" Greg said out loud as he stomped towards his front door and stabbed the intercom. "Fuck off!" he enunciated clearly, so that anyone within hearing, the bus queue included, should be in no doubt of his attitude to uninvited callers.

"Gre —?"

Greg removed his finger from the intercom, cutting off the reply. Only the first three letters were communicated, but that was enough for him to suspect he recognised the voice. He pressed the intercom again.

"Amanda?"

"Yes."

Oh, rapture! Greg buzzed the door open, ran down the stairs to greet her. She was still locked out; the mechanism hadn't sprung — first gripe for his landlord, he thought. He pulled open the door. A number 266 bus pulled up, right on cue.

"Hi," she said, looking a little nervous.

"Hi!" He tried to suppress his delight at her unexpected visit; he didn't want to be too obvious. But his eyes seemed determined to smile. "Come up," he said.

"No, I'm not staying."

Greg nodded: as you like. He stood there in his briefs and waited for Amanda to explain why she'd called round. She seemed reluctant.

370

"Are you sure you won't?" he asked, since she couldn't seem to think what to say. "I could give you the tour. It won't take long."

She shook her head. He waited.

"I forgive you, Greg. I want you to come home. That's if you'd like to."

The smile that had been evident in Greg's eyes swept across his whole countenance.

"Wait," Amanda said, her eyes serious. "Before you say anything, there's something you should know. You're not the only one who's cheated. I have too."

The elation plastered on Greg's face froze in place. What was she saying? Cheated? He couldn't believe it. She'd been so irate when she thought she'd rumbled him.

"When?" he asked.

Amanda hesitated. "About an hour ago." She shrugged apologetically.

Greg was dumbstruck. He wanted to say, "You're joking?" and she'd look deathly serious, like she was looking now, but only for a moment, and then she'd relax and break into a grin and he'd exhale in relief and laugh, and then they'd both crack up and they'd fall into each other's arms, and everything would be all right again.

But Greg said nothing. He'd lost the power of speech. And Amanda didn't relax, just continued looking deathly serious, till she finally said, "I should get back to the girls," and made off towards her car.

For a few moments, Greg didn't move. It appeared he'd lost that ability too. He stood half naked at his half-open door, like a flasher lacking conviction. A passing pedestrian did a double-take, snapping Greg out of his fugue. He pushed the door shut quietly, so as not to disturb the other residents, then climbed the stairs to his flat.

He was right to think he'd have trouble sleeping that night. But it had nothing to do with the streetlamp outside his window.

CHAPTER
EIGHTEEN

How often morning brings with it clarity. Not for Greg. Twelve hours after Amanda's announcement, he still didn't know what to think. He'd gone to work, as usual, but he was on autopilot. He'd sat down at his desk, powered up his laptop and stared with bloodshot eyes at his screen. He'd worked out that it must have been the bloke from the restaurant Amanda had slept with. What was his name? *Ben*, that was it. Good-looking bastard, Greg remembered. A good-looking bastard who's had your woman. How does that make you feel?

Numb.

Well, you know who to blame, don't you? he castigated himself. What's good for the gander, and all that.

"Congratulations."

Greg looked up to find Dan standing over him, extending his hand. Did Dan know that Amanda had forgiven him? How could he? Reflexively, Greg shook.

"It's only what you deserve," Dan added.

To have Amanda cheat? That seemed a little harsh. Though, you could also argue, fair.

Clearly Greg's confusion was etched on his face. "You haven't read your emails, have you?" Dan asked.

He shook his head in wonder. "You know, as Regional Sales Manager, you're going to have to get into the habit."

Greg stared at Dan. "Seriously?"

Dan shrugged. "Well, I suppose you could ask your PA to read them . . ."

"No, I mean . . . *me?*"

"Yeah," Dan agreed. "Hard to credit, isn't it? When we both know there was a much better candidate."

Greg nodded. "Strap-On," he dead-panned.

Dan smiled. "Thank fuck she didn't get it! Anyway, well done. And don't forget who put in a good word for you."

"Strap-On."

Dan rolled his eyes and turned to head back to his desk.

"Dan!" Greg called after him. "How did it go with Sarah?"

Dan considered his response, thinking back to his homecoming the night before.

"I'm in the spare room."

"Pretty well, then."

Dan didn't disagree. Keeping up appearances. "At least we're still under the same roof," he said, recalling Greg's fate.

"Amanda came to see me last night," Greg said. "Told me I'm welcome home."

Dan beamed. "Mate! That's fantastic."

Greg raised a cautioning hand. "We're not out of the woods yet. Far from it."

"You'll get there."

Greg wondered whether that was true.

"So, is now a good time to ask for a pay rise?" Dan asked.

"Well, Dan, I'd love to help," Greg sat back in his swivel chair, adopting a corporate voice, his hands clasped behind his head, "but budgets are tight and economic conditions tough. That said, I like you, Dan, and we don't want to lose good men. So, leave it with me and unless you bring it up again, we'll say no more about it." Greg dropped the persona, reverted to himself. "How was that?" he asked.

Dan smiled. "All too plausible."

"Course you can, mate," Greg relented. "If it's got anything to do with me."

Dan nodded his thanks, though it didn't escape his attention that Greg had given himself an out. For all Greg's stated good intentions, Dan doubted he'd notice his pay packet putting on weight. In his experience, as soon as someone became a senior manager, they *became* a senior manager. Their empathy for the lower ranks they'd just escaped was instantly erased. Dan had promised himself that, were he promoted, he wouldn't allow that to happen to him. It was a problem he'd be spared now.

He went back to his desk. So far this morning, he'd woken up in the box room and been passed over for promotion. All in all, it was not one of his better days. And yet Dan felt fortunate. It could have been so much worse.

Greg too considered his lot. The door was open for him to rejoin his family. And the years of hard graft he'd put in on behalf of the company had finally been recognised. He should feel exultant. So why didn't he? Was it simply because Amanda had cheated? That rankled him, to be sure, yet nowhere near as much as he would have expected. She'd only done it because she thought he had. A small part of him even bore her a grudging respect. But what if she'd got a taste for it? What if she were tempted to do it again? Well, he wasn't. Why should she be any different?

But this, it dawned on him, was not the sole cause of his malaise, not even the primary. He tried to imagine his new life: Regional Sales Manager, south-east, arriving home in his shiny Lexus, being met at the door by his loving partner (dreadful word) and their two wonderful daughters. There was something wrong with this picture. It didn't ring true. And not just because he'd be lucky to get home before the girls were tucked up in bed. The truth was, he did not believe that they could simply pick up from where they'd left off when Greg had gone to the conference.

It needed something more, something else, to put things back. No. To put things *right*.

Sarah cruised the Waitrose fresh-meat section faced with her daily dilemma. What to feed her family for dinner? She estimated that, over the course of her marriage, she had cooked more than five thousand meals, even taking into account holidays and Dan's chilli con carne (his signature dish, as he liked to describe it; the only thing he knew how to make). She had long ago — fifteen years, in fact — exhausted her repertoire. Everything since had been repetition.

She considered the other shoppers. How many of them had cheating husbands? she wondered. More than were aware, that was for sure. Perhaps some of the women were themselves cheating. Sarah hoped so. It seemed only fair, though she'd never contemplate it. She just wasn't built that way.

A voice roused her from her reverie. "Sarah! I've been meaning to give you a call."

Sarah looked up to find her friend, Veronica, pushing a shopping trolley. Bottles of Chardonnay clanked against each other.

"Veronica. How are you?"

Veronica was in no mood for niceties. Or small talk. "You know that Ruby and Russell are dating?"

Sarah stared at her. "Oh, I doubt it," she said.

"I've seen them with my own eyes — snogging." Veronica imbued the word with a sense of her distaste.

Sarah frowned. Either Russell was bi or in deep denial. "It won't be serious," she offered reassuringly.

Veronica snorted, in a somewhat equine manner. "I consider it serious. I do not want that boy associating with my daughter."

That boy? She might as well have slapped Sarah across the face. Sarah felt her cheeks burn. "And what is wrong with my son?" she asked stiffly.

"You know perfectly well."

Sarah regarded Veronica blankly, which was all the invitation Veronica needed.

"He is a sexual deviant."

"What?"

Veronica cast a glance about, but the only person within hearing was a store attendant and, in her opinion, he didn't count.

"Bondage," she hissed. "You told me so yourself."

Sarah laughed. "I told you it was harmless."

"Disturbing enough for you to keep an eye on him."

"That was your idea!"

"Who knows what further depravities you uncovered!"

"None," Sarah said coldly. "And, anyway, it was Dan." It was only as she said it that Sarah realised the truth of this statement. Good God, she thought, why didn't that occur to me before?

At this point, Veronica could have accepted that there had been a miscommunication, apologised for any aspersions incorrectly cast, and backed down with good grace. But then she wouldn't have been Veronica. "Well, I wouldn't be surprised if Russell's degenerate, the example his parents set!"

It wasn't often Sarah spluttered. She spluttered now. "I'm sorry?"

"His father into bondage; his mother having an affair!" The look of disbelief on Sarah's face thrilled the woman who, minutes earlier, had been her friend but was now well on her way to losing that designation. "Didn't think I knew your little secret, did you?" Veronica crowed.

"I have no idea what you're talking about."

"Russell told Ruby he'd caught you with your lover."

Sarah was gobsmacked. Why would Russell say such a thing? Spread such malicious lies? And then she remembered the look he had given Sarah and Veronica's husband when he'd encountered them on the stairs. She knew it was an inappropriate response, but that didn't stop her; she burst out laughing. "That was Tony."

"My Tony?"

"Yes."

"You bitch!"

"I beg your pardon?"

"Having an affair with my husband!"

Sarah snorted. "With his BO? Don't be ridiculous!"

"He has a problem with his glands!"

"I'll say," Sarah agreed, in a less than subtle aside.

Veronica was outraged. "Anyway, he wouldn't have an affair with you. He has more taste!"

Sarah was just about prepared to overlook Veronica's denigration of Russell. It had been a misunderstanding after all. But this was a character assassination too far.

"Let me tell you something about Tony," she informed Veronica. "He came to my house the other day and made a pass at me."

"You're making it up!"

Sarah was conscious of the store attendant within earshot and raised her voice. "Your husband told me he likes to be spanked. Sound familiar?"

It was Veronica's turn to look stunned.

Sarah bestowed a "fuck you" smile upon her former friend, tossed a tray of mince into her basket and strode away triumphantly. She hadn't been looking for a fight, but one had found her and, to Sarah's mind, she'd won it by a knockout. She felt rather smug, a curious emotion considering it was her husband who was the adulterer. But, fortunately, Veronica didn't know that.

Molly and Lauren were squabbling, Jess came in from the back garden trailing mud, and a burning smell wafted from the oven — Amanda had put the chicken tenders on too high. Of course, this would be the moment that the doorbell would ring.

Amanda shut her daughters, Jess and the chicken tenders in the kitchen and went to see who it was. Wiping her hands on a tea towel, she opened the door to find Greg standing on the doorstep. Seeing him took her by surprise. It shouldn't have; they had unfinished business. But she'd expected a call, or a text, or a hurt silence.

"Hi," she said, unable to gauge his mood.

He nodded perfunctorily; he didn't smile, she noticed.

"This is for you," he said. He held out the lunch box Lauren had left behind when Amanda had collected the girls from McDonald's.

Amanda didn't like to tell him she'd already bought another. Still, Lauren was always losing them; a spare would come in handy. "Thanks," she said.

Greg seemed unsure what to say next, or even whether anything needed to be said.

"I'll see you around," he finally remarked, making as if to go.

Wait. Stop. Don't go, Amanda wanted to say. Instead, she asked, "Is that it?"

Greg turned back. "What more did you expect?"

Fair question. Amanda didn't know. Some sort of reaction to the news she'd given him last night, she supposed. But apparently this was it. He'd decided not to come home.

Greg walked to his car. He cast a look back at Amanda. His face was without expression but she read defiance in his features, challenging her to criticise. She cursed herself for underestimating male pride. Resigned, she closed the front door. It clicked sadly shut. She stood in the hall a moment, recomposing her face into "happy Mum", bracing herself to face the pandemonium in the kitchen and unsure whether she still had the strength, now she knew Greg no longer wanted to share the journey with her.

Molly looked up as Amanda wearily entered the kitchen.

"Was that Daddy?" she asked.

"Yes," Amanda admitted. "He was returning this," she chastised her younger daughter, tossing the lunch box on to the table. Lauren attempted a penitent look. She's getting better at that, thought Amanda; must be all the practice.

"Didn't he want to see us?" Molly asked.

It hadn't struck Amanda before, but Greg hadn't asked after the girls. "He was in a hurry. He said he's looking forward to seeing you soon," she lied, forking the chicken tenders' charred corpses into the pedal bin.

Lauren shook the lunch box. It rattled. "There's something inside," she said.

"Probably the week-old remains of your lunch." Greg could at least have cleaned it out. Amanda took the lunch box from Lauren, expecting its contents to comprise an empty sandwich bag smelling of tuna, a rotting apple core and a sucked-dry yoghurt pouch. But there was just a single item inside and it was none of the above.

Curious, Amanda thought, taking out a small, heart-shaped, velvet box. She turned it over in her hand. Molly and Lauren watched, enthralled, as Amanda tentatively flicked the box open. Lying on a satin cushion was a silver ring, set with a single diamond, which sparkled and shone under the kitchen lights.

"It's beautiful," Lauren whispered in a reverent tone.

"It's an engagement ring," her mum said, confused.

"Why would that be in Lauren's lunch box?" Molly asked.

Why, indeed? Amanda played back what Greg had said as he'd handed the lunch box over: "This is for you."

An engagement ring? For her?

Amanda realised she hadn't heard Greg's car drive away. She ran out of the room. Molly and Lauren exchanged a look. What had possessed their crazy mum now?

Amanda threw open the front door to find Greg in the porch, leaning nonchalantly against the wall, as though this scene had been inevitable.

He regarded her seriously. "One thing I have to know," he said. "Did it mean anything?"

Amanda knew exactly what he was referring to. "You know it didn't."

Greg considered this, then nodded. He understood completely. A smile broke across his face and kept on going. It reached Amanda and infected her too. For a moment, they just stood there, taking one another in, beaming like old friends meeting after a long separation which, in a way, is exactly what they were. They fell into each other's arms and kissed, long and deep, grateful to return to a place each had feared they might never visit again.

"I love you," Greg said, clinging to Amanda for dear life.

"Don't you ever forget that again," she threatened.

Greg grinned. He knew there was no risk of that. And Amanda sensed it too. They kissed again, not passionately — there'd be plenty of time for that — but tenderly, savouring the gentleness.

Greg caught sight of a movement out of the corner of his eye. He nudged Amanda. She followed his gaze. Peering round the door to the kitchen were Molly and Lauren, not quite willing to trust the evidence of their eyes. Greg and Amanda smiled, widened their hug to invite their daughters in. The girls needed no further bidding. They tore across the hall and leapt, squealing with delight, into their parents' arms. The din brought Jess running too, leaving muddy footprints in her wake. The labradoodle barked with glee to see Greg restored to the family huddle. Greg clutched his family to him. Jess pawed at them all. And Amanda found she didn't give a toss about the mud.

Sarah heard the front door, then voices in the hall. Dan must have run into Russell, given him a lift home. Throughout the day she'd kept checking her phone, expecting a message from Dan informing her of the outcome of his interview. She'd heard nothing. Which meant either that he hadn't got the job, or that he wanted to give her the good news in person. No. It meant he hadn't got the job.

Dan's face betrayed no emotion as he entered the kitchen, Russell close behind. People said Russell looked like his mother but, at moments like this, when Sarah saw them side by side, oblivious of being observed, she was struck by how similar father and son were — the slope of their shoulders, the tilt of their heads. She felt a surge of affection — for Russell. She still couldn't look at Dan without thinking of Lynda. She wondered whether she'd ever be able to.

"Hey, Mum. What's for tea?" Russell asked, as he always asked on arriving home from school.

"Your dad's doing chilli con carne," she announced — news to Dan as well as Russell. Dan just nodded, accepting the commission. He was hardly in a position to complain.

"Cool," Russell declared, rifling through his rucksack. For his homework, Sarah wondered? Russell pulled out his iPhone. He looked at his mum, expecting to be berated.

"Ten minutes, then you get on with your prep," she said.

Russell grinned, headed out of the room.

"And don't make me have to remind you!" she called after him. Funny how Russell could accurately estimate ten minutes when that was how long it was until *Sherlock* started, but otherwise had no sense of time.

384

"How was your day?" she asked Dan casually. Let him decide what he wanted to tell her.

"They offered the job to Greg," he said.

"Oh, Dan, I'm sorry." Sarah didn't have to feign sympathy. She knew how much Dan had wanted that promotion — enough to dare to dream that it could be his — and Sarah had wanted it for him. He deserved it. The blood, sweat and tears he'd shed for that firm. Well, sweat, anyway. He was a trooper. Perhaps that was his problem. His bosses considered him an infantry-man, not a commander.

Dan shrugged. "I told the board he'd be the best choice. After me. Apparently, the Chairman mentioned that when Greg went to see him — to turn the job down."

"He turned it down? Why?"

"Because I want to spend more time with my family," Greg explained to Amanda as they sat in the kitchen, sharing a glass of wine. A bottle, actually; they weren't stinting. "Regional Sales Manager means being on the road every day. Late hours. I think it's more important I be at home."

Amanda smiled, leant across the table to kiss him. Molly and Lauren, eating their mother's second batch of chicken tenders, shot disapproving glances their way. The girls had been prepared to tolerate snogging in the cause of reunification, but now their parents were back together there was no further excuse.

"You don't mind that I didn't consult you?" he asked, taking her hand in his.

Amanda shrugged. "If you didn't want to take the job, there was nothing to discuss."

"It would have meant a pay rise. Which might have come in handy when the girls leave Addlington Road."

"You want them to go private? Say 'yah' instead of 'yeah'? Develop an eating disorder? I reckon being a close-knit family is the best start we can give them."

"Well, that's just as well. Cos we can't afford the fees now."

Amanda smiled.

"There was another reason I turned the job down," Greg confessed. "I couldn't see myself doing it well. I'm not a manager. I'm a salesman. That's what I love: selling, persuading people to my point of view, even when they're sceptical."

"You're very good at it," Amanda said, not referring to Greg's job at all.

He grinned. "Well, you know, it's actually only possible if, deep down, it's what the other person wants too."

"Mmmmmm," Amanda mumbled, retaining some scepticism. But her eyes were smiling. "So who's your boss then?"

"I told them I'd have to discuss it with you first," Dan said to Sarah.

"You're in two minds?" she asked, surprised.

"I need your approval. It would mean longer hours."

Sarah understood. He was warning her that he would often be away from home, and she wouldn't know

386

where. The perfect cover if he were wanting to have an affair. Another affair.

"You'd make a good manager," she said.

"I think so."

"Better than Greg."

"Possibly."

"You deserve it."

"Is that a yes?"

Sarah weighed her response. The question was whether she could ever trust him again. The answer was clearly no. But were those grounds to refuse him?

"You changed after you came back from the conference," she observed.

Dan looked hangdog. "I know. I'm sorry."

But that wasn't what Sarah had meant. "No, I liked the man you became. I'm just sorry about what caused it."

Dan offered no defence; he had none.

"I am furious with you, Dan, be under no illusion. But I don't want this to end our marriage. I've invested too much to allow it to be destroyed by some little tramp."

A part of Dan wanted to leap to Lynda's defence, to tell Sarah that she wasn't like that. Fortunately, a larger part told him to keep his trap shut.

Sarah considered him a moment, then came to a decision.

"I put a bottle of champagne in the fridge," she said, "just in case. I suppose we ought to drink it."

Dan's eyes expressed his gratitude. "Thank you," he said; he wasn't referring to the champagne.

Dan found the bottle at the back of a shelf, tucked behind some celery, hidden there, he suspected, in case the news hadn't been good. He poured them each a glass. Sarah raised hers in a toast.

"To your success," she said.

"To us," Dan countered.

Sarah hesitated, then decided she could endorse that sentiment. They chinked glasses and drank.

If Sarah were honest, she preferred Prosecco, but long ago some slick adman had hoodwinked a gullible public into believing that, without a specifically French sparkling wine, all celebrations fell flat. And like *moutons* we all follow, she thought.

"I may look for a job," she announced, thinking aloud. "Part time. Working for a charity. That's what women over the age of forty do, isn't it, when they need an interest but don't need an income?"

Dan looked sceptical. "I can't see you on the till at the Oxfam shop, haggling over 50p for a chipped China mug."

Not really her style, Sarah had to admit, worthy though it was. "There must be other options," she said. "Citizens Advice?"

"You'd be good at that."

Sarah rather thought she might be. And she sensed that she would find it rewarding, helping the disadvantaged to hack through the forest of bureaucracy that stood between them and their entitlements. At the very least it would restore her self-esteem, which had lately taken a knock.

"I am sorry," Dan reiterated.

Sarah held his gaze. "You know, you're going to have to stop saying that. It doesn't gain anything with repetition."

Dan nodded apologetically. They sat in silence a moment.

"Did you ever consider leaving me?" she asked.

He pondered his response. "Not seriously," he said. "It wasn't like that."

That sounded about right. Sarah felt a sudden melancholy, envy for the joy she felt certain Dan had experienced, and sorrow for the fact she hadn't.

"How did we let this happen to us?" she asked.

Dan noted her use of the plural. Sarah did too. She wasn't absolving him of guilt, but acknowledging that he alone was not responsible for the fate of their marriage.

"I think we took our eye off the ball," he offered.

It was true. They'd lost sight of what was important: each other. They'd started out in love. So much love that they were surprised when Russell came along and they discovered they had more to share. But they hadn't worked on replenishing their reserves. They'd thought they had enough to see them through. They were like gardeners who don't tend their plants, who take it for granted that they'll bloom this year because they always have in the past. But just as shrubs need light, water and cultivated soil, so love needs romance, tenderness and care. Without nurture, it too can wither and die.

"I won't cheat again," Dan said. "I promise."

"Don't promise what you can't guarantee."

"Then I promise I'll try."

It wasn't much but it was something. Whether it would be enough, only time would tell. Dan had tasted forbidden fruit and he might be tempted again. But if they worked on making their marriage stronger, they might avoid that moment. Or at least postpone it.

They sipped their champagne in silence. Yep, Prosecco got Sarah's vote.

Children are very adaptable. Within half an hour of their parents' reconciliation, Molly and Lauren had grown used to the idea. They'd sensed that this was a day on which the usual regulations were relaxed; they'd asked if they could watch TV. This was happening so often now, the exception was replacing the rule.

Amanda and Greg sat in the kitchen, just enjoying being with one another. Amanda turned her hand, watching the play of light on the diamond in her ring.

"Are you sure you want to get married?" she asked. "You never have in the past."

"I know," he agreed. "Everyone tells you it's the happiest day of your life. But I've always had this irrational fear of standing at the altar and a small part of me wondering, 'Could I be happier than this?' And unless I knew with absolute certainty that I couldn't, then I shouldn't go through with it."

"That doesn't sound irrational to me. But it would never happen."

"No?"

"We're not getting married in church."

Greg nodded: fair enough.

"You think you're over that fear now?" Amanda prodded.

"I guess we'll find out. I think I'm ready."

"After thirteen years, two kids and cheating."

Greg shrugged apologetically. "Hey. We each have to find our own path."

Amanda smiled. Greg took her hand.

"What about you?" he asked, "As I recall, you were never keen either."

"I don't think there's much risk I'll turn into my mother." Amanda thought of Margaret, who had spent most of her married life desperate to keep a man she could no longer give herself to. My poor mum, she thought. But Margaret hadn't been the only reason for Amanda's reluctance, she now realised. "I think I sensed that you weren't ready. I trust you now."

Greg leant across the table and kissed her.

"Do you want to go to bed?" he asked. "With me," he clarified, in case she had anyone else in mind.

Amanda grinned.

And then she nodded.

Fortunately, the episode of *Friends* that the girls were watching was followed by another, so their parents' absence went unnoticed. And the noise they made unheard. And they were noisy. It turned out that "just engaged" sex is even better than "make up" sex. Greg was going to have to rewrite his all-time top ten again. "In with a bullet at number six . . ."

CHAPTER
NINETEEN

Weddings are stressful occasions, which is why, along with sex and death, they are such a staple of TV comedies. Planning a wedding can be the test of any relationship, the couple arm wrestling, sometimes literally, to get their way. Greg and Amanda didn't fall out once. Amanda had strong views on how she wanted her nuptials organised, and Greg simply caved. He merely desired two things. First, that Amanda be happy, which by acceding to her every wish he pretty much guaranteed. And second, that, come the hour, he should be in no doubt that this was indeed the happiest day of his life. And that was out of his control, in the lap of the gods.

If surveys are to be believed (and most aren't, especially those in which people are asked how often they have sex), then the average wedding costs in the region of twenty thousand pounds. Amanda and Greg's was significantly cheaper — not because they were tight, but because Amanda's perfect day did not require them to spend, in twelve hours, more than a hospital cleaner takes home in a year. She just wanted a simple celebration, an affirmation of their love and commitment before a select group of friends and relatives.

"Select" in the sense of real friends — not acquaintances, or friends of the Facebook variety — and only those relatives she and Greg actually wanted to see, not the second cousins they only met at weddings or funerals.

On the morning of the ceremony, Amanda woke up at 5.38a.m. Not that she was aware of it, but coincidentally this was precisely the hour she'd been roused all those weeks ago, on the day that Greg had left for the conference, setting in motion the train of events that would lead to their marriage. What caused her to wake so early was not nerves — she felt supremely confident about the step she and Greg were taking. Nor was it Greg, looking to start the honeymoon early — he wasn't lying beside her. In a nod to tradition, he had not spent the night with his bride-to-be, but had instead stayed with Sarah and Dan, his best man, in their box room, under a *Ben 10* duvet cover. No, Amanda would have slept soundly on until the alarm, set for 6a.m., but she was leapt upon by Molly and Lauren, who were even more excited than on Christmas Day. Because they were to be bridesmaids.

Amanda had considered driving herself to the register office, but her matron of honour (Geraldine) had baulked at this. The bridesmaids had lobbied for a horse-drawn carriage. Amanda met them halfway — actually, closer to her end of the spectrum — she booked a limousine. She'd briefly toyed with the idea of a stretch, since it would comfortably accommodate the whole bridal party, but had rejected this on the grounds that a) it was naff, and b) the car would likely reek of vomit regurgitated by the previous occupants, doubtless a hen party that had been ferried to a nightclub just hours earlier. In the event, the "limousine" turned out to be a Ford Mondeo, driven by a recently arrived refugee who'd left his three wives in Saudi Arabia — a very nice man, but with scant knowledge of geography. Or technology — he couldn't get his Sat Nav to work. Geraldine had to resort to barking instructions from an A to Z, while Amanda sat giggling in the back, and Molly and Lauren pretended to be princesses and waved to passers by.

Amanda had allowed Greg to choose the music to be played in the register office. He'd gone traditional — The Proclaimers' "Let's Get Married". Guests took their seats to the stirring strains of the myopic Scottish twins and awaited the bride's arrival. Traditionally late, it seemed. But, actually, they'd got caught up in a one-way system Geraldine had not anticipated and were struggling to find their way. Amanda's giggling took on a slightly manic edge. The mother of the bride, who was following the bridal Ford in her own car with her friend, Joyce, wondered why they were taking such a circuitous route. Were this a TV drama, guests at the register office would have begun to fret that Amanda was having cold feet, but she rang Greg to explain and all was cool. Finally, as The Proclaimers were reprising their anthem, the double doors at the back of the room sprang open and all heads turned to see . . . Margaret's friend, Joyce, scuttling to her seat, embarrassed to be the momentary centre of attention.

And then came the bride. Like all brides are supposed to look, and happily many manage, Amanda looked radiant, beautiful. For those who care about such details, she was wearing a Stella McCartney rose-toned snake-jacquard A-line dress. It had cost more than she'd admitted to Greg, but, even had he known the real price, he'd have considered it worth almost every penny; she looked stunning. As he watched his bride progress towards him, the groom broke into a grin — because he realised that he had never needed to fear this moment. There was not one scintilla of doubt in his mind. This was not the happiest moment of his life, but the third. It was surpassed only by the birth of the bridesmaids, who waved at him now from behind their mother's skirt as they escorted her up the aisle.

Amanda arrived at the front on the arm of her mother. When Amanda had asked her mum if she would give her away, Margaret had shed a tear, touched by the honour, but sad that the man she still loved was no longer alive to perform that duty himself. She wiped away another tear now. She was so happy for her daughter. Margaret loved Greg — if not like a son, then not like a son-in-law, either; somewhere in between. She had never doubted that he would do right by her younger child. And so, ultimately, it had proved. Margaret stood back as Geraldine stepped up to Amanda's side.

Geri recalled her own wedding day. She was confident that Amanda and Greg would be as happy as she and Dave had thought they were going to be. Her sister deserved it, she thought. And so did Greg. She mugged at him; he winked in return.

As is the modern style, the bride and groom had written their own vows. Amanda undertook to love, honour and cherish Greg. He went further, pledging also to obey. We'll see about that, Amanda thought.

And, with that, it was done. The registrar pronounced them husband and wife, Amanda and Greg kissed like newlyweds, then scooped Molly and Lauren into their arms as the guests broke into applause. The bride retraced her steps up the aisle, but this time on the arm of her husband. Greg had deliberated long and hard about the music that should accompany their departure. He thought he'd got it just right. Amanda was less sure. She shot him a glance that said, "What the fuck is this?" Greg had gone rogue. It was Leonard Cohen's gravelly-growled cover of the Irving Berlin standard, "Always", the saccharine lyrics tweaked to reduce their sugar content, the Canadian songster pledging a love that was:

Not for just a second, or a minute, or an hour,
Not for just a weekend and a shakedown in the
  shower.

A love that was for ever. The sentiment appealed to Greg's warped sense of the romantic. He shrugged apologetically at Amanda, who rolled her eyes indulgently.

The man I love, she thought.

They emerged to the cheers and well wishes of family and friends throwing biodegradable confetti.

396

And then it was back to the house for the reception. This was the main reason for the delay between engagement and wedding: they had wanted to host the celebration themselves, in their newly made-over back garden. It had been a calculated risk — that the work would not be finished, or that the weather would be British — but the gods smiled on them. It was a pristine September day. The trees looked resplendent in their autumn coats, their leaves golden red and not yet shed, burnished by a cloudless sky that seemed to be showing off, goading summer by boasting, "*This* is how you do blue!"

Guests mingled on the landscaped lawn, admiring the rockery, its water feature providing a tinkling accompaniment to the relaxed chatter, while young children played in the sandpit. Molly and Lauren passed among the assembly, serving canapés and accepting compliments on their performance as bridesmaids. Returning to the party from what Americans term a comfort break, Greg took a moment to survey the scene. He spotted Russell with his girlfriend; what was her name? Greg wondered. Ruby — that was it. Apparently she was having something of a hard time at present; her parents had recently separated. A pretty girl, Greg thought, as he noticed Russell's eyes settle on one of the bar staff they'd employed — a handsome Czech lad. Greg smiled to himself; Russell will find his place, in his own good time.

Greg turned and noticed one of the wedding guests standing on his own. Understandable; he didn't know anyone there — apart from Greg and, to a lesser degree, Amanda. She'd been sceptical when Greg had proposed inviting Howard. The receptionist at the hotel Greg had briefly lived in? (And the hotel she'd visited with Ben, she hadn't added.) But Greg maintained that Howard had played his part in their story and, because Greg was being so amenable about everything else, Amanda had agreed.

Howard had been delighted to see Greg when he'd dropped by the Clifton Motor Inn, even more so when Greg told him the reason for his visit. Howard generally didn't feel comfortable among other people — something of a drawback for a hotel receptionist. He'd intended to duck the wedding, making a late excuse for his absence. But, as it turned out, he'd had the day off and nothing better to do, and it was kind of Greg to think of him, so here he was. But he felt something of a spare part. He'd give it another ten minutes then slip away. That's when Greg appeared at his side.

"Howard? May I ask you a personal question?"

Howard was a little taken aback. "Yes," he guardedly agreed.

"Are you straight?"

Howard was more than a little taken aback. Questions don't come much more personal than that.

"Yes," he allowed.

"Seeing anyone?"

Howard was tempted to point out that that made two personal questions, but instead he answered — cautiously. "No."

"Like to?"

Still cautious: "Possibly."

Greg grinned. "There's someone I want you to meet." He led Howard across the garden, towards his in-laws.

"Margaret!" Greg called out, to Howard's horror. The woman must be pushing seventy! (It was a good thing sixty-three-year-old Margaret could not read minds.) "May I steal my sister-in-law away for a moment?"

Thank fuck for that, thought Howard.

Greg introduced Geraldine and Howard, giving them little assistance in starting a conversation. "You two should get on; you both take few prisoners," was all he told them. And then he left them to it. Most likely they'd have one of those embarrassing party encounters, which limp on long past the point at which conversation has curled up and died, until one of the participants makes a feeble and transparent excuse about the need to top up their wine, or pee, or leave. But there was an outside chance that they'd manage to find a point of connection. Five minutes should tell. Ten minutes later, Greg noticed Geri and Howard chatting animatedly, helping themselves to a couple of glasses of wine from the waiter who'd caught Russell's eye.

On the other side of the lawn, Amanda sought out Sarah for a private word. "I wanted to thank you," she told her friend.

"Oh, you're welcome," Sarah said, before she frowned. "What for?"

Amanda looked round the garden, filled with family and friends — and joy. "Making this possible."

Sarah smiled. "I don't think this is down to me."

"More than you'd imagine."

Sarah wouldn't allow it. "No. You two always loved each other. You just needed reminding."

Amanda considered that, then nodded; she'd buy that.

"How are things with you two?" she asked.

Sarah's eyes sought out Dan, standing with Greg, who was having a laugh at his friend's expense, probably about his best-man's speech, which Dan had delivered in the form of a Powerpoint presentation. It had been sweet and sincere and not particularly funny, a little like Dan himself, Sarah thought with fondness.

"We're a work in progress," she told Amanda. "So far, so good." Really quite good actually. A few weeks earlier Sarah had found herself feeling sufficiently forgiving, and amorous, to invite Dan back into the marital bed. They were tentative at first, a little like strangers, not quite at ease with each other. But that had meant they could wipe the slate clean, begin again and avoid slipping into tired and trusted routines.

Sarah was not about to spill the details to Amanda. She was too shy for that. Too shy generally, she once would have thought. But not in the bedroom; not any more. She'd recently purchased from Amazon, in a plain brown wrapper — so much more discreet than shopping at Waterstones — *The Joy Of Sex*, a book she'd remembered, as a child, finding under her parents' bed. This had been "revised and updated for the twenty-first century", which, as far as Sarah could work out, involved the male model shaving off his beard — admittedly a vast improvement. She'd bought the

400

book as a giggle; she thought she and Dan might get a few laughs out of it. They'd got a lot more than that. Now she was waiting for *The Illustrated Kama Sutra* to arrive.

"Is Greg going to this conference next week?" she asked.

Amanda knew what Sarah was referring to: a two-day seminar in Leeds on IT marketing in the digital age. "No. Dan said he could be excused. We're taking the girls to Disneyworld. Our honeymoon; their treat." She paused. "I suppose, as Regional Manager, Dan has to go."

"Yes. He's assured me I have nothing to be concerned about."

"Well, if Greg won't be there to lead him astray . . ."

Sarah smiled. There is that, her expression said. "You know the woman Dan was seeing works for a marketing agency specialising in IT?" she asked.

Amanda shot her friend a glance. "Do you know whether she's going to be there?"

"Dan left the conference brochure out. It lists the delegates who are attending."

"And? Is her name there?"

"I haven't looked. Yet. I might."

"And then again . . ." said Amanda.

"And then again," Sarah agreed.

Amanda smiled sympathetically. A work in progress, she thought. But then, aren't all marriages?

That night, after the last of their guests had left and the over-excited but exhausted children had been put to bed, Amanda and Greg stripped off their wedding clothes down to their birthday suits, and christened their new spa. Amanda found a bottle of champagne that had escaped her mother's attention and poured herself a glass; Greg cracked another can of JD and coke, and sat back, allowing a jet of hot water to pummel his lower back. The fairy lights he'd strung round the garden competed with the stars overhead to see which could provide the more romantic setting.

Does married life get any better than this? Amanda wondered. She hoped so; it was only their first day. But, as Sarah had said earlier, so far, so good.

She caught Greg staring at the heavens. Thanking his lucky stars, she thought — and so he should.

In fact, Greg was trying to identify the Plough and other constellations that he remembered from his childhood. Was that the North Star there, that bright light twinkling? Or was it a plane beginning its descent into Heathrow? He became aware of Amanda watching him.

"Mrs Beavis," he said.

Amanda rolled her eyes. They'd been through this; he knew she intended to keep her maiden name. It wasn't so much feminism, though there was that too; it was more the hassle of informing banks, credit card providers, the DVLA — that and having to learn a new signature. Greg had teased her, saying it showed she still didn't fully trust him.

She thought about that now. Yes, she trusted him. She trusted him to love, honour and cherish. Not to obey, but then she wouldn't really want that. It sounded too much like servitude.

She put aside her glass of champagne and eased across the spa, the aerated water bearing her aloft. She bumped up against Greg. They exchanged a moist kiss. He draped his legs around her hips and pulled her close. Their bodies slithered against each other. He licked a water droplet from her breast.

"Have you ever made love in a spa?" he asked, his voice a little throaty.

"No," she said, "and I'm not about to start now."

"It's our wedding night!" he protested, sounding more than a little like Homer Simpson.

"The girls are gonna use this."

"Ohhhhh . . ."

Greg looked plaintive. Amanda felt her resistance crumbling. At most it had been half-hearted.

"Well, all right, but afterwards you'll have to change the water."

"Deal."

Compromise: the secret of a successful marriage.

It was not the best sex Amanda and Greg had ever had, but it was right up there — the third time this year they'd cracked their all-time top ten. Not a bad start to married life.

Sarah lay in bed, the after-tremor of her most recent orgasm still reverberating. Tomorrow Dan would leave for Leeds, and a night away from home. She'd resisted the impulse to check the conference brochure, to see whether Lynda's name was among the list of delegates. She'd decided she didn't want to know.

Dan had invited her to take the trip with him. But a marketing seminar in Leeds sounded about as much fun as a mammogram. Sarah had declined. Not for that reason, but because, long term such a strategy was untenable. She couldn't hold Dan's hand twenty-four/ seven. More to the point, she didn't want to. She'd rather hold on to her self-respect.

Earlier that evening, as he'd been cooking the evening meal — coq au vin, recently added to his expanding repertoire — Dan had reiterated his promise to be faithful. Sarah hadn't doubted her husband's sincerity, just his ability to deliver on this pledge. She cast a glance at him now, lying beside her, sated, sound asleep. In repose, his face looked serene, without guile. We don't even know ourselves, she thought, so to what degree can we ever know another human being? We may think we do, but the truth is we know only that part that they choose to present to us. The rest we have to take on trust.

And with that unsettling thought, Sarah handed herself over to sleep.

Dan spotted Lynda almost as soon as he walked into the hotel bar. They hadn't had any contact since she had ended their affair. On the flight up to Leeds, he'd wondered how he would feel on seeing her again. And how she would react.

She was with Liz, and a couple of men Dan didn't know, probably sales reps seeking to hit on the two women. She must have been aware of his gaze because she looked up and her eyes immediately found his. She smiled coyly and Dan was reminded of why he'd been attracted to her. But back then he'd been vulnerable. He and Sarah had not been as strong as they were now. Lynda whispered something to Liz, then excused herself from the group and made her way across.

"Hi," she said.

"Hi," Dan replied. "Fancy seeing you here."

"Do you?" Lynda asked, but with a twinkle in her eye to show she was messing with him.

Dan smiled. "How have you been?"

Lynda shrugged, non-committal, "Oh, you know."

He didn't, but he let it pass.

"How about you?" she said. "Still married?"

That was so her, always straight to the point. "Still married," he admitted.

Lynda nodded and smiled. For Dan's sake, she was pleased to hear it. "I saw in the trade press that you got that promotion," she said. "Congratulations."

"Thanks." Then, remembering the part she'd played, "I owe you one."

Lynda considered her near-empty glass. "I don't mind taking it now," she said.

Dan hesitated. How would Sarah react if she knew he were having a drink with Lynda? Though that's all this was — a drink with an industry colleague . . . who happened to be a former lover. Even with that proviso, harmless. Dan held his hand out for her glass.

He and Lynda spent the rest of the evening catching up. It felt easy — relaxed and comfortable — but not dangerous, not a threat to the happiness and stability that he and Sarah were edging towards.

Approaching midnight the bar was beginning to get rowdy. The lights were dimmed, the music was loud and most of the delegates were drunk. A good time to leave.

Dan and Lynda waited in the hotel lobby for a lift to take them to their respective floors. Dan was struck by a sense of déjà vu; they'd played this scene before. For the first time that night, he felt a hint of discomfort. He mugged at Lynda to mask his self-consciousness, but by so doing merely drew attention to it. She grinned in empathy. At long last a lift arrived, sparing them further embarrassment.

Dan reached his room and inserted his key card. He pushed open the door and considered what he'd tell Sarah about tonight. Would he mention seeing Lynda, having a drink with her, having more than one? Probably not. Some things were better left unsaid.

He let go of the heavy door. As it swung slowly to, closing out the dim illumination from the corridor, a shadow was cast on to the wall of Dan's room. It looked a little like the outline of someone with him. But, there again, maybe it was nothing. Just a trick of the light.

Acknowledgements

While writing this novel, my wife, two daughters and I were living in a one-bedroom cottage overlooking Bungan Beach in Sydney. (Unlike the rest of the book, that bit's not made up.) Good friends lived next door: Michael and Sarah Peschardt, who offered me a room in which to write. Without their kindness I doubt I'd have completed the manuscript. Their dog, Bella, kept me company and listened to me reading aloud, only occasionally expressing scepticism. Eugenie Furniss of literary agency Furniss Lawton offered to represent me on the basis of my first few chapters and gave me valuable guidance. Rebecca Saunders of Little, Brown "got" the book from the start — exactly what you'd hope for from an editor. Rebecca's enthusiasm has been shared by publishers Catherine Burke of Sphere in the UK, and Louise Sherwin-Stark and Justin Ractliffe of Hachette in Australia. I must acknowledge my wife, Lisa Clothier. That's not just expedient; she's been a sounding-board, cheerleader, critic and shrink: the works, in other words. A number of friends offered advice and encouragement, among them Alvaro del Pozo, Kate Buchanan, Julian Pulvermacher, Trevor

McCurdie, Sarah McCurdie, Lizzie Hodges, Grant Boston, and the guys at Independent Talent: Michael McCoy, Paul Stevens and Tiffany Roy. Last, but not least, in fact of greater significance than they're probably aware: Justin Ciabatti, Joshua Ciabatti and Mel Sachs of Sky Personal Training in Mona Vale, Sydney, who kept me sound of mind and trim of figure while I moaned about the vicissitudes of the writing life (look it up, Josh).

Thanks, each and every one of you.